Jane and the Prisoner
of Wool House

ALSO BY STEPHANIE BARRON

Jane and the Unpleasantness at Scargrave Manor:
Being the First Jane Austen Mystery

Jane and the Man of the Cloth:
Being the Second Jane Austen Mystery

Jane and the Wandering Eye:
Being the Third Jane Austen Mystery

Jane and the Genius of the Place:
Being the Fourth Jane Austen Mystery

Jane and the Stillroom Maid:
Being the Fifth Jane Austen Mystery

Jane and the Prisoner of Wool House

~Being the Sixth Jane Austen Mystery~

by Stephanie Barron

BANTAM BOOKS

NEW YORK·TORONTO·LONDON·SYDNEY·AUCKLAND

JANE AND THE PRISONER OF WOOL HOUSE

A Bantam Book / December 2001

Library of Congress Cataloging-in-Publication Data

Barron, Stephanie.
Jane and the prisoner of Wool House / by Stephanie Barron.
p.   cm.—(Jane Austen mystery ; 6th)
ISBN 0-553-10735-6
1. Austen, Jane, 1775-1817—Fiction.   2. Portsmouth (England)—
Fiction.   3. Women novelists—Fiction.   I. Title.
PS3563.A8357 J345 2001
813'.54—dc21   00-046735

Published simultaneously in the United States and Canada

Bantam Books are published by Bantam Books, a division of Random
House, Inc. Its trademark, consisting of the words "Bantam Books" and
the portrayal of a rooster, is Registered in U.S. Patent and Trademark
Office and in other countries. Marca Registrada. Bantam Books, 1540
Broadway, New York, New York 10036.

This book is dedicated with love to my uncle,
Charles Cornelius Sibre,
A Heart of Oak
Who has sailed many a voyage with Nelson's Navy
From the comfort of his armchair

Editor's Foreword

WHEN JANE AUSTEN CREATED THE CHARACTER OF LOUISA MUS-grove in her final novel, *Persuasion,* she endowed the young woman with a "fine naval fervour" that present readers might trace to the author's experience of the port towns of Hampshire between 1806 and 1809, a period of considerable naval warfare in which her two brothers—one a post captain and the other a master and commander—were engaged. Austen took up residence in Southampton in the autumn of 1806, but her knowledge of the Royal Navy began as early as her seventh year, when she was sent briefly to school in Southampton with her sister, Cassandra, and cousin Jane Cooper. A few years later, elder brother Frank left home for a stint at the Royal Naval Academy in Portsmouth, and the Austens' collective naval fervor was unleashed in earnest. The fortunes of Frank and younger brother Charles would occupy a large part of Jane's energy and correspondence throughout her life. Both men ended their careers as admirals—Frank, as Admiral of the Fleet.

Jane and the Prisoner of Wool House is the sixth of the manuscripts to be collated and edited from a collection of papers discovered in 1992 in the cellar of a Georgian mansion outside of Baltimore. I find the present account to be one of the most fascinating I have been privileged to handle—because it places Jane Austen firmly in the midst of a world she knew intimately, admired profoundly, and cherished for its domestic virtues as much as its military importance. Her observation of naval men—their preoccupations, their endurance, their zest for hard living—is rife in these pages, as it is in her two "naval" novels, *Mansfield Park* and *Persuasion*. In this account, we may trace her steps through the streets of the port towns she would revive years later in fiction, and find the originals of Austen's characters among the naval men of her acquaintance.

In editing this volume, I found several works of significant aid. Deirdre Le Faye's edition of Austen's letters (*Jane Austen's Letters,* Oxford University Press, Oxford, 1995) was, as always, invaluable. *A Sea of Words* by Dean King (Henry Holt, New York, 1995) was a useful lexicon for translating the terms of art relevant to Nelson's navy. J. H. and E. C. Hubback, descendants of Francis Austen and the authors of *Jane Austen's Naval Brothers* (Meckler Publishing, Westport, CT, 1986, reprinted), are greatly to be thanked. *Naval Surgeon: The Voyages of Dr. Edward H. Cree, Royal Navy, as Related in His Private Journals, 1837–1856* (Michael Levien, editor; E. P. Dutton, New York, 1981) was absorbing and informative. *Band of Brothers: Boy Seamen in the Royal Navy* (David Phillipson; Naval Institute Press, Annapolis, 1996) enlightened me regarding the Young Gentlemen at sea during the late Georgian period. *Men of War: Life in Nelson's Navy* by Patrick O'Brian (W. W. Norton & Co., New York, 1974) offered a pithy and lighthearted survey of fighting ships. But nothing compares to the tome that is *The Oxford Illustrated History of the Royal Navy* (general editor, J. R. Hill; Oxford University Press, Oxford, 1995). If time permitted, I would be reading it still.

I am deeply grateful for the generosity and scholarly depth of Dr. Clive Caplan and William C. Kelley, members of the Jane

Austen Society of North America, who shared their knowledge, resources, and enthusiasm for Austen's naval connections with me in conversations and letters over the past few years. The "fine naval fervour" of Austen's most intelligent fans is a constant inspiration.

Stephanie Barron

Jane and the Prisoner
of Wool House

Chapter 1

A Passage
Down the Solent

HAD I SUFFERED THE MISFORTUNE TO BE BORN A MAN, I SHOULD have torn myself early from the affections of my family and all the comforts of home, and thrown my fate upon the mercy of the seas.

That fresh salt slap, as bracing as a blow; the bucking surge of wave upon wave, a riderless herd never to be bribed or charmed into complaisance; the endless stretch curbed by no horizon, that must unfold an infinite array of wonders before the eyes—exotic climes, benighted peoples, lost cities set like rubies among the desert chasms—oh, to sail the seas as my brothers have done before me! Free of obligation or care beyond the safety of oneself and one's men—free of the confines of home and earth-bound hopes and all the weight of convention like an anchor about one's neck!

Casting my eye across the extent of Southampton Water to the

New Forest opposite—verdure indistinct behind a scrim of morning fog—I shuddered from suppressed excitement as much as from the chill rising off the sea. From my position on Southampton's Water Gate Quay I might dip my hand for a time in the cold current of English history. Southampton Water, and the Solent that runs between the mainland and the Isle of Wight just south, have ever been the point of departure for great adventure—for risk, and high daring, and fortunes made or lost. Here the troops of King Henry embarked for the battle of Agincourt; here the Puritan colonists hauled anchor for the New World. It is impossible to stand within sight and sound of the heaving grey waters, and be deaf to their siren call; and not for Jane Austen to resist the force that has bewitched so many Hearts of Oak.

A forest of masts bobbed and swayed under my gaze: men o'war newly-anchored from Portsmouth; merchant vessels and whalers from the far corners of the Atlantic; Indiamen, rich and fat with the spoils of Bombay; and a thousand smaller craft that skimmed the surface of the Solent like a legion of water beetles. Hoarse cries of boatmen and the creak of straining ropes resounded across the waves; a snatch of sea-chanty, an oath swiftly quelled. The smell of brine and pitch and boiling coffee wafted to my reddened nostrils. This was *life*, in all its unfettered boldness—and these were Englishmen at their most honest and true: a picture of glory enough to drive a thousand small boys from their warm beds, and send them barefoot to the likeliest ship, hopeful and unlettered, ill-fed and mendacious as to right age and family, for the sake of a creaking berth among the rats and the bilge-water below. Were I returned in spirit to the days of my girlhood, a child of seven sent to school in Southampton—I might be tempted to steal my brothers' Academy uniforms, and stow away myself.

"Are you quite certain you wish to accompany me to Portsmouth, Jane?" enquired my brother Frank anxiously at my elbow.

I turned, the pleasant reverie broken. "I should never have

quitted my bed at such an early hour, Fly, for anything less. You could not prevent me from boarding that hoy at anchor, if you were to set upon me with wild dogs." It was necessary to suggest bravado—the hoy, with a single mast bobbing in the swell, was rather a small coasting vessel when viewed against the backdrop of so much heavy shipping: and I am no seawoman.

"The weather shall certainly be brisk," my brother persisted doubtfully. "The wind is freshening, and I fancy we shall have rain before the day is out."

"I do not regard a trifling shower, I assure you—and the air is no warmer in our lodgings. Mrs. Davies is of a saving nature, and does not intend that we shall ever be adequately served if our discomfort might secure her a farthing. My mother felt a spur beyond petulance and imagined ills, when she took to her bed after Christmas. She knows it to be far more comfortable than Mrs. Davies's fire."

"I must lay in a supply of fuel for our own use," Frank murmured. "I had done so, in December, but the faggots disappeared at an unaccountable rate."

"That we shall lay to sister Mary's account," I replied sardonically. "It cannot be remarkable that so cold-hearted a lady must require a good, steady fire. Her frame should lack animation entirely, Fly, without external application of heat."

He looked at me in hurt surprise. "Jane!"

"Not *your* excellent creature, my dear," I said quickly. "I speak entirely of *James's* Mary! You know that I have never borne her any affection, nor she but a pretence of the same for me." I would to Heaven that my brothers had possessed the foresight to marry women of singularity, in their names at least. Two of the Austen men having chosen Elizabeths, and another two, Marys, we are forever attempting to distinguish them one from the other. My elder brother James had brought his unfortunate wife, Mary, to stay with us in our cramped lodgings over Christmastide. This was meant to be a great treat: but my relief at the James

Austens' departure far outweighed any pleasure won from their arrival.

Frank grasped my elbow. "Steady, Jane. The skiff approaches."

A long, low-slung boat with two ruddy-faced fishwives at the oars had swung alongside the Quay. It bobbed like a cockleshell in the tide, and I should as readily have stepped into an inverted umbrella. I summoned my courage, however, so as not to disoblige my excellent brother.

"Pray take my arm," Frank urged. "It is best not to step heavily— and not directly onto the gunwales, mind, or you shall have us all over! Just so—and there you are settled. Capital."

Frank stowed himself neatly beside me on the damp wooden slat that served as seat, and began to whistle for wind. I attempted to ease my grip on the skiff.

As the two women bent their backs to the task of conveying us across the water to the single-masted hoy—which, despite its diminutive nature, Frank asserted might serve as a respectable gunboat in any but home waters—I struggled to maintain my composure. I had never crossed the Solent much less been aboard a ship, before; but I refused to earn the contempt of the British Navy. I should throw myself overboard rather than admit to a craven heart, or plead for a return to shore.

It had long been my chief desire to be swung in a chair to the very deck of one of my brothers' commands—the *Canopus,* when Frank captained her, or the *Indian,* should Charles ever return from the North American Station. But we had always lived beyond the reach of naval ports; and our visits to the sea were matters of bathing and Assemblies. My mother's decision to settle with Frank in Southampton, a mere seventeen miles from the great naval yard at Portsmouth, must ensure frequent occasion for familiarising myself with ships, and sailors' customs, and all the ardent matter of my brothers' lives, that have demanded such sacrifice, and conveyed so much of glory and regret.

Charles, my particular little brother, has been Master and Commander of his sloop in the Atlantic for nearly three years—but is not yet made Post Captain.[1] When he will find occasion for an act of brazen daring, a risk to life and limb such as might draw the Admiralty's approval, none can say. Charles may only hope for another American war. The Admiralty's attention has heretofore been trained upon my elder brother Frank—who has been Post Captain these seven years. But of late, the Admiralty appears to have found even him wanting.

Frank suffered the distinction of serving under the Great Man, Admiral Lord Nelson. His third-rate eighty-gun ship, the *Canopus,* was destined to meet the combined French and Spanish fleets in 1805; but the Admiral, insensible that he should fall in with the Enemy off the headland of Trafalgar, and being desperately in need of water and stores, despatched my brother to Gibraltar in search of the same. Frank returned several days after the decisive action, to discover some twenty-four hundred British sailors wounded or dead, nineteen of the enemy's vessels captured or destroyed, the remnant of the Combined Fleet under flight—and the Great Man, wounded mortally by a musket shot.

Frank's failure to engage the Enemy in so glorious a battle—a day that shall live forever in English hearts—was a bitter blow. Not all his subsequent victory at Santo Domingo, his prize money and silver trophies, his marriage to little Mary Gibson, may supply the want of distinction—though the affectionate hearts of his sisters must rejoice in the intervention of Divine Providence.

The skiff mounted a determined hillock of wave, slapped firmly into the trough beyond, and sent a shower of frigid green water into my lap. I could not suppress a slight exclamation of shock at the sudden wet and cold, and Frank's head came round to stare at me. I smiled weakly in return, my hands still clenched on the rough

---

1. Although accorded the courtesy title of captain, a master and commander was an officer one rank below a full captain. He usually commanded a vessel smaller than a Royal Navy post ship, one that carried fewer than twenty guns. A post captain, however, was a full-grade officer entitled to command a post ship. He held a place on the navy list, which ranked and promoted officers by seniority; a master and commander did not.—*Editor's note.*

wood of my seat, and hoped desperately that I should not disgrace myself.

The hoy loomed—the oars were shipped—and Frank's warm hand was reaching for my own. With a deep breath to hide my trepidation, I picked my way across the skiff's slatted bottom—quite in want of caulk, and welling with water—and allowed myself to be hauled upwards by the hoy's master.

A weathered face, pinched and crimson with cold, the eyes two agates against the light of morning—if he was akin to most of the seamen plying the Solent from Southampton to Portsmouth, he would bear his female supercargo little affection. But his boat, in comparison with the lighter craft I had just quitted, appeared ample and sturdy; I heaved a shuddering sigh of relief and sank against the side. Frank jumped across the widening gap of water between skiff and hoy, clapped the master about the shoulders, and said, "What do you make it, Finley? Two hours, in this wind?"

"She's bearing south-south-east, Captain," the master replied, with a doubtful eye to his straining canvas. "We're forced to beat and beat, I don't reckon."

"The wind will shift in another quarter-hour," my brother replied, "and then we shall see what your poor tub might do. Crack on, Finley!"

With a grin in my direction, Frank swung himself into the bow, as though the frigid spray could not daunt him, nor the February wind cut through his good naval coat. It is a trifle worn, that coat—he is the sort of man who considers of refurbishing his dress only when it is in rags about him—but the gold epaulettes of his rank shone brightly upon his shoulders. His face was thrust out into the gusts and swell, his whole countenance alight, and his aspect that of a hunting dog let off its lead. My heart leapt with pleasure at the sight of him. It has been many months since Frank was turned onshore, and the landsman's lot does not sit well with him. But on this raw wintry morning he was once again the brave and reckless older brother I adored as a girl—the boy we named *Fly* for his trick of spurring his horses to breakneck speed—the boy who set off alone for Portsmouth at the age of twelve, and could never bear dry land thereafter. Frank has more courage at the bone and more good English commonsense than any other Austen; and though he spares less thought for weighty matters than my brother James, and wastes less on frivolous ones than brother Henry, he is quite the truest heart I have ever known.

The mate hauled anchor; the sails rose up the mast; the canvas swelled with wind; and faster than I could have believed, Southampton slipped away behind us. My involuntary grip on the hoy's gunwales eased; I breathed more steadily, and was capable once more of observation. Never had I been privileged to travel so swiftly, in such relative silence. No wheels rattled, no horses' hooves rang like mallets on the paving-stones; we were sped by merest air, the fresh strong wind buffeting my bonnet. I grinned foolishly at the hoy's master, as though he were an angel bent on conveying me to Paradise.

"How do you like it, Jane?" Frank asked, crouching low as he made his way into the body of the hoy. "Are you warm enough?"

"I shall never be warm enough while winter holds sway in Southampton." I wrapped my arms more firmly in my cloak. "The south of England provides quite the most penetrating damp of any I have known, though the locals will protest so much. Southampton may be rated high in the esteem of the Fashionable for its bathing and medicinal waters, but the Fashionable, you will allow, are not prone to bathe in February."

"Not by design, certainly," Frank returned, "although I recollect some few who have bathed by misadventure. More than one pleasure party has ended with your Fashionable beaux headfirst in the drink. But you are not indisposed? Not queasy in your workings? You do not feel the slightest threat of a fainting fit coming on?"

Poor Fly. He has been closeted too long with his Mary; and as she is increasing, and much prone to swooning after a hearty meal, Frank is grown convinced that all women are prey to it.

"Not in the slightest," I assured him. "I am admirably situated here; you may return to the bow with equanimity."

"Pray join me," he urged. "The sensation of wind and movement is delightful. I shall keep one hand firmly on your arm, never fear, Jane; you shall not risk the slightest injury."

I found courage enough to attempt it, and soon stood with my brother in the hoy's farthest extent. Here, the views of the Solent and its encircling landscape were unimpeded. Frank's eager hands made figures in the air: to the larboard side, the peaceful settlements of Netley, and Lee-on-Solent, and Gosport spilling down to the sea; to starboard, the last fringe of the New Forest; and ahead, the Isle of Wight looming like another country. Portsmouth commanded the headland directly opposite the island; and beyond them both, roiled the broader waters of the Channel, where Frank had mounted blockade against the French for so many tedious years.

"How diminished is civilisation and comfort, how false the air of security, of a town viewed from such a vantage," I observed. "What might be taken, on dry land, for the power of commerce and Kingdom, appears the merest foothold at this distance. How greater still the diminishment, when all the wide waters of the ocean are at one's back!"

"I have always believed," Frank added, "that could kings and emperors reign solely from the seas, and suffer the overruling might of Nature to humble and command them with every gale of wind, they might then regard themselves in the proper light. The vastness of the world is an acute corrective, Jane, for over-weening vanity! As it is for many land-borne ills."

I studied him soberly. "You miss a ship, Frank. Confess as much. You long to put to sea, however near Mary's time and however comfortable your present circumstances."

"You forget the inadequacy of Mrs. Davies's fire, Jane," he returned with brusque humour. "There is little of comfort in *that*."

"We shall be gone from hired lodgings in a fortnight," I said dismissively, "but your malaise shall prove as strong. The lease in Castle Square—that fringe you are so busily knotting for the parlour curtains—the bedsteads you turn, and the conveniences you fashion in your restless, tidy, sailor's way—they are nothing more than make-work, a sop to fill your time. You are unhappy, Frank. I am more convinced of it now, having seen you once again in your element, than I have been for many weeks. Though I have long suspected the cause."

He offered no reply—only stared across the heaving water, his eyes narrowed. Salt spray had dried in a haphazard pattern of white droplets on his collar; his auburn hair was ruffled into curls by the force of the approaching rain. It is hard for such a man—trained from boyhood in every nerve and sinew to pursue the Enemy, to engage and subdue him—to subdue, rather, his own ardent spirit to the necessities of fortune. Frank is become like a powerful horse, honed for the Oaks or the Derby, that is put to plough the same featureless length of turnip patch day after day. Having won a little prize money, he saw fit to marry at last the lady who had waited so many patient months for his return from sea; and being a gallant son, he required his mother and unwed sisters to take up their abode in his company. Southampton was chosen, the treaty struck for a house in Castle Square; that house entirely refurbished; and our prospects of happiness in our situation, very great—but a plan for domestic happiness must prove inadequate to one of Frank's temperament.

He is a man accustomed to commanding three hundred tars, at least, in the midst of the greatest fleet on earth. He has chased the Enemy across every ocean on the globe, and seen the colours of French ships struck at his desiring. Now he turns and turns without employment, surrounded by too many muslin skirts, and the tiresome frivolities of a watering-place, with its Assemblies and circulating libraries and occasional theatrical play. He slips away to Portsmouth whenever convention will allow, and haunts the naval yard, where constant intelligence of the better fortunes of his brother officers—who possessed the luck to distinguish themselves with Nelson at Trafalgar—must poison his heart like gall. He bears so constant an aspect of forced cheer—such unfailing interest in the tedium of domestic life—that my heart aches for him, as must any heart of discernment and feeling.

"It is only that . . ." He faltered, and glanced down at his reddened fingers where they gripped the bow. "That is—you must be aware, Jane, from the intelligence of my letters in the year '05, how ardently I pursued the French Admiral, Villeneuve—across the Atlantic to the West Indies, and back again; how many months I spent vigilant, on blockade, before his Fleet even broke out of Brest. After having been in a state of constant and unremitting fag, to be at last cut out by a parcel of folk just come to join Lord Nelson from home, where some of them were sitting at their ease for months—"

"It is lamentable," I said quietly. "We all feel your misfortune acutely, Frank."

He shifted in the bow, unable to tear his eyes from the Solent. "I do not profess to like fighting for its own sake—and Mary is thankful to Heaven that I avoided the danger of that battle—but I shall ever consider the day on which I sailed from Nelson's squadron as the most inauspicious of my life."[2]

There had recently been a rumour, I knew, that the First Lord of the Admiralty, Lord Grenville, had confidentially assured our acquaintance Lord Moira that the first fast frigate available should be given to Captain Austen. But as several fast frigates had subsequently gone to others, I placed no confidence in rumour. Like Patronage and Connexion, those twin hounds of a naval career, Rumour will forever abandon one prospect to bay after another more likely.

"Have you no word of a ship?" I enquired.

Frank's eyes slid towards mine and were as quickly averted. More than any gentleman in my circle, Frank is incapable of deceit. He *must* look conscious when he should prefer to be inscrutable.

---

2. Frank's words to Jane closely echo sentiments he first expressed a few days after Trafalgar in a letter to his then-fiancée, Mary Gibson, written from the *Canopus* while off Gibraltar.—*Editor's note.*

"You *have* heard something!" I seized his arm. "It is intelligence of a ship that takes you to Portsmouth, and not 'concern for an old friend' as you would have Mary believe. Why have you said nothing of your prospects at home?"

"Because I cannot be easy in the subject," he replied. "You know very well, Jane, that dear Mary is as solicitous for my credit as any woman—but she cannot like the idea of my putting to sea when she is so near her time. Indeed, I cannot like it myself."

It was true—the birth of Frank's child was barely two months off; and as it was Mary's first lying-in, and the young woman's apprehension of childbed exceedingly great, he should have been a monster to wish for a ship at such a time. Yet he *did* wish it. A man's heart may yearn for what his sensibility would disdain.

"Mary talks of nothing but fast frigates," I observed. "She is as zealous on your behalf—as buoyed by hope at the slightest portent of Admiralty favour—as any midshipman preparing to pass for lieutenant. But I shall undertake to conceal your prospects from her, if only you would impart a tenth of the whole to me."

"Mary is an angel," Frank returned with fervour, "but had I suspected, Jane, how much my affections for my wife would anchor me to shore—how little I should like my duty when it must come—how torn in my soul I should feel at the prospect of embarking—I declare I should have remained single to the end of my days, and suffered less in regret than I do presently in indecision."

"Naturally you must feel it so," I observed. "Any man would say the same—though I speak only of such men as have hearts. But consider, my dear, how little service you should do your wife by remaining fixed at her side. Such a position cannot advance your career or the prospects for your family. You must return to active service. Mary will agree. Was it not just such an eventuality that urged you to secure your sisters as companions for your wife? You have done the utmost to ensure her comfort, and must be satisfied. Now tell me of this ship you believe may offer."

The hoy surged over the crest of a precipitous wave and flung itself into the gulley beyond; I clutched inadvertently at the bow, salt spume in my face, and felt my brother's shoulder brush close against my own. Gosport was now hard off the larboard side, and the white-painted houses of the Isle of Wight, clearly discernible. We should be anchoring in Portsmouth harbour soon.

"She is a fifth-rate," Frank said low in my ear, "forty-eight guns, and new-built but six years ago: the frigate *Stella Maris*. I have seen her some once or twice, coming out of the Rock, or putting in at Malta. Perfect lines! Built for speed. So maneuverable and sure at coming about, that she has taken French prizes that ought to have out-gunned her. The better part of her seamen are rated Able, and she boasts some first-class gunnery."

A frigate. The very thing for Fly. Having served so long in a ship of the line, as Flag-Captain under an admiral, my brother, I thought, deserved to cut a dash. Every young buck of spirit craved a fast frigate. They were the eyes of the fleet—they fought the majority of single-vessel actions—they were despatched at a moment's notice to every corner of the globe. Frigate captains were the pirates of the Royal Navy: seizing enemy ships, flying into guarded ports on midnight raids, convoying merchantmen at the behest of the Honourable Company, and culling a share of Bombay profits as a result.

"On which station does she sail?" I enquired.

"The Channel. I should never be farther than a few days from home, should I be wanted."

I raised my hands as though in applause—or prayer. I could no more suppress my delight than I could stifle hope. "The very thing! How could we wish for anything better! You shall make your fortune, Fly, as many a worse fellow has done before you!"

The sun shone briefly in my brother's countenance; then a shadow crossed his face once more, and all light was extinguished. "I have not told you the worst, Jane," he informed me heavily. "There is the matter of Tom Seagrave."

"Tom Seagrave?" I furled my brows with effort. "I do not recollect the name."

"He is a post captain like myself," Frank replied, "but well before our elevation, we shared a berth as Volunteers on the *Perseverance*. By the time I was made midshipman, Tom had already passed for lieutenant; I served under him on the *Minerva*. There is no one like the fellow for dash, and bravery—he has always been called 'Lucky Tom Seagrave' in the Navy for the number of prizes he has taken. But luck, Jane, has very little to do with Tom's career. He has more pluck at the bone than most squadrons put together, a fighting captain for whom the men would die."

Frank had never been a man to flatter or praise where praise was not due; I must take it, then, that Captain Seagrave was a paragon of naval virtue. And yet I read trouble in my brother's looks.

"And what has your old friend to do with the *Stella Maris*, Fly?"

"He is her captain."

"Her captain? But I thought the ship was to be given to *you*."

Frank's grey eyes were bleak. "And so it may. Tom Seagrave is presently in Portsmouth awaiting court-martial, Jane. He is charged under Article Nine of the Articles of War."

I waited mutely for explanation.

"Article Nine states that no enemy officer or seaman is to be stripped of his possessions or abused in any way, when an enemy ship is taken," Frank said carefully. "Some few weeks since, Seagrave fell in with the *Manon*, a French thirty-two-gun frigate, just off Corunna. He engaged her; the *Manon* returned his fire gallantly; but the sum of it is, her mainmast was carried away and she struck her colours after a matter of an hour."

"Well, then!" I cried. "There can be nothing shameful in such a victory, surely!"

My brother's countenance remained set. "The French captain suffered a mortal wound, Jane—*after* the *Manon* had struck and the fellow had surrendered his sword. Seagrave is charged with murder."

"But why?" I gasped. "The Admiralty cannot believe he would kill a defenceless officer in cold blood! What reason could he find?"

The master of the hoy called harshly to his mate, and Frank's eyes shifted immediately to the sails. The canvas had slackened;

the vessel had slowed. A massive three-decker, a first-rate by its gun-ports, was anchored to starboard with an admiral's white flag at the mizzen; we had achieved Portsmouth harbour.

"You see my dilemma, Jane." Frank's voice was barely audible over the cries of sailors skimming across the water from ship to ship. "You see why I make no mention of my prospects at home. It is a damnable bargain! I may have my frigate with the Admiralty's blessing—"

"—provided your old friend hangs," I concluded.

Chapter 2

Dr. Wharton's Comfort

23 February 1807,

cont.

~

PORTSMOUTH IS A SAD PLACE IN THE ESTIMATION OF THOSE WHO look only for beauty in a landscape; it offers no grandeur in its edifices, no promenades worth speaking of, no sweep of land that might draw the approving eye. It is a town of tight and jogging lanes quite crammed into the east side of a horseshoe, whose western leg is Gosport; a small ell of a place enclosing a secure harbour, with the deep-water anchorage of Spithead immediately across the Solent. The landward side of town is girdled with drawbridges and moats, the fortifications deemed vital to the preservation of the Kingdom's naval stores; but the effect must suggest a medieval fortress, it confirms the desperate activity of war and frowns upon frivolity. The commercial streets do nothing to soften so martial an aspect—Portsmouth's shops are schooled to the business of ships, the men who command them and the men who build them.

There are chandlers, and tailors adept at the fashioning of uniforms, and purveyors of all such items as are necessary to a sailor's trunk—cocked hats, round hats for everyday wear, preserved meat and portable soup, Epsom salts and James's powders, nankeen and kerseymere waistcoats, black silk handkerchiefs, combs and clothes-brushes, tooth-powder, quadrants, day-glasses, log-books, Robinson's *Elements of Navigation* and *The Requisite Tables and Nautical Almanac.* Portsmouth may boast a few butchers and grocers, but they cannot look very high in their custom, the pay of the naval set running only to modest joints, and such comestibles as are cheaply in season.

Four coaching inns serve the well-heeled traveller come south for embarkation: the Crown, the Navy Tavern, the Fountain, and, of course, the George. I do not believe there is a town in England that cannot claim a *George.* It was to this latter that my brother intended to repair, to procure us both a light nuncheon before seeking the home of Captain Thomas Seagrave. I thought it likely that Frank did not wish to put the Captain—or his wife, did Seagrave possess one—to the trouble of feeding those who came to condole.

"There is the *Stella Maris,*" Frank said quietly as we were rowed into the quay. "Cast your eyes upon *that,* Jane. Everything prime about her."

I gazed in silent absorption at the single-decker's closed gun-ports, her soaring triple masts. I knew nothing of the subtleties of ship design; I should have to accept Frank's assurances regarding this one. But the ship was certainly an article of spirit, rocking gently at her moorings like a swan come to rest: sails close-furled in the shrouds, quarterdeck bereft of life. Only a handful of men moved purposefully about her. The rest of her crew would be on shore leave.

"You can see where the foremast has been shipped and re-paired," Frank observed. "Splinters dashed from the poop railing and tops, as well—it is a French habit, you know, to train their guns on the masts and rigging, rather than the hull as we should do. I should like to see the damage the *Manon* took! She must be moored somewhere near about; the *Stella* will have towed her into port—but such trifles as this trim little frigate sustained, would never leave Seagrave dead in the water."

He halted abruptly in this speech, as though his words risked an ominous construction; and we spoke no more of the unlucky action, nor of the trim little frigate, until the George was gained and our nuncheon consumed.

As this was my first visit to Portsmouth, Frank was all enthusiasm in conducting me through the streets once we quitted the George. He had first come to the town as a boy of twelve, a hopeful scholar at the Royal Naval Academy; he had returned some part of every year thereafter, and must regard it as almost a home. He was longing, I knew, to gain the naval dockyard in order to observe the ships presently building in the stocks; to meet with old acquaintance and learn the latest intelligence of war; to finger lengths of cordage and brass carronades and talk with spirit of his views on gunnery. I had heard Frank's opinions on the subject before, and might have engaged in such a conversation, with a remarkable air of possessing knowledge well beyond my grasp—*Three broadsides every five minutes, and better by G-d if we can manage it*—but Frank was inured this morning to the lures of his profession. He led me unswervingly from the broader main street, into a crooked little lane halfway down its extent, lined with steep and leaning houses shoddily-built. In one of these, we thought to find Captain Seagrave.

"I should mention," Frank informed me as we stood upon the steps, "that Seagrave possesses a wife—a lady of birth and independent fortune. I believe she married to disoblige her family, however, and was cut off."

I nodded once in comprehension. The door swung open to reveal the harassed visage of a girl in apron and cap, several strands of blond hair trailing down her reddened face. Remarkably, she bore a black patch over one eye.

"Missus says as how she's not at home," this apparition supplied without preamble. "You may leave yer cards if you've a mind."

"It is Captain Seagrave we seek," Frank said firmly. "Pray tell him that Captain Austen has called."

"Yer can tell 'im yerself," the slattern retorted.

"That will be all, Nancy."

The maid skittered aside as though she had been prodded with a fire iron, to reveal an upright figure barely discernible among the shadows of the foyer. From his bearing alone—correct, unfussy, and economical in its containment—I should have known him instantly for an officer of the Royal Navy; but the smile that lit my brother's countenance was assurance enough.

Frank stepped forward and seized Captain Seagrave about the shoulders. "Tom! It does my heart good to see you!"

The man before us broke into a grin; he returned the pressure of Frank's hands with a clap of his own. "Austen! You rogue! I thought you well out of Portsmouth this age—on convoy duty to the Indies, some said, though I had heard you were relieved of the *Canopus*. Is Charles Yardley in command of her, then? She'll not be well served. Yardley's a craven fool."

"You'll not hear me say you nay, Tom," my brother replied with a laugh. "I might almost suspect the Admiralty of wishing the old *Canopus* at the bottom of the sea, in placing her in such hands. But it *has* been an age since we met!"

"Off Minorca, was it not? A year since?"

"More," Frank replied grimly. "It was the thirty-first of October, 1805, and I had at last come out of Gibraltar in search of the Admiral's fleet. I encountered you first among all the victors of that action."

There was no need to distinguish *which* admiral the two men would discuss, or what action; with Nelson gone, the details of his passing were forever enshrined in glory.

"You look well, Frank," Seagrave said in a softened tone. "I might almost believe that shore leave agrees with you. And you are married, I understand! Is this, then, the pretty bride you've brought to meet me?"

I blushed. The shadows of the foyer must be heavy, indeed, could Tom Seagrave flatter me so. This past December I achieved the age of one-and-thirty, and any bloom I might once have claimed has entirely gone off.

"Mary sends her most cordial greetings, to be sure," Frank interposed, "—but at present, she is indisposed. May I present my sister to your acquaintance? Miss Austen, Captain Seagrave."

I made my courtesy to the gentleman, and received his bow in return. Like so many officers of the Navy, Seagrave possessed a weathered face, deeply lined, with crow's-feet about the eyes from gazing long at the horizon; his hair was grizzled by the sun, his skin the color of mahogany. He was, I thought, a few years older than Frank; or perhaps his various fortunes had hardened his countenance in a manner that Frank had yet escaped. It was a handsome face, all the same, as a beast's carved in stone will forcibly draw the eye. In gazing upon it, I judged that Tom Seagrave was formed for command, and decisive action, and coolness in the extremity of battle; but having viewed his countenance, I could no longer dismiss the idea of the man shooting an enemy point-blank, in cold blood. By his looks, Seagrave required only sufficient provocation.

A door into the hall burst open at that moment, and two boys of perhaps six and eight rushed headlong into the room to fall in a tangle about Seagrave's ankles. From the open doorway there emanated a baby's insistent wail, and the tired voice of a woman attempting to hush it.

"Charles! Edward!" Seagrave cried as he hauled his sons to their feet. "Mind your manners. We have visitors. What will they think of you!"

"But, Papa!" the elder boy exclaimed. "Nancy says that the *Defiant* has signalled. She leaves the harbour for Spithead, and we must be on hand to see her go! Look, I have my spyglass from

Malta. Cannot we run down to the Sally Port? She shall be gone if we do not make haste!"

"*Please,* Papa!" the younger boy added.

"Go, then," Seagrave said with good-natured impatience, "but mind you look after your brother, Charles. Edward—your boot is unfastened; you will be asprawl in the gutter, and you do not take care. I expect you both in time for dinner!"

Edward ducked around me; Frank made a teasing jab to corner Charles; and our little party was almost overrun as the two boys bowled through the door.

"They should be at sea by this time, Tom," Frank said, looking after them thoughtfully. "Cannot you secure good places?"

Something in Seagrave's countenance hardened. "It is rather difficult at present," he said abruptly. "Circumstances—"

For an instant, the grim spectre of the gallows hovered before all our eyes, though no one had yet dared to broach the subject of Seagrave's disgrace. A considered delicacy, I thought, prevented the two men from discussing the matter in the Captain's own lodgings, and before a lady. I hastened to turn the conversation.

"But they are full young, surely? Would their mother consent to part with them at so tender an age?"

"Pshaw!" Frank retorted with disgust. "I have known Young Gentlemen of five to come aboard. It is every stout lad's dearest wish to put to sea, Jane! If I am fortunate enough to have a son—"

"I wish to Heaven the boys were in the Indies at this very moment," Seagrave said flatly. "It would do them both good to be lashed to the t'gallants. They might even learn to read, Frank, from sheer boredom! God knows they learn little enough here!"

Frank laughed aloud, quite at home in all the squalor and noise of such a household, though it bore not the slightest resemblance to his own. Perhaps, however, it was very like to the confines of a ship—in which my brother had spent the better part of his life. Frank is nearly three-and-thirty; he went to sea (rather tardily, for the Navy) at the age of fourteen. Nineteen years is a considerable period in the life of a man. It must witness the better part of his character's formation—shape his ideas—confirm what is steady or vicious in his nature. How little we at home understood of Frank's way of life!

The wailing from beyond the parlour door increased, but Captain Seagrave paid it little mind; Nancy the maid screamed at some poor unfortunate in the depths of the scullery; and it appeared we should remain, for the nonce, in the front hall. I understood, now, why Frank had taken such care to procure tea and ham at the George well before seeking his old acquaintance; we had felt the full force of the Seagraves' hospitality in achieving their front step, and must be satisfied.

"Should you like to walk down to the dockyard, Frank?" Seagrave enquired. "I have an errand that way, and might converse with you as we go."

"A capital idea!"

Seagrave glanced at me. "Perhaps Miss Austen would prefer to rest in the parlour. I shall summon Louisa—"

"Pray, do not disturb her," I said, in hasty consideration of the squalling infant. "I am well able to amuse myself in exploring the shops hereabouts. Frank might rejoin me in an hour."

"Louisa would like nothing better than a turn upon the High," Seagrave insisted firmly. "It would do her good to get a breath of air. She is too much confined, and forever fancying herself ill. If you will but wait a moment, Miss Austen—"

He disappeared within the noisy parlour, and a low murmur of conversation ensued. Frank, I thought, might have intended a word for my benefit in the interval, but that Seagrave reappeared in the hall almost directly. I had only time to glimpse a swirl of ruffled muslin—Mrs. Seagrave, I suspected, had not yet exchanged her dressing gown for more formal attire, though it was nearly one o'clock—before the Captain cried, "Excellent! She would be delighted to accompany you, Miss Austen, if you will but spare her a moment to fetch her bonnet. I am sure she will attend you directly. If you should like to take a seat here in the hall—the maid is at present engaged in tidying the parlour—"

"But of course," I murmured, and settled myself on the single Windsor chair the foyer could boast. I have always detested Windsor chairs. "Pray do not tarry on my account, Frank. I shall be quite happy to await Mrs. Seagrave."

"Expect us in an hour, Jane. Any later, and we'll find the passage back to Southampton too cold and wet for bearing. The rain cannot hold off forever." Frank squeezed my gloved hand, settled his cockade hat, and pulled open the door. A bow from Captain Seagrave—and the two men were gone.

I had a full quarter-hour to calculate the depth of dust on the picture frames before the distant sound of feet descending a staircase alerted me. The hallway's farthest door was thrust open— Nancy's black patch and sullen countenance appeared—and behind her, the lady who must be Louisa Seagrave.

She was a tall woman, almost equal to her husband in height; and though, to judge by the infant's cries, she had recently been increasing, her gown hung upon her emaciated frame. Her hair was dark, and drawn back without the slightest attention to style or arrangement, in a severe knot at her nape. Though her features were good, and I might trace the remnants of a vanished beauty, it was rather as one might conjure the memory of summer from the frame of a leafless tree. There was about her a palpable air of defeat mingled with defiance, as though she knew herself to have suffered a mortal wound, but was prepared to fade without ceding the slightest quarter to her enemies.

I rose, and moved by an obscure sensation of pity, extended my hand.

"Good day. I am Miss Austen. And you must be Mrs. Seagrave. How good of you to consent to walk with me in town!"

"The kindness is entirely yours, I am sure," she returned abruptly. "Have you any particular errands you wish to complete? A direction you thought to pursue?"

"None whatsoever," I replied cheerfully. "As this is my first visit to Portsmouth, everything is of interest to me."

"Then you are more easily amused than I." She could not disguise the bitterness in her words. "Portsmouth is a wretched hole, Miss Austen, with nothing to recommend it. May I ask what place you call home?—Or are you as itinerant as every naval woman in my acquaintance?"

"I am presently settled with my family in Southampton," I replied.

"Ah. *Southampton.* They have libraries there, I believe. All you will find in Portsmouth are essays on the calculation of longitude." Her grey eyes glinted as she pulled on her gloves. They were doeskin, the color of mulled wine—and like much about Louisa Seagrave, of the highest quality and the shabbiest use.

"Have you lived here long, Mrs. Seagrave?"

"Three years. But I do not intend to endure it a fourth. I shall remove to Kent when my husband is again at sea."

She lifted her head as she said this, as though in defiance of courts-martial and all the Articles of War—or perhaps it was a courage flung at the husband who would attempt to rule her. "Shall we go, then?"

"With pleasure," I said drily, and followed the lady to the street.

THE RAIN BEGAN PERHAPS A HALF-HOUR AFTER WE HAD ACHIEVED the High. In the interval before the deluge, however, I had time enough to establish that my companion was the only daughter of a viscount; that her schooling had been accomplished at a fashionable establishment in Town; that she had become acquainted with Tom Seagrave at the age of seventeen, during a period at Brighton; and had married not long thereafter. The air of elopement hung over her terse explanation; the match had been accomplished without the sanction of her parents. It was clear to me, however, that if Louisa Seagrave did not exactly regret her headlong alliance with the dashing Captain, she had suffered greatly from social diminution. At the time of their union, Tom Seagrave had been only a lieutenant, with a lieutenant's meagre pay; success, and further steps in rank, had swiftly come—he was not called "Lucky" for nothing—but the early years had proved a period of deprivation. The connexions so swiftly thrown off, at seventeen, were reckoned a greater loss at three-and-thirty. Doors that should have swung open for the Honourable Miss Carteret were closed to Mrs. Seagrave; and she had only learned to value the rooms beyond, once they were locked against her. Her pride had suffered in the exchange, and not all the years of marriage, or the birth of three children, could heal the wound of a cut direct from a former intimate acquaintance.

Now, with her husband being brought under a charge of murder, even her tenuous claim to the naval world must be threatened, her last foothold on safe ground, crumble beneath her. Louisa Seagrave had chosen to regard her fellow officers' wives with a coldness bordering on contempt—and given half a chance, they were sure to return the favour.

"There is Mrs. Aubrey," my companion observed, as we attempted to cross to the far paving, "with her hair newly-dressed on the strength of her husband's prizes! I do not think Sophie Aubrey has exchanged two words with me this winter; however, Captain Aubrey is not without troubles of his own. One ship at least has sunk under him, and he has been a prisoner of the French; there is some muttering, as well, regarding debts and a recklessness at cards. We may assume that Mrs. Aubrey avoids us out of sympathy for my husband's case, or horror at the threat of commiseration. She is a proud creature, Mrs. Aubrey—but not one of those who would laugh behind their hands as I attempt to pass. I assure you, Miss Austen, that there are many who would! Captain Seagrave may not chuse to regard the abuse—or perhaps he does not perceive it; he hears them call him 'Lucky,' and believes the word to be hurled without enmity. But I have quite given up promenading alone. I do not wish to invite insult. The women of Portsmouth forget whose daughter I am!"

She possessed intelligence, for all her self-absorption; a woman possessed of less might have suffered less pain.

When the rain commenced to fall, we hurried up the street, rejecting several sailors' taverns before achieving a pastry shop of Mrs. Seagrave's preference. She had fallen silent by the time we turned into it and secured a table; her gaze was fixed on the street beyond the window. Such a description suggests an attitude of placidity, however, and that would entirely mistake the case. My companion's fingers moved restlessly over the surface of our table, and her grey eyes were grown feverishly bright. I almost suspected a hectic fit, or the onset of fever. Certainly, from the aspect of her thin face, her mind was much disturbed.

"Are you unwell, Mrs. Seagrave? Have we attempted too great an exertion?" I enquired, as she pressed one shaking hand to her lips, and closed her eyes.

"A faintness—there is a bottle in my reticule—"

I reached for the embroidered bit of silk, and withdrew a flask of elixir—*Dr. Wharton's Comfort.* "I shall fetch you a glass."

"With water, if you would be so good—"

She poured a quantity of drops into the water I procured, and drank it down entire. I surveyed her countenance with some anxiety, but forbore from interrogation; and in a few moments, she had recovered herself. Her skin was still as sallow, but the restless activity of body and brain had eased.

She did not replace the bottle of medicine in her reticule; but neither did she speak of her indisposition. "A little refreshment is all I require. Will you take tea?"

"With pleasure."

"Mrs. Huddle! A pot of tea and some fresh cakes, if you please!"

She was determined to proceed as though nothing untoward had occurred; and as her guest, I could not do otherwise than to oblige her.

"I understand that Captain Seagrave has been lately much at sea," I ventured. "You must have endured long periods of confinement with your children. How do you pass the hours, Mrs. Seagrave?"

"I read." She glanced at me swiftly, as though in expectation of mockery; the naval wives of Portsmouth, I must assume, could not regard a patron of the circulating library as worthy of their notice.

"And which do you prefer—prose, or poetry? Letters, or horrid novels? For my part, I find little to choose between Mrs. Radcliffe or Madame d'Arblay, and the verse of Scott; they are all words enough to surfeit on. Were I to face extinction by flood or fire, I should spend my final moments immersed in a book."

"I could not admire *The Lay of the Last Minstrel,* tho' everyone would be talking of it; I far prefer Southey to Sir Walter Scott. What think you of Coleridge?"

"He is a poet more to a gentleman's taste," I replied, "and I cannot like his habit of eating opium. But Southey's *Madoc* is certainly very fine."

"Do you believe so?" she enquired with an air of penetration. "I enjoyed the first quarto; but I detect a falsity in the Azteca girl— who in aiding the White Man, destroys her husband, her father, and herself. Such cataclysmic vengeance cannot be credited. The variations in life and fortune depend as much upon coincidence as design. I will not accept a Fate that exists solely for the convenience of the Author."

Here was matter for the strictest debate; and so we whiled away the better part of three-quarters of an hour, over tea and marzipan, in the liveliest conversation. The rain's cease at last occasioned a consultation of our watches, and the recollection that I was to have met my brother at the Seagraves' some time since.

Louisa fortified herself with a second dose from her little bottle before proceeding home; but when I would express the most active anxiety, she would hear none of it. "You have been a greater tonic, Miss Austen, than a gallon of Dr. Wharton's," she declared. "I am starved for good company—the conversation of interesting people, with a wide knowledge of the world and a liberality of ideas!"

"That is not good company," I gently replied. "That is the best. Pray do not hesitate to call, Mrs. Seagrave, if you happen to visit Southampton. Though we are at present quite cramped in hired lodgings, we shall be settled in Castle Square in a fortnight, with all our books about us. You and I might look into them together."

A brisk walk of seven minutes achieved her doorstep; and there we found the two Captains settled in chairs drawn up to the parlour fire. The little Seagraves had not yet returned, though they must be wet quite through, in standing upon the seawall as the *Defiant* slipped her moorings. With an exclamation of annoyance, Louisa Seagrave despatched the slattern Nancy in search of her sons, and accepted the charge of her infant in return.

We exclaimed over the baby, a fine, fat little girl of seven months; and made our *adieux* not three minutes later. I had time enough, in turning back for a final glance, to observe the animation dying from Louisa Seagrave's countenance as she followed our progress through the window; and I felt a pang. I had cheered her solitude a little; but her troubles were too fixed to dissipate entirely in an afternoon. I wondered that such a mind—restless for matter, and admirably equipped for discernment—should succumb so completely to an oppression of spirits. If I might be forgiven such a judgement, Louisa Seagrave had no *right* to encourage weakness. Its ill effects were evident all about her: in the neglect of her home, the mismanagement of her children and servants, the suppressed violence of her husband. Where she might have done measurable good through a determined strength, she merely contributed to the oppression of the household.

"Well, Jane?" Frank enquired, as we hurried through the misty air to the Portsmouth quay, "how do you like my friend?"

"I like him very well indeed," I said with effort. "He is all that you describe: open, warm in his expressions, and manly in his spirit. But I cannot think him happy in his choice of wife, Frank. They are both strong-willed, and must vie for dominance. It cannot be a peaceful household."

"Seagrave was never formed for peace, Jane," my brother replied satirically, "and remember that he is much at sea. I do not think that he and Louisa have spent more than a twelvemonth, all told, in each other's company—and they have been married fifteen years! I could wish her capable of greater support, however," he added, "in Tom's present pass. He don't admit it, but he is more anxious about the court-martial than I should like."

I studied my brother's countenance as he handed me once more into the hoy. An expression of trouble had replaced his usual cheer; his brother officer's concern, it seemed, was catching. We should both have much to hide from little Mary.

"Is the Captain aware that you have been offered his ship, Frank?" I asked him quietly.

"I would not tell him for the world, Jane." Frank did not tear his gaze from the open water beyond the harbour's mouth; Portsmouth was at his back, and I fancied he preferred it so. "Pray God I am never obliged to."

Chapter 3

The Lieutenant's Charge

Tuesday,
25 February 1807
~

I FIND MYSELF RATHER UNWELL THIS MORNING, OWING, IT MUST BE assumed, to the thorough wetting I received yesterday evening, as Frank and I returned up the Solent. It was a weary, tedious business, with the rain pouring down and the wind in an unfavourable quarter. The hoy's master was forced to come about with such frequency, that we might all have been sailing on the carapace of a giant crab, sidling backwards into Southampton Water.

Owing to the lateness of the hour, a great fuss was made of us in Queen Anne Street, when at last we achieved our lodgings; Mary was anxiety itself, believing us both gone to a watery grave off Spithead, or set upon by pirates, and threatening to advance her labour on the strength of it. My mother went so far as to quit her bed and appear in the parlour to remonstrate with Frank—a gesture she has not considered of since the New Year at least. The most sensible member of the household, our landlady Mrs. Davies, proffered steaming soup and a fresh cutting of cheese, which we gratefully accepted. But it cannot have been earlier than ten o'clock by the time we mounted the double flight to our rooms, our candles guttering in the draughts; and I had been shivering with chill for an hour since.

And so, the morning not yet advanced to eight o'clock, the rain still coursing against my windowpane, and Frank alone abroad of all the house, I have propped myself against the bed pillows and taken up my little book. My nose is streaming and my head feels as though it has been stuffed inside a sack of goose feathers, the mere thought of which ensures a breathless sneeze. A cold in the head is nothing, of course, compared to one which chooses to settle in the lungs, and I must account myself fortunate—I shall certainly *look* far more ill than I truly am. But that thought fails miserably to comfort me. I had passed most of the autumn in poor health, having contracted the whooping cough after an unfortunate exposure in Staffordshire. My ailment occasioned considerable alarm in my mother's breast—her anxiety rose the higher with every whoop—so that by Christmas she was grateful to count me among the living, and herself impervious to such an ignoble complaint. Had I malingered any longer, she might have insisted upon carrying me off to Bath, for a medicinal turn about the Pump Room; and that I could not have borne.

I sneezed once more, and reflected on the efficacy of hot liquid in banishing all manner of ills. I might have ventured downstairs in my dressing gown and petitioned for a pot of tea—but a bustle from the hall suggested that our very own Jenny, the excellent creature who has been with us since our days in Lyme, and who shall serve as maid in the hired house in Castle Square, had already procured me one. I called admittance at her knock—her freshly-scrubbed face, pink from the ice in the washstand this morning, peered around the door—and the heavenly scent of steeped China leaves wafted through the air.

"Writing again, miss?" she enquired, as though much inclined to scold. "The time I've had, scrubbing black ink from your bed sheets! And no fire, yet, in the grate—what *does* that foolish Sara do with herself, I'd like to know, when she should be tending to you all? And you perishing from that drenching you got at Captain Austen's hands, I've no doubt! I'll look to the fashioning of a mustard plaster this morning, if you will be so good as to keep to your bed. There's little of advantage to take you abroad today, I'm thinking, with the weather so wet and nasty!"

I thanked her through the muffled folds of a cambric handkerchief, and sent her to the depths of the kitchen in search of mustard. The tea was ambrosial. I sipped it contentedly as my pen moved over the page.

The weather has often been wet and nasty in Southampton this winter; so sharp and chill, in fact, that on the worst occasions we have not ventured out-of-doors even to attend Sunday service. Such a moral lapse in the wife and daughters of a clergyman should be deemed inexcusable, did we possess a team of horses and the conveyance suitable to our station; but we do not, and a slippery progress through the ice and mire of the streets is not to be thought of. My brother ventures out to skate in the frozen marshes, and kneel alone in his Sabbath pew; on every street corner he may meet with a friend, and learn all the most urgent naval gossip.

In returning from church, Frank will often carry in his train a solicitous acquaintance, come to comment on his wife's blooming looks, and enquire about his mother's health. These occasional bursts of friendship and information do much to break the monotony of our routine and loosen the stranglehold of winter; but they are too brief and narrow in their content. Our acquaintance in Southampton is mostly derived from Frank's professional circle, and though I possess a fine naval fervour, and will assert that sailors are endowed with greater worth than any set of men in England, I must admit to a certain weariness in their society. They are entirely taken up with battle and ships, and with the advancement of themselves and their colleagues up the Naval List; and though dedicated to the preservation of the Kingdom, and possessed of noble hearts and true, they are, in general, a population whose schooling ended at roughly the age of fourteen. I had forgot, until my chance encounter with Louisa Seagrave, how much I craved the conversation of intelligible people—of those whose world is made large by the breadth of their ideas. As the years advance upon me, and my monetary resources grow ever more slim, I have begun to feel the walls of these rooms—whatever rooms I chance to inhabit, they are all very much of a piece—press inwards upon me. I am stifling from the limitations penury must impose, like a candle shut up in a coffin. I am desperate to lead a different life, and yet know that all possibility of exchange is denied me.

My heart whispers that I should have been better pleased with my lot, had I never formed an acquaintance with the Great—had I not sampled the dangerous delights of a certain notorious gentleman's world, or shared some particle of his confidence. I am sure that my sister, Cassandra, believes the same. But one cannot wish a hundredth of one's experience undone, any more than one might command the heart and will of another; and though I might lament the change, in having traded the summer beauties of the Peaks and all the elegance of a ducal household in Derbyshire, for the damp and draughty lodgings of winter in Southampton, I could not desire Derbyshire unseen. I might recognise the pernicious hand of regret clutching at my entrails, but I confess that I prefer a sense of loss—and its attendant spirit, depression—to ignorance of my own heart.

I have heard nothing of Lord Harold Trowbridge since parting from him at Bakewell last September. I have no expectation of a furtherance of our acquaintance. Indeed, in regarding the inner oppression that so often follows a sojourn in his company, I have lately begun to wonder whether I should leave off the acquaintance entirely. But I have not the heart for a formal break in friendship, nor, indeed, the strength. Hope of once more encountering The Gentleman Rogue, I confess, is one of the few impulses that sustains me in such a raw and unlovely February.

But perhaps, like Louisa Seagrave, I have little right to submit to such weakness. Mine is too sharp a character to invite melancholy; I have always despised those poor honies, who languish in boredom on a procession of sophas, and fancy themselves ill. Such behaviour must argue a lack of inner resources, a sinking of the female mind. And yet what, of a sustaining and nourishing nature, have I sought out this winter in Southampton? I subscribe to a circulating library; I read aloud to my mother. I devote myself to planning the shape and composition of our garden in Castle Square. I choose green baize for the dressing-room floors and consider of the size of beds. But I have not ventured inside the theatre in French Street; I have not danced since quitting Bath; and I have entirely left off my attempts at novel-writing. The creatures of my pen afford me no amusement in this despondent season. Their caprice and wiles cannot dislodge the mental dullness and spiritual weight that have dogged me, now, for too great a period—dogged me, in varying degree, since my poor father's death, and the end of so much that was comfortable in our domestic arrangements.

There is nothing unusual in a period of lowness during the winter months. And I have been more than usually bereft of companionship—my sister, Cassandra, having gone to my brother Edward's estate in Kent for Christmas. Edward's wife, Elizabeth, being but recently delivered of her tenth child, there is much to do this winter at Godmersham—what with the little boys too young to be sent away to school, and the little girls in want of a governess, and the eldest child, Fanny, on the verge of quitting the school-room altogether. I am certain that Cassandra must have her hands quite full, and may forgive her the letter that arrived only Friday, postponing her descent upon the South until April, several weeks after we shall have undertaken the move to Castle Square. I could not wish her to suffer the same lassitude and confinement I have myself endured, and may hope that she enjoys a pleasant interval of dancing at Chilham, and the luxury of claret with her dinner, and much coming and going in my brother's equipages, before the monotony of home life must once more descend.

But I am sick of cities and towns, of the rumble of cartwheels on paving-stones, of the ceaseless babble of harsh conversation, of muck and commerce and an end to all peace. I would give a good deal for one breath of fresh air—for the sharp green smell of bruised clover, the sight of snowdrops poking through the warming earth; for the call of a curlew, and the rushing chatter of a stream. In the blessed quiet of a country lane, or before a wide-flung window, I might recover somewhat of my serenity, and learn to sustain myself in the affections of my family alone. I might cease to yearn for love that is beyond hope. I might even be able to write again.

This rush of confidence, scrawled in the pages of my little book, was spurred, I know, by Louisa Seagrave—by her own air of disappointed hopes, of throttled ambition. The love of a brash man, and a headlong union of two brilliant spirits, accomplished little towards her happiness. She is more earthbound and compassed now—by obligation, duty, the bonds of family—than the young girl beating her wings against a viscount's cage could possibly have imagined. I pity her; I recognise in her the human condition; and I return once more to the conviction that life's burdens may only be overcome by a summoning of inner resources: by a dependence not upon others, but upon the qualities of spirit and mind.

I resolve to do better. I resolve to leave off depression, and embrace what I may of good in my lot. I possess, after all, life and health—or should, but for this abominable cold—and am not so far reduced in circumstances as to admit of shame. There might yet be cause for rejoicing in the years ahead; much of worthy and fruitful endeavour, that might contribute to the happiness of my family and increase my own respectability. It cannot be so seductive a prospect as the life of a woman of fortune—one, for instance, allied to all the resources of a duke's second son, a confidant of the Crown—

But I must banish the thought. It is as illogical, as unlikely, as improbable as one of my own creations—a Lizzy Bennet, perhaps, in conquest of a Mr. Darcy, or a Marianne triumphant over a Willoughby reformed. Such things may only be permitted in novels.[1] They wither in the harsh light of truth as a bloom in exile from the hothouse.

Better to exchange the contemplation of my own troubles for those of my brother Frank. It is impossible not to consider, upon waking, of the thoughts that so engrossed my attention as I fell off to sleep; impossible not to rise, and throw aside the bedclothes, and recollect that Frank had intended an early breakfast before setting off in search of Tom Seagrave's first lieutenant. It was this man—an officer by the name of Chessyre, who had sailed with Seagrave against the *Manon* as well as two previous commands—who had laid the charge of murder against him. Frank, having gained some understanding of the matter from his conversation with his old friend, thought to comprehend it still better by a close interrogation of Seagrave's accuser.

"I cannot fathom a man who would so betray his captain," Frank had said, as we beat up towards Southampton last night in the rain-lashed spray, "and a man, too, who was loyal to Seagrave beyond any other—a man Tom counted as friend! It does not bear consideration, Jane. There are niceties—there are forms—to the conduct of naval life; and I should sooner hang myself at the yardarm, than behave as Chessyre has done! He has displayed himself as the very worst sort of scrub, and deserves to be run out of the Navy on the strength of it!"

"Are you at all acquainted with the Lieutenant?" I enquired.

"Not in the least. He's a fellow well past the next step—shall probably die in his present rank—a competent first lieutenant, mind you, but nothing brilliant in his action or understanding. Seagrave might have had a host of ambitious young fellows at his call, all eager for the chance to take a prize, and show their mettle before the Admiralty; but Tom chose to offer a hand to his old shipmate, and ensure that Chessyre earned a comfortable berth at a time when he most required it. Not that Tom said so much in his

1. Jane refers here to characters in *Elinor and Marianne* and *First Impressions*, which had not yet achieved their final manuscript forms as *Sense and Sensibility* (published 1811) and *Pride and Prejudice* (published 1813).—*Editor's note.*

own behalf, mind you—but I am well enough acquainted with the service to understand the case."

"And you regard Chessyre's laying of information as the basest ingratitude?—Regardless of whether there is truth in his accusation, or not?"

"I think I may be allowed to recognise truth when I meet it, Jane," Frank replied with an air of impatience. "Tom Seagrave is as frank a soul as ever breathed. He described the *Stella*'s engagement with the *Manon* in every particular—and for my part, I credit his claim that it was entirely above-board. The court-martial cannot help but do the same! Are they likely to believe the word of an aging lieutenant, over the best fighting captain the Navy has seen since Nelson?"

Frank did not appear to require an answer, and I offered him none. I knew too little of courts-martial, or Admiralty boards, or anything so subject to Influence as this body of men who promoted or scuttled one another's careers with seemingly equal caprice. Frank may possess the best will in the world, and the most open of characters—but he has been formed by the naval conceptions of rank and seniority. The presumptions of a junior must appear akin to mutiny; they threaten the Divine Order of Naval Things. I could not look for a dispassionate account from such a quarter.

My brother had related some part of his conversation with Seagrave; but having heard it, I could not declare with Frank that only one judgement was open to the court-martial. There were gaps and inconsistencies in the tale that must trouble an impartial listener, and a clear requirement for further intelligence, if Seagrave's innocence was to be established.

Just after Christmas, Tom Seagrave sailed out of his anchorage at Spithead under sealed orders. He was instructed to open his packet only upon achieving a certain position near Lisbon; but having progressed so far as Corunna, some leagues north of the Portuguese port, he fell in with the *Manon*. The French frigate possessed only thirty-two guns to Seagrave's forty; and moreover, her gunnery was not equal to our Captain's, who soon had the satisfaction of seeing four gaping holes below the *Manon*'s waterline. With the French ship taking water fast, and her mainmast carried away, Seagrave brought the *Stella Maris* across the *Manon*'s bows, and prepared to board her.

Seagrave led his men, including Chessyre, into the French frigate, and fought his way to the quarterdeck at great risk to himself. There he discovered the French captain lying as though dead, and approximately one hour and forty-three minutes after the commencement of action, the French colours were struck. But prior to the moment of this glorious capitulation, an event occurred which greatly disturbed the crew of the British frigate: a small boy perched high in the shrouds—where no Young Gentleman should be during the heat of battle—plummeted with the *Stella Maris*'s roll to the deck below. Upon examination, the child was found to have been shot through the heart by a French marksman mounted in the *Manon*'s tops; and the rage this deliberate injury caused among the seamen was impossible to describe.

The savagery of the boarding party, and its success in carrying all before it, may thus be credited to a desire for revenge; but revenge may be carried beyond reason. Certainly Lieutenant Chessyre would have that this was so. When the Captain of Marines undertook to secure the survivors of the French ship's crew, for conveyance as prisoners of war back to Portsmouth, it was discovered that Porthiault, the French captain, had been stabbed through the heart by a British dirk—and the blade was certainly Tom Seagrave's own. Seagrave expressed astonishment at the fact; owned that he had missed his dirk from its scabbard in all the confusion of the boarding party, but could not say how it came to be found in the corpse of the French captain.

It is customary, after the taking of a prize, to send the enemy ship home to port under the command of a junior officer. Seagrave appointed Lieutenant Chessyre commander of the *Manon,* and ordered him to return to Portsmouth with the French prisoners, while Seagrave pursued his appointed course south towards Lisbon; and so the two officers, and the two frigates, parted company. Seagrave despatched with Chessyre a letter to Admiral Hastings, his commanding officer, describing the action and detailing the British casualties; he also enclosed a letter intended for the mother of the dead boy, which Chessyre swore solemnly to deliver.

It was only upon Seagrave's return to Portsmouth some weeks later, that he learned he had been charged with a violation of Article Nine of the Articles of War, for the murder of the surrendered French captain, Victor Porthiault. Chessyre had laid charges with Admiral Hastings within moments of achieving Portsmouth; and he claimed, moreover, to have witnessed the murder himself.

"And what motive does he ascribe to Captain Seagrave, worthy of so brutal an action?" I had enquired of Frank.

"Chessyre would have it that Tom blamed the French captain for the death of the Young Gentleman. The lad was a great favourite, it seems, and no more than seven. Chessyre claims that Tom Seagrave forgot himself in a rage at the Young Gentleman's murder; and that he stabbed the unfortunate Porthiault at the very moment when the Frenchman gave up his sword."

"But how dreadful! And Seagrave?"

"—Denies it. He is convinced that Porthiault was already dead when he and Chessyre discovered him on the *Manon*'s quarterdeck."

"But the dirk, Frank!"

"The dirk is a problem," my brother agreed. "Seagrave, in boarding an enemy ship, should have brandished his sword. He claims that the dirk—a smaller blade altogether—was pulled from its scabbard in a moment of confusion during the fight with the French; and that he neither knew the person who seized his dagger, nor how it came to end in Porthiault's chest."

"And how does Captain Seagrave account for the Lieutenant's charge?"

"He is charity itself in speaking of Eustace Chessyre. Tom will have it the fellow mistook him for another, in all the smoke and madness of the boarding. Chessyre was mistaken in his account,

Tom believes, and will own as much during the course of the proceedings."

"Is a recantation likely, Fly?"

My brother sighed heavily and dashed a spate of rain from his cockade. "Certainly Seagrave's superiors do not live in expectation of it. There was *that* in Admiral Bertie's looks, when he spoke of posting me into the *Stella,* that cannot urge me to be sanguine. The Admiral should never have imparted so much of a confidential nature did he not find the case against Seagrave compelling in the extreme."

"But surely there must be someone besides the Lieutenant who might testify as to what occurred!" I cried. "I cannot believe the two men to have stood alone on the French quarterdeck!"

"The rest of the boarding party being engaged in hand-to-hand combat, Jane—or in striking the colours—there was naught but confusion. You cannot have a proper idea of such an action, my dear—the great clouds of black smoke from the guns, carrying across the decks and obscuring sight; the cries of the wounded underfoot; the shouting of men made savage by death, and spurred into ferocity. When all is conducted on a platform that is constantly pitching, from the wash of the sea and a lower deck fast taking on water, you may understand that no one among the boarding party can swear to what might have happened. They were taken up with the business at hand—averting a pike in the gullet or an axe in the skull."

"Of course," I murmured. "And so it is Seagrave's word against his lieutenant's."

"So it would seem," Frank replied grimly. "But I mean to learn from Chessyre what cause he finds, to fire such a shot across Seagrave's bow! His commanding officer, and an old friend, too! He should be stripped of his rank and his uniform!"

I HAD NO DOUBT THAT FRANK SHOULD SWIFTLY SECURE THE LIEUTEN-
ant's direction, from among his naval acquaintance in Southampton,

and that the morning might find him in full possession of Chessyre's history before it had grown very much in the telling. But I hoped, as I drained my tea, that Frank had not gone in search of the man alone. The Lieutenant's actions argued for a desperation of character—and if Tom Seagrave had not murdered the Frenchman, it seemed entirely possible that Chessyre *had*.

Chapter 4

A Morning Call

24 February 1807,
cont.

~

I COULD NOT LONG ENJOY THE LUXURY OF LYING AMIDST THE BED-clothes, however much I might sneeze or Jenny scold: for I had recollected that it was Tuesday—and that we expected our dear friend and future companion in Castle Square, Martha Lloyd, before the morning should be out.

Martha is the eldest sister of my brother James's wife, Mary, but as unlike that shrewish article as the human frame is to a butter churn. She has formed the dearest part of my acquaintance for most of my life, having spent her youth in close concert with the Austens in Hampshire. Martha is the daughter of a clergyman, and is cousin to the Fowles of Kintbury—the very Fowles I might once have called family, had my sister Cassandra's betrothed survived his voyage to the West Indies so many years ago.[1] Martha's younger sister, Eliza,

1. The Reverend Thomas Fowle (1765–1797) became engaged to Cassandra Austen in 1792 but died of yellow fever in San Domingo five years later while serving as naval chaplain to his kinsman, William, Lord Craven.—*Editor's note.*

being the wife of the Reverend Fulwar-Craven Fowle, Martha might consider the vicarage at Kintbury as very nearly a second home; and thither she had repaired for the Christmas season. Her mother having passed away not long after my father's death, Martha may claim no other home, and has consented to form a part of our Southampton household.

Cassandra and I will thus know the pleasure of regarding Martha as very nearly a sister, a position we have long desired her to claim. There was a time when we believed it likely she should marry our Frank—but, however, the attraction between them, if indeed it existed, came to nothing. Martha is now in her early forties, some eight years Frank's senior; and with middle age, has acquired the dignity of a lady who dresses in lace caps and black satin. The difference between herself and Frank's rosy-cheeked bride is material, I assure you.

Among her many admirable qualities, Martha brings to our household the accomplishments of a cook, and a compilation of receipts, written out in her own hand, of such comestibles as she has learned to value through the years. In our present dismal weather, Martha should find the journey south from Berkshire cold and tiring; she would wish for a good dinner. As my mother was unlikely to quit her sickbed to procure a joint for Mrs. Davies's cook, I had better look to the business myself.

I rose and dressed for breakfast, sedulously avoiding my reflection in the glass that hangs over my dressing table. The pain of a chapped nose is more than enough to endure, without the added injury of ill looks. But I found that the tea had partially restored me; I felt a greater vigour, from my interval of writing amidst the bedclothes. I could not regard my diminished appearance as reason enough to remain within doors: not one woman in eighty may stand the test of a frosty morning, after all, and my watering eyes and reddened nose should occasion no very great comment on the streets of Southampton.

"Jane!" Frank's Mary exclaimed, as I entered upon the breakfast room, "I did not think to look for you this morning! And you are dressed!"

"I am quite well, Mary, thank you."

"You are hardly in looks, my dear," she declared, with utter disregard for my pride. "I am sure that you have a fever. Pray—come and sit beside the fire."

My brother's bride is a well-grown young woman of one-and-twenty, with a fresh complexion and vivid blue eyes; her hair is glossy, neither brown nor gold, but curling delightfully over her untroubled brow. Mary possesses good health, considerable good humour, and just enough of understanding to please her Frank without attempting to master him. She is not so high-born as to regard a seafaring life with contempt, nor yet so vulgar as to cause the Austens a blush; fond of dress without turning spendthrift; willing to listen to whatever novel I might chuse for our evening's entertainment; and desirous of her husband's credit before and beyond everything. Mary Gibson of Ramsgate, without the warm affections of a brother to praise her, might never have secured my interest; we are too unlike to pass as friends, without the intimacy of blood to unite us. But when I consider the flush of ladies Frank might have pursued—the grasping, prattling, heedless crowd that populates every sailors' ball in every port, and that is mad for officers of any stamp—I consider him as having chosen very well indeed. He certainly could have chosen far worse.

The weight of Mary's child is now impossible to conceal, however much she might let out the seams of her serviceable blue muslin; but she has gained in prettiness what she sacrifices in elegance. A perpetual air of happiness follows her; it is only when talk of her confinement arises that her visage is clouded, and exuberance fled. I am sure that she fears all manner of ills—pain, of course, and the death of her child or herself. Worse than all these, however, is the terror of Frank's possible absence at sea, during the interval of her childbed. She never speaks of it before him, but the women of her household are privileged to know everything.

She chatters to us without check or caution, as she might confide in a pack of hounds snoring before the hearth, and never considers of the fact that our loyalties—like our confidences—might be divided between husband and wife.

"Frank has been out early, and brought back kippers!" Mary exclaimed with delight. "And a quantity of fuel for the fire. He purchased nearly a cord of wood from a carter and had it sent round to our lodgings. But now he is gone out again. Should you like some fish?"

"Perhaps not just yet."

I adopted the chair near the fire and reached for the plate of toast our landlady had provided. Frank had certainly discovered Chessyre's lodgings, then, and might even now be closeted with the Lieutenant.

"I intend to walk out in order to procure a suitable dinner for Martha," I observed. "And you, Mary? Have you any plans for the morning? A visit, perhaps, among your acquaintance?"

"I shall accompany you to the market, if you have no objection. Mrs. Davies is quite insistent as to the efficacy of boiled eggs, for one in my condition. She assures me that there is nothing like a boiled egg for throwing off a fainting fit, in the evening; but she urges me to choose them myself, so that I might be certain they are wholesome."

I raised my brows with feigned interest. I thought it probable that a surfeit of dinner occasioned Mary's swoons, and might argue for a stricter diet; but lacking personal experience of the lady's state, I could not presume to offer an opinion. The addition of an egg or two, to the quantity of food she consumed, was unlikely to make much difference.

"Lord, how it does rain!" she cried. "I do not envy Martha Lloyd her journey on such a day. I own that I had thought the South would be pleasanter. Did not you, Jane?"

"Having spent most of my life in Hampshire, I may profess to be acquainted with its habits. I expect a severe March, a wet April, and a sharp May," I returned. "But we may hold out hope for June, Mary. What would England be, after all, without her June?"

"Scotland," she said promptly, and dissolved in giggles at her own wit.

OUR PLAN OF ATTEMPTING THE STREETS DIRECTLY AFTER BREAK-fast was forestalled, however, by a visitation of ladies from the naval set, who had recently claimed our acquaintance. No less than three of them descended upon our lodgings at eleven o'clock—such an early hour for a morning call, that we were taken by surprise in the very act of tying our bonnet strings, preparatory to quitting the front hall.

"Mrs. Foote!" Mary cried with pleasure, at the sight of the small-est lady among the party—a pink-cheeked, dark-haired creature very close to herself in age. "I had not thought you abroad, yet! What a stout woman you are! And how is the precious child?"

"Elizabeth is thriving," returned Mrs. Foote. She had been brought to bed of her fourth daughter only before Christmas, and looked remarkably well—an example that must prove encouraging to those in a similar state. From long acquaintance with the Foote family, and their various troubles, I sincerely wished them happy, and rejoiced to see the lady in health. Mary Patton had married Edward Foote only four years previous; she was his second wife, the first—an illegitimate daughter of a baronet—proving too unsteady for the care of her household or children. Having exchanged Pat-ton for Foote, Mary has been increasing without respite ever since.[2] As the Captain already possesses three children from his first unhappy union, he must certainly be accounted a prolific pro-genitor.

2. Jane is indulging in a pun. A patten was the small metal ring strapped onto ladies' shoes to elevate them from the mud of the streets during the winter sea-son.—*Editor's note.*

"And you, Mrs. Austen?" enquired Mrs. Foote, with an eye to Mary's figure, "are you in health?"

"Excellent health, I thank you. My poor sister Jane is not so well."

"You have taken a cold," said a faint voice at my shoulder. I curtseyed in the direction of Catherine Bertie, Admiral Bertie's daughter—who, though nearly ten years my junior, has already lost her bloom to the effects of ill-health. "Pray, let me offer you my vinaigrette."

"What she needs is a good hot plaster," declared a lantern-jawed woman of more advanced years. "I am Cecilia Braggen," she added, as if by way of afterthought, "wife to Captain Jahleel Braggen. I do not usually force acquaintance, you may be assured; but I am come expressly on a matter of some urgency, and must solicit the aid and benevolence of you both. May we beg a seat in your parlour?"

"Of course!" Mary breathlessly replied, and led her visitors within.

I glanced at Mrs. Foote, who returned an expression of amused condolence; however urgent the matter to Mrs. Braggen, it could not command the entire sympathy of her companion.

"Jane," Mrs. Foote whispered, as we moved to follow the others, "do not feel obliged to satisfy her in the least regard. I fell in with the woman as I progressed along the High. She could not be turned back. But I am come myself to press you all most urgently— your mother and Miss Lloyd included—to join us for an evening party at Highfield House on Friday."

"Friday? We should be delighted!" I cried. "I may answer for the others—we have no fixed engagements."

"That is excellent news. And perhaps we shall have cause for celebration! Edward confides that Captain Austen may soon be posted to a frigate!"

"How very unlucky that the intelligence should already have spread so far," I murmured uneasily. "There is just that degree of doubt in the case, that I should not wish the matter canvassed too soon. Mary, as yet, knows nothing of it."

"Then I shall not breathe a word," Mrs. Foote returned in a whisper. "Better that the full joy of it should burst upon her unawares!"

". . . most distressing implications for the entire port," Mrs. Braggen was exclaiming, as we joined the three women in Mrs. Davies's parlour. "Nineteen of the prisoners have fallen ill already, and with no one to nurse them, the situation will soon grow desperate! You cannot conceive the conditions in which they lie; the inclement weather must sharpen every discomfort. I have undertaken to organise our little society in shifts for the remainder of the week; but we are sadly pressed for hands. May I count upon each of you for at least a few hours—today or tomorrow, if convenient?"

I looked at Mary's pallid face and anxious eyes, and saw her palms pressed against her stomach. "Of what are you speaking?"

Cecilia Braggen wheeled upon me. "Of the French prisoners of war, confined in Wool House. There are forty of them held there, in a room fit for at most half that number; and they are all shaking with fever. The men who guard them—Marines, for the most part, and decidedly ill-educated—appear indifferent as to whether the poor fellows live or die. But I am persuaded that if disease is allowed to ravage the prisoners' ranks unchecked, it may soon spread to the Marines themselves—and you know what Marines are. The sickness will be all over the streets of Southampton in a thrice. We must act to stem the tide, before it is too late!"

"Mercy!" whispered Catherine Bertie. She held her vinaigrette to her flaring nostrils, and closed her eyes.

"But surely the French will soon be exchanged," Mrs. Foote observed most sensibly. "I am sure they should fare far better on their native shores."[3]

"I have it on good authority—from no less a personage than your father, Miss Bertie—that an exchange is not to be thought of

3. In the Napoleonic period of warfare, it was customary to hold prisoners of war only briefly, in expectation of a bilateral exchange in which officers of both sides were sent home. Common seamen, however, sometimes lingered in prison for months.—*Editor's note.*

before May. So you see where we are. I have presented my arguments most vigorously to the Admiral, and he agrees that we must attempt everything for the prisoners' comfort, and our own safety. He has offered me the services of his shipboard surgeon, a Mr. Hill."

"You would have us to nurse the French officers presently held in Wool House?" I repeated, for the sake of clarity. "What an extraordinary idea!"

"Do you speak French, Miss Austen?"

"A little," I replied, revolving the idea in my mind. I had just been struck by the possible utility of a nurse, and the method by which I might serve my brother and Tom Seagrave. "Do you happen to know, Mrs. Braggen, from *which* of the captured prizes the Frenchmen hail?"

Cecilia Braggen stared. "I have not the slightest idea, Miss Austen! And I would not have you to expect an officer among your charges. The officers are all housed in good naval families. I speak, in the case of Wool House, of common seamen."

"I do not believe that Captain Austen would wish his wife to risk exposure to illness at such a time," observed Mrs. Foote gently, with a glance for the anxious and tongue-tied Mary. "And for my own part, I cannot undertake to carry all manner of disease into the nursery."

"Father would certainly forbid it in my case!" cried Catherine Bertie, "however much he might recommend the charity, in the general way. You must know, Mrs. Braggen, that I have never been strong—and the winter months are replete with danger for a lady of delicate constitution!"

"It appears, Mrs. Braggen, as though you have won the heart of but a single recruit," I told the hatchet-faced lady. "Pray inform me at what hour I must report for duty."

Chapter 5

The Odour of Chessyre's Fear

MARY AND I WERE GRANTED A REPRIEVE OF SEVERAL HOURS BEFORE
I should be expected to take up my new vocation; at present, Mrs.
Braggen's serving woman—a close confidante, it seemed, of many
years' standing—was in attendance upon the surgeon, Mr. Hill. I
should have laughed aloud at this sacrifice of a personal maid, in
testament to Mrs. Braggen's devotion to her adopted cause, had
Catherine Bertie not warmly assured me that dear Cecilia had worn
herself to a fag end in nursing the sick at Wool House. She had ab-
sented herself from its noisome interior merely to solicit the aid of
her naval sisters. I might expect her return in the midst of my own
service—the better to instruct me, I suspected, in the finer points
of contagion.

Mary and I bid the ladies *adieu*—assured Mrs. Foote that we
should not fail her on Friday evening—and tarried only long
enough in the hall to be certain of escaping our departing friends.
Happily, the rain had dwindled to a fine mist, exactly calculated to

freshen Mary's complexion and add a springing curl to the wisps of hair escaping from my bonnet. And so we set off.

My first object was to select a joint suitable for Martha's delectation, and order it sent home to Mrs. Davies; my second was to ensure that my brother's wife did not come to any harm in the public market, where she intended to examine every egg ever laid by ardent hen. At the last, if time permitted, I intended a healthful walk up the length of the High—which in Southampton runs the entire extent of the ancient center of town, from the Quay at water's edge, north to the very Bar Gate. Southampton, like its sister, Portsmouth, has always been fortified with broad, stout walls and the Keep so necessary for the defence of the realm; all the efforts at improvement—the Polygon that ambitious builders would tout, as the next Fashionable locus for Gentlemen of Means, fine shop fronts along the broad sweep of the High, the modern villas erected in the hills beyond the town, by sailors turned once more on land—cannot disguise the pleasant utility of a stone escarpment twenty feet tall and eight feet wide, perfectly suited for a promenade in view of the sea. The garden of our prospective house in Castle Square is bordered by the city's battlements, and from its height—achievable by flights of steps at several points along the wall's length—one might gaze at the New Forest beyond. The sea washes steadily at the great wall's foot; and I imagine that in warmer months—my window flung open to the night air—I shall fall off to sleep amidst the gentle susurration of the waves, and dream that I am rocking aboard one of my brother's ships.[1]

So absorbed was I in this pleasant thought, that I was almost propelled headlong into the arms of the brother in question, as he

---

1. Present-day visitors to the probable site of Austen's house in Castle Square may still walk the wall that bordered what was once her garden but will notice that the sea has long since receded. A public-works land-reclamation project filled in the estuary that once divided this part of Southampton from the New Forest.—*Editor's note.*

stood outside the door of the Dolphin Inn, gazing earnestly upwards at one of its bow windows.

"Frank!" I cried; and, "Dearest!" exclaimed Mary at the same moment.

He turned, and appeared not to recognise us, so absorbed in thought was he. But then his expression changed; he shook off abstraction and mustered a smile. "You have caught me out, Mary, in a private dissipation—I never *can* pass the Dolphin without remarking upon the strange picture by way of a ship, that they have propped there in the window; a very strange ship, from its construction, and hardly one I should consent to command. The wind is filling the sails from entirely the wrong quarter, to judge by the ensign; and how any fool of a painter could expect such a craft— but enough, you are laughing at me, and no husband worth respect should consent to be laughed at."

I was convinced, from an intimate knowledge of my brother's ways, that some other object had drawn his eye to the Dolphin's window; but I forbore to question him. Over Mary's head, his gaze slid anxiously to my own; but I preserved my serenity of countenance, and he appeared relieved.

"You are in time, Mary, to renew your acquaintance with Captain Sylvester," Frank told his wife. "See—he is just coming along the opposite side of the High, and Mrs. Sylvester with him. Should you like to cross, and say how d'ye do?"

Mary expressing her willingness to perform this small social duty, we had soon exchanged one paving for another, and stood in a tight little knot of the Navy, while the Sylvesters—he a hale fellow of perhaps fifty, she a smaller article with an expression of bird-like intelligence—offered all that was solicitous regarding Mary's condition and Frank's shipless state. Our direction being consulted, the couple then obligingly turned back in order to accompany us on our way to Queen Anne Street. Amidst all the chatter of, "When do you expect to be removed to your home?" and, "When may we visit you in Castle Square?" and, "Pray allow me to relieve you of the burden of your eggs, Mrs. Austen—" an exchange of Captain Sylvester for Frank was made at Mary's arm. I found my brother at my side.

"I have seen him," he murmured low in my ear. "I have found him out. *Chessyre.*"

"He lodges at the Dolphin?"

Frank nodded abruptly. "It was no very great matter to learn his direction. The whole town may know it, provided they frequent the more disreputable taverns and houses of ill repute by the quayside. Mr. Chessyre, I find, is intimately known in certain circles that should never gain admittance to the Dolphin."

"And you spoke to him? You learned the truth of the engagement?"

"You possess far too wide a knowledge of the world, Jane, to assume that truth is so easily secured," my brother replied grimly. "Do not sport with my understanding by undervaluing your own; I am not in the humour for it."

Mary's laughter pealed delightedly before us; Captain Sylvester— or his diminutive wife—must be roundly entertaining.

"What did Chessyre say?"

"Very little. For a man much given to boasting when disguised in drink, he preserved a Delphic silence in his own rooms. I prodded—I pleaded—I threatened by turns; but the Lieutenant remains obdurate in his charge of murder. He would have it that Tom Seagrave demanded blood for blood, at the death of his Young Gentleman; and therein lies the end of the matter."

"And did Chessyre witness murder with his own eyes? Or does he merely assume the act, from the dirk's being first in Seagrave's possession?"

"He insists he saw the Frenchman, Porthiault, hold out his sword in surrender; that Seagrave took it, as is the custom, as the French colours came down; and that while the enemy captain stood defenceless, Seagrave cut him to the heart." Frank's voice was heavy. So determined a recital—complete with facts, and clear in its account—looked quite black indeed.

"Then why did Chessyre say nothing against his captain until he reached port?"

"From fear of Seagrave. To hear Chessyre tell it, he might as well have thrown himself into the sea, as accuse the man aboard his own ship. I cannot blame him for keeping silent, if there is truth in his charge. Such an act of murder—for that is what every man of feeling must hold it to have been—would urge the Lieutenant to believe Seagrave on the verge of madness. I confess, Jane, that having seen Chessyre—having heard his account with my own ears—I comprehend the grim looks of Admiral Bertie. So harsh a testimony could well sink my friend."

"And do you believe it, Frank?"

He was silent just that instant too long. "I confess I do not know what to believe."

"Will none of Seagrave's crew give Chessyre the lie?" I cried.

"None has come forward. It is possible that they are all in the most fearful indecision."

Much would be required, for a man to risk the contempt of the Admiralty—the loss of confidence were he proved wrong—the negative consequences for his career. Silence, in such a pass, would seem the wisest policy of all.

But silence was not my brother's choice.

"Jane, the Captain's trial is to be held two days hence on board Admiral Hastings's ship, moored in Portsmouth harbour. I intend to be present for the proceedings—and to offer my most fervent testimonial as to the worth of Seagrave's character."

"The case shall turn upon evidence, Frank, and not upon a judgement of character. If you would clear Captain Seagrave's name, you must learn why his lieutenant intends him to hang."

My blunt words occasioned little more than a grunt of displeasure from Frank; he could not love the duty that must destroy the honour of one man, or the other.

"You have but two choices," I persisted. "To regard your friend as innocent, or to believe Lieutenant Chessyre's charge. If the latter— your friend's cause is lost. If the former—then we must consider the possibility that the Lieutenant would shift guilt upon the Captain, because he is mortally afraid of being charged with murder *himself*."

"Chessyre?" Frank cried, as one amazed.

"I can account for his actions in no other way—excepting the spur of truth. And you will not allow him to speak from truth."

"But why should Chessyre kill the French captain? Seagrave has never suggested that he did; and if Seagrave did not see the hand that struck Porthiault down, then how may we accuse Chessyre of the act?"

"I confess the entire affair confounds reason. I am almost persuaded that both men are mired in half-truths and prevarication. No other construction may be placed upon events."

"A very simple construction might be placed upon them," Frank countered grimly. "Shall I tell you what it is? Eustace Chessyre is an aging man. He has been thirteen years a first lieutenant, and is unlikely ever to achieve a further rank. Two younger men in Seagrave's command—second lieutenants, both of them—have been promoted to master and commander from beneath Chessyre's eye. He told me so himself. The success of his subordinates has made him bitter, Jane. He has been passed over, from among the ranks of his own men. He cannot bear the indignity—and he blames Seagrave for its accomplishment. He regards his captain as blocking his advance—as deliberately thwarting Chessyre's career—when by all accounts poor Tom has done nothing but look out for the man in his progress through the service."

I considered this theory. "And thus we find the goad to murder. You believe the fellow nursed his grievance, and merely awaited opportunity to exact revenge?"

"If he was so struck by Seagrave's act—if indeed he witnessed the Captain's hand strike down an enemy officer after receiving that officer's sword—then why did he not denounce my friend at the very moment? Instead we find him appointed commander of the French prize, and beating back to Portsmouth without a murmur."

"That is very singular," I admitted.

"Chessyre had several days' sailing time to consider of his story, before appearing off Spithead in the captured prize. He might have walked the *Manon*'s deck with any number of devils, Jane; he might have been tortured in his mind up to the very moment of going over the side with Seagrave's letters, and only cast his lot for murder as he gained the Admiral's ship to convey his intelligence."

"He took a formidable risk. What if the British seamen under his command denied the charge against their captain?"

"They probably knew nothing of Chessyre's intent while yet in Portsmouth; they should have been sent out to regain the *Stella* once the prize was secured. Chessyre seized his moment, convinced that he should be safe."

"—Acting solely from revenge?"

"And from interest, Jane. A healthy and hopeful self-interest. Eustace Chessyre thought to be made master on the strength of this action—and if Seagrave were removed from the *Stella*, why should not Chessyre command her? A temporary appointment, perhaps, but one that might satisfy so embittered a man. Never mind that masters and commanders are never posted into anything higher than a sloop: Chessyre was in the grip of delusion."

"He should better have thrust the dirk into Seagrave's heart," I observed, "and assumed command of the *Stella* while yet on the high seas."

Frank was silent an instant in consideration. Then, with his eyes fixed upon the rain-splashed paving-stones at our feet, he said, "It is one thing to strike down an enemy in the heat of battle; it is quite another to kill a man in cold blood with whom one has sailed year after year. If pressed, I should say that Eustace Chessyre is not above plotting what is devious; he may calculate, and lie, and attempt to turn misfortune to every advantage—but I do not think he would do murder outright."

"How kind you are!" I cried. "How judicious! The court-martial had better employ your powers of pleading on behalf of your fellow man, Fly. To say that the Lieutenant preferred Seagrave to die at the hangman's hands, rather than his own, is so much flummery. I wonder your man can live with himself!"

"He certainly does not live in comfort," my brother said. "I have been long enough at war to recognise the stench of fear; it dogs the gundeck before every engagement, it sleeps in the hammocks of unsound men. Chessyre's room was rank with it, Jane. The man is awash in terror, and sinking fast."

I halted on the street and stared at Frank. "And what do you believe him to fear? Discovery in deceit?"

"I cannot say. Something more powerful than myself, or all the threats I might bring to bear. But in parting with the fellow, I urged him to consider his course—to judge if it were sound—and pressed my direction into his hand. We might yet hope for a visit from the Lieutenant, and a reversion of events, before Thursday morning."

We walked on, each of us silent, until achieving the turning for Queen Anne Street. There my footsteps slowed, and I gazed down the broad sweep of the High to the huddle of buildings that fronted the Quay. One of these—a squat, square stone structure of ancient date, with a peaked brick roof and windows barred with iron—was Wool House.

"What we require," I told my brother, "is an impartial witness to the French captain's death."

"That is exactly what we shall never have," Fly retorted.

"Do not be so certain, my dear," I replied. "*Never* is an unconscionable period."

Chapter 6

Wool House

WOOL HOUSE DATES, I AM TOLD, FROM THE FOURTEENTH CENTURY, when Southampton was a far smaller port than it now appears, and the town's habitation was contained entirely between the Water Gate and the Bar. It was built during a period of warfare and constant strife; a period, too, of thriving commerce, when the wool from England's great herds travelled across the sea to weavers in Flanders, and thence to the princes of Florence. Wool House once formed the hub of this trade—a meeting place for the Wool Merchants Guild. They were warm men, quite plump in the pocket, and if indeed it was they who soldered bars to the building's window frames, we may comprehend the value of their fears.

In the interval of five hundred years that stretches between those times and ours, the incidence of warfare borne in ships across the Channel has hardly diminished; but the wool trade has found other weavers to surfeit, other backs to clothe, and fewer pockets to line with guineas. Wool House itself has served many uses: as a customs house, as the offices of the local constabulary, and most recently, as a gaol for prisoners of war. The bars once intended to keep miscreants *out,* now serve to hold them within.

I turned into French Street, as though merely another lady intent upon securing seats in a box at the pretty little theatre that stood some distance beyond; and lingered before the double black doors that fronted the Water Gate Quay. Two Marines in scarlet dress stood to either side of the arched portal; one was rigid with his sense of duty, but the other allowed his gaze to stray insolently over my form. Without even a second perusal, he dismissed me as unworthy of his attention.

"Pray tell me, sir," I said in an accent sharpened by suppressed indignation, "whether Mr. Hill, the surgeon, is within Wool House? I have undertaken to assist him in his ministrations to the French."

The Marine's gaze returned to my countenance with an expression of slow amusement, but his companion—somewhat senior in rank, from his appearance—relaxed his stance and bowed.

"You will find the surgeon within, ma'am—but allow me to urge you to reconsider. Wool House is not a suitable place for a lady."

He possessed a kindly visage, and his glance was direct; it held neither presumption nor arrogance, but merely the most active concern. I managed a smile.

"May I enquire as to your name?"

"Major Morrissey, ma'am."

"I am Miss Austen, Major," I told him, "the sister of Captain Austen of the Royal Navy—and I fully understand the dangers to which I expose myself. But were my brother laid low on enemy shores, I should wish him to be equally served by the hand of some French lady."

"Step lively, Stubbs," the Major urged his subordinate, "and shift the door for the Captain's sister!"

A heavy block was moved—an iron ring turned—a bolt thrown back—and the massive oak doors suffered to swing slowly inwards, while my two protectors lowered the muzzles of their guns to prevent the sudden escape of anyone within. I hesitated an instant on the threshold, my eyes overcome by the blackness of the interior, then took a few steps forward.

"Knock three times on the oak when you wish to be let out," Major Morrissey urged, "and mind you don't exhaust yourself, ma'am. Recollect that in their right senses, these fellows would as soon blow your good brother to pieces as take a cup of gruel from yourself."

With a screech of protest as painful as a sinner's wail, the heavy doors swung closed.

I was conscious of an awkward silence, as of conversation abruptly cut off, and then a resurgent murmur of male conversation, and a guttural bark of laughter. The dimness within was not so heavy as I had at first supposed; there were, after all, several barred windows punctuating the massive stone walls, and through the bleary panes of glass a little light must penetrate. Two or three candles burned in niches high above the prisoners. But the room was darkest at my feet, where so many men lay side by side. It was as though the shadows emanated from the sick themselves, to hover like a gathering of souls in the rafters above.

It was as well that I had stopped short just beyond the room's threshold—for there was barely space to walk among the pallets. I stifled a gasp of disbelief as I gazed about me—how many men had Mrs. Braggen described? Forty, in a room better suited for half that number? At least ten were arranged around two tables at the rear of the room, playing at cards; but they alone were upright of the entire assembly. The rest lay in suffering at my feet, some as still as death, some moaning piteously for water. Others thrashed about as though pitching with the roll of the waves; and I saw, with failing looks, that these men's legs were bound with hemp to prevent them kicking at those who would aid them.

The atmosphere, though cold and damp, was sharp with the smells of blood and human waste, and putrefying wounds; with the heavy must of unwashed men. The animal odour of tallow mixed chokingly with the charcoal smoke from a single fire at one side of the chamber. There had recently been meat roasting somewhere on a spit.

I felt my gorge rise, and fumbled in my reticule for a handkerchief. Cecilia Braggen was right to fear the spread of contagion,
when it found its source in such a room.

"Qu'est-ce que vous voulez, madame?" cried the voice of one grizzled
old card player.

"Le médecin," I returned, after an instant's panicked retrieval of
my schoolgirl French. *"M'sieur Hill. Est-il ici?"*

A small figure rose up from the floor like Beelzebub, and saluted
me with a bow: Mr. Hill, I did not doubt. He was spare of form, with
a periwig affixed rather carelessly on a bony head; shirtsleeves
turned back, forearms bare, and a heavy black apron over his shirtfront and trousers. I should have known him for a naval surgeon in
a moment; his very air suggested shipboard economy.

"You one of the naval ladies, I trust?" he enquired without preamble.

"My name is . . . Miss Austen," I stammered. "And you are . . . Mr.
Hill?"

His eyes surveyed me shrewdly; it was a measuring glance, as my
brother Edward might assess the points of a prospective hunter,
and I quailed at the surgeon's calculation of my fitness or courage.
The awful truth of my careless undertaking had fallen full upon
me. When Mrs. Braggen proposed the duty this morning, I accepted with the view to a little French conversation. I thought to
soothe a fevered brow, and discover, in the process, whether any of
the *Manon*'s crew was held at Wool House. But I found myself in
the midst almost of battle. There was nothing of frivolity here; no
easy passage for deception. These men represented the harsh
spoils of war, in all their misery and deprivation; and however soon
they might be exchanged, I should not lightly forget them. I fought
the impulse to turn and pound heartily upon the door in expectation of the Marines.

"You are some relation to Captain Frank Austen?" Mr. Hill enquired.

"His sister, sir."

The surgeon wiped an instrument absently on his canvas apron, and nodded. "I met with the Captain some once or twice, while serving in the Indies. You'll do. Pray follow me."

I took up the basin he thrust into my hands, and commenced to spoon weak gruel between the cracked lips of one unshaven face after another. And presently—as though I had been no more than an insect that came to light upon a table—I was dismissed from the interest of the French, as care for their own consuming anxieties superseded the novelty of my presence. The card players returned to their gambling, and the sick to their pitiful moaning. I followed Mr. Hill in a sort of macabre dance, stooping and rising, from one sad pallet to the next, and felt that the line of suffering should never come to an end.

The contagion was of a peculiar kind: some of my patients were o'erspread with red spots; others suffered trembling so acute, they could neither stand nor hold a spoon; all were racked with fever. But I detected no inflammation of the lungs—no catarrh, that might be manifest in coughing; whatever the ill, it could not be laid to the account of Southampton's raw weather.

"What ails these men?" I whispered once.

"Gaol-fever," replied Mr. Hill grimly. "A common enough complaint, when so many are forced to shift together like beasts in a barn. But there is little a surgeon may do for such a malady. I have bled them; I have given water; and for the rest—God shall provide."[1]

From the look of the poor wretches lying about the floor, all that God was likely to provide, I knew, was a foreign grave.

WE WORKED IN SILENCE, BUT FOR THE FEW WORDS OF DIRECTION Mr. Hill deemed necessary. I emptied chamber pots through the barred windows into the Southampton gutters; I cleaned wounds

1. Gaol-fever and ship fever were the common names for typhus—an acute infectious disease caused by a rickettsia transmitted to man by the bite of fleas or lice. Typhus is not to be confused, however, with typhoid fever—a malady caused by a bacillus found in unpasteurized milk.—*Editor's note.*

with rags dipped in hot water; I pressed cold compresses against fevered brows; and once, to my horror, I was required to hold steady the shoulders of a man while Mr. Hill probed his angry flesh for the bullet buried there. Far from interrogating the assembled enemy, I was tongue-tied with pity and horror. At this rate, I thought despondently, I should learn nothing that might support Captain Seagrave's claims of innocence.

My passage among the pallets had revealed one item of intelligence, however. Members of the *Manon*'s crew were certainly among the inmates of Wool House. I learned this not from any words of French that were spoken, but from a lady's skill at observing the fine points of dress. It is a seaman's habit to embroider ribbons upon his shiny tarpaulin hat; the ribbons invariably bear the name, in bright letters, of the ship that he serves. Four at least proclaimed the *Manon*. Three lay by the sides of men tossing upon the floor; but the last still rested upon the head of a fellow who seemed in better health than his brothers.

He was sitting up, shaky and weak, and though desperate to consume some hot broth, looked unable to hold the spoon that Mr. Hill had afforded him. I judged him to be a seaman, of perhaps fifty years or so; but whether he should be rated Ordinary or Able, I could not entirely say.[2] I inclined towards Able: from the length of his hair, which was knotted in a queue that reached to the middle of his back, I suspected him of naval pride; and, of course, there was the hat, with its handsome red ribbons embroidered in blue and white. *Manon.*

I took bowl and spoon from the man's shaking fingers and helped him gently to eat. His jaw trembled as the broth trickled into his mouth, and he closed his eyes. *"Merci, madame."*

2. An Ordinary seaman was a man with little experience of the navy or of ships. He was paid less than a sailor rated Able, a designation accorded men who had mastered the skills required for the working of ships. The French navy probably employed different terms and standards from the Royal Navy in this regard; but Austen would have used the designations familiar to her. —*Editor's note.*

"De rien," I replied.

His eyes flew open. *"Vous parlez français?"*

"Un peu, seulement. Il y avait beaucoup de temps . . ."

He fluttered a thin hand in dismissal of my excuses. His red-rimmed eyes were dangerously over-bright. *"Avez-vous du papier?"*

Did I have paper? I stared at him in consternation. I could not have understood the words correctly.

"Pour les lettres," he insisted. *"Je voudrais écrire à Provence . . ."*

Letters home. But of course. He was probably illiterate, and would depend upon the skill of others to despatch his intelligence to France. Somewhere in the south of that country, there might be a wife or a child—someone who could fear him dead, were it not for the arrival of a missive penned in a strange hand. A whisper of excitement rose up within me. For surely this fellow—so recently taken prisoner—must desire to relate every detail of the *Manon's* engagement with the British? Should he not be likely to recount, in tedious detail, the moments that led to his ship's capitulation?

"I shall find you paper," I said without regard for French or English, and set down the man's bowl. His gaze followed me in hopeful confusion as I hurried towards Mr. Hill.

After whispered consultation, the surgeon accepted the few coins I pressed into his palm and sent an urchin to a nearby tavern. The appearance of writing materials a quarter of an hour later occasioned a surge in health, an increase of life and energy among the ailing. A few moments bent over my pen, and I was surrounded by such men as could drag themselves near to watch my hand move across the cheap foolscap. Had the supply of paper not been swiftly exhausted, I might be writing to France still. A tedious job I should have found it, for the mind of your common sailor is in general unimaginative.

The fellow whose duty I first undertook, was direct in his wording and naive in his aims. He wished only to inform a lady named Marguerite that he was alive—that he was confident he should soon be returned to Boulogne—that he desired her to remain chaste—and that she must not, on any account, sacrifice the red-backed rooster to her mania for *cassoulet*. I managed to convey as much of these varying sentiments as my pitiful mastery of French would allow, and then enquired: "Do you not wish to tell her anything of the engagement in which you fell prisoner? It was with the *Stella Maris,* was it not?"

My seaman pursed his lips and emitted a peculiarly French sound somewhere between an expectoration and a whistle, as if to say, *"Tant pis."* He had done with defeat; he was marshalling his strength for a return to battle; he could not reflect upon ships that were lost. Why discredit the Emperor's glory, by sending news of so ignominious an engagement? All these sentiments and some I could not fathom were contained in that single syllable, that sputum of contempt. I folded the sheet of paper in disappointment.

But directly I had sealed the edges with tallow, my services were implored by others too ready to relate the particulars of the *Manon*'s loss. And here I discovered, to my chagrin, the limits of schoolgirl French.

I had never been taught the sort of terms that might prove useful in such a pass—the French that should distinguish the differences among guns, or describe the varying weights of shot, or convey the particulars of sail and line. I struggled to decipher the full sense of *vient sous le vent,* which I took to mean "coming under the wind," when (I later learned) it meant "coming into the lee." I could not attempt to explain "seizing the weather gauge" in any language. And I knew nothing of the *patois* that reigned supreme among the denizens of the gundeck. I was on the verge of despair, when a quiet voice at my shoulder said in English—

"I believe I might prove of some assistance, *madame.*"

My face flushed with effort, my ears ringing with a multitude of voices, I turned to glare at the man propped against the stone wall. And managed to utter not a word of acknowledgement or thanks, being overcome, of a sudden, with confusion and surprise.

He was too weak, I imagine, to sit upright without assistance, and his dark eyes glittered at me through half-opened lids. He wore breeches of a colour indeterminate in the dark, and a white linen shirt oddly at variance with the soiled garb of the men about him; his fine hands rested lightly on his knees. It was the hands that drew my attention, after those first words of English; they had certainly never hauled a line, nor pulled this man upwards into the shrouds. He had recently shaved. His features were fine. There was a quirk of humour about the full lips, and strength in the cut of his chin. I must be staring at a French officer—inexplicably left to sicken and die among the ranks of his own men. But where was his uniform, or the marks of authority?

"You speak English," I managed.

He bowed his head—a gesture of courtesy, the habit of a gentleman. "I might translate for your pen. There are niceties, there are *forms,* to a life at sea with which a lady like yourself could not be expected to be familiar. . . ."

Niceties. Forms. How often had I heard those words? He might be my very brother Frank; he had been cut from the same mould. "Certainly you may assist me. I should be glad of the help. Are these your shipmates?"

"What few remain. Most of the *Manon*'s crew are held at the large naval prison in Portsmouth—you know it?"

I nodded assent. It was a fortification that dated from the Norman era; twenty generations of British prisoners might have rotted there.

"But your navy has had too much luck, and that prison is full of the French; and so we are sent here, along with others of different vessels, to await the exchange."

"You are not a common seaman," I said awkwardly, "and yet I do not observe the uniform of an officer."

"We are all equal in defeat, *madame,*" he retorted gently. "But perhaps that is a French belief—the equal right of men to suffer and die. When something more of value is at stake, however, we prove as selfish as the rest of the world."

He smiled—a flash of white in that dim and awful room—and I felt a wave of giddiness rise from my feet to my cheeks. I could not help smiling back.

"You were writing to the sister of Jean-Philippe, I believe," he resumed. "Something about the *Stella* luffing, and the wind being three points off the bow, and the *Manon* incapable of carrying royals."

"Yes," I stammered. "Luffing. Is that what *vient au lof* meant?"

His eyelids drifted lower, as though he would fade with weariness. "I would write to all of them myself," he murmured, "but I can barely hold up my head. *C'est une fièvre de cheval . . .*"

I rose and went to him in some anxiety. His forehead was clammy, his limbs trembling with the effort he had brought to bear on conversation. "You should lie down," I said sternly. "You require rest."

"A little water, if you please."

I hesitated—Mr. Hill did not like cold water on a fevered stomach, believing it to cause retching; I fetched the man some lukewarm tea instead. He drank it without complaint, sighed, and closed his eyes again.

"*Madame,*" cried Jean-Philippe, the young seaman who had wished to write of luffing. "*Madame, s'il vous plaît—*"

"*Un moment.*"

The Frenchman's eyes flicked open. "You are very good, with your paper and your broth. May I ask what is your name?"

"I am Miss Austen."

"And I am Etienne LaForge," he murmured. "You may call me ship's surgeon. It is as good a name as any for me. Has M'sieur Hill determined the nature of this illness?"

"Gaol fever."

"Ah. It is as I suspected. Pray continue with your letters, *mademoiselle,* and I shall supply whatever words you deem necessary—"

I recommended writing; and in a very little while, possessed a greater understanding of the *Manon*'s last moments than the *Naval Chronicle* should be likely to procure.[3]

3. The *Naval Chronicle* was a journal published twice annually from 1799 to 1818. It detailed Royal Navy actions as well as other topics of interest relating to the sea, with maps and illustrations.—*Editor's note.*

It would appear that Captain Seagrave had learned his tactics at Nelson's foot, for like that great departed naval hero, he was a proponent of gunnery and of crossing an enemy's bows with complete disregard for peril. Seagrave laid the *Stella* yardarm to yardarm with the French frigate, and brought his full broadside to bear at point-blank range—only four hundred yards of heaving water lay between. The destruction rained upon the *Manon*'s hull was dreadful, for the British crews displayed greater accuracy than the French in training their guns. Where the *Stella* received a quantity of grape in the rigging, to the detriment of her masts and canvas, the *Manon* took several balls below the waterline, and was shipping water faster than the pumps could work. A mere forty minutes into the action, three of the French guns had been dismounted, and were rolling about the deck with every pitch of the waves, at immense hazard to the men; two unfortunate sailors found their feet crushed beneath the weight.

Seagrave seized his moment. He brought the *Stella* across the *Manon*'s bows; his boarding party, with their pikes and axes, fell upon the French crew; and within moments, the poop, quarterdeck, waist of the ship—all were overrun—and the colours struck.

"You will not find great willingness to fight among the French sailors at present," LaForge observed, when Jean-Philippe had fallen silent. "We preserve too well the tragedy of Trafalgar. It is accepted truth that British guns will always prevail. We prefer to run rather than engage; then we might save our ships as well as our lives."

"But the *Manon* did not run. And how many men were lost?" I enquired, my eyes trained upon the foolscap.

Jean-Philippe did not reply. I glanced over at the French surgeon.

"Thirty-four were killed outright. Eighty-seven were wounded," LaForge said.

"Seamen? Or officers?"

"We lost only one officer—*le capitaine*, Porthiault. The rest—our lieutenants and midshipmen—are housed in Portsmouth and Southampton, if they have not already been exchanged."

"Your captain! That must have been a great loss."

LaForge's head moved restlessly against the stone wall. "I tended his body myself."

"He was killed in battle?"

"But of course." He turned to stare at me. "You thought it possible he died of fright at the sight of the Royal Navy? It is hardly singular for a captain to be killed, when he is exposed to the enemy guns. Officers maintain a position on the quarterdeck, you understand, in the path of every well-aimed ball."

"If you tended his body, Monsieur LaForge—you must have seen the nature of Porthiault's wound?"

"I begin to suspect that you have a taste for the macabre, Miss Austen." The dark eyes—so deep a brown that in the flickering candlelight, they appeared almost the colour of claret—held my own. "You spend your liberty in the stench and squalor of Wool House, ministering to the sick; and you are morbidly concerned with the history of a man's last agony. You interest me very much. What can have excited your curiosity?"

I had no desire to inform the *Manon*'s crew that a British captain was charged with the murder of their captain. If they were at all akin to British seamen, I might very well have a riot on my hands.

"It is only that my brother is a post captain," I said lamely, "and I suffer considerable anxiety on his behalf."

"He is presently at sea?"

"No—but he is likely soon to be."

LaForge stared at me quizzically, unconvinced.

"And . . . and we possess a considerable acquaintance among the officers of the *Stella Maris*. The action has been of no little significance in Portsmouth."

"I see. You wish to carry all the smallest details of the noble Porthiault's end to your next card party. I am afraid that I cannot increase your delight, Miss Austen. I was below decks, throughout the action."

"You saw nothing?" I murmured in disappointment.

"The surgeon's place in battle is always the cockpit deck,"

LaForge said by way of reply. "I was entirely taken up with amputation, you understand—two men had suffered crushed feet, from the dismounting of the guns, and there were arms and legs torn away. I did not emerge on deck until I had dressed the last wound."

How unfortunate, that the most articulate and sound observer of the naval battle should be below decks throughout the action! I stared at Etienne LaForge with consternation; and at that moment a timid hand brushed my elbow. Jean-Philippe.

"*Ma lettre?*" he enquired. "*C'est finie?*"

"*Mais oui,*" I replied, and folded it swiftly. "Did any of the *Manon*'s crew observe how your captain died, Monsieur LaForge?"

"You are very interested in a fellow who was no better than a fool, and who is now feeding sharks off Corunna, Miss Austen."

His voice—formerly so weak and gentle in its expression—fell like a lash upon my ears. I looked up, and dripped hot tallow across my fingertips.

"I listen to the talk of the Marines outside, from time to time," he said slowly, his half-lidded eyes never leaving my face. "They say that the captain of the *Stella Maris* has been charged with murder. I thought I imagined their words—in the rages of fever, you understand, much may be distorted—but now I am no longer certain. Is that man accused of the death of Porthiault?"

I nodded. "Captain Seagrave is charged with having killed Captain Porthiault after the *Manon* struck. He is to go before a court-martial on Thursday. The outcome is . . . uncertain."

LaForge pursed his lips. "A pity. Seagrave is a gallant fellow—a Heart of Oak, as you English say. Clever in his tactics and fearless in their execution—he fought like a tiger, as though all the hounds of hell were at his back. Are you in love with him?"

I gasped incredulously. "You mistake me, sir! Captain Seagrave has long been a married man!"

LaForge lifted his shoulders dismissively. "There must be some reason you concern yourself."

"The Captain is my brother's fellow officer. I am acquainted with his wife."

"Ah." The surgeon's voice was now faintly mocking. "The bosom friend of the wife. I understand. But you do not believe this Seagrave killed *le capitaine*. And neither do I, Miss Austen."

I studied the amusement at his mouth, the strong chin, and knew that the man was sporting with me. He was, after all, the French ship's surgeon; if any had examined Porthiault's body before it was sent over the side, it should be LaForge.

"How do they say that Porthiault died?" he asked.

"That is a point under dispute. Captain Seagrave would have it the man was already dead when the colours were struck. Others insist that Porthiault died by Seagrave's hand, *after* the *Manon*'s surrender. Seagrave's dirk was buried in Porthiault's heart, but Seagrave will have it that he never touched the man! It is a difficult tale to credit—"

With effort, LaForge leaned towards me. He spoke very low. "Porthiault did not die from the knife to his heart. He died from the wound to his head."

"His head?" I repeated. "But the dirk—"

"A small hole at the base of the skull," the surgeon continued, "oozing blood as the chest wound could not. The chest wound was given *after* death. I tell you, I examined the body before it was delivered into the sea."

"A musket shot, then? Fired during the battle?"

There was a glint of something in LaForge's narrowed gaze. Then his shoulders lifted again in that most Gallic of gestures. "There is nothing very wonderful in this. Your own Nelson—the Hero of Trafalgar—died in much the same way."

It was true. A French marksman had aimed for the jewelled star pinned at the Admiral's breast, and wounded him mortally.

"Seagrave said the Frenchman lay as though dead when discovered on the quarterdeck. He thought the man had been stunned by a falling spar. Why, then, thrust a dirk into his heart?" I mused.

"For vengeance? Or . . . the desire to make it appear as such? This Seagrave was not alone, *hein*?"

"He was not. His first lieutenant stood with him."

The man held my gaze. Despite the fever, despite his weakness and the lazy arrangement of his limbs, Etienne LaForge was taut as a bowstring. He knew the end to which I must be brought; but he preferred that I reach it under my own power.

"You saw him!" I declared. "You saw Eustace Chessyre near Seagrave on the quarterdeck. You were not below throughout the battle, as you claim."

"I do not know the man's name." He glanced over my shoulder warily and lowered his voice to the faintest of murmurs. "There was a great deal of sea in the cockpit deck, you understand. The pumps could not keep up with it. Those British guns—how they love to kiss the waterline! I was forced to pile my patients at the foot of the gangway, and to plead for help in shifting them; otherwise, I feared they should drown. And I am not in the habit of saving a life, to lose it to the sea."

"You went up the gangway to beg assistance."

"The waist of the ship was a chaos of men," LaForge said faintly. "I turned and glanced up at the quarterdeck, where the Captain already lay dead. It was then that I saw him."

"Seagrave?" I whispered.

"The British captain was being set upon, by our second lieutenant, Favrol; the two were fighting *du corps à corps*."

"So the ship had not yet struck."

The surgeon shook his head.

"Seagrave was alone?"

"For all the good his support did him—he ought to have been. But no, *mademoiselle*, the Captain had an officer at his back. I did not, at the time, observe the rank—but I recognised him later. He was master of the ship that carried me prisoner into this British port."

"Lieutenant Chessyre," I breathed.

"Very well. I observed him, bent over *le capitaine* Porthiault, while Seagrave and Favrol were at each other's throat; he knelt there a moment—his arm rose—and when he stood, Porthiault's sword was in his hand."

"What of the colours?"

LaForge shook his head. "At such a time—who can say when the *Manon* struck? All was confusion. But know this, *mademoiselle*"—his voice became almost indistinct—"when the officer rose from Porthiault's side, the dirk was in my captain's breast. I would swear on my mother's grave that it was not there before."

My breath came in with a hiss. LaForge's eyes widened in alarm; he raised a feverish hand to his lips.

"*Mademoiselle*—do not betray us both. More than one man's life may hang upon your discretion."

His fingers dropped heavily to his side.

"But why thrust a blade into the breast of a dead man?" I murmured, with a swift glance around the shadowy chamber.

"Must I always translate for you, *mademoiselle?* The word is not *why,* but *who.* Who among all the men of the British Navy would wish your Seagrave to hang? For that was certainly Chessyre's object. He did not strike for vengeance against the French, but from motives none may penetrate. This was no act of war, Miss Austen. Your Seagrave was betrayed from within."

Chapter 7

Messenger to Portsmouth

24 February 1807,
cont.

~

I RACED HOME THROUGH THE DARKENING STREETS, INTENT UPON
finding Frank and relating all that LaForge had told me. I must
have looked a trifle mad among the sedate ladies and aging sailors
that made their careful way along the High; in the darkness and
stench of Wool House I had become like one of Mrs. Radcliffe's
desperate heroines, with Etienne LaForge my cryptic prisoner of
the keep. I do not think that I would have accorded the Frenchman's words the same horrific weight, had he not presented a failing aspect. There is something chilling about the word *betrayal*
when uttered by a sinking man, particularly against the backdrop
of ancient stone walls. LaForge had chosen his moment—and his
auditor—well.

My brother was established with Mary before the fire in Mrs.
Davies's sitting-room; at the sight of my flushed face and heaving
breast, he rose at once in alarm.

"Jane! You are unwell!"

"Nothing I regard. A trifle fagged from haste."

"But where have you been, my dear?" Mary enquired.

"At Wool House. Tending the French prisoners laid low with gaol fever."

"Gaol fever!" Frank's countenance darkened. "Have you lost your reason, Jane? To expose yourself to such a scourge, when Mary's health—and the health of our child—is certainly at stake? I forbid you to go so close to my wife as twenty yards, madam, until we may be certain that you have not contracted the disease! No, nor so close as fifty yards to our mother, given her delicate state of health! I am in half a mind to procure you a room at the Dolphin until we may be sure that you are clear!"

"Banish her to London, Fly, and permit me to serve as chaperone," said my dear friend Martha Lloyd as she sailed into the room. "I might recommend any number of places in Town, and Jane and I could enjoy the Season at a safe distance from little Mary—provided, of course, that gaol fever does not carry Jane off. But I confess to a sanguine temper on that head. I have little fear of seeing any of us come out in spots. It has always been a man's complaint."

I embraced Martha with joy, and enquired as to the safety and comfort of her descent upon the south; declared her in excellent looks after her visit to her sister—a compliment she turned aside with asperity—and took her bonnet into my own hands for safekeeping.

But the niceties of welcome had eluded my brother. Frank took one furious stride across Mrs. Davies's small parlour and turned in frustration at the far wall. He appeared to be itching to draw someone's cork; his hands were clenching and unclenching in a fine demonstration of the pugilist's art. I was not to be forgiven my improbable charity. In such a mood, he was unlikely to credit anything I might say.

"Oh, my dearest," Mary cried, "do not be thinking of sending Jane away! I confess that I cannot do without her!"

Her plump hands were pressed against her mouth; she stared at Frank in dismay. I do not think she had ever witnessed a display of her husband's temper; but I have an idea it is very well known among Frank's colleagues in the Navy. He did not survive the mutinies at Spithead in '97, nor yet a gruelling chase across the Atlantic and back again in pursuit of the French, without driving his men and himself to the point of collapse.

"Damned foolish!" he returned, with fine disregard for our landlady's peace. "And why? Because Celia Braggen—that lantern-jawed, jumped-up busybody whose husband is the worst sort of scrub—required it!"

"Jane only went to that dreadful place to spare me the trouble, Frank," Mary stammered. "I thought it very kind in her to oblige Mrs. Braggen, and save me from giving offence!"

"I shall call upon that Harpy in the morning, and offer my opinion of her presumption," he muttered.

"Then pray let us dine on the strength of your conviction, Frank—it does not do to meet a Harpy on an empty stomach." Martha's attention was given entirely to drawing off her gloves. "Jane may sit at the farthest remove from Mary and the fire both, as punishment, and your mother have her meal on a tray. They do not offer much in the way of sustenance, in your southern coaching inns; and the smell of that joint makes me ready to weep with vexation."

"Frank," I interjected, "however angry you may be, I must have a word with you at once. It is a matter of the utmost urgency."

My brother's brows were lowered over his frigid grey eyes. He glanced at Mary; she threw me a frightened look, but gathered up her sewing without a word. Martha placed a hand at her elbow, and was just saying comfortably as the door clicked behind them, "I hear that the talk in Southampton is all of short sleeves for the summer—" when I sank down into a chair.

Frank listened this time without interruption. I told him of Etienne LaForge, and the scene the French surgeon had witnessed on the *Manon*'s quarterdeck; I told him of the blood from the head wound, and the lack of same from Porthiault's chest. I told him, moreover, of LaForge's final charge: *This was no act of war. . . . Your Seagrave was betrayed from within;* and then I waited for some reaction from my hot-headed brother.

He was silent for the length of several heartbeats. He thrust his hands into his pockets and stood before the fire, his gaze fixed unseeing on the print of Weymouth that hung over Mrs. Davies's mantel.

"This French dog—this *surgeon*—would have it that Chessyre deliberately made Tom look a murderer. To what purpose, Jane?"

"I cannot say."

"The notion of skullduggery is common enough, I grant you, among the French. But I hesitate to credit it."

"Do you prefer to believe that Tom Seagrave lies?" I protested. "One or the other—Seagrave or Chessyre—must be acknowledged as duplicitous. You require a witness who may speak without prejudice; I have found you one. Why will you not consider all that he has said?"

"Because what LaForge would claim is utterly beyond reason. Why should Chessyre thrust Seagrave's dirk into the French captain's breast? —And well after the man was dead?"

"To ensure that his charge against Seagrave would be amply supported by evidence—evidence observed by Englishmen and French alike. Can you think of any reason, Frank, why Tom Seagrave should be the object of such a plot?"

But Frank did not immediately reply. He bent and stared into the fire, though the heat from the faggots he had procured was considerable. "On Chessyre's part, I might put it to the account of envy—the desire to see a successful man ruined, and repay trust with betrayal."

"It seems such an awful act," I murmured, "for one man to effect from spite alone. There ought to be another hand behind it—another force, that bent Chessyre to his will."

Frank stared at me. "A plot, you said. You used the word as a politician might. You think it possible, Jane, that someone unknown has deliberately worked through Tom's subordinates to ruin his career?"

I smiled thinly. "Believe me, Frank, when I assure you that similar outrage has been known to occur. How well acquainted are you with the details of Seagrave's service?"

"No more than what every man may know. Tom was at the Nile, where he commanded a ship of the line. He was also at Trafalgar—and distinguished himself among all others on that glorious day. Since then he has been posted to the Channel station, having a rare old time ruffling Boney's feathers and seizing ships off the coast of Spain. He's worth twenty thousand pounds, at least."

"You do not ruin a man's reputation within the Navy for twenty thousand pounds. You ruin him for the satisfaction of seeing him disgraced before those he values beyond everything in the world."

Frank nodded in assent. "The history of this whole affair must argue an intimate enemy."

"Has he family? Connexions? Some force for Influence that might work on his behalf?"

"An elder brother employed by the Honourable East India Company out in Bombay. I met Alistair Seagrave in India once—a fair-spoken, intelligent man who cuts something of a dash. But the family were never very Great, Jane. The father was a clergyman. That was an early bond between Tom and myself—the likeness in our childhoods."

Of course. The constant hours of learning Greek at the knee of a stern and kindly man, when one had much rather be gone to sea.

"And does Alistair Seagrave know aught of his brother's trouble?"

"No letter could reach him in time. The voyage round the Horn is uncertain in winter; several months at best. I should not like to predict when he might learn of it. After all is . . . decided, perhaps."

"But you think Tom Seagrave would request his brother's help?"

"I cannot say. Even did Tom hope to prevent Alistair learning of it—from diffidence, or shame, or pride—they possess common acquaintance enough that his brother cannot remain in ignorance. The Navy and the Honourable Company are forever in one another's pockets."

"Is it at all likely, Frank, that Mrs. Seagrave's family is behind the project? For you know they have considerable standing in Town, and cut her off when she married to disoblige them."

"Why attempt to scuttle Tom Seagrave now, when the marriage is fifteen years old? They had better have despatched assassins on the night of elopement."

"True. It does not seem likely. But whom, then? Has he enemies you could name?"

Frank threw up his hands. "Are you certain in your mind that we must credit this Frenchman?"

"Monsieur LaForge is no friend to Eustace Chessyre. That must be accounted an advantage."

"He's managed to complicate matters considerably."

I laughed. "Then his work is disinterested at least. What possible advantage could LaForge find in destroying Chessyre's reputation? Even the Lieutenant's name was unknown to him. LaForge was cautious enough in his manner, as befits a man who has witnessed what is strange among his enemies; but I detected nothing of deceit. He offered the evidence of his own eyes."

"Eustace Chessyre professed the same," Frank observed.

I was resolutely silent.

My brother sighed. "I suppose I must disclose the whole to Tom Seagrave. He deserves to face the court on Thursday with as much intelligence as he may; he deserves to know that his subordinate betrayed him. A letter despatched express is in order, I think."

"It is possible that Seagrave may supply the reasoning behind Chessyre's act, and resolve the affair entirely."

Frank hesitated. "Would your Frenchman consent to testify before an English court-martial?"

"We can but enquire."

"And he refuses, we shall take a sounding of his deceit. The man may merely be raving, after all, and when pressed on the morrow, deny all knowledge of his tale. But I shall petition Admiral Bertie for LaForge's release, and carry him with me down the Solent on Thursday."

"Let us hope he will survive so long."

"If you are nursing him, he can do nothing else." Frank's tone was much softened from the abuse of a quarter-hour previous. I suppressed a smile, and rose to join the others in the dining parlour.

"Jane—"

I turned at the door.

"I regret what I said regarding your activity at Wool House. I know you undertook the effort solely with a view to aiding Seagrave's case. I am deeply grateful for all that you have done. But—"

"Never fear, my dear," I said. "I shall sit in the chair farthest from your bride."

MY MOTHER FELT WELL ENOUGH, ON THE STRENGTH OF MARTHA'S return, to rise from her bed and descend—in all the fuss and state of vinaigrettes, wool shawls, and needlework—to the dining parlour.

"—Tho' I shall not take a chair next to Jane," she insisted fretfully, "on account of the French; nor yet next to Mary, on account of the baby."

"Dear ma'am!" cried Martha with hearty good humour. "We have divided you between us! May I enquire what has laid you low, since my going into Berkshire?"

"I cannot like winter"—my mother sighed—"and I fear this shall be my last. Such dreadful spasms, Martha, in my side! Such flutterings at my heart! It is as much as I can do, to take a little tea and bread once each day; and with dear Cassandra gone, nobody pays me very much heed—tho' I am decidedly failing."

As my mother was, if anything, in better looks now than she had been when Martha quitted Southampton for her sister's home in Berkshire, I could not blame my friend for her aspect of astonishment. The simple truth is that my mother is dreadfully bored in her present situation. She does not like being a guest in someone else's house, particularly if she must pay for the privilege; and the raptures of Frank and Mary's young married life are proving a trial. I have hopes of her amendment, however, when once we are established in our own home. A Castle Square entirely under her command, with Frank returned to sea and Mary at an utter loss as to the rearing of her infant, might give scope to my mother's ambitions. We might live to see her abandon her bed at last.

"Where is dear Frank?" my mother enquired. "Has he deserted the family table yet again?"

"A pressing matter of business," I supplied, "has detained him. But he begged that I should make his excuses, and urge you all to partake of dinner without regard for his absence."

Mary lifted her fork with alacrity. We should have another swoon before the evening was out.

"I do not blame dear Mary for the neglect I have endured," my mother assured Martha; "for she has her own indisposition to attend to—tho' for my part, I did not lie upon the sopha half so much for any child, and I bore no less than nine! But I could wish that *Jane* were more attentive. There is nothing very much to occupy her, now that Trowbridge fellow is gone off again. A most unsteady, disagreeable man, Martha! Always flying about the Continent in carriages not his own, on business that must not be mentioned, at the behest of some unsavoury character such as the Prince of Wales. I never speak of Trowbridge, of course—but I shall always say he used my daughter remarkably ill. Were I Jane, I should die of a broken heart."

Little Mary's eyes were very wide in her round face; her countenance was all pity and regret. I suspected I had risen considerably in her estimation for having Suffered a Disappointment.

"How happy your return has made me, Martha!" my mother

cried. "I might almost think myself restored to the Hampshire of old, with your dear, departed mamma and all my friends about me!"

"You *are* returned to Hampshire, madam," I observed crossly. "It is some centuries now since Southampton formed one of the county's principal beauties. There is nothing wrong with you, as you very well know, that a little activity should not cure. You are too much indisposed. Fresh air is what you require."

"I know that *some* have called you heartless, Jane, but I did not suspect you of cruelty." My mother dabbed at her eyes with a square of lawn. "When I am gone, you shall consider—too late, alas!—how advisable were your words."

"The joint," Mrs. Davies announced, entering the room with admirable timeliness—and, "Here, my dear Mrs. Austen—pray sit by me!" cried Martha, with an anxious look for myself. "I am sure that I may coax you to take a little of mutton!"

And so we sat over a joint rather underdone, and debated with all the appearance of interest the minutest activity of Martha's Berkshire connexions. I heard more than enough of hunting, and the business of a country parish, to suffice for several dinners; laughed at Martha's pointed jokes, where Mary entirely failed to comprehend them; and listened for the sound of an express messenger's horse on the cobbles of East Street. The halloo and rap at the door came before we had done with the nuts.

Frank's voice was heard in the corridor—a clink of spurs and a horse's neigh; and in another instant, my brother was seated at table, intent upon the cooling joint.

"You're looking very well, Mamma. Descending for dinner agrees with you. May I serve you more of mutton?"

My mother closed her eyes and raised one hand in mute protest. "It was very ill-turned," she remarked. "I wonder how Mrs. Davies came to choose such a leg. She buys food on the cheap, I've no doubt, and saves the cost of our board."

"But it was Jane—" stammered Mary, her cheeks flushing.

"Captain Austen, sir."

We turned as one to look at the parlour doorway, where Jenny, our housemaid, stood twisting her large hands in her apron. The girl made such a picture of guilt and regret that I was certain she had killed Mrs. Davies over some dispute in the scullery, and now meant to make a clean breast of it.

Frank set down his knife. His countenance had begun to show the harassed expression of a man desperate for victuals. "What is it, Jenny?"

She held out a card that had once been white, but was now grubby with over-fingering. "The officer did seem most urgent that I should give you this. But I was that taken up with the washing, and Mrs. Davies did want me to dress the mutton, on account of Miss Lloyd coming from such a distance, and the day being so dreadful. 'I'll just put this card in me pocket,' I says to myself, 'and give it to the Cap'n when I sees him—' "

Frank took the card and studied it with a scowl. Then his countenance changed.

"When did the Lieutenant call?"

Jenny looked all her misery. "Quarter past one o'clock, it must've been, while you and the Missus was out walking. I ca' remember the time, because the butcher had just called round with the mutton as Miss Austen bought special. I hope as I did no wrong—"

"That remains to be seen," Frank said in clipped accents. He stuffed the card into his coat and rose from the table. "Forgive me, Mary—Mamma—ladies. I am called away and may not tarry."

"But, dearest—" Mary protested. "You have had nothing since breakfast!"

Had Chessyre summoned him to his rooms at the Dolphin? Or did Frank hope to seek him there, and learn the purpose of the Lieutenant's call? My eyes sought my brother's face, but his countenance told me nothing. He was intent upon retrieving his cockade from the table by the door.

"A little cold meat upon my return shall do very well," he said over his shoulder. "I beg you will not wait, but retire as usual. Forgive me."

"But whatever is the matter?" Mary cried. "It is too unkind, to call you from your dinner! And a mere lieutenant, too. I wonder you regard it!"

The sound of the outer door closing must stand as reply.

Chapter 8

Mr. Chessyre Vanishes

Wednesday,
25 February 1807

~

MY BROTHER DID NOT RETURN UNTIL THE EARLY HOURS OF THE morning. I knew of the length of his absence, from Mary's small movements about the boarding house—her stealthy descent of the main stairs by the light of a taper, not long after midnight; the occasional squeak of a poorly-oiled door hinge, as she peered unavailingly from the parlour out into the hall; and then her faint rap on my own door, rousing me instantly from the bedclothes. Her face was pale, her expression miserable, in the flickering light of her poor flame.

"May I come in, Jane?"

"Of course."

She slipped through the doorway, and the taper went out.

I groped for my candle in the darkness, then coaxed a flame from the embers of the fire. I set the light on the mantelpiece and turned to stare at Mary. Her thick hair hung in a plait down her back. Her shift was of pink flannel, and voluminous. One finger was lifted to her mouth; she was worrying at the nail with her teeth. Distracted with exhaustion and fear, she looked a disconsolate child up long past her bedtime. I took her hand and found it cold as death.

"He has not come home," she muttered. "Nearly three o'clock, and he has not come home! What if the worst has happened, Jane?"

Violence was not an unreasonable worry; a seaport overrun with sailors released from men o' war was not always the safest of habitations. We had often caught a faint echo of the revels at quayside—the drunken laughter and occasional shrieks, the explosions of breaking glass. But I trusted Frank to know how to defend himself. His uniform alone must demand respect of any fellow seaman.

"You should try to sleep, my dear," I told Mary gently. "Frank shall come to no harm."

"It is not *harm* I worry of, Jane," she retorted bitterly. "Oh! That everyone would cease to treat me like a child! It has been many years since I enjoyed the privilege of innocence, I assure you. In my own home—in Ramsgate—I was accustomed to regard myself as quite the eldest of the family; my advice was sought, and my opinions respected. I know that I am not half so clever as you, nor half as kind as Cassandra—but I am not a simpleton!"

"My dear Mary!" I cried in return, "I have never regarded you as one! Could my brother have loved a fool? It is only that you are a full ten years younger than myself, and younger still than your husband—"

"—and you are a decade junior to Martha Lloyd," she returned impatiently, "yet you do not suffer her to treat you as anything but her equal in sense and experience. I am sure that it was always so, when you were but four years of age and she fourteen! You have never allowed anyone to regard your opinions as of little account, Jane. Confess that it is true—and accord me the same privilege you have always seized for yourself."

"Very well." I sank down upon the foot of my bed. "I shall tell you that you have every right to worry, and to remain sleepless. Frank's behaviour is abominable. He should have considered of your feelings, and sent a boy with a note, long since. You have my permission to scold him roundly when he reappears."

"Scold him—Lord, how can I? He is only a man, and must behave as any man would." She took a turn upon the carpet, unable to meet my eyes. "I simply expected—that is, I hoped . . . we have been so happy, despite the suddenness of this child—but he is restless, turned on shore. My mother warned me how it would be."

"How *what* would be?" I enquired, bewildered.

" 'It is always the same with the Navy,' Mother said. 'They cannot keep their breeches on.' Those were her only words of congratulation, Jane, when I pledged myself to Frank."

"Forgive me, Mary, but your mother is a fool." I raised a hand to forestall her protests. "Frank may be a post captain, with all the glories and perfidies attendant upon that rank, and all the dubious practise of a lifetime spent at sea; but I would remind you that he was known in Ramsgate as *the captain who knelt in church*. Do not let the fears of the dark hours cloud your judgement. Frank has hardly sought solace in another's arms."

"Then why would not he disclose his business?"

I drew her down to sit beside me, and felt her trembling—with anger, or cold? The air in the room was quite chill, and I wished for the means to kindle a good fire; but that was several hours distant, at least. All Frank required to entirely lose patience with me, was that Mary should fall ill as the result of her night's walk. He should not hesitate to blame the French of Wool House, Cecilia Braggen, and Mr. Hill together. I must get her back to bed at any cost.

"Frank learned some distressing news while visiting in Portsmouth," I began. If Mary's understanding demanded respect, and a degree of trust in keeping with her position, then I ought to accord her both. "A fellow captain, a man Frank has known from his earliest years in the service, is to appear before a court-martial Thursday on a charge of murder. Frank is seeking intelligence on his friend's behalf. He hopes to clear his colleague. It is nothing less than this honourable purpose that has drawn him from home tonight—and no strumpet's charms. You must endeavour to think better of him, Mary, than your mother does."

"Court-martial? On a charge of murder?" Mary's brow cleared. "Surely you do not refer to Captain Seagrave?"

"I do," I replied, astonished. "Has Frank told you of his misfortune?"

"Not a word. I was not aware that Frank was acquainted with Lucky Tom. But you must know that the *Stella*'s engagement with the *Manon* is the talk of the Navy! I have heard of nothing else, all February. Mary Foote is never done speaking of it; but she is quite the Captain's warmest advocate, and must insist he could never kill an enemy in cold blood. She is one of the few naval wives who *do*."

"And what do the rest say?"

"As much, or as little, as any party of women with their husbands' interest to divide them." Mary glanced at me sidelong. "Some are moved by malice, others by jealousy, and still others by satisfaction at seeing the Captain's luck turn."

"You would imply, I imagine, that they dislike Seagrave's wife— and rejoice in her misfortune. Louisa Seagrave intimated as much, when I spoke with her Monday."

"You met Mrs. Seagrave?" Mary's curiosity succeeded where all my words of comfort could not, in dispelling her anxiety for her husband. "She actually consented to receive you?"

"Is such behaviour so extraordinary in a naval wife?"

"Quite the contrary. But Louisa Seagrave has never comported herself as a matron of Portsmouth, nor sought the company of those who do. She has a reputation for oddity, Jane. Mary Foote declares that she is going mad."

Mad. Was that the trouble I had glimpsed in the confectioner's shop—the trembling hands, the distracted air, the refuge sought in a medicinal draught? Was the brilliant Louisa Seagrave unsound in her mind?

"I wonder that Frank did not tell me of his friendship with the

Captain," Mary mused to herself. "He is grown so secretive this winter."

I hesitated. What could, and should, be revealed? Nothing of the possible posting to the frigate—for Frank seemed determined to refuse it, were Seagrave to hang. "He did not wish to disturb your thoughts, Mary, when you have so much else to occupy you. The move to Castle Square, the infant's arrival—"

"And this is naval business, and therefore the province of men," she concluded resignedly. "Has it ever occurred to you to wonder, Jane, why men insist on taking the full burden of their work and families entirely upon themselves?"

"Recall, my dear, that Frank has spent the past twenty years in living solely for himself," I replied gently. "He has been a solitary fellow, and the business of sharing a life is entirely new to him. Give him time. Once your husband is again at sea, you will be positively overwhelmed with the duties you are expected to undertake."

"I suppose you are right. But it galls me to learn, Jane, that he is disturbed in spirit on behalf of his friend—and could not feel it right to confide in me."

Choosing, instead, his sister, I thought, *for the long passage down the Solent. Yes, I see how it is.*

Mary looked me full in the face. "Does Frank believe that Seagrave will hang?"

"He is doing everything in his power to ensure the reverse."

"Then he is the first of my acquaintance to do as much."

"In what manner has Seagrave offended the Navy, to garner so considerable a contempt?" I asked her.

"He has taken more prizes than other men, and not solely among the French." I caught the ghost of a smile in the darkness. "It is said that Tom Seagrave is one of those sailors, Jane, who cannot keep his breeches on—and the Service cannot forgive him for it. There is such a thing as *too much* luck."

"I see," I replied. And considered anew the reputed madness of Lucky Tom's wife.

~

FRANK WAS CERTAINLY RETURNED, AND IN ADMIRABLE FRAME, WHEN I descended to the breakfast parlour before eight o'clock. He had shaved, and changed yesterday's shirt for a fresh; his uniform coat was brushed and his shoe buckles polished.

"Well?" I enquired from the doorway. "Did you discover the sinister lieutenant?"

"Neither hide nor hair," he replied cheerfully. "The fellow has done a bunk. I regard Seagrave's innocence as accomplished, Jane—for you cannot have a charge of murder, nor yet a court-martial, without you call a witness; and I cannot find that Chessyre is in Hampshire."

"Perhaps he has taken passage on an Indiaman," I said idly, "and hopes to make his fortune without recourse to hanging."

"Should you like some coffee?"

"Tea, I think, against the morning. You disturbed Mary last night, Frank, with your prolonged absence; I hope she is well?"

"Sleeping yet." He consumed a bit of bacon. "I confess I had no intention of being gone so long. I went round to the Dolphin directly I quitted this house, but was told that Chessyre was out. When I had cooled my heels a full half-hour, the Dolphin's proprietor—a man by the name of Fortescue, Jane, you must recall him, with a stooped back and a balding pate—suggested I might discover my man in a particular establishment near the Quay, one apparently more to his liking."

Frank glanced at me over the rim of his cup; his grey eyes were dancing with devilry. "I have visited any number of sinkholes in my time, Jane—in Malta and Santo Domingo and Calcutta and Oporto; and I shall not hesitate to declare the Mermaid's Tail the very worst of its kind in Southampton. It is no secret where it sits—anyone may approach, provided he possess a strong stomach and an air of insouciance—and so I doffed my hat to the immense woman who sat inside the door—all red satin and moustaches—paid my five shillings' admittance, and prepared for delight."

"Chessyre was not within?" I concluded patiently.

"He was not. I lifted several sodden heads from stinking tables, the better to scrutinise their features; consoled one poor midshipman crying piteously into his beer; lent a pound to another who had just sold his last shirt—and upon further interrogation of the Moustached Proprietress, learned that Mr. Chessyre had not been seen at the Mermaid's Tail in at least three days."

"Perhaps his taste in sinkholes has changed. I find nothing in this to silence alarm. Frank, how can you be so certain that Chessyre has fled?"

"Ah—but I am coming to that bit," he assured me.

At that moment, Jenny appeared in the doorway; she had brought me tea and a quantity of soft rolls fresh from the oven. I sighed with contentment and prepared to endure the remainder of my brother's story.

"I managed to secure a guide to our lieutenant's haunts—a fellow of perhaps eleven, who works as potboy in the Mermaid's Tail. He was a likely lad, with the sharp chin and quivering nose of a weasel; he pocketed my money and led me through a warren of alleyways and foetid corners that I should never have believed existed outside of London. I poked my head into gin rooms and gambling hells and the offices of moneylenders; I visited cockfights and nunneries, and went so far as to interrogate a member of the Watch.[1] By this time, you may well believe, I had felt the loss of my dinner, and sought a poor sort of meal in the company of my young guide; the taverns were beginning to close, and I thought the boy should be sent home to bed. It was a quarter past one o'clock when I returned to the Dolphin—"

"—and was told that Lieutenant Chessyre never sought his room last night," I concluded.

1. *Nunnery* was the cant term for a bordello. Its proprietor was called an "abbess."—*Editor's note.*

Frank's visage turned pink. "At this point I must confess that I engaged in an unpardonable subterfuge. I intimated to Fortescue that I was Chessyre's captain—that he was due to sail—that he was wanted at Spithead before the turn of the tide, or should be left aground—and in general, I made so much of a public fuss, that Fortescue agreed to unlock the Lieutenant's door."

"Well done," I murmured. "You examined the premises?"

"And determined that he had flown. The room was neat as a pin. It looked as though the man had been absent some hours already. The bed had not been slept in. There was not so much as a change of clothes, Jane, in the wardrobe. I rounded upon poor Fortescue and demanded to know whether he had mistaken the room! The fellow was quite put out. He had begun to suspect that he had been bilked of gold; for Chessyre had not settled the tenth part of his account, I understand."

"—And has left any number of enemies behind him, but no direction for future enquiries!"

"He did, however, leave *this*." My brother flourished a crumpled sheet of paper as though it might have been his sword. The sheet had been torn in eighths, and laboriously pieced together with sealing wax. I took it from Frank and frowned over the scrawl of smeared blue ink.

"When *will* you heroes learn to command a legible fist?"

"When we are afforded a desk that does not heave and roll with every swell."

I glanced up. "You believe this to have been written at sea?"

"Method, Jane!" he declared patiently. "Observe the heading."

"His Majesty's Prize Manon, *in the Bay of Biscay, 13 January 1807,"* I murmured. " 'His Majesty's Prize'—this was written after the French ship had struck! I suppose it is in Chessyre's hand?"

Frank shrugged. "I suspect as much. I found it discarded among some other papers in his room. Give it here, and I shall attempt to read it aloud. It is a monkey's tangle; I am in some hopes you may make sense of it."

I have done all that was required, and congratulate myself that I shall not disgrace you. It is the sole aspect of the affair I may regard without distaste, for the perfidy—

I write to inform you of the recent action between His Majesty's frigate *Stella Maris,* commanded by Captain Thomas Seagrave, and the French vessel *Manon,* off Corunna on the eleventh of this month—a date that shall live forever in my mind as the death of Honour—

I have the honour to inform you that the paltry sum, the benefices you pledged, are as nothing when measured against the diminution of Self I have been required to endure, and that if we cannot come to a more precise understanding, as to the value of a man's Honour, however sacrificed and besmirched—

There was no signature affixed, and no direction.

"A letter from one unknown to another," I murmured, "and certainly unsent. He never intended it should be read."

"No."

"But this is vital, Frank! It assures us that Chessyre worked against his captain at the behest of another. Taken in company with the French surgeon's history, it smacks strongly of a plot. There cannot be two opinions on that point!"

"It was not a letter for Admiral Hastings to read, that much is certain. Though the author mentions the engagement, his thread descends swiftly into recrimination."

I handed the piecemeal sheet carefully to my brother. "I must confess that I feel pity for the man. He is so divided in his soul! The writing smacks of torment. It is all pride and impudence, contempt and self-loathing. His conscience is uneasy. He has done *that* with which he cannot be reconciled; and he would blame the hand that moved him."

"Save your pity for Tom Seagrave," Frank told me brusquely. "Chessyre suffers from shame and pride, certainly—but he is perverse in his desire to bargain with his mover. Having sacrificed his Honour, as he puts it, he is ready to profit from the loss."

"A man who fears the future may bargain with the very Devil." I looked at my brother thoughtfully. "And you did say that he seemed mortally afraid. Do you think that he sent some version of this letter?"

"Not from the *Manon,* certainly, though this was written at sea. He was bound for port himself, and must arrive before any missive he could have pressed upon a homebound ship. I wonder that he wrote it at all."

"Perhaps he merely attempted to order his thoughts."

"A draft, you mean? Of a letter he later posted from Portsmouth? It is possible, I suppose."

"His employer—if such we may call him—may have demanded the most immediate intelligence of Chessyre's deed."

"I comprehend, now, why he said so little during our interview yesterday. He could not speak for himself; he moved under the prohibition of silence. His honour, we must assume, extends so far as the protection of his conspirator."

"Then why did he call upon you here, Frank? It cannot have been with a view to reiterating his refusal."

Frank glanced at me swiftly. "You think the man experienced a change of sentiment?"

"Why else consult with a superior he had spurned but a few hours before?"

"Remember that Chessyre is a mercenary creature. He may have thought to put a price on Thursday's testimony."

"So much coin for Seagrave's guilt—for he must already have been well paid for the construction of the evidence—and so much more, for a subsequent avowal of Seagrave's innocence?"

"It might assuage his conscience, at the same moment it lined his purse."

"And he could not hope for advancement in his naval career, did he recant of his charge," I added thoughtfully. "Even did Chessyre profess himself confused—mistaken—unwitting in his accusation— he must be regarded as highly unsteady by the panel. He must be cashiered for calumny at least."

My brother was silent an interval. Then he sighed. "I am too simple a man for prognostication. Chessyre is fled, Jane; and what Chessyre intends for the morrow must remain in question."

I sipped the last of my chocolate. "We ought, nonetheless, to take measures against the worst that Chessyre might do."

"Your French surgeon?" Frank cocked his head. "Very well. I shall go this morning to Wool House and petition Mr. Hill for the loan of his patient."

"Will Admiral Bertie consent?"

"Admiral Bertie is so adamant in his refusal to credit any French-man of disinterested good, that he warns me soundly to be on my guard, and thinks it very likely your surgeon shall not receive a hearing before Seagrave's court. We can but try."

I set aside my breakfast plate without further ado. "Then I shall accompany you."

"There is not the slightest need."

"On the contrary," I retorted. "I have been ordered by Martha to procure a box for the theatre tonight; and Wool House lies in my way. You cannot thwart me in this, Fly. Mrs. Jordan is to play."[2]

"Mrs. Jordan!" he cried. "And poor Mary has not seen the inside of a theatre in weeks. It was always her chief delight. I secured the promise of her affection, you know, during the interval of a play at Ramsgate; and must always accord the theatre my heartfelt grati-tude."

"Then it is decided. You shall make another couple of our party, and I shall walk out with you now in the direction of French Street. I only stay to discover my bonnet."

"I hope Mary may not swoon," Frank added. "The crush, you know, is likely to be fearful if Mrs. Jordan is to play."

"Let her swoon, and welcome!" I said in exasperation. "A lady in

2. Dorothea Jordan was one of the most accomplished comic actresses of the late Georgian period, a regular performer at Covent Garden and Drury Lane. For many years the mistress of William, Duke of Clarence (later William IV), she bore him ten children before their parting in 1811.—*Editor's note.*

an interesting condition has so few opportunities to shine in public; and Mary, in fainting charmingly, might divert the attention of all assembled from a royal mistress. Think what delights she shall have in store! A play, and a personal act of considerable distinction! When one is grown old, and sources of satisfaction are few, it is much to relive one's youth in recounting such a tale."

Chapter 9

Scenes Played in French Street

I MOUNTED THE STEPS TOWARDS MY ROOM IN SEARCH OF MY BON-
net, a parcel clutched to my breast. Martha was in the act of descending, and the staircase being narrow, one of us must be forced
to give way. I elected the office, and pressed myself flat against the
wall.

"I have ordered of Mrs. Davies a good dinner," she told me, "and
begged that it might be early, on account of Mrs. Jordan. I do hope
we may secure good seats! Do you think that your mother might be
persuaded to make another of the party?"

"I do not think wild dogs could keep her from French Street. It is
exactly the sort of amusement calculated to drive her from her bed."

"She has been very low," Martha mused, "but I cannot make out
any symptoms of decline. Perhaps a change of season, coupled with
a change of domicile, will offer amendment."

"Was she very pitiful when you begged admittance this morning?"

"I counted only three sighs and one dab at the eyes," Martha replied, "but you know that talk of an early dinner must always raise her spirits."

"True. Had I recollected the fact earlier, we all might have spent the winter months in tolerable good humour."

I have known Martha Lloyd since I was fourteen. It was in 1789 that her mother, a clergyman's widow, settled in Deane and rented from my father the neglected parsonage; and though the Lloyds very soon removed again, to Ibthorp, the bond of our friendship endured. It is true, as Mary says, that Martha is ten years my senior, and might be supposed to have found a better companion in a girl closer to her own age; but there has hardly been a time when Martha and I did not share a good joke, or chatter about our acquaintance, or dispose of our friends in marriages they should never have thought of for themselves. Martha is as much my sister as Cassandra could be—more, in some respects, because she so often shares my turn of mind. We two have lain awake far into the morning, after many a ball, abusing everyone within our acquaintance, and have never failed to move each other to laughter.

But if I cherish her for her ready understanding and convivial spirit, I must acknowledge that her true value lies far beyond these. Martha, at forty, has honed and measured her strength. She has watched her younger sisters marry and have the joy of children; she has presided over the deathbed of her mother, and seen her buried; moved alone and penniless into the world, to take up a home without the slightest assurance of its permanence; and never has she complained or expressed a wish to exchange her lot.

"Frank intends to walk into French Street, though not so far as the theatre," I informed this paragon of female virtue. "Should you like to join us?"

"With pleasure. Too many hours confined in a carriage must cripple a woman of advanced years; I should benefit from the exercise."

"We might return by way of Bugle Street," I added thoughtfully, "and look in upon the house in Castle Square. I cannot convince myself of its being habitable without the constant reassurance of my own eyes."

"Surely the renovations are finished! Or have the painters been too often pressed into our neighbour's service?"

The Marchioness of Lansdowne—the neighbour whom Martha chuses to regard so familiarly—presides over the Gothic folly immediately adjacent to our house in Castle Square. She is everywhere acknowledged as a former courtesan, and as such, is permitted an eccentricity of behaviour that should be shocking in a female gently bred. She drives a diminutive team of eight ponies, each pair tinier than the next, and is much given to rouging her cheeks. Her husband the Marquis has taken a kindly interest in the Austen project of renovation—as naturally he must, being our landlord. The Marchioness's favoured house-painter has been pressed upon us for the improvement of our rooms. It is a family joke that when not required about the Marquis's walls, the painter must often be tending to the Marchioness's face.

Martha peered at me narrowly. "Whatever are you clutching to your breast, Jane? A foundling in swaddling clothes, that you intend to lay at the Marchioness's door?"

"Eggs," I replied. "Mary *would* buy several dozen in the market yesterday, and now finds that they bring on bilious attacks. She begged that they be hidden from sight as soon as may be. And as Frank intends a visit to Wool House, I thought they might better be used in treating the sick."

"Frank at Wool House? And after such a demonstration of temper?" Martha's eyebrows rose. "That *is* a reversal. You know that I can never ignore an opportunity to observe your brother reformed and penitent. Naturally I shall come."

I WAS BETTER PREPARED TODAY FOR THE STREAMING STONE WALLS and the dreadful stench of illness. The surgeon Mr. Hill chanced to be standing by the oak doors as we entered; and the turn of his expression at the sight of me was painful to behold. It was too much like relief to be mistaken for his usual reserve, though it vanished as swiftly as it appeared. I knew, then, how much the surgeon felt the Frenchmen's fate in his heart—how much it galled him to be able to do so little.

Frank bowed, and paid his respects to Mr. Hill; enquired of the surgeon's career since they had last met in the Indies; then introduced Martha to Mr. Hill's acquaintance. I lent half an ear to these pleasantries while my eyes surveyed the room.

Seven of the pallets, at least, were empty this morning. I did not enquire as to their occupants' fate; I was reasonably assured that I knew it. One of the missing was the young seaman whose letter I had transcribed only yesterday: Jean-Philippe.

With a chill at the heart, I glanced swiftly around the darkened room in search of the one man we could not afford upon any account to lose. I failed to discover his face. He was not lying in the shadows, nor yet propped against the stone wall; nor was he among the card players grouped around the table. Surely he was not—

"I am astounded to see you here again, Miss Austen," said Mr. Hill, "and deeply grateful."

I collected myself and curtseyed to the surgeon. "I could not stay away, Mr. Hill, and I have brought with me a companion. Miss Lloyd has consented to assist us."

"We have brought eggs," Martha declared. "They should be coddled over a moderate fire and served upon toast—provided, of course, that your men are capable of keeping their victuals down?"

Mr. Hill straightened. "I am happy to report that several of them seem equal to the task of taking a little sustenance. And I may say that I am well-acquainted with the process of coddling an egg."

"Then you are a better man than most," Martha retorted, and moved off in the direction of the fire.

"Pray tell me, Mr. Hill," I attempted. "The French surgeon— Monsieur LaForge. Is he . . ."

"—Attempting to shave by the light of that far window," Mr. Hill replied.

I followed his gesture with a queer little catch in my throat and a sensation of relief. The corner in which Etienne LaForge sat was difficult to plumb with eyes adjusting to Wool House dimness; but I discerned his clean profile, the spill of dark hair over the broad brow, the delicate hands poised with the razor. He looked and seemed stronger at a distance of twenty-four hours. Not for him, the coarse black shroud and the common pit dusted with lime.

He had ceased his ablutions and was staring at me intently. I found that I blushed, and looked away. With my brother beside me, purposeful in his intent of securing LaForge's witness, I felt almost a traitor to the Frenchman's confidence.

"Captain Austen has been telling me of Captain Seagrave's case," Mr. Hill persisted. "Most extraordinary. I had no notion we harboured such celebrated prisoners in this dreadful place. I did not even know that LaForge was a surgeon. I might have secured his assistance in treating the sick; but, however, he has been almost unable to stand upright before this."

"He is improved, then?"

"I am happy to say it. I lost several men in the early hours of morning, Miss Austen." He shook his head in weariness and regret. "It is always thus; a man will go out with the night's ebb tide, as though he cannot wait for dawn."

Frank was listening to our conversation without attempting to form a part of it. His eyes roamed over the assembled pallets, but his countenance evidenced neither shock nor distaste; the scene before us must resemble the usual squalor of the lower decks. He had often seen men in suffering before.

"I have given my consent to your brother," said Mr. Hill, "for this small liberty of Monsieur LaForge's. He shall accompany Captain Austen to Portsmouth on the morrow."

"You are not his gaoler, surely?"

"No—but I remain his doctor," returned the gentleman shrewdly. "He goes with Captain Austen on one condition: that I might form another of the party. I should not wish LaForge to suffer from exposure in the hoy."

"You are very good," I said. "But there remains one other person's consent we must seek."

"Admiral Bertie's?"

"Etienne LaForge's," I replied.

THE BUSINESS WAS CONCLUDED WHILE MARTHA CODDLED TWO dozen eggs.

LaForge was brought forward, his white shirtsleeves rolled high and his jaw wiped clean with a reasonably fresh towel. He stood easily before my brother, regarding him with the faint expression of amusement I had detected the previous day. For support he chose an ornately-carved walking-stick, ebony with a silver handle—so precious a thing must surely be his own, carried out of the *Manon*. He leaned upon it with all the careless disregard of long use.

While the two gentlemen conversed, I undertook to assist Hill with his patients—it seemed the least I could do for the harassed surgeon. My brother's interrogation did not require many minutes.

Frank bowed; the Frenchman nodded—and with a slight glance over his shoulder, returned to the place where he had been sitting. I thought his countenance somewhat sobered. But before I had occasion to consider the man and his moods, my brother was at my side.

"He does not deny his story, at least," Frank said without preamble. "What he told you yesterday in the vestige of fever, he is very happy to report with a clearer head to a panel of British officers. He attempted to bargain, naturally—but I could promise him nothing. I told him merely that I would exert myself on his behalf, and so I shall."

"What sort of price does one put upon the truth?" I asked curiously. "Exchange to France? A quantity of gold?"

"Neither. He merely begs to be allowed to remain in England, a free man. I suppose there are many who cannot love the Monster Buonaparte."

"But it is agreed? He sails with you tomorrow?"

"Quite early." Frank's grey eyes moved over the face of the prisoner beside me; I had been attempting to feed the man an egg, but found him unequal to the task. "The trial is settled for eleven o'clock, you know, and I should like to be arrived in good time. I must write to Admiral Hastings aboard the *Valiant,* and request permission for LaForge to come aboard."

"I should like to accompany you, Fly."

"To the court-martial? Don't be absurd. It is not the place for a lady," he said stiffly.

"Not to the *Valiant* itself, but to Portsmouth."

"Jane, you do not know what a dreadful thing it is to see a man hang. It is entirely possible that if things go badly—not at all in Seagrave's way—that the sentence will be carried out immediately. It is the tradition in the Navy."

"Then Louisa Seagrave will undoubtedly require a companion," I rejoined with equanimity. "Think, Frank! A lady in such a state! With her little children all around her, and no support but a surly maidservant in a black eyepatch! It is not to be thought of. Certainly I shall go."

Frank's lips parted, but he failed to voice a word. An appeal to the feelings of a lady must always reign paramount in his mind, however strong his attention to naval *niceties* and *forms.*

I handed Mr. Hill the remnants of coddled egg. There was a spark of humour in the surgeon's grave eyes as he took charge of spoon and bowl.

"This is become quite a pleasure party," he observed. "A morning's diversion on the Solent! Do not neglect a hearty breakfast, Miss Austen. It is the surest safeguard against seasickness."

"I should never ignore the advice of a surgeon," I said, and prepared to attend Martha to the French Street theatre.

THE PALE SUNLIGHT THAT HAD GREETED THE DAY WAS SOON FLED, and succeeded by the usual Southampton drizzle we had come to abhor. I feared the night would prove far too wet for my mother's health, and that a diminution of our evening party must be the result. Nothing short of widespread revolution, however, should prevent me from seeing the play in French Street. I had found too little enjoyment this winter, and meant to have my share of amusement.

I have long been a devotee of good hardened real acting, and though I may win contempt for preferring a Comedy to a Tragedy, I own that Mrs. Jordan is exactly the sort of player to please my taste. She is bright and light and sparkling; ingenuous in her air, despite the increase in grandeur that has attended her notice from the Duke. She delivers her lines with so lively a humour, that one might almost believe the words to have sprung directly from her wit, rather than the pen of a Kotzebue or an Inchbald. I had once been disappointed in a glimpse of her at Covent Garden, while on a visit to my brother Henry; I could hardly credit my good fortune in finding the lady descended upon Southampton, and must assume that some imminent embarkation aboard a royal yacht had occasioned Mrs. Jordan's removal hither.

Despite the delay occasioned by our visit at Wool House, Martha and I were in good time to procure seats for our entire party. The hearty dinner Martha had ordered was duly laid at an early hour; my mother descended to table for the second time in as many days—an unprecedented honour—and insisted that the rain was nothing she must regard. By seven o'clock we were all established cosily in a hack chaise, pulled up before the theatre doors in a long line of similar conveyances. The downpour was considerable, and Frank was so gallant as to *offer* to carry me across the wet paving-stones. I declined, and splashed my slippers regrettably in achieving the foyer.

Such a crush of local worthies! Such a display of fine silks and sateens, of feathered headpieces and naked shoulders! How one was frozen from the draughts that flooded through the doors, and yet toasted unbearably when too near the roaring fires! The danger of spilled claret from a neighbour's glass, trailing like blood down a skirt of white lawn—the danger of an inflammation of the lungs, to so much goose-fleshed womanhood! I had elected to wear a sober gown of blue sarcenet with long sleeves, several years behind the fashion; what it lacked in daring exposure, it more than compensated in warmth. My hair was pulled back in a simple knot, and bound with ribbons of a similar colour; it was nothing very extraordinary in its arrangement. I felt positively dowdy; and suffered, of a sudden, from an access of shyness.

The sensation was increased when a broad-shouldered, chestnut-haired fellow jostled my arm in attempting to ease by me. He glanced at my face, muttered an apology, and swept on with only the barest civility of manner. I thought his countenance familiar. There was a mix of worldliness and contempt in his eyes that struck me like a blow. I had seen this man before.

"Frank! Frank—"

My brother turned from assisting his wife with her pelisse.

"That gentleman by the staircase, ascending to the boxes—with the woman in dark grey. We are acquainted with him, surely?"

The chestnut-haired man had a hand under the elbow of his fair companion. I had not noticed her previously, a testament to my confusion; she was extraordinarily lovely, with a haunting, fine-boned beauty. Her cheekbones were high; her nose aquiline; her deep-set eyes heavily lashed. A luxuriant mass of gold hair trembled elegantly above her nape; her ears were two pink shells. And though she was dressed in dark grey, with complete sobriety and disregard for ornament, the lines of her gown could not disguise the exceptional in her figure. It was a wonder that every male eye was not turned the lady's way. Her companion bore her along like a prize he had seized.

"By Jove," Frank murmured. "That is Sir Francis Farnham—a member of the Navy Board. I wonder what he is doing in Southampton?"

"Seeing to his ships, one must assume."

"He should far rather work his coded signal lines from a safe distance," Frank retorted.

"You would refer to the Admiralty's cunning flags, which communicate intelligence from London to Portsmouth?"

"Sir Francis never goes near the water if he may help it, and thus is a great advocate for telegraph—and every new form of jiggery-pokery the Admiralty may advise. It is said they contemplate a signal-line that will run the length of the Kingdom—God help them when the wind blows too strong!"[1]

"You seem quite familiar with the effects of Sir Francis's administration," I observed.

"I made the Baronet's acquaintance some years ago in Kent, when I commanded the Sea Fencibles; I warrant he will not remember me now. He is grown so very great in Influence!"

"Ramsgate," I said thoughtfully. "That is where I have had a glimpse of him."

"He does not observe," Frank persisted, craning his neck; "he has already ascended. I shall seek him out during the interval, however. Sir Francis governs the Transport Board, and I should dearly like to consult with him on the matter of those Frenchmen in Wool House. The Transport Board holds authority, you know, over prisoners of war."

"His wife is very lovely."

"Wife! That is Phoebe Carruthers; Trafalgar widowed her. Perhaps Sir Francis hopes to secure her as his second lady—though I should have thought him capable of attaching a woman of greater fortune. He is handsome and rich, and Mrs. Carruthers possesses little more than her beauty."

"Many men are happy with less."

"I wonder at her sensibility, Jane. I should not have thought her in a humour for play-acting."

1. Frank Austen is referring here to the Royal Navy's semaphore system of communication, which only replaced the older form of signal-flag communications in 1816. "Telegraphy" refers not to the electrical system of transmission invented by Samuel Morse in 1837, but to a series of signal towers that relayed orders from the capital to the coast.—*Editor's note.*

"And why is that?"

"Cannot you see that she is in mourning? It was her son—the Young Gentleman—who fell dead from the shrouds on the *Stella Maris*."

BUT BY THE TIME WE HAD WITNESSED MRS. JORDAN'S SKILL, AND laughed until our sides ached, and stood once more to seek the foyer—Frank's project of appeal on behalf of the French prisoners must perforce be postponed. Sir Francis Farnham and his companion were gone.

Chapter 10

A Morning's Pleasure Party

Thursday,
26 February 1807

~

IF FRANK RECEIVED ANY REPLY FROM TOM SEAGRAVE TO HIS EXPRESS
of Tuesday evening, I was not informed. My brother was unwont-
edly silent this morning as we sailed down the Solent. It was so early
that the dusk had barely lifted from the New Forest, so early that
the faint winter light had no power to warm me, and I huddled in
my old pelisse while the frigid spume raced across the small vessel's
hull.

Etienne LaForge was braced in the bow of the boat drinking
great draughts of fresh air. To him, the cold and wet seemed immaterial. He had donned this morning a black wool coat, serviceable
and unadorned. His hair, overlong from inattention, was bound at
his nape with black ribbon, and his countenance was alight with
freedom despite the manacles at his wrists. I had winced at the sight
of those bonds, heavy and remorseless about his fine hands; but I
did not question them. Frank had warned me that the French surgeon's motives must be suspect. It was possible, after all, that the

man had schooled his story to the hints I had given him—that having heard a little of Seagrave's court-martial from the Marine guards, he had fabricated Chessyre's perfidy with precisely this view to escape. Frank had no intention of appearing a fool; he had sacrificed reputation enough in taking Tom Seagrave's part. Did LaForge intend to hurl himself from the hoy halfway to Portsmouth, he should sink like a stone from the weight of his irons.

The Frenchman had bowed low, the perfect gentleman regardless, as we stood on the Water Gate Quay. There was no cause for LaForge to feel shame at his bonds; he was a prisoner solely from unhappy circumstance; yet I did not think there were many Englishmen who should have worn humiliation so carelessly.

"Miss Austen! Your taste for the macabre runs to hanging, I see. Shall you be very disappointed if the Captain survives?"

"Monsieur LaForge." I had bowed my head in acknowledgement of his greeting. "You must recollect the friend of the bosom—the Captain's wife. I go to Portsmouth solely to comfort her."

A twitch of amusement, peculiarly his own, had worked at the corners of his mouth. "*La pauvre petite.* But as I have agreed to tell whatever I know to whomever will listen—perhaps your comfort will be unnecessary, *hein?*"

We had now been underway nearly half an hour, and Gosport was fast approaching to the larboard side; the squat dark shape of the Isle of Wight loomed like an enormous turtle. Mr. Hill, as a sailor of long standing and a responsible gaoler, stood stoutly next to LaForge in the bow; the two men spoke but little. Given the tearing breeze, Hill's attention seemed fixed upon securing his periwig to his skull. LaForge's eyes eagerly swept the horizon, as though he expected to find salvation there. My brother was engaged in steady conversation with the vessel's master—a conversation that consisted mainly of assessing the wind and clapping on sail—and so I was alone amidships, with my gloved hands clenched upon the edge of my seat.

Mr. Hill chanced to look around—chanced to furl his wizened face in a smile, which I returned—and that swiftly it seemed the two men could not sustain the picture of lonely self-sufficiency I presented. As one, Mr. Hill and Etienne LaForge picked their way over coils of rope, dodged taut lines and shuddering canvas, and settled themselves beside me.

"That is better." Mr. Hill sighed with relief, and dropped his hands to his sides. The gusts of wind in this part of the vessel were greatly diminished in relation to the bow. "I never wear my wig at sea if I can help it; but circumstances this morning must dictate the strictest attention to propriety. One cannot present a ragged appearance before Admiral Hastings."

"You look very well, sir," I assured him. "You shall disgrace no one in your present guise."

Etienne LaForge raised one eyebrow. "Is it not the custom for surgeons to look pitiful and go in tatters? I had thought it was requisite to appear as the dregs of humanity, a testament to impoverished circumstance."

"Surgeons are a mixed lot, I warrant you," replied Mr. Hill equably. "Five drunkards for every sober man, most without the scantiest learning, and not a few fleeing charges of murder at home. But you have seen the same in the French Navy, surely?"

"*Zut*," cried Monsieur LaForge, "you ask me to impugn the honour of the French? Never! Besides, I cannot claim to be a real surgeon. I am versed in the physical sciences, not the sawing of bones; I was pressed into service aboard that ship, and know very little of the navy, French or otherwise."

"Aha!" said Mr. Hill with satisfaction. "I thought there was something peculiar in your air, sir. Too much the gentleman to be merely a sawbones—there was the matter of your attire, that handsome walking-stick, and all those books you brought from the *Manon*. Great intellect is not often wanted aboard ship."

"Nor evident in the conduct of its sailing," LaForge retorted. "That is one blow to French honour I may freely give."

I remembered that the same bitterness had marked his views of the dead captain, Porthiault. LaForge had called him a fool, and evinced no regret at the man's violent passing. He wished, as well, to remain in England rather than return to France. Life under the Monster's claws must be brutal beyond enduring.

"I myself fell in with the Navy purely as a view to research, you know," continued Mr. Hill. "I am a passionate ornithologist, and one cannot stay at home and hope to master the subject. Was the *Manon* your first berth?"

"Yes," returned LaForge abruptly, "and I pray God it may prove my last. Having seen the inside of Wool House, I have no *grande envie* to see the rest of the world."

"And where in France do you call home, *monsieur?*" I enquired.

"The Haute Savoie," he replied, "not far from the Swiss border. It is a beautiful country, quite unlike your England."

"And yet you wish to exchange the one for the other," I rejoined, stung.

"Beauty is not the sole recommendation for a *méthode de vivre,*" he said. "Whether I remain in this country, or flee to another, I am not likely to see my Haute Savoie again."

This last was muttered in so low a tone, I could not be certain I had heard the man correctly; but when I would have begged his pardon, and asked him to repeat his words, he turned the conversation by exclaiming, "I commend you, *mademoiselle,* for an excellent sailor. *Vous avez de pied marin.* No sickness, no cries of womanly fear at every movement of the boat—it is in your blood, yes? You enjoy the sea as your indomitable brother?" He gestured at Frank, who was still engrossed in the matter of sails.

"Who may regard the constant life of the waves and be unmoved, *monsieur?* Who may witness the ebb and flood of the tide and not yearn to be carried far from shore, to know the multitude of peoples and places about the globe?" I enquired wistfully. "I should dearly love a man's experience of the sea, but must be content with stories of my brothers' wanderings."

The master of the hoy shouted suddenly to his mate; the canvas was reefed, and the vessel slowed as it turned. We had achieved the entrance to Portsmouth harbour once more—to starboard, the ships at anchor off Spithead; to larboard, the mass of build-

ings tumbling towards the quay. Within the sheltered port itself were anchored a few men o' war. One of these, I knew, must be
the *Valiant,* with its signal flag for court-martial fluttering at the
mizzen.

"And there, I presume, sit the rest of the *Manon*'s complement,"
observed Etienne LaForge wryly.

My eyes were drawn to the massive stone prison that rose forbid-
dingly above Portsmouth—a prison in which perhaps hundreds of
French sailors languished in expectation of exchange. I had not
spared it a thought on Monday. Were the men within ill and de-
spairing? And had they anyone to write their letters?

"Steady, Jane," my brother said at my elbow as the hoy dropped
anchor. "You will not scold us if we do not accompany you to the
quay. Our course lies with Admiral Hastings's ship—the *Valiant,* just
to larboard there. The irregularity of LaForge's circumstance is
such that we ought not to delay in paying our respects."

"Of course," I replied with intrepidity, as though the experience
of two days on the water had made me a seasoned sailor. Frank paid
off the hoy while Mr. Hill handed me into the cockleshell of a skiff;
Monsieur LaForge's hands, after all, were bound.

I TOOK TWO WRONG TURNINGS BEFORE I PETITIONED FOR AID, AND
found my way at last into Lombard Street. Once there, I managed
to distinguish the Seagrave household from its companions in the
uniform row of small cottages. This is a more remarkable feat than
it sounds, for all passage of the narrow lane and entrance to the
residence were blocked by a stately and expensive carriage. Two
sets of arms—both unknown to me—were empalled on the panels,
surmounted by the bloody gauntlet of the baronet.[1] Not all of

---

1. Jane refers here to a heraldic shield that has been split down the middle to
accommodate the arms of the lady's family, to the right, and the gentleman's,
to the left. The gentleman is presumably a baronet, for the symbol of the
bloody gauntlet is traditionally accorded to that rank.—*Editor's note.*

Louisa Seagrave's acquaintance among the Great had ceased to notice her, it seemed.

I hesitated on the paving-stones before the door. If Mrs. Seagrave already entertained a visitor, I could scarcely be wanted. I did not like the duty that awaited me in any case, and should relish the opportunity to avoid it. The lady must be presently in a pitiable state, and the visit of a relative stranger might oppress rather than sustain her. Surely, if the lady of a baronet had come to call—

All these excuses and more flooded into my mind; but I will confess that I was troubled most by Mary's careless suggestion that Mrs. Seagrave was going mad. Bodily illness I may face without blenching, and all manner of infirmity or dereliction; but a soul unsound in her mind is the most terrifying of spectacles. My own brother George had been born without his full wits, and was banished while still a child to the care of strangers paid well to maintain him. We rarely saw him, and spoke of him still less. I glanced over my shoulder at all the bustle of Lombard Street, the carters shouting for passage against the claims of the elegant equipage, the maidservants trudging over the wet stones in their pattens. When I looked back at the Seagraves' door, the choice was made. Louisa Seagrave was standing at the window, staring at me.

I had taken passage down the Solent. I could not turn from a fellow-creature in torment. I smiled at her, stepped up to the door, and pulled once upon the bell.

The door was immediately flung open by two dark-haired boys who scuffled and shoved at each other in their haste to be first to greet the visitor: Charles and Edward Seagrave. Charles's stock was undone and trailing down his shirtfront; Edward, the younger child, had a bright smear of jam across his forehead. A hunk of bread torn from a loaf was still clutched in his fist.

"Have you any news of Papa?" he demanded without preamble. "Has he been akidded?"

"*Acquitted,* you imbecile," retorted Charles. "Of course he has! Papa could never be guilty of murder, whatever Nancy says." His large grey eyes, heavily lashed and startlingly like his mother's, turned full upon me. "I've seen you before. You came with Papa's captain friend. You'll be wanting Mum—only she's shut up with Aunt Templeton, the old carcase."

"I won't go into Kent!" Edward cried shrilly, and dashed his bread at my feet. Involuntarily, I stepped backwards off the threshold. "Not without Papa! Aunt Templeton is a *monster!*"

A delicate clearing of a throat—apologetic and half-hearted—alerted me to the presence of a third person in the dimly-lit hall. I craned my head around the two boys—Edward was now crying bitterly, and Charles was berating him in furious whispers—and glimpsed the shining domed head of an elderly man, exquisitely dressed in silk knee breeches and a coat of black superfine.

"I beg your pardon," he murmured, coming forward with one hand outstretched. He made me a deep bow in the fashion of thirty years ago, his right leg extended painfully behind him, then raised his quizzing glass to survey my figure. "I am Sir Walter Templeton. Forgive the . . . ah . . . *high spirits* . . . of the little boys. They are quite overset by events in this house. Quite unruly. There is no managing them. So my wife, Lady Templeton, assures me."

His words, although stern, were uttered in such failing accents that I wondered at his true convictions: he might have been reciting a verse learned by heart.

"Not at all," I replied. "I am quite used to boys and their antics. I am happy in the possession of no less than six nephews at present, and shall undoubtedly be blessed with more."

"How very fortunate," Sir Walter managed. "I was never so happy as to possess a child of any kind. It has been . . . a great sorrow." He glanced down at young Charles, and his elderly face creased in an angelic smile, rendering his countenance unexpectedly carefree and childlike.

"Uncle!" cried Edward. "You promised that we should make paper ships today, and launch them off Sally Port!"

"So I did," he declared, and laid a hand upon Edward's shoulder.

Then casting a furtive glance at me, he added, "I cannot like the oppression of the household at such a time. I thought it best to divert the children with a little harmless sport."

"Excellent notion," I agreed—and would have said more, but that the door at the far end of the entrance hall was thrust open with a bang, and the housemaid Nancy hastened forward, her one good eye balefully upon me.

"Leave yer card!" she barked. "The Missus is seeing no one today, as any fool with a heart should know. Disgraceful, to call at such a time, with the Master about to swing at the yardarm!"

"He's not!" cried Charles angrily.

Nancy rounded upon the boy with her hand raised, and found her wrist firmly seized by Sir Walter Templeton.

"That will do, my girl," he said in a voice somewhat stronger than previous. "Pray be so good as to present the lady's card to Mrs. Seagrave."

The maid no doubt intended a stinging rebuke, but Sir Walter had released her and was already steering the two boys firmly towards the kitchen, muttering in quiet tones about the Sally Port, and the necessity of fetching a quantity of paper from the nursery. I proffered the offending card, and grudgingly, the maid took it.

"If your mistress is otherwise engaged this morning, I shall wait for her reply."

An ejaculation from the parlour doorway must serve as answer enough.

"Miss Austen! You are come again to cheer my solitude!" Louisa Seagrave cried. "Pray do not give the slightest attention to that ill-bred slattern, but hasten to the fire. You must be perishing of cold. Do I understand the situation correctly? Are you only now disembarked from the Southampton hoy?"

I drew off my bonnet and gloves, handed them to Nancy—who crushed them under her arm with a snort of contempt—and crossed the hall. "I am. My brother could not be absent from Portsmouth on such a day; and when I learned of his intention, I begged to join him. Do I disturb your peace unforgivably?"

"Not at all." Her fingers, when she clasped my own, were chilled to the bone. The parlour fire could not be adequate. Her face was sallow, her breathing hectic, and her entire appearance one of the deepest suffering; but I could not judge her *mad.* "You know, then, where my husband is gone. You know that a few hours alone may decide it."

"A few hours—and all the most active intelligence of his true friends, exercised upon his behalf," I declared. "You must not sink, Mrs. Seagrave—you must not give way. Let us talk of books; let us dandle the baby—let us walk out into the cold, if we must! But I shall not allow you to sink!"

"You are very good," she murmured, and swayed in the doorway. I caught her arm and helped her into the parlour beyond—it was a small room, rather dark, with a single round table placed in the center and two or three chairs arranged around it. I settled Mrs. Seagrave on the sopha crammed into the bow window, and turned to face the second lady standing silently near the hearth. The mistress of the magnificent carriage, I presumed.

"Pray forgive my weakness, Lady Templeton," Louisa Seagrave murmured, "and allow me to introduce Miss Austen to your acquaintance."

Her ladyship was an austere personage, thin and tall, with a magnificent carriage to her head and a pair of glowing dark eyes. I should judge her a quarter-century junior to her husband, and where the Baronet was all diffidence and kindly hesitation, she was all decision and contempt. Like Louisa Seagrave, Lady Templeton was dressed entirely in black, though of an elegance the Captain's wife should never achieve. She did not waste her smiles upon a woman only just disembarked from the Southampton hoy; it was unlikely we should meet again, and a baronet's wife must always be sparing in her notice. A stiff nod, which I returned with my usual courtesy, was all the acknowledgement I received.

"I suppose you are one of Mrs. Seagrave's naval connexions?" she enquired.

"I am fortunate enough to have two brothers presently serving His Majesty," I replied.

"And their rank?"

"The elder is a post captain, the younger a master and commander."

This intelligence effectively thwarted further attempts at conversation. Nothing less than an admiral, it seemed, would do for a Lady Templeton. But her business was hardly with me; I could be ignored as a flaw in the paintwork, or a bit of thread discarded upon a table.

Her ladyship pulled on her gloves and grasped her reticule. "I may not tarry any longer, Louisa. I have wasted far too much time as it is. You know what Luxford shall be in such an hour. I may only repeat that I am not in the habit of brooking refusal. I expect you to afford my arrangements the consideration they warrant, and to vouchsafe a reply to the inn by midnight. Sir Walter and I shall be forced to start for Kent no later than ten o'clock on the morrow. Pray attend to the hour. You were never a punctual child; I hope the years have effected some amendment."

Mrs. Seagrave pressed her hand against her eyes. "Will you not stay, and take refreshment? I believe that Sir Walter intended some project for the boys' amusement—"

"Nonsense," returned Lady Templeton briskly. "Sir Walter must attend me to the George at once. We have not the time for frivolity. We are not come upon a pleasure party, I would have you know."

"Charles and Edward take such delight in Sir Walter—"

"I should prefer to see less of delight, and more of self-control! They could do with firmer management, Louisa. We shall procure a tutor post-haste, once they are removed to Luxford. I certainly cannot be expected to set up as nursemaid, however much Sir Walter may enjoy his second childhood!"

Louisa Seagrave's lips parted, as though she would muster some reply; but then her sallow face flushed an unbecoming red, and she fell back into silence.

"I shall not wait for that wretched girl you chuse to call a maid-servant, but shall show myself out," Lady Templeton concluded.

"The horses cannot be expected to stand long in this damp weather. Gibbon will be exceedingly angry."

Louisa Seagrave struggled to her feet. "We must not make poor Gibbon angry; he has suffered too long already in your service."

If Lady Templeton caught the barb beneath the simple words, she did not chuse to evidence it.

"I thank you for your attention," Mrs. Seagrave continued formally, "and wish you every conceivable comfort on your journey into Kent; but I cannot say whether it shall be in my power to accept your kind—"

"Do not be a fool again, Louisa."

The abrupt warning, delivered without softening civilities or the slightest attempt to guard their subject from contempt, stopped Mrs. Seagrave's pleasantries in her mouth. She bowed her head, and made no effort to escort her visitor to the door.

My gaze followed the upright, formidable figure of her ladyship as she swept into the passage; and when the door had slammed with finality behind her, I could only look to the Captain's wife with silent pity.

"You have been honoured with a glimpse of my paternal aunt," she told me with a shaky laugh. "I learned only yesterday of the passing of my father—Charles, Viscount Luxford—at Richmond three days since; he is to be buried Tuesday at Luxford House, in Kent."

"You have my deepest sympathy," I said. "The loss of a parent must always be felt. I hope that he did not suffer long?"

"He died of apoplexy, after too rich a dinner; and I am sure that no man died happier than Father. He was always the sort to relish a good meal."

It was difficult to know how to greet this intelligence. I was uncertain whether Louisa Seagrave possessed a brother who might accede to the title, or if the estate was entailed upon another—whether she had seen her father since her headlong marriage, much less this redoubtable aunt. She was breathing heavily, as though under the spur of considerable emotion. She certainly had not met her relation with composure; but whether love, remorse, or hatred ranked uppermost in her spirits, I could not determine.

"Lady Templeton wishes me to accompany her and Sir Walter into Kent. She thinks it necessary I pay my respects."

"That must be natural."

"There was never anything natural in the connexion between myself and my family, Miss Austen," Mrs. Seagrave retorted with asperity. "To think that I must *now* make my appearance in Kent, with my little boys in tow—the heiress returned like a bad penny, with her questionable progeny behind her—and at such a time!"

"Heiress?"

"My father has no sons, and the estate is not entailed. Lady Templeton thinks it likely that Charles— But I cannot be tiring you with such tedious family business. I shall not speak of it. Tell me what you have been reading, Miss Austen! I hear that Mrs. Jordan was in the theatre at French Street; did you happen to see her play?"

There was in her whole manner a feverish inattention to word and air that suggested the gravest anxiety. I had no notion how long a period Lady Templeton had demanded for the presentation of her schemes, but surely little of constructive activity had been accomplished in the Seagrave household this morning. Scattered about the room were signs of occupation too swiftly abandoned: a novel face downwards against a seat cushion; a boy's stick and hoop thrust into a corner; needlework hastily set aside. Mrs. Seagrave had been working at something—a small gown of dimity, no doubt for the new baby. Such is the desperate occupation of a woman's hours, while men decide the fate of the beloved, and all of existence may be summed up in a single word—*guilty*. We women sew, as though the world entire must hang upon a thread.

"Should you like some refreshment? A glass of wine?" I enquired. "Let me fetch you one."

"No—that is, perhaps a small draught of Dr. Wharton's Comfort. It is there, on the Pembroke table—" She gestured towards the center of the small room. I collected the blue bottle, uncorked it, and offered it to her. She did not wait for a glass of water, but tipped the flagon's neck between her lips.

Whatever Dr. Wharton had prescribed, it appeared to answer her affliction. Louisa Seagrave sighed and stopped up the bottle's mouth with a hand that trembled only a little. "That is better," she whispered. "I shall do."

I sank into a chair. She remained standing, her sharp profile turned towards the front windows, in the direction of the sea. "They will fire a gun," she murmured, "if he is to hang. It is no distance at all, from Lombard Street to the quay. We shall hear it. Can it be that any in Portsmouth is deaf to the sound of guns today? But perhaps they shall take him across to Spithead, and hang him there."

"Do not speak of it," I urged her. "It shall not come to that."

The restless eyes returned to mine. "You cannot believe him innocent! My dear Miss Austen, make no mistake. My husband *deserves* to hang."

It was the one pronouncement I had least expected, and I could find not a single word to answer it. I stared at her, horror pricking at my spine. Perhaps she *was* mad.

"He killed that poor fellow as surely as though he fired the ball himself."

She knew, then, of the wound to Porthiault's temple. And yet Seagrave himself had never mentioned it when he described the French captain's last moments. He had merely spoken of a blow to the head—some wound undiscerned, that had stunned the man or killed him outright. It was Etienne LaForge who had examined the skull, and located the hole from the ball. But if Louisa Seagrave could speak of it so readily . . .

"Your husband has told you this?" I whispered.

Her lips worked, and then her entire countenance crumpled with the fierce violence of grief. "He did not need to say a word. I know the love he bore that child. I witnessed it every day, in the diminished affection he gave to his own sons—in the flight of all love and honour from myself! I did not have to be told."

"The child," I repeated, as comprehension broke. "You would speak of the Young Gentleman! The boy who took a musket shot, while aloft in the shrouds, and was dashed to the decks with the roll of the ship. But why—"

"Master Simon Carruthers," Louisa Seagrave said. "Nearly two years he was in my husband's keeping, and dearer to him than any child in the world. A bright, healthy lad with a courageous heart, a shock of blond hair, a ready grin. The boy's father—Captain Carruthers—was a great friend of Thomas's, and killed at Trafalgar. Simon's place on the *Stella* was meant to be a great favour, a mark of esteem. Do you know what they do to a lad of that age, when he dies in battle? Do you?" Her voice was shrill, as though she teetered on the brink of hysterics; it demanded of me some answer.

I shook my head.

"They toss him overboard without a word of farewell, without a prayer for his parting soul. He slips astern like a sprig of jetsam, and is lost to the fishes and the rocks. No mother may bathe his body for burial, or stand by his graveside with a posy for remembrance." She covered her face with her hands and began to sob wretchedly. The sound was guttural and harsh. "Such dreams as I have had, Miss Austen! Such visions of decay—the nightmares that haunt my sleep! *'Those are pearls that were his eyes . . .'*"

The high, piping voice of six-year-old Edward, raised in protest as his uncle Sir Walter was torn from all the delights of boat launchings at Sally Port, drifted through the ceiling from the nursery upstairs. I shuddered. It was horrible to think of such innocence blasted, and made food for fishes.

"But a French musket brought down the boy. Surely you cannot—"

"Seven years old. But seven years old! No stouter than one of my own boys should be." She turned upon me as a wolf might avenge the baiting of her young. "Simon Carruthers should not have been at sea. I blame my husband! As who could not! He is guilty of the grossest folly—guilty of abuse and murder! It was Thomas who would have the boy torn from his mother at the tender age of five—Thomas, who being denied his own sons to parade about the quarterdeck, must borrow the heir of a hero, and throw the child into all the violence of a fighting ship in the midst of a brutal war. Madness, this crush of young lives in the gun's breech, like the maul of apple blossom beneath a booted heel! Can you bear to think of his mother, Miss Austen?"

His mother. The beautiful Phoebe Carruthers, in her gown of dark grey, her mass of golden hair. I had thought her a sort of Madonna when I glimpsed her in French Street last night, before I even knew of her mourning. Strange that a woman with every cause for grief should venture to a play.

"Are you at all acquainted with Mrs. Carruthers?"

"One cannot reside in Hampshire, and yet be ignorant of Phoebe Carruthers," Louisa Seagrave replied. "She is reckoned the most beautiful woman of the naval set; certainly she has suffered the most. The entire Admiralty is at her feet, I understand, from respect for her courage. Even Thomas—"

She broke off, and stared at her hands. "You think me bitter, no doubt. You think me vengeful and cruel to urge my husband's sacrifice. There are some, I know, who do not hesitate to call me *mad*. But I cannot view the Navy's folly, Miss Austen, without I declare it criminal. I would not give my sons to Thomas when he longed to take them to sea. I refused him—and my refusal has long divided us. It is the rock upon which our marriage has broken. But I am justified in that poor child's death! And if God is yet in His Heaven, Tom will hang for what he did."

There was a bustle in the hallway and the parlour door swung inwards to reveal my brother. Behind him I detected the forms of Mr. Hill and Monsieur LaForge. All three were subdued; and from the turn of Frank's countenance, my heart sank. I feared the worst.

"Mrs. Seagrave," he said with a bow, "pray forgive an intrusion so unannounced. We thought it best to inform you—"

"Oh, God, pray tell me at once!" the lady implored.

Frank hesitated, and his eyes sought my face. "Captain Seagrave's court-martial has been suspended by order of Admiral Hastings."

"He is free, then?" Mrs. Seagrave asked faintly.

"For the moment. But he remains under charge. Suspension, I am afraid, is not the same as acquittal." Frank glanced over his shoulder at the pair on the threshold. "I must apologise for carrying strangers in my train, and thrusting them upon you at such an hour. Mrs. Seagrave, may I present Mr. Hill and Monsieur LaForge, two gentlemen who have been most active on your husband's behalf."

Louisa shielded her eyes as the gentlemen made their way into the room, then sank once more upon the sopha. From her attitude, she might be overpowered with relief and thankfulness; I alone of the party must suspect the truth.

"The Lieutenant, Mr. Chessyre, failed to appear?" I enquired of Frank in a lowered tone.

"Mr. Chessyre is dead," my brother returned without preamble. "He was murdered last night in a brothel beyond Southampton's walls, his body discovered only this morning."

I pressed one hand to my lips in horror.

Louisa Seagrave began to laugh.

Chapter 11

The Source of the Trouble

"THAT IS A VERY ILL YOUNG WOMAN," MR. HILL DECLARED AS WE stood in Lombard Street almost an hour later. We had subdued Louisa Seagrave's hysterics, and partaken of the dry sherry and iced cakes the maidservant had thrust upon us, however little appetite we felt for them.

"If she were my wife," the surgeon continued, "I should engage a private nurse and demand absolute quiet. Her children should be taken from her care, and a strict control placed upon her diet. A tour in the Swiss Alps might answer the case, if safe passage could be managed."

"Is the complaint a nervous one?" I enquired apprehensively. Even to Mr. Hill I dared not voice the idea of madness.

"Perhaps it began as such. But she has not helped her situation by consuming so much of laudanum. It is a tincture that carries its own dependence; more and more of the stuff is required to achieve a salutary effect; nightmares and waking terror swiftly follow; and the total destruction of the bodily frame must eventually result. She should be weaned from it as soon as may be." He shook his head grimly.

"You mean Dr. Wharton's Comfort? But surely that cannot be harmful. It is stocked in every stillroom in the land. Babies take it from their wet nurses' hands, to comfort them in crying."

"Laudanum is a tincture of opium, Miss Austen," enjoined Mr. Hill brusquely, "and no less vicious than what may be eaten in a Chinese den. I suggest, Captain Austen, that you speak to your friend about his wife."

"I expect to meet him within the hour," Frank returned, "but it is a delicate subject. Perhaps if you would be so good as to vouchsafe an opinion—in a professional capacity, of course . . ."

"I can do nothing unless I am expressly consulted," said Mr. Hill, "but I stand willing to perform the office."

Frank bowed. Mr. Hill clapped LaForge on the shoulder.

"We two shall take a nuncheon, Captain, and await you and your sister at the quay. Our French colleague deserves a toast to freedom, before he is immured once more in walls of stone."

Our French colleague looked almost prostrate with apprehension. He had attempted too much in his weakened condition. I smiled encouragement at LaForge. "Did you speak before the court, *monsieur*?"

"I did," he returned with feeling, "but I wish that I had not. My tale served no purpose in freeing your captain—he was no longer in danger—and it exposed me most decidedly."

"Exposed you? In what manner? I confess I do not understand."

"A man has been killed, Miss Austen. This Chessyre who lied about murder. I am the sole remaining person who professes to know the truth. That is not a healthy position, *hein*? You see before you a man in terror for his life, *mademoiselle*."

"I suspect you take too much upon yourself, LaForge," said Mr. Hill drily. "A good lunch should defray the worst anxiety. Pray come along and allow me to buy you a glass of claret. There must be smugglers enough along the Channel coast to provide us with refreshment."

I could not be so sure that the answer to a Frenchman's care must always be found in wine. I reflected, as I watched the two men proceed up the street, that there were worse habitations than a comfortable gaol of stone.

"NOW, FRANK," I CHARGED, AS WE STEPPED SWIFTLY INTO THE High, "you must tell me everything you know about the proceedings against Seagrave and Mr. Chessyre's death. Relate the particulars without exception."

He told me then of the ships of Seagrave's squadron drawn up at anchor off the harbour, in the strait of the Solent opposite to Spithead; of the signals that flashed from each to each, and the air of unhappy expectancy that pervaded the crews assembled on deck; of the solemn looks of the empanelled officers—a vice admiral, a rear admiral, and Admiral Hastings, Seagrave's commanding officer; of how Frank was forced to cool his heels while the court convened, his spirits oppressed by the gravest anxiety for his friend's fate.

My brother has never commanded a ship that has struck to the enemy, or been wrecked upon a stormy coast; and thus he has been spared the indignity and suspense of a court-martial.[1] He had supposed that his ardent wish of speaking to Seagrave's character, and delivering a witness in the form of Monsieur LaForge, might be exercised at the first opportunity; but, in fact, he was forced to await the court's pleasure, while the charges against his friend were read out. Next Mr. Chessyre was summoned, and found to be absent; a tedious interval ensued, while the Admirals deliberated their course; and at last, Captain Seagrave was called before the panel to give his account of the *Stella*'s engagement with the *Manon*.

In relating the latter, Frank became so enthralled with the details

---

1. A court-martial was automatically held for the commanding officer of any ship lost at sea or taken by the enemy, to determine whether dereliction of duty was the cause.—*Editor's note.*

of battle that he quite forgot for a period the point of his recital, and I was forced to endure all the tedium of broadsides and their timing, until we had left the High Street behind and turned towards the Portsmouth naval yard. It was there we intended to fall in with Captain Seagrave, before undertaking the passage back up the Solent. I felt compelled to interrupt my brother's effusions regarding the excellency of the *Stella*'s guns.

"Mr. Chessyre," I supplied. "When did you learn of his unhappy fate?"

"LaForge had delivered his account of the French captain's end, to considerable shock among the officers and much muttered consultation. There were those among the assembly inclined to discredit the surgeon, as a Frenchman and a dog; but others, more sanguine, expressed the view that LaForge should hardly have fabricated such a story about a British officer completely unknown to him. I believe that Seagrave might have received a complete acquittal at about six bells, and put the affair at his back, if it had not been for a lad rowed out to the *Valiant*. He handed Admiral Hastings a note from the Southampton magistrate. Hastings broke the seal and read it silently to himself—appeared immensely struck—and handed the note around the panel. At length, Vice-Admiral Black read the intelligence aloud.

" 'Compliments of Percival Pethering, magistrate of the City of Southampton, who begs to inform the commanding officers of the Channel Squadron, that Mr. Eustace Chessyre, commissioned first lieutenant of His Majesty's frigate *Stella Maris*, was found dead this morning at eighteen minutes past six o'clock. Due to the irregular nature of the gentleman's passing, an inquest into Mr. Chessyre's death will be called by His Majesty's Coroner not later than Wednesday next.' "

"So much for Seagrave's acquittal," I murmured as we approached the towering portals of the naval yard.

"Indeed. It was clear that more than one man present considered Tom the very person to have throttled Chessyre to death."

"Was he throttled, then?"

"With a garrote. It is decidedly a man's weapon." Frank threw me so troubled a look that my heart turned over with pity. "This death comes hard on the heels of your Frenchman's story. Do you think it possible, Jane, that I spurred Tom Seagrave to *murder* when I sent him that express?—That I gave him every cause to avenge betrayal?"

"It is what the court-martial will hasten to believe, certainly. But I regard Chessyre's death in a different light altogether."

"That being?"

"The sinister glow of conspiracy. You said that when you met the man he was mortally afraid. He came to you but a few hours later, and disappeared when he could not secure an interview. Chessyre meant to recant his testimony, Frank—to expose, perhaps, his employer—and he was killed to quell his conscience."

"Jane! You have read far too many horrid novels!"

"Then I suggest you adopt the practise. You reveal a distressing naïveté, Fly, with regard to the ambition of evil men. Think how much more useful Chessyre shall be, dead instead of alive! Rather than exonerate his captain, he shall seal his fate."

Frank's countenance was wooden with disbelief. "But how are we to expose such a plot—if indeed it exists?"

"You must look into Seagrave's personal affairs. You have the means to do it, Frank. You know his colleagues—how he stands at home and at sea. From the men who esteem and serve him, the men who despise and mistrust him, we shall learn the answers we seek."

"You would ask me to spy on Tom!"

"It would not be the first time, I assure you. Someone—someone who bears him no goodwill—has learned his habits long since." My steps slowed as we approached the iron portal of the naval yard. "We may assume that Chessyre did not act on the spur of the moment. His plans were set before ever the *Stella* hauled anchor off Spithead. I should dearly like to know the nature of Tom Seagrave's sealed orders. Is it customary to sail in complete ignorance of one's duty, as he did?"

"I should not call it customary—but neither is it so unusual.

Sealed orders are adopted when the duty at hand must be undertaken in extreme secrecy. They are intended to keep the ship's destination from being common knowledge among the crew, which might talk too freely among their mates onshore."

"You have no idea why the *Stella* was sent to Lisbon?"

"Tom has never said. I should never think to ask. These were *sealed orders,* Jane."

"I admire your delicacy," I said wryly, "but must consider it ill-placed in such a turn. You must begin to ask questions you personally abhor, Frank, if you are to save your friend. Who should despatch him on such a duty?"

"Admiral Hastings. But the directive might come from the Admiralty, in London—from persons unknown to Seagrave himself."

"I see," I said thoughtfully. "Careful planning, and the simple employment of an established system for despatching ships, might answer the case of conspiracy. I wonder if the engagement with the *Manon* was intended as well?"

"Absurd!" Frank cried. "Now you *have* gone too far!"

I wheeled upon my brother with ill-concealed impatience. "Etienne LaForge is afraid for his life, Frank. After what occurred in Southampton last night—can you blame him?"

Chapter 12

A Sparring Among Friends

"Austen!"

My brother withdrew his gaze from my earnest visage and peered about the yard. A gnarled figure under a battered cockade was advancing upon us.

"Admiral Bertie!" Frank cried. "I did not know you was to be in Portsmouth this morning! We might have come down in the hoy together! How d'ye do?"

"Fair enough, Captain, fair enough—though I could wish my legs in better trim. The gout has nearly crippled me; this is what comes of shifting too long on dry land. I cannot recommend it!"

The Admiral has long been intimate with Frank, but now forms a part of our family's Southampton acquaintance, in company with his invalidish daughter, Catherine. I felt a rush of affection at the sight of his weather-beaten countenance framed by an old-fashioned powdered wig. In his kindly manner and hearty goodwill, the Admiral must always recall my father, though he lacks the subtlety of my father's understanding.

"Nothing would do for Catherine but that I should be driven down from Southampton in the trap," said he, "and all the while I was longing for the roll of the sea! Good day to you, Miss Austen. You look a picture."

A picture of *what*, might better be left undisclosed; the wind and persistent damps of February cannot have improved my complexion.

"I hope you left Miss Bertie in good health?" I enquired.

"A slight cold, nothing to refine upon. But I should better be enquiring after yours! I understand that you have spent several days with my surgeon, Hill, among the prisoners of Wool House. He speaks your praises whenever we chance to meet. There is no better nurse than Miss Austen, so Hill says, throughout the Kingdom."

"He is an excellent man. The French are in good hands."

"Pity. I could wish them in worse. Your brother, Miss Austen, should treat them as they deserve—eh, Austen? He should nurse them with a few good broadsides apiece, and scuttle what he could not tow!" The Admiral smiled at his little joke, and Frank attempted the same.

"My sister has proved the value of charity," he said, "in procuring the testimony of the French surgeon. I thought Monsieur LaForge should have achieved Tom Seagrave's acquittal—but was sadly disappointed."

"I understand the proceeding has been suspended." The Admiral drew a snuffbox from his coat and procured a pinch of fine grey powder. "Bloody business—meaning no disrespect, of course, Miss Austen." He sneezed resoundingly.

"None taken, sir, I assure you. *Bloody* is only too apt a term in the present case."

The Admiral looked slightly startled at my freedom; Catherine Bertie, it must be supposed, should never have uttered an indelicacy. She should sooner have fainted at the blow of an expletive.

"It looks very black for Seagrave," the Admiral went on—"his sole accuser throttled on the very day of his trial! I wonder old Hastings did not string him up directly. Still, we must afford the man an opportunity to explain himself. With the Southampton magistrate putting in his oar, however, we may expect a delay. There will be all the dispute of jurisdiction and authority, and Seagrave shall go free on the strength of it, I'll be bound."

I glanced at Frank, whose looks had taken a lowering turn. "Would you suggest, sir, that . . ."

"That Lucky Tom did for the scrub himself? Shouldn't wonder at it." The Admiral let out a bark of laughter. "After all, the Captain ran a Frenchman through with his own dirk, and after the colours came down, too. One cannot vouch for Seagrave's temper.—Nor, I understand, for his whereabouts last evening." Bertie raised one hoary eyebrow significantly.

"I beg your pardon?" I managed.

"The Captain will not say where he was last night," the Admiral repeated, "nor allow his wife to be questioned. Hastings has just told me of it. Asked Seagrave himself. Seagrave replied that as the court-martial was suspended, he considered himself above the necessity of an answer. Damnable cheek! Should be resigned the service."

The alteration in Frank's countenance was suddenly dreadful. Some thought of the express despatched on Tuesday—of Seagrave's taking the news to heart—of Frank having put, as he phrased it, a spur to murder—all were evident in his looks.

"I understood that Captain Seagrave meant to fix quietly at home until this business was concluded," he said stiffly.

Admiral Bertie shook his head. "I confess I cannot be sanguine as to his chances, Frank, when the court-martial is resumed. As it certainly must be. We shall have you in the *Stella* yet."

My brother was on the verge, I am sure, of refuting such an ill-timed hope—but I glimpsed Thomas Seagrave over Frank's shoulder and clutched at the sleeve of his coat, forestalling any answer he might have made.

The Captain had come to a halt some ten paces from our little party, and eyed us with a mixture of anger and mortification. He was resplendent in full dress uniform; his white pantaloons shone with brushing, and the gold at his shoulders gleamed. That he had overlistened some part of the conversation, I am convinced; and that he misapprehended the tenor of it was obvious.

"Ah, Tom," Frank said, his visage suddenly scarlet. "There you are. You are acquainted with Admiral Bertie, I believe?"

Seagrave inclined his head; the Admiral barely acknowledged the courtesy, and an awkward silence fell.

"I must leave you here, Austen," Admiral Bertie said abruptly. "Hastings is most pressing in his desire to take refreshment, and I cannot keep him waiting. My compliments to your wife. Good day, Miss Austen."

"Admiral."

He strode off without a backwards glance: the clearest example in my experience of a mind uncomplicated by subtlety. Such an one is distinctly suited to the pursuit of the Enemy—he will have the rules of engagement by heart, and follow them to the letter. Life, in its attacks and repulsions, must seem a simple arrangement enough. All the infinite shadings of circumstance and will, decision and restraint, are not for him. It does not do to think overmuch on the point of battle; but woe betide the pure of heart on dry land.

I glanced at Seagrave. Here was just such another; and he was aground and awash in the present perplexity of his fortunes. Even this little exchange between my brother and a senior officer was rife with betrayal and deceit. There is a brutal innocence in your seafaring men: tho' accustomed to all the savagery of conflict from a tender age, they know little of social intercourse. Tom Seagrave was ill-equipped to take a sounding of the depths of such waters. I sincerely pitied him.

"May I offer my heartfelt congratulations on the suspension of your trial, Captain," I attempted.

"You are too good, Miss Austen. Frank tells me you have been sitting some time with my wife. Pray, how did she take the news?"

I felt my cheeks flame red. There seemed an embargo on every answer. For lack of a better, I said, "She fell into a swoon. But we left her in good hope of recovery. Her maid attended her."

"I see." He drew his white gloves through hands made rough by constant exposure to the weather. "Louisa has not been well, for a twelvemonth at least, and I confess it wears at my heart. She abhors Portsmouth; and this wretched business has hardly contributed to her happiness. I thank you, Miss Austen, for your kindness to my wife."

"It was a pleasure, I assure you."

He appeared surprised, as well he might—there can be few that found aught in Louisa Seagrave to redeem the caprices of her temper.

"I wonder, Captain," I added, "whether you have consulted a reputable physician? For Mrs. Seagrave does appear a trifle . . . thin." I had chosen my words; *uneasy in her mind,* or *most dependent upon laudanum,* must be discarded as ill-advised. "Mr. Hill, the naval surgeon, remarked upon her . . . nerves. I am sure that he—"

"She will not bear a consultation," Seagrave said abruptly, "though I have urged her repeatedly to it."

"You must bring her to Southampton one day. I am sure the airing would do her good."

"Yes," he replied, but his gaze fell to his gloves and he appeared less open than before. Perhaps he could not trust his Louisa amidst the delights of a watering place.

"Tom," broke in my brother with some urgency, "the Admiral tells me you were questioned as to your movements last night."

"I was."

"Why did you not tell them that you were at home?"

The Captain smiled thinly. "I saw no reason to prevaricate. I was not at home. Though for all the good my activity did me, I should better have sat by the fire."

Frank slapped his thigh in irritation. "You went in search of Chessyre. I should never have sent you the contents of that express! The shock must certainly prove too great—"

"Betrayal, particularly among friends, must always seize us unawares. A lifetime of experience cannot inure us to each new perfidy."

Seagrave's accent was cold to the point of ice; but my brother appeared oblivious. "Tom, you must own the truth before it is too late. If you killed Chessyre in an affair of honour—"

"I wish that I had. I did not. You may chuse to believe me or no, Austen—it is all one with me."

Again, Frank flushed. "I am happy to find you value the good opinion of your friends so highly!"

"The idea of friendship, it seems to me, has suffered an alteration. I once called Eustace Chessyre *friend;* but he might better have thrust my dirk into my back than Porthiault's chest—my end might have proved less lingering. I cannot forgive him for it."

"Good God, Tom, will you build your gallows in the very naval yard?" Frank hissed.

"And then there is Frank Austen," Seagrave continued harshly, "whom I have also called friend. Frank Austen, whose desire for a fast frigate is everywhere known, whose ties to the Admiralty are so very good, whose efforts to clear me of dishonour must provide an occasion for the most officious and public spectacle of interference, and raise him in the esteem of everybody who has eyes to see—good, noble, avaricious Frank Austen, who should as soon steal a man's livelihood as shake his hand!"

"Tom!" my brother protested, aghast.

"Damn all friends, I say!"

And Tom Seagrave stalked off without a word of apology.

My brother stared after him. "I have half a mind to call him out! This is the basest ingratitude—and after all I have done, too!"

I restrained him with one gloved hand. "It is a hard thing for an independent man to utter thanks. Seagrave must know himself indebted to your goodness; he shall reflect, and regret his harsh words, when anger has passed. Surely you see so much?"

"I see nothing but a man determined to go to the Devil," Frank muttered. "He might at least have told us where he was last night."

"As to that—" I said, "surely it is obvious?"

Chapter 13

Mr. Pethering Pays a Call

"NOTHING ABOUT THIS WRETCHED BUSINESS IS OBVIOUS TO ME," Frank commented bitterly as we made for the Portsmouth hoy.

I glanced at him sidelong. "There is a woman in Seagrave's case, Fly. Men never plead silence on the subject of their movements without they fancy themselves honour-bound to shield a lady's virtue. In their ponderous reticence they succeed in exposing that which they would most protect."

"You suspect poor Tom of an illicit attachment?"

"Why else would your friend refuse to say where he was last night?"

"For any number of reasons! A man may have his privacy, after all!"

"Tom Seagrave has been careless in defending his; he must not be surprised to find it invaded. Mary tells me that Lucky Tom is everywhere known as a taker of prizes—not all of them ships. The ladies of her naval acquaintance regard Captain Seagrave as one who cannot keep his breeches on."

Frank snorted. "Mary does not understand the meaning of the phrase."

"I fear she does."

My brother saw me safely into the hoy beside Mr. Hill, the surgeon; Etienne LaForge already sat in the bow, his manacled hands held before him like a penitent's. The Frenchman's face was flushed, his expression turned inwards. He was in the grip of fever or anxiety—the one hardly distinguishable from the other.

"I do not mean to make out that Tom is a saint, Jane," my brother persisted. "I do not have to tell you what the Navy is. Women are left at home, to commit every kind of folly in un-guarded idleness, while the men exist without sight of England for years, sometimes, at a stretch. Neglect and thoughtlessness may ac-count for every kind of misery on both sides. But Tom has always seemed happy in his wife."

"His wife, however, is hardly happy in her husband." I drew my brother a little apart from the others and spoke in a lowered tone. It was imperative, now, that I acquaint Frank with Louisa Seagrave's opinions regarding the Captain. He was astounded; nothing in life had prepared him for such bitterness of feeling on the part of a spouse; and he seemed to feel her betrayal as though it were his own.

"Is she mad?" he cried. "When Tom is most in need of support, *she* must go blathering to a recent acquaintance that he deserves to hang! The woman can only be bird-witted!"

"She is anything but," I replied evenly. "Her wisdom in revealing so much to a relative stranger must, of course, be disputed; but I believe her to have spoken from an agony of spirit that would not be gainsaid. Remember that she never accused Tom Seagrave of the French captain's murder. She is most unhappy in her union; she cannot respect or confide in the man who shares her fate; she does not approve of his way of life, and will not entrust her children to his care at sea. So much is certain. It remains for us to determine how much weight to accord her words."

"None at all, if I am to be consulted," Frank muttered belligerently.

"She is a shrew and an ungrateful wretch, and Seagrave should be quit of her directly."

"Frank—"

He turned upon me. "You cannot take her part, Jane. You cannot wish the man to hang, simply because a boy of seven was killed in battle. Boys of every age are dropped over the side; it is the nature of war."

"Then women are well out of it," I retorted bitterly. "You must not apply the coldness of a man's heart, trained to command and to hurl lives into the breach, with the tender feelings of a mother."

"Louisa Seagrave has done the reverse," Frank declared, "and the application is ill-judged. I know for a fact that Tom was most seriously cut-up about young Carruthers's loss; he felt the lad's death acutely. But if he were to feel every such death in excess of its due—"

"—he should be incapable of command," I concluded bleakly. "I quite see your point."

We sailed up the Solent with the wind on the quarter and the threat of storm ominous at our backs. I could not be easy; my mind had received new information. I considered of my brother's life in a harsher light. I knew, of course, that he was daily witness to scenes of brutality; that he lived in the closest proximity with the baser instincts of man; that he was constantly exposed to mortal danger. But his love for the naval life had superseded every objection in the hearts of his family. We saw that Frank could not do otherwise than he had done, and the honour he had won seemed recompense enough for sacrifice. I had never considered, however, that he must play at God. Each action—each decision as captain to engage the Enemy—must bring with it the certainly of death for some among his men. My brother lived with the consequences as surely as he lived by the noon reckoning. I could not gaze at his beloved profile—already aged unnaturally by privation and war—without feeling equal parts pity and pride confounded in my heart.

We sailed on in silence for a period, the rough seas slapping and tugging at the hoy's bow. Mr. Hill fell sound asleep, with his hands clasped over his breast; Etienne LaForge sat slumped by his side, looking quite ill. It was probable that the excitement and fatigue of the morning had sapped his strength, already delicate from prolonged fever; he could not achieve Wool House too soon. I burned with indignation at the thought of the Frenchman's incarceration; his precarious health demanded a decent room with clean linen, a steady fire, and adequate victuals. I must speak to Admiral Bertie. The surgeon should be housed as an officer, in the home of a naval family. Perhaps Mr. Hill—or even Mrs. Davies—might find the man a room. . . .

At my side Frank expelled a heavy sigh. "Lord knows I should prefer that Tom carry a *tendre* for a lady not his wife, than to suppose him a murderer—but it seems an unhappy choice."

"You were ready enough to believe the latter while disputing in the naval yard."

"Perhaps I was over-hasty there. A lesser man might kill for vengeance, but Tom did not earn his reputation through impulse and unreason. I should be surprised, upon reflection, did your Frenchman's tale of rank betrayal overrule Seagrave's good sense."

"This murder was not, however, the act of a hasty man," I observed thoughtfully. "Death by impulse requires a knife or a pistol—something carried against attack, and deployed without thought, in the heat of passion or self-defence. But a garotte—"

"—would suggest that Chessyre's killer came upon him from behind. That he crept up by stealth, and slipped the iron band deliberately about his neck, and pulled it taut. Yes, I quite seize your meaning, Jane. The murder was determined, organised, and carried out with despatch. That much is of a piece with Tom's usual tactics in war."

"Then a casual brigand we must discard. Three choices remain to us," I concluded. "Either Chessyre was killed by his companion in plotting, to prevent him divulging all he knew; or he was killed by Tom Seagrave, from vengeance. Or lastly by one of Seagrave's friends, who thought to tip the scales of justice in the Captain's favour by weighting them with the corpse of his accuser."

"I cannot like the character of such a friend."

"But can you put a name to him, Frank? Some old shipmate of Seagrave's, perhaps?"

My brother shook his head in the negative.

"Excepting, naturally—yourself," I said.

OUR RETURN TO MRS. DAVIES'S LODGING HOUSE WAS ATTENDED with unexpected ceremony.

As the hoy dropped anchor in Southampton Water, and the skiff set out from the Quay to meet us, I observed a singular figure clutching the gunwales amidships. He was tall and spare—so spare that his narrow back curved like a fishhook over his protruding knees, and his thin wrists sprang from his coat sleeves like stalks of spring rhubarb. The master of the hoy, in observing this apparition's approach, muttered under his breath.

"I'll not be taking that delicate article anywhere on the Water, Cap'n, and I'll thank'ee to tell him so."

His eyes narrowed against the wind, Frank clapped the master on the shoulder. "I doubt that gentleman has a voyage in view."

The skiff came alongside; the oarswomen shipped their blades; and the reedy fellow glanced at us beseechingly from under his broad-brimmed hat.

"Captain Austen, I assume? Miss Austen?" He evinced no interest in Mr. Hill or Etienne LaForge, who were waiting patiently for a seat in the skiff.

"You have the advantage of me, sir," Frank replied.

The gentleman ducked his head in acknowledgement. "Forgive me—I feel most unwell—that is, a trifle indisposed—the motion of the seas—" He swallowed convulsively and clutched once more at the skiff's sides. "I am Mr. Percival Pethering, Magistrate of Southampton, and I wish to speak with you, Captain, on a matter of utmost urgency."

"Am I to suppose," said Frank with undisguised amusement, "that you have braved the seas in order to apprehend me? Then shift your position, sir, that I might hand my sister into the skiff."

"Naturally!" cried Pethering in an agony of consciousness. His hands remained fixed at the skiff's sides, his skeletal form immovable. "Only too happy to oblige! Provided, of course, that this cockle does not overturn. . . ."

"And you do not attempt to stand upright, all will be well." Frank avoided the satiric looks of the oarswomen, and placed his hand under my elbow. "Lightly, Jane, lest Mr. Pethering be indisposed."

I cast him a chiding look. Fly is merciless in his abuse of the lubbers everywhere about him; he cannot resist this natural tendency towards superiority in matters naval; but Pethering held a temporal power that warranted respect.

At the moment, however, the magistrate was incapable of taking offence. He was recumbent over the skiff's far side, being sick into the sea.

We managed to achieve the Water Gate Quay without further incident. My brother assisted Mr. Pethering—who was most unsteady on his feet—from the skiff before even myself. The magistrate stood upon the stone pier drawing great gusts of salutary air, as though life, in all its miseries and joys, was newly granted him.

Frank stepped easily to shore and bowed to the magistrate. "You are come upon the matter of Mr. Chessyre, I think?"

"I am, sir. You have learned of his brutal end already. But we shall defer our speech until the lady"—this, with a nod for me—"is safely returned to your lodgings."

"My sister is entirely in my confidence, sir," Frank told him stiffly.

"Pray do not regard me in the slightest, Mr. Pethering," I said.

The magistrate hesitated. His small eyes shifted from Frank to myself, as though in the most acute indecision. Viewed in full, his countenance appeared drawn, his features sharp, his teeth very bad. I guessed him to be no older than myself, but the wispy tendrils of hair escaping from his hat suggested a man approaching his dotage. There was about Percival Pethering a pitiful air of ill-health, of seclusion within doors, of embarrassments nursed in the most painful solitude. He was not the sort for decisive action or lightning-swift thought.

"Very well," he conceded abruptly. "We shall talk as we go, and save your wife the trouble of accommodating an interview."

"You know of my wife?" Frank returned, with the first suggestion of unease.

"It was she who told me where you might be found. I have been waiting for the hoy's return this last hour at least. You may judge from that how serious is the case."

"As murder must always be," Frank observed.

I was in danger of being led away from our companions of the morning without so much as a farewell; I turned, and found the two surgeons preparing to cross from the Quay to the far paving-stones where Wool House loomed.

"*Adieu, monsieur,*" I told LaForge.

He looked very ill; but nonetheless he carried my gloved hand to his lips with an excess of courtier's gallantry. In this, as in everything, his manners belied the humbleness of his professed station; and I wondered again at his being in such a place and among such company.

"Mr. Hill," I murmured to the surgeon, "we must contrive between us to improve Monsieur LaForge's circumstances. He ought to be exchanged at the earliest opportunity; but he is most pressing, my brother tells me, in his desire to remain in England. Cannot we secure a more salubrious lodging? He ought not to be allowed to sleep another night on those chill stone floors."

"I quite agree," Mr. Hill returned wryly, "but I fear in the case of a prisoner of war, comfort is the very last consideration. I shall write to Admiral Bertie tonight, and plead LaForge's case; your brother has requested that I should refer the Frenchman's desire to remain in this Kingdom to Bertie as well."

"I shall urge Frank to write to the Admiralty. He is not without acquaintance among the Great. We shall see what determined activity may do."

"Improvement, of whatever nature, cannot come too soon," Mr. Hill observed. The shrewd narrow eyes flicked from my countenance to LaForge's. "Our colleague in justice has grown quite despondent since his appearance before the panel. Lowness of spirits cannot help a case of dubious health. I shall prescribe brandy as soon as I am within Wool House's doors."

"You are very good," I said with deep sincerity.

"Jane!" cried my brother. "We try Mr. Pethering's patience."

Mr. Hill bowed; I curtseyed, and without another word turned to my brother and the magistrate.

Frank all but raced up the steep pitch of Southampton's High. He was considering, I knew, of Mary's anxiety—of her fears for himself, and of the magistrate's intent. Mr. Pethering proved unexpectedly equal to a sailor's brisk stride. I followed along in the wake of the two men, and bent all my effort at attending to the questions of one, and the replies of the other.

"May I enquire, Captain Austen, as to your conduct last night?" the magistrate began.

"My conduct? I was engrossed by the performance of Mrs. Jordan, in the French Street playhouse, as my sister and wife shall attest."

"That play should have ended by half-past eleven, and all of you been returned to East Street by midnight at the latest. Did you stir from your home afterwards? Put the ladies down at the door and proceed alone to some haunt only you are aware of?"

"I did not, sir."

"Do you generally display so domestic a devotion?"

"In general—yes. I am in the habit of rising at an early hour, Mr. Pethering, and such habits require a settled and tranquil life."

Frank's tone was easy enough; but I knew my brother, and found his words were watchful.

"I understand you sent an express messenger to Captain Seagrave's house in Portsmouth on Tuesday evening."

"Seagrave is a very old acquaintance. I am often in communication with him—when we are both aground on dry land."

"But an express—an *express* would argue a certain urgency, Captain Austen."

"Would it?" Frank posed airily, as though constantly in the habit of spending more than he ought on his correspondence. "I confess that I am so often at sea, Mr. Pethering, that I am not able to keep abreast of the usual forms and charges of landsmen."

"At sea. Yes, indeed. I imagine you must often be at sea. May I enquire, sir, as to the nature of the intelligence your express conveyed?"

"Gentlemen never look into the contents of each other's mail," my brother replied with heat.

The magistrate abruptly changed tack. "You have heard already of Chessyre's murder, though the body was discovered only this morning and you have been in Portsmouth all day. How, pray, did you learn of it?"

"In much the same manner, I imagine, that you learned of my express. From the mouths of innocent men. The messenger you sent to Portsmouth this morning was the agent of my discovery."

The magistrate glanced sidelong, his appearance for all the world like that of a long-beaked marsh crane. "So you are not above perusing *my* correspondence, though I may know nothing of yours. I see how it is. But my message, Captain Austen, was for Admiral Hastings alone."

"I was aboard the *Valiant* at the moment the Admiral learned of Chessyre's death. Your note was read aloud to all in attendance at the court-martial."

"Your friend Seagrave's court-martial," Mr. Pethering reiterated pointedly.

"I was not aware there was any other, sir."

"You are deeply concerned in that unpleasant affair, Captain

Austen. I wonder that you risk your reputation and standing—a man of your pronounced domestic virtue—in such a cause."

"I should always support a brother officer," Frank replied tautly, "particularly when I believe him unjustly accused. But I do not think, sir, that an affair of military justice falls within the scope of your power."

Here my brother was on uncertain ground. It was true enough that the original charge on Seagrave's head—the killing of the French captain after the surrender of the latter's ship—fell to the disposition of his naval superiors. That crime, if crime it were, had occurred at sea aboard one of His Majesty's vessels. The murder of Lieutenant Chessyre, however, was another kettle of fish. Chessyre had died in Southampton proper, while relieved of his duties and turned upon shore. The disposition of his case must be considered the magistrate's; and anyone Mr. Pethering suspected of evil should fall within the temporal law, be they naval or no.

We turned into East Street and progressed the brief distance to Mrs. Davies's establishment. The magistrate seemed disposed to ignore, for the nonce, Frank's challenge to his authority. He preferred to pursue a different line.

"If Captain Seagrave ranks so high among your friends, Captain Austen, one must presume that Eustace Chessyre was chief among your enemies."

I stumbled slightly at a loose paving, and both men turned.

"It is nothing," I cried. "Pray do not regard it."

Frank flashed me a brief smile; he must know that anxiety had tripped me up, not an obstacle at my feet. "I date my acquaintance with Mr. Chessyre only from Tuesday, and thus must consider him neither as a friend of the bosom nor an enemy of the heart. To what do your questions tend, Mr. Pethering? Or should you like to enter my lodgings, and discuss them further?"

"You need only explain this, Captain Austen," Mr. Pethering replied, "and I shall trouble you no longer." With the air of a conjurer he withdrew a square of paper from his coat pocket and thrust it towards Frank.

"That is my card," my brother observed, without taking it from Mr. Pethering's bony hand.

"Indeed. It was found upon Chessyre's corpse—one of the few things the man seems to have kept about him."

"I gave it into the Lieutenant's keeping on Tuesday."

"You met with him?"

"On . . . an affair of business."

"You have written your direction upon the reverse, I see. Did you expect Mr. Chessyre to call in East Street?"

"He did call. Unfortunately, I was not at home." Frank's lips had set in a thin line; he was holding his temper in check only with difficulty.

"How very inconvenient. One wonders what the Lieutenant might have said. Were you very pressing in your invitation, Captain, to seek out your lodgings? Or was the matter of business you wished to discuss better concluded . . . behind the Walls?"

"Good God, man, if you wish to accuse me of murder—then do so at once! I am confident you will be made to look a fool!"

But the magistrate was studying my indignant brother with calculation. He neither accused nor offered quarter. I understood, suddenly, that he hoped to frighten Frank with his suspicions—and draw forth some intelligence presently withheld. The contents of his express to Captain Seagrave, perhaps?

"Pray come inside, Mr. Pethering," Frank said at last. "My sister is greatly in need of a warm fire and a glass of claret after her passage up the Solent, and I cannot believe you likely to refuse either."

"I never take wine," the magistrate rejoined. "It is most injurious to the health, in my opinion. But I should not say nay to a glass of warm gin, if you have any in the house."

"It shall be sent for directly."

THEY WERE CLOSETED IN MRS. DAVIES'S BEST PARLOUR NEARLY three-quarters of an hour. I sat with Mary before the fire in the dining parlour adjacent, while she tried to attend to her sewing, and threw it down again; chewed at her fingernail, and sighed her impatience. I thought I glimpsed the stain of tears about her pretty eyes; some trouble with the child she carried, or a depth of anxiety for Frank must be the cause. But when at last she spoke, her voice held only fretfulness.

"And so Tom Seagrave's accuser was murdered, and must bring the magistrate to our very door! Thank God my mother has no notion of the scenes to which I am daily subjected—the indignities and sufferings quite thrust upon me, and in my delicate condition! I am sure that Mamma would carry me off to Kent directly, without stopping for a word of explanation; and I am in half a mind to summon her!"

I studied her petulant young face over the edge of my book. "Mr. Chessyre called at this house in search of Frank on Tuesday. It was Chessyre who occasioned Frank's absence from home that night, and Chessyre you must thank for your extreme anxiety then. Mr. Pethering, the magistrate, knows that Frank solicited an interview with Chessyre on Tuesday morning; he has found Frank's card among Chessyre's things. As Tom Seagrave's friend, Frank must be counted among Chessyre's enemies. Must I speak any plainer, Mary, or will the recital do? Your husband is in the gravest danger of being accused of murder."

Her mouth formed itself into a tragic *O*. "Frank went in search of the Lieutenant Tuesday night? When I could not sleep?"

"He sought the man throughout the quayside, and among the most unsavoury circles; but failed in the end to meet with him. Tom Seagrave should consider himself greatly obliged to Frank, once he learns of the energy exerted on his behalf—" I broke off. Mary's hand was now pressed to her lips, as though she were ill, and her eyes had filled with tears. "I have upset you. What a wretched thing in one who professes to be your sister! Pray forgive me—"

"So *that* is why she came in search of him."

"Who came?"

Mary shook her head. "She would not give her name. A very *vulgar* sort of person, Jane. Indeed, I believe one might refer to her as a...a..."

"Barque of frailty?" I enquired.[1]

"Not nearly so well-bred as that! She was quite disreputable in her person, and her clothes were in rags. I must confess that she *smelled*, Jane, most disconcertingly. No, I am afraid we must call her simply a jade, and leave it at that. 'As much as my life is worth,' she insisted, 'to speak to Captain Austen; but I *must* do it.' I thought her quite out of her senses."

"Wherever did you meet with such a woman?" I enquired, bewildered.

"She came to Mrs. Davies's kitchen door, just after breakfast, and asked for Frank."

"How very unfortunate," I breathed.

"Mrs. Davies felt it her duty, she said, to summon me—Captain Austen being from home." Mary's countenance was scarlet; she must have presented just such a picture of consciousness and mortification in our landlady's kitchen. I apprehended, now, the source of those tears I had suspected in the poor girl's looks, her misery and thoughts for her mamma.

"And did she state her business?"

"She would not, though I pressed her most severely. I thought at the time that she was simply surprised to find that Frank had a wife—that he had suggested otherwise, on a previous occasion in her...company. But I wonder—"

"You did not learn her name?"

Mary's eyes slid away. "I suppose in common decency I should have requested it, Jane, but I will own that I was so dumbfounded by her appearance that I wished only to be rid of her. I told her that

1. *Barque of frailty* was the cant term for a mistress or courtesan.—*Editor's note.*

Captain Austen was from home, and that if she refused to disclose her business with my husband, she must seek him on another occasion. She wrung her hands, and insisted that she was in terror of her life—she looked most pitiful, Jane—but in the end, I shut the kitchen door, and she took herself off."

I could imagine the scene without considerable effort. Young Mary—unequal to the display of pride that Mrs. Davies would require—sailing past our landlady with her chin quivering, to spend the remainder of the morning in her empty bedchamber.

"Do you think it possible," Mary enquired of me, "that this person sought Frank with regard to Chessyre?"

"Anything, in this sordid business, is possible," I replied with unhappy candour. "Frank was open in his effort to secure the Lieutenant, the night before the man's death; from my brother's account, he searched the quayside for some hours, asking directly for Chessyre. Any with ears to hear and eyes to see, would know that the one man was concerned with the other."

Mary did not reply. She appeared lost in sorrowful reflection; the young bride's quick remorse for hasty judgement, I presumed.

There was the sound of a distant door thrust open, and the murmur of voices quick and low; then a decisive thud in the passage to the street as the house turned its back upon Mr. Pethering. Another instant, and my brother strode into the room, his countenance considerably lighter than it had been when we parted.

"I do not believe we have the slightest cause for worry," he declared without preamble. "Mary, my love, have you been dreadfully disturbed in spirits? I must beg your pardon for occasioning anxiety, and lay the whole before you without delay."

"Spare your breath, Frank," she replied with energy, "for I am well-acquainted with the business."

My brother shot me a look of hurt surprise; he had not believed me so unreliable a confidante; but Mary hastened to disabuse him.

"Would you take me for an ignorant child? Am I to remain unconscious of a subject that has engrossed the better part of my acquaintance these many months, solely because my husband did not chuse to speak of it? Fie, Frank! That you could credit me for a goose! I wonder at your opinion of my understanding."

Frank begged forgiveness; Mary wept a little into her square of lawn; and I was spared a further indulgence of bridal humours, by the urgency of the matter at hand.

"Pray tell me, dearest Frank, what that dreadful man Pethering would lay at your door," Mary begged.

"He had hoped to disturb a desperate murderer in his plans for flight," my brother answered calmly, "but was forced to conclude, from my sanguine air and excellent head, that I had nothing to do with the Lieutenant's sorry end. I pointed out that any number of lodgers in this establishment might vouch for my presence last evening; and proceeded to inform the magistrate that I thought it likely the man was killed in a brawl."

I raised my brows at this, but elicited not the slightest notice.

"Pethering required an explanation for the presence of my card among the man's things, and I told him that I had called upon Chessyre at the Dolphin during the course of Tuesday morning. I fancy he already knew as much. What he hoped to learn was the substance of my express to Tom Seagrave."

"And did you disclose it?" I asked.

Frank hesitated. "I had no choice, Jane. Pethering warned me that he shall soon call a coroner's panel to enquire into Chessyre's death; and I shall be forced to give evidence. I could not very well lie to the man in my own home."

"You might have pled the constraints of honour, and purchased your friend a few more hours!" I protested. "The magistrate now knows what the Frenchman saw. And what he saw is motivation for murder enough!"

"What Frenchman?" Mary cried, bewildered.

"I am done with preserving Tom Seagrave!" Frank retorted. "He has not been open; he guards all in a cloud of secrecy; he impugns the disinterest of his friends. It is not enough that I should be suspected of dangling for a ship; I must now be expected to lie for him! I wonder you can suggest it, Jane!"

My brother rose, and quitted the room with a bang of the door. Mary stared after him in perplexity.

"Frank is to have a *ship*? Why did he say nothing of this to me?"

"Perhaps we should start with the Frenchman," I sighed.

Chapter 14

A Turn for the Worse

~

I awoke not long after seven o'clock to the sound of a fist hammering at the front door.

My ears strained through the dawn stillness for the issue of so much commotion—caught the tramp of sleep-dulled feet along Mrs. Davies's lower passage—the murmur of conversation—the thud of the heavy oak. There was an instant's silence, and then the same ponderous tread of a woman long past her prime, mounting the steps and making for my brother's bedchamber.

Another express. From Portsmouth, perhaps?

Mrs. Davies would not be pleased to have lost her final hour of rest in the presentation of Captain Austen's mail.

I threw back the bedclothes and stretched my warm feet to the cold drugget. There was little point in attempting further sleep; I had tossed throughout the night, my dreams consumed by a dimly-lit room and the glittering, half-opened eyes of a whispering Frenchman. There was something he meant to tell me—some message he sought to convey—but either the noise in my head was too great for hearing, or his French was become suddenly unintelligible. I could not make out the sense of his words.

Must I always translate for you? Etienne LaForge enquired wearily. *Chessyre is dead. I shall not long survive him.*

I drew my dressing gown about my shoulders. The palest light seeped through the clouded windows; a bank of heavy fog pressed down upon the house. It was an hour for lying curled in a huddle of warm blankets; but I could not be easy in my mind. The Frenchman's words haunted me. Was I a fool to accord such weight to the spectres of fancy? Perhaps in my younger days I might have shrugged off this nocturnal warning; but the wages of experience are caution. I have learned that what waking thought may not penetrate, the slumbering mind will illumine. I am hardly the first to credit the notion—the English language is replete with aphorisms that would urge a troubled soul to retire with worry, and find comfort in the dawn. For are we not "such stuff/As dreams are made on, and our little life/Is rounded with a sleep"?[1]

Chessyre is dead. I shall not long survive him.

I twitched back the curtains and strained to make out the street below. My eyes have never been strong, and in the grey light every outline was indistinct; but even I could not mistake the horse and rider lingering there. The express messenger had been instructed to wait. His mount snorted and tossed its head; its breath showed white in the frigid air. At that moment, I caught the sound of my brother's door bursting open, and the quick light race of his feet along the passage. The reply, then, would be urgent. I must dress and discover what intelligence was come before Frank entirely quitted the house.

I let fall the curtain and broke the thin layer of ice in my ewer. I avoided the image of my own face in the glass; the persistent cold in my head could not improve my looks, and its effects were most determined before breakfast. One could only hope that by

---

1. Shakespeare, *The Tempest*, act IV, scene 1, line 148.—*Editor's note.*

this evening's party at Captain Foote's the swelling of my nose would have diminished. The view of a lady's complexion by candle-light, in any case, is vastly to be preferred to the glare of day.

"Jane!" My brother's voice came quick and cutting beyond the door. "Are you awake?"

"Of course." I admitted him immediately. "What news, Frank—good or bad?"

"The magistrate has called the inquest into Chessyre's death for nine o'clock this morning. Tom Seagrave shall be in Southampton within the hour."

"Oh, no! Poor Louisa!"

"I understand she intends to remove with her children to Southampton, the better to observe her husband's misery. It was she who drafted this letter; I must suppose that Tom did not wish to seek my aid. His wife shows less of injury, and more of sense. I replied that I shall endeavour to secure her accommodation at the Dolphin."

So Louisa Seagrave had determined to decline Lady Temple-ton's offer, and the funeral party in Kent. There was little enough of choice remaining to such a woman, I thought: an interval among relations one could not love, or the prospect of a husband's public disgrace. Either event should involve her in consuming shame; so proud a creature must be prey to every mortification. Dr. Wharton's Comfort should be sought all too often in the coming days.

"I shall leave my card at the Dolphin this morning," I said thoughtfully. "She *must* receive every consideration at such a time. It seems hard in us to abandon her to solitude this evening—but I do not like to give up the party at the Footes', even in so persuasive a cause. We go out so little during the winter months—and Mary has looked forward to it so."

"Devil take Louisa Seagrave!" Frank retorted savagely. "She may sit in contemplation of her disloyalty to Tom, and see whether she finds reason to blame herself for his present fate. Had she told the magistrate that her husband was at home Wednesday night—"

"She should have perjured herself without improving his chances," I interrupted with equanimity. "Do not make her the proxy for your own unhappy conscience, my dear."

The door to my brother's bedchamber slammed harshly in reply. From the floor below came the clang of an iron pan and the first heavy odours of bacon fat and boiling coffee; our faithful Jenny should be gone in search of fresh rolls.

Frank's furious voice shouted for hot water—and then like the strain of an uncertain bird, came Mary's placating tone. I pitied them both. Frank must regard himself as in some wise responsible for his friend's debacle. He had told Seagrave that which should make him murderously angry; and he had given Percival Pethering all that was required to clap the man in chains.

Frank would certainly attend the inquest; but I should be spared the discomfort. I had played no part in the body's discovery, I had witnessed nothing that must be disclosed, and I will confess that I felt consuming relief. I had no love for a coroner's panel—they are, in my experience, the product of haste and officiousness, spurred by information that is at best incomplete and, at worst, mendacious. In the present case, I could wager on the unhappy outcome. This should be Tom Seagrave's last day of liberty.

The thump of a boot hurled with vicious force thudded against my bedchamber wall; I heard a bell ring at the other end of the hall. My mother was awake, and demanding the most current news; she should be all agog at the flurry of misfortune among our acquaintance. But I could spare the matter only a part of my mind. Frank might be thrashing in the grip of rage; Louisa Seagrave, bound for the Dolphin; her husband, destined for misery—but I intended to appear at an evening party, and must endeavour to be a credit to my family.

Martha Lloyd—ingenious at the trimming of headdresses—had promised to accompany me to Pearson's, the milliner in the High, for a perusal of exotic feathers. A turban must be requisite for a lady of my advancing years: something dignified and imposing, with a swag of braid and a peacock's plume not unsuited to a gown of Prussian blue sarcenet. I fear that I am quite past the age of appearing all in white, regardless of season; such an attitude may be permitted only among pale consumptives or determined vestals, and I have never aspired to either station.

I turned back into my room and pulled my shift over my head, heedless of the draughts.

MY CONSCIENCE WAS NOT SO BEWITCHED BY THE PROSPECT OF dissipation, however, that I ignored the duty of sending my card up to Mrs. Seagrave at the Dolphin when Martha and I passed the inn later this morning. I declined to wait, having bade the footman not to disturb the lady; and trusted I should have the pleasure of receiving her in East Street before very long.

"Where is the inquest to be held?" Martha enquired in a voice better suited to the graveyard.

"At the Vine. It is much less public than this place, and the magistrate appears disposed to discretion, at least."

"Is your brother in any danger?"

I looked at my friend in some surprise. There was *that* in her voice that suggested the most acute anxiety; and I thought it hardly the disinterested concern of a fellow-lodger. Some remnant of youthful feeling for Frank must survive in Martha's breast; but it should never do to speak of it now.

"Far less than he should be upon the open seas," I told her easily. "He is a sensible man; he has nothing to hide; and I trust he shall convince every fellow on the panel of his probity and good sense."

Martha sighed. "For so much of difficulty to come at such a time! With the removal to Castle Square but a fortnight hence—and Mrs. Frank's baby so near its time—and there is the possibility of a ship, I understand? Our Frank may be posted before his wife's childbed? It seems he has been ashore but a few months, and they would be sending him off again! The Navy is governed by brutes and beasts, Jane!"

"I am sure Mrs. Seagrave must believe so," I said thoughtfully, and stared up at the inn's bow windows.

MARTHA'S SPIRITS SHOWED GRADUAL IMPROVEMENT AS WE MADE our way along the High—stopping here to finger a sprigged muslin, there to abuse a bonnet of atrocious design. The day was clear and bright, almost unnaturally so for February, but sharply cold. We were obliged to enter far more shops than we had originally intended, merely to keep warm. When at last we had all but stripped our purses bare, I proposed a bit of refreshment—and was turning for a pastry shop I knew of, tucked into Butchers' Row, when two small figures huddled on a neighbouring doorstep caught my eye. They were dark-haired, rosy-cheeked, and shuddering from the cold: both well-grown boys, not unfamiliar, and decidedly ill-clothed against the penetrating wind.

"Charles Seagrave! And Edward!" I cried. "You shall both of you catch your deaths!"

Charles, the elder, sprang upright like a jack-in-the-box, his grey eyes wide with relief. "It's the lady who called upon Mum in Lombard Street," he informed his brother. "When Uncle Walter was there. I have forgot your name," he admitted doubtfully, "though you know mine."

"Never admit to such an ignorance before a lady, Charles," I told him briskly. "It is the worst sort of offence a gentleman may bestow. I am Miss Austen, and this is Miss Lloyd. How do you boys come to be abroad, entirely alone, in such cold weather? Where is Nancy? Surely she attended you from Portsmouth?"

"Nancy is in charge of the baby," retorted Charles, "and good riddance, so cross as she is!"

Little Edward rose to his feet, his bare fingers thrust under his arms, his lips blue and chattering. "Please, m-m-miss, don't be telling our mum about our lark! She's resting after our journey from P-p-portsmouth, which was bang-up jolly if you ask me—four post horses hired from the G-g-george, and everything prime about 'em! How we ratt-tt-tled along! We made the distance in under two hours!"

"Am I to understand that your mother is as yet ignorant of your absence?" I enquired in an awful tone. "That you are both abroad expressly without permission?"

Martha choked upon what I guessed to be a laugh. The brothers quailed. Charles threw his arm about Edward, as though his thin nankeen jacket might supply the want of warmth in the younger boy's own.

"We only meant to have a look around town," he protested. "It's our first visit to Southampton! We've been down the High to the Quay, and seen all the ships, and poked our noses into the dockyard—though it's a poor thing indeed compared to Portsmouth's," he concluded contemptuously.

"Not even Nancy knows of your going?"

He shook his head.

"They shall be all in an uproar at the inn," murmured Martha beside me.

"We intended to return ages ago!" Edward cried. "Only—we could not find the High once we had visited the bathing machines. We are most dreadfully lost."

I did not have the heart to tell them that the High Street was but a hundred yards away. Both boys were shivering violently now. Edward looked upon the verge of tears.

"Come along," I said with a sigh. "Miss Lloyd and I shall treat you to hot chocolate and honey cakes in that pastry shop opposite, while I beg some paper and a messenger of the proprietor."

Crows of delight interrupted my declaration. I endeavoured to look stern.

"We shall send a note to the Dolphin attesting to your whereabouts and safety—but the very moment your last drop of chocolate is drunk, my fine fellows, it is off to the inn with you and no mistake! You require hot water bottles and warm possets, and you do not wish to die of an inflammation of the lungs."

Suitably subdued, the boys preceded us into the pastry shop, and commenced to eat with a voracity that suggested young wolves. I secured my paper and pen, and began to compose a note for Louisa Seagrave while Martha kept up a stream of nonsense calculated for the boys' amusement. But not all their talk was of spillikins and hoops, or the dashing naval actions recently reported in the *Gazette;* little Edward must be constantly reverting to the subject foremost in the boys' minds: the judgement hanging over their father's head.

"Charles and I have determined to run away to sea if Father hangs," he informed us as he tucked into an apple pasty.

"Edward!" his brother hissed in a quelling tone. Possessing eight years to his brother's six, he was necessarily more cautious, and knew the value of discretion. "They will tell Mum straightaway! Only you mustn't," he added for our benefit, "for it is our only recourse, as I'm sure you're aware, being of the naval set yourselves. If Father hangs, we shall be tossed overboard in a manner of speaking. I mean to say—no connexions worth having, and no influence with the Admiralty. We shall have to make our way if we mean to advance."

Martha gazed at Charles doubtfully. "I am sure your father— even supposing the worst should happen, which I do not admit for an instant—would wish you to serve as support for your mother. She should be in ever greater need of you, if she were . . . alone . . . in the world."

"Muzzer thall go into Kent," Edward declared through a mouthful of pastry. "We thould be more of a burden if we thayed." He swallowed mightily. "Besides, I cannot support Aunt Templeton. She means to engage a tutor for us! As if we did not know all we needed to learn, already! She is an ape-leader! Poor Uncle Walter— how he must suffer it!"

"He is shot of her for now," returned Charles, "and must be having a jolly time of it. But I for one shall *certainly* run away to sea if we are bound for Luxford!"

I met Martha's eyes over the heads of the two boys. She raised one eyebrow. At that moment, the bells of St. Michael's Church, adjacent to our seats in the shop's bow front window, tolled half-past eleven o'clock. The inquest into Mr. Chessyre's death must be concluded, or nearly so.

I was suddenly sharply impatient to know what the judgement might be, and determined to place the boys in Martha's charge—they were getting along famously, for Martha has always been a slave to children's amusement—and set off in search of Fly. I gathered up my paper parcels—one held a pair of gloves in dark blue satin, quite unlike my usual wear, but perfectly in keeping with the iridescent hue of the three feathers I had chosen under Martha's instruction—and motioned for the reckoning. Pray God I had sufficient coin to satisfy the ravages of two healthy young predators.

"Jane," observed Martha in peering through the window panes clouded with February cold, "is not that Mr. Hill I see before us? He looks worn to a fag end. I should judge that travel by sea does not agree with him—a curious recommendation for a naval surgeon, I am sure!"

The thin frame, the narrow, black-clad shoulders, the periwig—indeed, it could be none other than Mr. Hill. I set down the gloves and hurried out of the shop to intercept him.

"Miss Austen!" The surgeon started at my address, as though lost in a brown study. "How well you look this morning! I should say that your cold is quite gone off!"

Martha appeared in the doorway, her parcels precariously balanced in her arms and the Seagrave boys hiding behind her skirts.

"Miss Lloyd, too! And you have been making a few purchases at the milliner's, I see—a pursuit that is always calculated to bring animation to a lady's countenance."

"We have been entertaining Captain Seagrave's sons," I informed Mr. Hill. "Master Charles, his heir, and Master Edward."

Both boys scraped their bows. Mr. Hill inclined his head benevolently.

"Your brother is well, I hope, Miss Austen? No ill effects from yesterday's voyage?"

"I do not think that Frank could ever suffer at sea. You might better enquire how he fares on dry land!" I scanned the surgeon's face. He looked very ill indeed. "But what of yourself, Mr. Hill? Are you quite recovered from your exertions?"

He hesitated. "I could wish our friend Monsieur LaForge to be in better frame. I sat up with him all night. The effort of achieving Portsmouth yesterday—his testimony on Seagrave's behalf—or perhaps simply the exposure to poor weather in his weakened state—"

Chessyre is dead. I shall not long survive him.

"You find me just returning from a consultation with Dr. Mount," the surgeon continued, "a physician of considerable reputation, and a great traveller in his day. He has seen many cases of gaol-fever—or ship fever, as it is also known. Even he cannot account for LaForge's symptoms. I confess that I am greatly disappointed; I had hoped for some inspiration. Instead, I have fetched only laudanum. It shall ease his suffering, at the very least."

"Then you think . . . you believe it possible . . ."

"That the man will die?" Mr. Hill gazed at me baldly. "I should never undertake to say, Miss Austen. It is a point that only his Maker may answer. I will tell you that his fever has increased; that from cramping in the bowels, he may take neither food nor water; and that his pulse is fluttering and weak. Indeed, he may have passed from this life while we stand thus, in talking."

I looked my indecision at Martha, then impulsively seized Mr. Hill by the arm.

"For God's sake, let us be silent," I said, "and reserve our breath for walking. Miss Lloyd must carry the young Seagraves back to the Dolphin, but I shall accompany you to Wool House. I cannot stay away."

ETIENNE LAFORGE WAS NOT DEAD; BUT HE LAY IN AN ATTITUDE SO narrowly approximating it, that I all but despaired of his life. The sharp brown eyes were completely closed, the jaw clenched in pain. He was drenched in sweat despite the room's raw atmosphere, so that his body was racked with chills. His ebony walking-stick lay by his side on the pallet, as though in the last extremity of existence, he would guard this one relic of home. He muttered fragments of French—phrases I could not always catch, or comprehend once I heard them. At times he seemed to be wandering in childhood; at others, he broke into bawdy song, and must be restrained or he should have attempted to dance. But for the most part he seemed torn with anguish, and struggled upright to cry aloud the name of Geneviève. His Beloved, perhaps? Left behind in the Haute Savoie— or in early death?

"Just so it has been," Mr. Hill muttered, "since eight o'clock last evening. I do not know how much more the human frame may stand."

Chessyre is dead. I shall not long—

I pressed LaForge's shoulders gently back onto his pallet and bathed his brow. I held a basin while Mr. Hill bled him. Where I knelt on the stone floor, the cold crept through my dress, deadening all feeling in my joints.

"He should not be lying in these dreadful conditions," I burst out. "None of them should. It is shocking that we treat men this way—as though they were slaves, or less than human. He should be moved to a proper bed, near a proper fire."

Mr. Hill did not meet my eyes. "Naturally. But his condition has declined so greatly, Miss Austen, that I do not think it possible to move him now."

"This is nothing like the usual course of gaol-fever?"

The surgeon shook his head. "Did I know nothing of the case before this, I should pronounce him poisoned. He suffers, I should say, from an acute gastric complaint quite unlike the troubles of a few days previous. His sickness is lodged in the bowels. It is that which causes him agony."

I felt my frame stiffen, the breath caught in my chest. "I once witnessed a death from poisoning. It was terrible to behold. Could something noxious have been introduced to his food?"

"But that is absurd! Why should anyone wish to harm a French prisoner? None but ourselves is familiar with even a particle of his history!"

"Monsieur LaForge was in despair yesterday at the suspension of Captain Seagrave's trial," I told the surgeon urgently. "When he learned the news of Lieutenant Chessyre's murder, he declared that his life was forfeit for having related what he saw aboard the *Manon*. He is the sole witness to an attempted plot. Do not you comprehend the matter?"

"But who—"

"Whoever killed Chessyre! Have you received a gift of food for the prisoners?"

Mr. Hill hesitated. "Your eggs, of course," he said slowly, "and a quantity of meat pasties from Mrs. Braggen's kitchen. They were sent in my absence yesterday. But surely Mrs. Braggen—"

"I should never accuse the lady or her household of ill intent. But if the food appeared in your absence—anything might have been done to it."

"Then why did not every prisoner who partook of the food fall dreadfully ill?"

"Because the poison was meant for only one man," I persisted.

Mr. Hill shook his head. "My dear Miss Austen, I fear that your imagination is run away with you. You have been overwrought. All this talk of murder—it may give rise to the most dreadful fancies—"

"There has not merely been talk! Two men are dead. One was killed at sea, another not a mile from this door. It is you, Mr. Hill, who persist in fancy. You must treat LaForge as though he were indeed a case of poison. It can cost you nothing, and may save his life."

The surgeon studied me shrewdly, then felt LaForge's brow with his palm. "Fever, a fluttering pulse, and a disruption of stomach and bowels. A purgative first," he said decisively "Ipecac, I think, or perhaps the more gentle tartar emetic. Then a cathartic, to flux the bowels. I should attempt cremor tartar, but for its strength; perhaps a solution of castor oil and medicinal rhubarb will prove more gentle in its effect. Once the system is cleansed, we may see what a strong dose of charcoal in milk may do for what has already been consumed. It is a property of charcoal to attach itself to metallic substances, such as are often found in your common poisons; the stuff may then be passed harmlessly enough."

"Can such doses harm him?" I enquired with trepidation.

"The combined effects shall work violently on his frame, and in such a weakened state—I should advise you, Miss Austen, to leave us for a period. I shall send word by messenger to your boarding house, once I am certain of the effect—whether it be good or ill."

He began to rummage in his black bag, purposeful now that he had determined his course. I rose, took one last look at the sufferer, and quitted that dreadful place.

It was ten minutes past two o'clock. I went directly to St. Michael's Church, halfway along my path towards home, and knelt in the silence of the nave. I prayed for the salvation of Etienne LaForge—prayed as I had not done for some months since, with a passion and a purpose that could not help but sing its way to Heaven. If asked, I could not have said why the Frenchman's case burned at me so. I hardly knew the man. But the thought of so much wit and understanding finding an untimely grave was suddenly insupportable. In praying for LaForge, I prayed for all that I loved: Frank and Mary and their unborn babe; for my mother, and Cassandra, and the sprawling family at Godmersham; even for Mr. Hill, unstinting in his work to save this foreign life. In this quarter-hour they were all of a piece with that Frenchman: beloved of somebody, and dying alone.

Chapter 15

The Naval Set

27 February 1807,

cont.

~

"A VERDICT OF WILLFUL MURDER WAS RETURNED AGAINST TOM SEA-grave," Frank said, as I entered Mrs. Davies's sitting-room at a quarter past three o'clock. "He is held at present in Gaoler's Alley, in expectation of trial."

I sank into a chair ranged against the wall and closed my eyes. "That is very unfortunate. You told the coroner's panel of your express?"

"I did. The magistrate knew enough to direct the coroner's questions. There was little of surprise in anyone's testimony; and Seagrave refused, again, to disclose his movements on Wednesday night."

"Did the charges of the court-martial arise?"

"Naturally. Percival Pethering has not the slightest authority in that case; but he sought to show that Seagrave had murdered his lieutenant—and all discussion of motive must involve events on the *Manon.*"

"And thus the panel was taught to regard Tom Seagrave as a man who is intimate with murder. No other outcome was possible. I feared as much." I stared up at Frank. "Monsieur LaForge has taken a turn for the worse. Mr. Hill suspects poison."

"Poison!" My brother's hand clenched spasmodically. "But who—?"

"The man who killed Chessyre, I suppose. Having despatched his conspirator, he could not allow a witness to survive."

"If he dies, Jane, his blood will be on our hands," Frank muttered. "It was we who urged LaForge to divulge what he knew."

"Then we must pray that he does not die," I said, and went to dress for the party.

"MY DEAR MISS AUSTEN! YOU DO US PROUD IN SUCH FEATHERS, I declare—we shall be as the moon outshone by the sun!"

Captain Edward-James Foote, hearty and weather-beaten as only a man in his third decade at sea may look, stood in his dress uniform under the sparkling chandelier in the central hall of Highfield House, and bowed to all our party. Captain Foote is a towering figure—quite suited to serve as model for some martial statue in bronze; and though forty years at least, is as yet handsome.

"And how is your delightful daughter?" I enquired, as I curtseyed before him. I had practised the movement in the privacy of my room, under Martha's tutelage, to be certain I should not disturb the wretched turban; but my heart and delight were not in it. I must be always thinking of Wool House, and the grim struggle undergone in its shadows. I had received a messenger from Mr. Hill just before five o'clock. Etienne LaForge had suffered greatly from the ministrations of castor oil and ipecac; he had refused to drink the potion of charcoal of his own will, and must be held down by two Marines while the dose was given; but Mr. Hill could detect no greater injury to the system. He saw nothing of improvement in the

Frenchman's condition, but neither did he see a persistent decline. LaForge had fallen into restless slumber, still muttering the name of Geneviève. I must hope for the best. And endeavour to turn my mind to other things—

"We were so happy to receive your daughter's visit last week, when Captain Austen brought her home from church; Catherine is most natural in her manner, and quite devoid of shyness." She was also small and frail for her age, and her looks were not equal to her brother's; but I saw no occasion for telling the father *this*.

Captain Foote raised one eyebrow. "I hope Kitty did not disgrace herself by seeming too forward? She did not bring you to a blush? Her mother, you know, was not entirely what one could have wished."

The unfortunate Nina Herries, long since fled to Calcutta with an officer of the Hussars. She had a fatal interest, it seemed, in the military orders—a fascination with uniforms that had better been outgrown in the nursery. Little Catherine was her second child, abandoned to a new mamma and a different home; but the change had been of marked benefit.

"Kitty was everything that was delightful—and all that I was not, at her age," I replied. "You need have no fears for the young lady, with such an example at home."

I glanced at Mary Foote as I said this, and felt the Captain's eyes travel fondly towards his wife. She looked brilliant in pale grey satin, her dark locks piled ingeniously upon her head. In four years of marriage she had spent barely six months free of pregnancy; but the practise appeared to agree with her. She was perhaps a bit more stout than the elegant young daughter of an admiral who had first caught Foote's eye; but the Captain's second adventure in marriage had proved him a gambler of good fortune.

I could feel Frank at my back, impatient to speak to his old friend; and so I passed on, and curtseyed to Mrs. Foote. She had only time to press my hand and murmur something about "delightful . . . so happy . . ." before Frank's Mary gave a little crow of pleasure, and was enfolded in her friend's embrace.

"You must come up to the nursery and see the baby," Mrs. Foote whispered to her, and received a giggle in return.

I made my way into the large and comfortable drawing-room of Highfield House. The villa on the outskirts of town was happily situated on rising ground, with a view of the sea from its upper storeys; it was adequate to the accommodation of seven children and occasional guests, and though quite modern in its style, looked everything that a growing family could wish. Nearly thirty people, I should judge, were already disposed about the room; a roaring fire ensured that those closest to the hearth should be roasted, while those at the farthest remove must suffer from draught. I discerned Admiral Bertie, engrossed in conversation with another gentleman by the cunning French windows; his daughter, Catherine Bertie, held a silk handkerchief to her nose, which appeared decidedly enflamed. The Lances—Mr. David Lance and his wife, whom I believe to be called Mary, as every woman of my acquaintance must be, who is neither an Elizabeth nor a Catherine—were sitting in very grand style at the far end of the room, as though expecting the rest of the party to pay court. And beside them—

Beside them, in the closest conversation, stood a man I recognised from his bold dark brows and his broad shoulders. Sir Francis Farnham, last glimpsed at the theatre in French Street, on the most intimate terms with David Lance. It should not be extraordinary; Lance had once been a prosperous merchant with the Honourable East India Company, and Sir Francis was something to do with the Navy Board. The two services were thick as thieves, my brother had always said. Frank had carried gold bullion for the Company himself on at least one occasion—a venture not strictly legal, but rich in its recompense and repeated so often in naval practise as to seem mundane. The Honourable Company depended upon Navy protection for its valuable convoys of merchant ships; and at times, in certain parts of the world, the Navy used Indiamen for the transport of men or victuals.

"Frank," I breathed to my brother as he approached, in excellent humour for the first time in days, "what exactly did you say was Sir Francis Farnham's post?"

"Farnham is Civil Administrator of the Transport Board," Frank replied. "He must spend a devilish amount of time in hiring merchant ships. The Navy uses them, you know, for the transport of goods and seamen. I expect that is why Sir Francis is in such close converse with Mr. Lance."

"Yes," I replied, "but it is Sir Francis I mean to speak to."

Frank's attention was claimed by a man in the uniform of a first lieutenant. Martha Lloyd appeared in the doorway, a trifle flushed from the exertion of climbing the Highfield House stairs. I motioned to her to join me.

"Courage, Martha. I espy a difficult acquaintance, and you know that we must pay our respects."

"Oh, Lord," she breathed. "Not the Lances! Why must they be so very grand? I do not wonder poor Mr. Lance hesitates to be seen in his brother's company. It is too great a mortification for so modest a man."

The "poor Mr. Lance" to whom she referred was a highly respectable gentleman of the Church—an old Hampshire acquaintance, and possessed of a living in our former neighbourhood of Netherton. It was through our good Mr. Lance that we had met the bad Lances, as we sometimes referred to them; for the clergyman's younger brother had gone off, in his youth, to India, and had made such a fortune there as Mr. Henry Fielding's novels satirise. He had married his partner's sister upon his return to England. The two possessed at least four children, all of them exceedingly delicate. They presided over a vast place known as Chissel House about a mile out of Southampton on the Bitterne side. David Lance is as keen as his name, and I will confess that I admired his wit and calculation; but I could not like his wife.

Frank and I had paid a call on Mrs. Lance some weeks previous. It was clear that she was rich—and that she liked being rich; and as we are very far from being so, she has determined that we are quite beneath her notice. She displayed her enormous pianoforte, and the view of her grounds, which are known hereabouts as Lance's Hill; and these two duties done, was entirely without conversation.

Martha grasped my arm. "Remember your feathers," she instructed. "They shall never shame you, at least."

We advanced upon the sopha; the gentlemen were engrossed in conversation. Mrs. Lance bestowed a distant nod, but failed to vouchsafe a greeting or evidence that she recalled my name or visage. Martha boldly advanced to claim acquaintance, and to talk in animated spirits of our good Mr. Lance; I curtseyed, and strained to overlisten the gentlemen's conversation.

". . . signal flags certainly are an immense improvement upon the usual speed of such . . ."

". . . understand these signals might be changed for purposes of encoding . . ."

". . . entirely secure . . . hardly subject to . . ."

Far from discussing vital matters of transport with the Honourable Company, Sir Francis was launched upon his favourite subject of swift communication. Mr. Lance was most attentive; but at that moment he happened to glance around—happened to catch my eye—and bowed most handsomely.

"Miss Austen!" he cried. "You should never wear any colour but that. It becomes you exceedingly."

"Thank you, Mr. Lance," I replied. "I find the shade encourages me to boldness when I most require it. Like the peacock, I carry my feathers forward when I should prefer to retreat."

He gave a swift look about the assembly. "I had not realised Foote's drawing-room was a battlefield! Whom would you tilt at?"

"Your friend, Sir Francis Farnham," I replied promptly, with an inclination of the head at that gentleman, who stared at me sardonically from his black eyes. "Though we are as yet unacquainted, I confess I have yearned to speak with him for some time, on the subject of prisoners of war. The Transport Board is responsible, I believe, for the care of the French? Or should I say—irresponsible?"

"Let me fetch you a glass of claret, Miss Austen," cried David

Lance with a gallant attempt to lead me away. "I am sure that you require refreshment. The heat of the room—"

"Stay, Lance," commanded Sir Francis. His imperious eyes had never wavered from my face. "I should like to hear the lady's concerns. It is because of the French I am come to Southampton, after all."

David Lance looked from Sir Francis's set face to my own, which I imagine must have been flushed with the ardour of my thoughts. He took a step backwards. "Very well. I should never come between opponents on the battlefield. Tilt away, Miss Austen!"

I lifted my chin, and with it, my feathered turban. Martha drew a sharp breath at my side, as though she intended to dissuade me; she had not bargained for dispute when she agreed to meet the Lances. I squeezed her gloved hand in a gesture that has always commanded silence.

"Am I right in believing I have the honour of addressing some relation of Captain Austen?" Sir Francis enquired, with ponderously calculated formality.

"There are two captains of that name—my brothers Frank and Charles."

"I am acquainted with the former. He commanded the Sea Fencibles, I believe, some years ago—and was stationed in Ramsgate. But presently he undertakes a very different duty, I understand. The defence of rogues and murderers."

"My brother is a steadfast friend, sir," I returned tartly.

"It has often been observed that one may know a man by the company he keeps."

I gestured around the Footes' close drawing-room. "Then you may learn in a single evening at Highfield House all you wish to know. My brother is perfectly acquainted with three-quarters of the party."

"His great friend Tom Seagrave, however, is not present. I understand the Captain was thrown into gaol this morning. It is a wonder he did not land there years since. Has your brother visited Gaoler's Alley?"

"He has. The support of a friend is no less a duty when it is afforded little respect, Sir Francis."

"It must call into question Captain Austen's judgement, however," Sir Francis observed. He had a broad smile on his supple mouth; he bent his broad shoulders attentively my way. Anyone in observing us would consider Sir Francis the most delightful of men, a true paragon of the Fashionable Set—and so attentive to the poor spinster with the ill-judged plumes. "I imagine the Admiralty will be forced to review their opinion of Captain Austen. They will wish to revise their estimate of his probity."

"I have every confidence in my brother, sir—as I have in Captain Seagrave's innocence."

"I shall take that as the most ardent recommendation of each man's worth, ma'am." He bowed, and made as if to turn away—but that I reached without hesitation for his sleeve.

"Pray enlighten me, Sir Francis, regarding an Admiralty matter that *does* happen to fall within your purview. Why are French prisoners, though no less men than ourselves, housed in such miserable conditions that they die of want and disease?"

My voice had risen with my passion for the subject; conversations all around me fell away and ceased. Sir Francis regarded me with one eyebrow quizzically raised. I drew breath, and blundered on.

"Surely we would not wish for British soldiers and seamen to be treated so abominably! If we cannot secure expeditious exchanges in the dead of the winter months, then we must ensure that the sick and wounded are placed in the naval hospitals at Greenwich or Portsmouth."

"Are you fond of causes, Miss Austen?" he enquired with a curl of his lip.

"Only when I discern injustice, Sir Francis."

He set down his wineglass with a care that suggested his temper was under tight rein. "I wonder that you dare to broach such a subject in the home of a naval officer. Those men you speak of so tenderly would as soon kill Captain Foote, and every other man in this house, as kiss your pretty hand."

Most of the naval set was utterly engrossed, now, by our spirited scene. I felt my cheeks grow warmer.

"The men I have seen are in no condition to stand," I replied evenly. "Indeed, there is one man at least who may not survive the night, he is in so wretched a condition; and he is a gentleman of some learning, too—a naval physician."

"Ah." Sir Francis risked a sneer. "There is a *gentleman* in the case. I should have suspected as much."

I flushed hotly. "You are impertinent, sir! Were my brother—a post captain in the Royal Navy—to end a prisoner in France, I should devoutly hope that he might receive better care than a Frenchman on these shores. Our care for the Enemy must stand as a testament of our government's humanity, despite the brutality of war. It *ought*, it *must*, to serve as example to the Monster in France, that English subjects are possessed of hearts!"

"Here, here!" cried Cecilia Braggen. She had advanced upon the conversation. "Are you plaguing Sir Francis about Wool House, then? Well done, Miss Austen! The conditions are a positive disgrace, and Sir Francis should know it."

The gentleman's expression shifted suddenly, from one of wooden tolerance—of indulgent impatience—to that of fleeting contempt.

"I have been to Wool House," he replied, "so recently as yesterday. It was to view Wool House that I came to Southampton. I agree that the conditions are dreadful; I have already ordered that the men should be removed to Greenwich, and turned over to the care of the naval hospital. They shall be conveyed thither on the morrow. And now, ladies, if you would allow me to conduct my Board as I see fit—and as I am far more capable of doing than yourselves—I should be greatly in your debt."

He turned his back and strode across the room without another word, so that I was left with scarlet cheeks and a desire to flee Highfield House that instant. *When* would I learn to govern my hasty tongue?

"I wonder what Mrs. Carruthers can be thinking," observed

Cecilia Braggen reprovingly. "To set her cap at such a man—vulgar, intolerant, and contemptuous as he is! I do not care how great his family was, or how considerable his late wife's fortune! He ought to be thanking us for the benevolence of our activity—for the sacrifice of our men, nearly every day! He ought to know what he owes the naval set!"

Curiosity overcame my mortification—I glanced up, and saw that Sir Francis indeed stood by Phoebe Carruthers's side. She wore tonight a gown similar to the one she had displayed in French Street—severe in its lines, untrimmed except for a frogging of black braid across the bodice—but her form was so magnificent, she might as well wear sacking and the world should cry admiration. She was speaking to Sir Francis in the most urgent tone, her eyes flitting from his countenance to my side of the drawing-room. Was it possible she understood a little of the scene that had occurred, and wished to know the particulars?

The golden beauty inclined her head to something Sir Francis said. Her countenance was unreadable; serene, or perhaps persistent in its coldness. And then her gaze came up to meet mine with an unfathomable look: nothing of humour or pain, neither wonder nor penetration. It was as though a wax doll had turned its painted eyes upon me. I shuddered, and at that instant Phoebe Carruthers's lips curled in the spectre of a smile.

Thanks to the efforts of his sister, Frank should never get his fast frigate *now*. I had made the name of Austen a laughingstock at the Navy Board; and the story would no doubt travel directly to the Admiralty.

"It is most improper," persisted Cecilia Braggen, without guarding her tone. "She should *not* appear in public—a lady in her circumstances. And the poor little fellow not two months gone!"

"You see, Miss Austen, I am as good as my word—I have fetched you a glass of claret." David Lance was kindly affecting insensibility to my confusion. He bowed slightly as he offered me the wine. "If I may be so bold as to comment—you might have chosen a more suitable adversary. Sir Francis is renowned for his harsh manners. Your feathers deserved greater consideration."

I murmured a few words of thanks—half apology, half dismissal—and suffered an added blow at the sight of Mrs. Lance over her husband's shoulder. She was tapping her fan against her palm in a considering sort of way, and her smile was everything of contempt and derision.

"JANE," SAID MARY FOOTE. "I UNDERSTAND THAT YOU SUFFER FROM the head-ache. Should you like to lie down upon my bed for a little?"

I had seated myself on a bench nicely screened by two large plants, in a passage just off the dining parlour. There, with a glass of lemonade and a biscuit I could not swallow, I might recover my spirits and my courage.

"You are too good," I told her, "but I shall soon be perfectly well. I suffer from an excess of folly, Mary, not head-ache—though the one may certainly bring on the other."

"We all *admire* the work you have done at Wool House." Her voice was gentle. "Admiral Bertie has been talking of nothing else. He tells us that you certainly have saved more than one life, Jane. Mr. Hill, the surgeon, cannot do without you."

"I fear poor Mr. Hill will pass a heavy night. One man was close to death when I left him this afternoon. We may regard this as the spur to my passionate plea, and dismiss the whole as a woman's hysterics." I looked up from my dry biscuit. "I may fault Sir Francis's manners, but must grant him a certain perspicacity. The French are to be conveyed to the hospital in Greenwich tomorrow. Sir Francis Farnham has disposed of my trouble, and I may retire from the field."

"Sir Francis Farnham has just quitted the house," she observed, "and taken Mrs. Carruthers with him; that is all I know of advance and retreat. It was quite an honour that he came, to be sure—but we much prefer the company of our friends. Never doubt your welcome in this house, Jane. I should vastly prefer your company to a thousand Phoebe Carrutherses. She is delightful to look at, of course—but she has no conversation!"

"I have never tried her talents in that way. We have never met. I had hoped to make her acquaintance this evening—but that must have been impossible." I recollected the coldness of her looks; I must be accounted among those she would henceforth cut direct.

"It *is* a fearful crush," Mary Foote observed naively. "I had no notion we had invited so many! I suppose Edward was busily commanding the presence of some, while I secured others. But I do not think either of us thought to send a card to Mrs. Carruthers. We assumed she was too deep in mourning. It must be that Sir Francis brought her."

"She has recently lost her young son, I understand."

"Yes. On the ill-fated *Stella*. I should not touch that ship for a kingdom, once Tom Seagrave is relieved of it—it is unlucky in its very knees! But poor Phoebe. Such grief as she has borne! She seems marked out by Fate."

"Her looks remind one of Helen of Troy; and I suppose that when one tempts the gods with beauty, all manner of evil may follow."

Mary Foote sat down beside me on the bench and patted my knee. "I have shown the baby to your Mary. She could hardly be pried from the nursery. I thought perhaps the sight of an infant might inspire her with delight; and that may do much, you know, to banish fears of confinement. We must all suffer them, to be sure, but we should never allow ourselves to be destroyed by them."

"No indeed," I replied. "And yet—it is not merely fear for herself. Mary fears for the child as well. So many young things are taken off in an instant! I recently knew of a family—in Derbyshire, where I passed some part of the late summer—that lost all four of its children within a year. Consider such unhappiness!"

"I could not survive it," Mary Foote said simply.

"But Phoebe Carruthers—"

"Ah, Phoebe. She is possessed of considerable resources. Or perhaps—perhaps it is only a coldness of heart. Young Simon was gone from her for nearly two years, you know, before his death. She had not seen the boy but for a fortnight here or there; and she must certainly have known, as we all do when our men put to sea, that this parting could well be the last."

"He was not a man," I observed, "but a little child. Mrs. Seagrave says—"

"Louisa Seagrave is mad," declared Mary Foote. "I know what you are going to say—that she refuses to risk her boys to the Navy's care—but some part of her resolve must spring from jealousy."

"Jealousy? Of Simon Carruthers?"

"Or his mother. It is everywhere known that Mrs. Seagrave believes poor Tom to be in love with Phoebe Carruthers."

"I see!" I sat a little straighter on my bench. A good deal was suggested to my understanding, most of it conjecture, but none of it implausible. "And is it known whether Mrs. Carruthers returns the Captain's affection?"

"Who can say? Phoebe preserves as perfect a silence as Delphi. One might read anything, or nothing, in her sublime features. But I have seen her several times of late in the company of Sir Francis; and as Sir Francis has lately lost *his* wife, and is possessed of a considerable fortune—more than ten thousand a year, I am told!—one must regard him as a better prize than a post captain." She gazed at me reflectively. "Is it true that Lucky Tom was seized and taken to Southampton Gaol?"

"Indeed," I assured her. "My brother visited him there today. Captain Seagrave is very low, as should not be extraordinary."

"And his wife has put up at the Dolphin, I understand. Edward fell in with her in the High Street at the very moment she was descending from her carriage. He says the little boys are fine fellows!" This last was said with a wistful air; for all her pregnancies, Mary had produced nothing but girls.

"Very fine," I returned with some amusement, "and despite their present trials, undiminished in both spirits and appetite."

178 ~ STEPHANIE BARRON

"You've paid a call, then?" Mrs. Foote enquired sharply.

"I left my card at the Dolphin this morning," I said, "but did not like to disturb Mrs. Seagrave. She must be involved in all the chaos of unpacking, for herself and three children; there are the servants to think of, and the ordering of dinner. But I shall certainly call to-morrow. She will require the support of many at such an hour."

Mary Foote sighed. "Then I must go as well, I suppose—though I am sure Louisa Seagrave has never warranted much attention from the naval set! We must consider it a kindness on behalf of Tom. For my part, I never believed him a murderer. I made the poor fellow quite a cause among my acquaintance! I shall look a fool, now—for of course the magistrate should never be wrong."

"I am afraid that magistrates are quite often wrong, Mary. Do not abandon your hero yet."

"Very well. But I depend upon you, Jane, for all the latest intelligence. If I *am* to look a fool, it were as well I should be prepared." She rose, and held out her hand. "The lion has gone, and taken his prize with him; so let us venture your acquaintance once more. I would not see those plumes wasted on my back passage, Jane. Martha would never forgive me."

Chapter 16

Nell Rivers

OUR HACK CHAISE WAS THE FIRST TO ARRIVE AT THE FOOTES' DOOR, once the carriages were summoned—a testament to its driver's impatience, one must assume, or the penetrating cold. Frank handed in his wife, then Martha, and then myself. When we were all settled, and Mary had begun an animated discussion of baby Elizabeth's manifold charms, to which Martha kindly attended, I asked Frank softly, "What do you know of Phoebe Carruthers?"

He started; perhaps he had hoped to doze on the journey home. "No more than anyone may know. She was orphaned early, and worked as a governess, I believe—in a very wealthy household somewhere to the north. There was threat of a scandal—an attachment on the part of the eldest son—that led to her dismissal. She married Hugh Carruthers not long thereafter. He was her cousin, you see."

"She is very beautiful."

Frank glanced at his wife sidelong, but Mary remained insensible. "If you like that proud, untouchable look—yes, I suppose that she is."

"Louisa Seagrave observed that all of Southampton was at Mrs. Carruthers's feet. 'Even Thomas,' she said, and then broke off."

"Did she?" enquired Frank with quickness. "They have been acquainted some years. Hugh Carruthers was a great friend of Seagrave's, I believe, and when he was killed by a ball aboard the *Téméraire,* nearly two years since, Tom undertook to give young Simon a step."

"Perhaps his esteem for Captain Carruthers now extends to his widow. Certainly Louisa Seagrave believes as much."

"You imagine her to harbour envy of Phoebe Carruthers? But she seemed to grieve so deeply for the boy!"

"Louisa Seagrave grieves for herself," I returned tartly, "and for the loss of an amiable marriage. She spoke of Mrs. Carruthers with pity, for the death of her son; that death must justify Mrs. Seagrave's refusal to send her boys to sea. She was unstinting, however, in her abuse of her husband for having showered young Carruthers with affection—at the expense of his own children."

Frank whistled sharply between his teeth. "She regards the woman in the nature of a rival."

"Mrs. Foote declares that it is so."

"What Mary Foote professes to know, all the world must see is truth," muttered my brother. "You suspect Mrs. Carruthers as the lady Tom Seagrave would shield? The lady in the case, as you put it?"

"He did say, with some bitterness, that he might better have remained at home for all the good he achieved Wednesday evening. What if he rode out to Southampton—not with the intent of murdering Chessyre, but of calling upon Phoebe Carruthers?"

"—Whom we know to have been occupied with Sir Francis Farnham in French Street," Frank cried.

"For at least the first of three acts."

"And so Tom, in finding her from home, suffered a disappointment!"

"Or arrived at her door in time to make the acquaintance of her latest escort."

"Then it is a wonder it was not Sir Francis found with a garotte about his neck," Frank supplied.

"I DECLARE, MISS! YOUR COLD IS MUCH IMPROVED." JENNY HAD TORN herself from the embrace of sleep quite early this morning, and her comfortable face was quietly cheering. She is nearly forty, our Jenny—as yet unmarried, and likely to remain so; plain of feature, ample in girth as she is in kindness. No one may equal her at frying a chop or dressing a salad; but the chocolate and rolls she carried this morning were all that I could desire.

"It will be the mustard plaster, I'm thinking," she continued. "It's just as well you employed it—what with that dreadful fever as the Frenchmen are spreading, and you so insistent upon ministering to them yourself, miss. I don't wonder Captain Austen was put out to find you'd gone to Wool House. But there, a lady must do her duty."

"Indeed," I replied. I sat up in bed and prepared to have my breakfast on a tray, like an indolent marchioness. I had never employed Jenny's mustard plaster, and had no intention of informing her of the fact. "Has any messenger come from Mr. Hill this morning?"

"No, ma'am."

I was sure that Jenny knew everything to do with our smallest concerns. From her piercing search of my countenance this morning, I guessed that she was disturbed in her mind—undoubtedly because of my correspondence with Wool House. Did she think me likely to lose my heart to a foreigner? Or was she nettled at the vagaries of Frank's temper? "I am afraid we are all a sad trial, with our adventures and our disputes. It is a wonder you put up with us, Jenny."

"I'd never call it a quiet household, what with your taste for murder and the Captain's for drabs."[1]

---

1. Jenny's long acquaintance with the Austen family—she had been in their employ since 1803—meant that she had witnessed Jane's involvement in the investigation of previous crimes, in Lyme and Bath particularly.—*Editor's note.*

I nearly choked on my chocolate.

"He did ought to be ashamed of himself! There's that poor young wife of his so far gone with the first, and her still a bride. I never thought I'd live to see the day when we should have women of the street lurking in the back doorway—but there, he is a man of the Navy, and we all know what they are. Mrs. Davies will never be done talking of it. If it weren't for the spoke I planted in her wheel, she'd have told all of Southampton."

"Did you see the young woman who enquired Thursday for the Captain?"

Jenny shrugged. "She weren't much to see. Long in the tooth and short on washing, if you ask me. But I knew it was her straight-away, when she come round again this morning. I told her to be off in three ticks, and no mistake!"

"This morning!" I thrust aside the covers and made to get out of bed. Jenny hastened to fetch my dressing gown. "Why did you not call my brother?"

"Captain Austen quitted the house at half-past six," Jenny returned with asperity, "no doubt upon business of his own. The Captain made sure to tell me I was not to disturb Mrs. Frank, and that I was to tell you he was gone to Gaoler's Alley." These last words were uttered with extreme contempt.

Gaoler's Alley. We had agreed last night, before retiring to our respective bedchambers, that Tom Seagrave should be interrogated on the subject of Mrs. Carruthers. Frank was doubtful that a direct assault might persuade him to yield a confidence he seemed so determined to keep. The lady, however, might save Seagrave's neck if she could swear before the magistrate that it was she he had sought on Wednesday night—and not Eustace Chessyre.

"Even so," Frank had told me doubtfully as we stood in the passage, "it cannot account for the entire period before the body's discovery. I do not know what we gain, Jane, by exposing Seagrave so dreadfully."

"He may stand the test of a trifling exposure," I retorted. "If you

intimate that we shall appeal to Phoebe Carruthers if Seagrave preserves his silence, he may well unbend to spare her the mortification."

And so my brother was not at home to answer the plea of a
Southampton jade. The woman had come in search of him twice. I
knew Frank well enough to believe it was not on business of a personal nature. This woman sought him as a certain authority. It was
imperative that we learn what intelligence she guarded.

"Would you know the woman again?" I asked Jenny directly.
"The one who wished to speak to my brother?"

She started, a slight frown between her eyes. "Happen I might.
But I'd'a thought you'd be glad to see the back of her, miss."

"So we probably shall," I murmured, "once we apprehend what
we have undertaken. Nonetheless, she must be found."

Jenny's gaze slid guiltily away. "The poor wretch begged me to
take a message to the Captain. I told her I wanted none of it. But
she stood her ground. All manner of nonsense she uttered."

"You must try to remember what she said. It is of vital importance, Jenny."

The maid hesitated. "Has it to do with the murder? Of that sailor
as all the town is talking of? He weren't a friend of the Captain's,
surely."

"The man accused of Mr. Chessyre's death may hang for a crime
he did not commit. And he is Captain Austen's dear friend. My
brother cannot bear to see an injustice done."

"You think the light-skirt as is skulking about the back door
knows summat she oughtn't?"

"Please try to remember what she said."

" 'My soul must be quit of it'—that was one part, like she had a
sin she needed shriving of. Of course, at the time, I reckoned she
meant the Captain. That her conscience was devilling her on account of Mrs. Frank."

"She gave you nothing? No note for Captain Austen's perusal?"

"I doubt as she can write, miss; and that sort don't go carrying of
cards."

"No," I admitted. Even with Jenny's sharp eyes as aid, the search for a single young woman in all of Southampton must be fruitless.

"I suppose we could ask at the Bosun's Mate," she said thoughtfully.

My head came up. "What is that? A tavern, of some sort?"

Jenny shrugged. "I haven't the slightest idea, miss. But that's what she said. 'Tell the Captain he must ask for Nell Rivers. The Bosun's Mate will find me.' "

"It does sound like a tavern. I shall just have to find it."

"You're never going into that part of town, miss! Not alone! I won't allow it!"

I handed Jenny my cup. "Then you'll come? Thank Heaven! I do not know how I should manage without you, Jenny."

The maid rolled her eyes. But she did not decline the office; and as she thrust her large frame into the passage, I saw that she was smiling.

WE SET OUT TWENTY-FIVE MINUTES LATER. I HAD TAKEN JUST TIME enough to dress and pen a swift note to Mr. Hill, begging the earliest news of the manner in which Monsieur LaForge had passed his night; I might hope for an answer upon my return to East Street. The bells of St. Michael's were tolling a quarter-past nine as we descended to the pavement. Jenny wore the hood of her cape well over her head, as though to ward off the impertinence of the common sailor; and though my bonnet presented a wide brim, and was secured with ribbon over my ears, I found that I could wish for a disguise as thorough as my maid's. It seemed unlikely that I could ever be taken for a slattern; but my appearance in such a part of town must occasion comment.

"Have you any notion, Jenny, which streets might be considered . . . of ill-repute? My brother spoke of the quayside—and of the district beyond the Walls."

"The quayside you know," Jenny replied. "It's a pother of houses for the common seamen, and a few taverns where food as well as drink is served. The Bosun's Mate might well be there, but I cannot say as I recollect the name. If that bit o' muslin hails from one of the nunneries, I'm thinking we should search out past the Ditches.[2] There's a snarl of lanes new-laid just there, and poor ramshackle places as no one should be proud of biding in."

From the High, we turned into Winkle Street and proceeded to the limits of the town walls. Just beyond where we stood was a platform for viewing the sea and the ships at anchor; to the north ran the Ditches. Beyond the drained moat lay Porter's Mead, an open greensward. Above the mead was a web of small alleys that sprang from Orchard Lane, a narrow thoroughfare running north in parallel to the High. It had received its name long since, and apple trees had given way to buildings of every description.

Our road was of recent construction, and in fairly good repair; but the jumble of houses that lined it on either side was cheap and poorly maintained. It is natural, I must suppose, that the situation of an ancient port such as Southampton—drawing every describable breed and rank to its shores—must encourage such a miscellany of habitation and circumstance. There is poverty in the country, of course; the clergyman of a parish must be intimately acquainted with the humbler forms of suffering, and I had witnessed a good deal of humanity's bleaker side in my youth. But the decay of a city's lower districts is something worse. Here it is not simply a question of want of bread, or of illness brought on the wings of bad weather; here it is a rotting from within: through drink, and violence, and every form of vice.

A woman emerged from a doorway opposite to toss her chamber pot into the gutter. She eyed us malevolently as we passed, and her gaze followed us down the street. Three chickens scurried before us, clucking anxiously; a cat trotted by with a fishhead in its

2. Southampton's medieval walls still enclosed a good part of the city during Austen's time, and the eastern wall was bounded at its far side by a drained moat. The Ditches, as this area was known, ran north from Winkle Street, which fronted Southampton Water, to Bar Gate, a distance of more than half a mile.—*Editor's note.*

mouth. I counted at least three men stretched drunkenly upon the pavement, and was sorry to note that one of them still wore the remnants of a midshipman's dress. From the distance came a high-pitched cackle of laughter, swiftly choked off, and then the wail of a child.

"Poor mite," murmured Jenny.

Almost every habitation along Orchard Lane was shuttered as yet against the morning. A man's face—dreadful in its haggardness—peered out through one undraped window, and a milk cart drawn by a donkey made its rumbling way along the ruts at the paving's verge. "It is an unsuitable hour for approaching a tavern," I observed doubtfully, "even did we find the Bosun's Mate. We ought to have waited until sunset, and brought my brother with us."

"Good mornin', ladies," said a rough voice behind us. "Lost yer way?"

Jenny started, and clutched at the market basket she carried; I turned with a rustle of skirts. It would not do to show alarm. We should occasion even greater notice than we already had.

"That depends, sirrah," I replied, "upon the quality of your aid. We are in search of a tavern called the Bosun's Mate."

He was a man of advancing years, yet still powerful in his frame; his face had been ravaged by pox in his youth, and his right arm was gone below the elbow. His grizzled hair was drawn back in a queue, and tied with a length of black ribbon. He stank of strong spirits, and his eyes were very red.

"We are searching for . . . my maid's young son," I added with sudden inspiration. Jenny stiffened beside me. She had never married, and the imputation against her virtue was deeply felt. "A lad of fifteen years, whom we believe is lying insensible in a place called the Bosun's Mate. Do you know it?"

"What happened to the young feller then?" our interlocutor enquired, his bleary gaze falling heavily on Jenny. "Run away from home?"

"He were avoiding the Press Gang," she answered stoutly. "And who wouldn't, I'd like to know?"

"The Press done fer me, in my time," said the drunkard darkly. "Crying disgrace, it is, the King sending ruffians to cart every able-bodied man and boy off to slave and die at sea. Not that it ain't a good life, mind. I'd be there still, if it weren't fer Boney taking the better part of my arm. But if the lad don't have a taste fer it—"

"He holed up in this here tavern," Jenny interposed, "but the pore lad were beaten silly by a lout with a grievance. We 'ad a note of the publican, sent to my lady's house bold as brass, and my lady were so good as to lend me her protection. Me being a woman with a reputation to keep."

I was stupefied by this exercise of wit on Jenny's part, and could only stare at her and await developments. They were not long in coming.

"And could yer man not come in search of the boy?"

"Dead," she said succinctly. "At Trafalgar."

The drunkard swept off his hat—or the one he imagined to be as yet on his head, but had lost some time since—with a grand gesture of his remaining arm. "Caleb Martin at yer service, good lady," he informed Jenny. "As who could not be."

She actually simpered at him. I deemed it time to retrieve the reins.

"Would you be so good as to direct us to the Bosun's Mate?"

"Gladly," he said, "provided I knew where it was. There's no pot-house o' that name in Southampton, and I've been inside of 'em all."

Studying his red-veined features, I could well believe the truth of this. I turned to Jenny. "Are you certain that was the name?"

She looked at me helplessly, then nodded. "It's not a common one, like the George, that a body could mistake."

"No. But a George we might have been certain of finding." I sighed. "Let us proceed up the street. Perhaps we shall encounter a person better able to assist us than Mr. Martin."

The fellow attempted to bow, and went sprawling on all fours. I winced at the impact of his poor stump against the paving-stones, but he seemed quite insensible to pain. From his position at our feet, he looked upwards and grinned—a gap-toothed, rather hideous smile that was nonetheless endearing. "Yer boy wouldn't be havin' a joke with yer now, would he?"

"Young Ned is capable of anything," Jenny told him with resignation. "I almost wish he'd been sent to sea. It might be the making of him—same as yerself, Mr. Martin."

"I only ask, because o' the name," he explained.

"The name?"

"The Bosun's Mate. Everyone in Orchard Lane calls old Jeb Hawkins that, on account of it being his station fer thirty year or more. You sure it wasn't a person yer boy meant, and not a public house?"

JEB HAWKINS LIVED IN A TIDY END OF CHARLOTTE STREET, WITH A neat front yard and a kitchen garden set out to one side. He kept a dog, which howled as we approached, and a few guinea fowl. He had evidently been up with the sun, and had been working about his place some few hours. We took courage and introduced ourselves; and rather than setting the dog upon us, he bade us welcome. He was just about to take his morning ration of grog, and would be happy if we might join him.

I should judge the Bosun's Mate to be roughly the age of sixty. A person of his prolonged exposure to the elements can never exhibit an unmarked frame; he was bent from hard labour, and his eyes were creased from gazing perpetually up into the shrouds. It is the boatswain's province on board ship to mind the sails and rigging, and report their condition daily to the first lieutenant; he is in charge, moreover, of all deck activity: the weighing and dropping of anchors, the taking of soundings, and the piping aboard of officers. The silver boatswain's whistle is a badge of honour among the able seamen, the highest distinction they may hope to attain. Frank has often said that a good bosun is worth his weight in Bombay bullion, and much of mutiny may be avoided in a ship that boasts the same.

"Mr. Hawkins," I began, as Jenny and I perched upon two rattan chairs he had set out on the grass by a small table, "I am uncertain whether we disturb you to any purpose. A young woman—a stranger to us—said that we might find her through the Bosun's Mate. I understand that is how you are sometimes called."

His thick white eyebrows lifted. "Are ye a naval lady, ma'am?"

"My brother is a post captain."

"And his name?"

"Francis Austen," I replied.

Mr. Hawkins nodded. "I've heard tell of yon. A grand, fighting cap'n, so they say, with none of your namby-pamby cut-and-run. Here's to the lad and his barky ship." He raised his tankard, and took a long draught. I glanced sidelong at Jenny; we appeared to be no forwarder.

"Are you at all acquainted with Nell Rivers?" I persisted gently.

The tankard crashed down with a thud. Eyes flashing, Jeb Hawkins thrust back his chair. "I'll not have ye meddling saints getting on the pore girl's back with all yer blather! She's not going to a Reform House, you hear? Not without Jeb Hawkins has something to say about it. Pore Nell's had enough to do, keeping body and soul together, and her the mother of three little 'uns, with no man about the place, without ye mealy-mouthed pisspots and all your bloody hymns! Be off!"

From the look on his face, he had been a bosun to fear indeed. Men must have quailed before the threat of his tongue, not to mention his lash; even in old age he could strike terror into a heart stouter than mine. Jenny was already on her feet, as though she meant to flee. But I reached out my hand in supplication.

"I am no missionary of God," I said quietly. "I come in search of Nell because she asked it. She says she is in fear for her life."

190 ~ STEPHANIE BARRON

The anger died out of his face. He settled once more in his chair and took a gulp of grog, scanning my countenance over the rim of his tankard. Then he sighed and set the loathsome mixture carefully on the table. A faint scent of rum laced the air.

"What do ye want wit' her?"

"That I cannot tell you."

"May not—or won't?"

"Twice in three days Nell has sought my brother urgently. There is a matter of great importance she wishes to convey. And yet Captain Austen declares that Nell is unknown to him."

"Many a man has said the same, to her sorrow," Jeb Hawkins observed.

I leaned towards the old man and held his gaze. "My brother *does not know* this woman. And yet she wishes to speak to him. Captain Austen was from home when she came today, and she was sent away in disappointment. I am come to relieve her mind."

Jeb Hawkins glanced from my face to Jenny's. Then he reached for a small ivory pipe, and settled it between his lips. "In fear for her life, you say? What has Nell to fear, in parting with such a bitter lot? She would be well out of her sorrows, and she found her grave."

"Surely while there is life in mind and body, there must be hope of amendment," I said.

He considered this. He rose from the table and ducked inside his small cottage to fetch a taper from his fire, then lit his pipe while standing in the doorway. I waited while the tobacco caught, and the smoke began to draw; I saw his narrowed eyes shift about the lane and then return to me. He lifted his shoulders in a gesture of surrender.

"I will not tell you where to find my Nell," he said. "I shall send word by a trusty boy. If she is truly in fear for her life, better that no one know where she bides."

"Tell her Captain Austen's sister begs the favour of a meeting," I suggested. "Tell her that I shall be walking with my maid near the Water Gate Quay. She might find me there within the hour. If she does not appear by eleven o'clock, I shall return to my lodgings in East Street. Please impress upon her that we are most anxious to hear what she has to say."

"I'll tell her." He took his pipe from his mouth and fastened me with a look. "But God help you, miss, if Nell comes to the slightest harm."

Chapter 17

What the Drab Saw

28 February 1807,
cont.

~

NELL RIVERS DID NOT KEEP US WAITING LONG. WE ACHIEVED THE Water Gate Quay inside of ten minutes, our steps hastened by a fervent desire to put the district east of the Ditches entirely at our backs. The Quay is a lengthy, imposing structure thrust well out into Southampton Water; it provides an excellent walk despite the constant bustle of embarkation and landing. Jenny and I took great gulps of fresh sea air as we paced the stones, and gazed out at the ships tearing at their moorings. A hulk there was such as I had not observed before, dismasted and deprived of its rigging. It rode at anchor like the ghost of glory, mournful in its fractured state, a vessel becalmed for the rest of its days. I wondered at its purpose. Such ships are sometimes found at Spithead, for the lodging and training of landsmen and young officers; it was these that had seen the worst of the mutinies in '97. But a hulk was a rarer sight off Southampton.

In contrast, I picked out an East Indiaman, which we learned from the chatter of small boys agog at the sight, had anchored but an hour before. She was broad of beam and low in the water with a considerable cargo, all her gay flags flying. The harsh calls of sailors echoed across the water, and skiffs were continually plying between the ship and the Quay. It was so busy, in fact, that I considered the coming interview with satisfaction. We might shout the particulars of murder and dissipation at Nell Rivers with impunity. No one should overlisten our conversation.

I turned and studied Wool House, a stone's throw opposite. So few hours ago I had watched Etienne LaForge enter that dispiriting place; and now he might be dead. Had I time to enquire of Mr. Hill, before Nell Rivers should approach? It was as I debated the question that I espied a small, dark-clad figure exiting the massive oak doors—the very surgeon! And bound on his way up Bugle Street! My heart leapt—I almost made to race after his figure—but that the sight of a second man stopped me. Tall, with chestnut hair and brows that must always suggest malevolence, his broad shoulders concealed today by a black driving cloak with many ruffled capes. Sir Francis Farnham, quitting Wool House. He was certainly accompanying Mr. Hill. Had he disposed of the French prisoners? Were they even now bound for Greenwich, and the seamen's hospital?

But as the two men rounded the corner of French Street and made to mount the High, my interest was seized by another pair of fellow-travellers: two boys with curling dark hair and purposeful looks, their figures almost overwhelmed by serviceable wool cloaks of blue. They sported diminutive cockades, and each had a small midshipman's trunk hoisted upon his shoulders. Charles and Edward Seagrave. They waited on the paving-stones while a coach-and-four rumbled past, then crossed to the Quay. Little Edward was struggling under the weight of his trunk; it teetered upon his shoulder and very nearly overset him. His brother paid him no regard, but made deliberately for the steps leading down to the water. Good God, did they intend to be rowed out to a ship?

I gathered up my skirts and was on the point of dashing after them, when Jenny said urgently in my ear, "Miss! There's the very woman! By the foot of the Quay. She is staring about like a rabbit in a snare. Shall I fetch her?"

I had so far forgot Nell Rivers as to emerge almost from a reverie. I dragged my gaze unwillingly from the Seagrave boys—young Edward was even now disappearing down the steps in his brother's wake—and turned to search for the figure Jenny would indicate. The woman had certainly espied us; and the expression of relief on her countenance was remarkable. It was as though she had been racked in a painful childbed, and we were her deliverers. I cast one last look towards the steps, hesitated an instant, then took Jenny by the arm and hastened down the Quay.

She was both shorter and smaller than myself, a slip of a thing with a sharp, pointed face. One eye was blackened and bruised from the impact of a fist. Her hair was unwashed and ill-dressed; she wore a kerchief over it, like a common fishwife, but her dress was at once grander than one of these and more horrible in its cheapness. She was arrayed in a manner designed to reveal her charms, and her occupation—even so early in the day—must be obvious to everyone. It occurred to me that such a woman must have limited funds, and could hardly spare the coin to purchase a modest gown for daily use, when her money must be invested in her trade. And she had children, the Bosun's Mate had said; three little 'uns, without a father. Such a family must run to considerable expense.

"Are you Nell Rivers?"

"Are you the Cap'n's sister?" she asked in a low and hurried tone. "The one as asked to speak with me?"

"I am Miss Austen," I said. "You have twice begged an interview with my brother, and found him not at home."

"I meant no 'arm, as God's my witness," she said, crossing herself fumblingly. "I only thought as he might be needing to hear what I know."

"Is this a private matter?" I asked her severely.

She shook her head. The furtive, rabbity look that Jenny had described was returned in force. "Will the Cap'n hear me, now?"

"He is regrettably engaged this morning," I replied, "in the service of a friend accused of murder."

Nell Rivers blenched white, and staggered a bit as though she might swoon.

"Here." I grasped her arm. "You must rest a bit before you may speak. Lean against this pier." There were pilings along the Quay, and a low stone parapet that served as viewing box for every urchin in Southampton with a lust for the sea. I directed her to a seat, and sank down beside her.

"Dad said as you were a real lady," she muttered. "I'm that ashamed—"

"Mr. Hawkins is your father?" I looked up at Jenny, whose expression was aghast. "I think perhaps you should tell me what you know."

Nell glanced at me sidelong and shook her head. "It's as much as my life is worth to speak. I daren't."

"Am I right in thinking you know something of an officer whose body was found in the Ditches—Mr. Chessyre, lately first lieutenant of the *Stella Maris*?"

She gasped, and pressed her hand to her mouth.

"Are you going to be sick?"

"No. It's just that dreadful—the thought of poor Eustace."

"You were acquainted with him?"

Her head bobbed. It was sunk so low into her bosom that I could not read her countenance. "Four year or more. We was mates."

"I see."

She fell silent, and I feared she might dissolve into weeping; but a second furtive glance informed me that she merely awaited initiative on my part. I reached for my reticule and extracted a shilling. Nell's head lifted and her eyes widened. I pressed the coin into her palm, and her fingers closed.

"Eustace was with me the night he died." Her eyes were swimming with tears. "He was that afraid. That's why he left the Dolphin, and come to set up with me. He'd done some dishonour, he said, and to try to put it right would only make things worse. He'd have to run for it, he said, only he needed some blunt. I said I'd help."

My opinion of Eustace Chessyre—already low—sank even further at this. Having failed to win his fortune from crime, the scoundrel thought to earn it off a woman's back.

"I'd never seen pore Eustace so jumpy in his skin. He wouldn't go out, but must hide in my room; he'd start at every sound, allus looking over his shoulder. Fair gave me the shudders, so it did." Nell shuddered now, in recollection.

"He told you nothing of what he'd done?"

"Not a particle. When I tried to wheedle it outta him—so as to make him easier in his mind, like—he give me this." She pointed to her blackened eye.

"Nothing? Not a word, not a hint of what his dishonour entailed? No . . . names . . . of anyone who might have been involved?"

Again she shook her head.

"Well," I said, attempting to hide my disappointment, "at least we know where he was the night he died. Have you thought of telling the magistrate this?"

She looked suddenly wild, and half rose as if to spring. "I'll be clapped in gaol!" she cried. "They've no love for a whore, them judges, and they'll lock me away."

"Calm yourself," I said. "I did not intend to throw you into alarm."

"I only asked for the Cap'n because Mrs. Bidgeon—she runs the Mermaid's Tail, where I work sometimes—said he was combing the quayside for news of Eustace. I told Eustace as much, thinking maybe it was Austen he'd dishonoured, and that he ought to lie low; but he just laughed. 'It's too late,' he said. 'I can't help him, nor him me. I've told off the Devil, and the Devil will have my neck for it! We'll all go to the Devil together!' "

Nell dashed away her tears with one worn hand. "I'd never seen him like that—down and beaten. Like he'd been trod on by a pack o' dogs. It scared me to death, and scares me still. When I heard they found his corpus—"

"Had he left you? Left your house, I mean, before he died?"

She gaped at me as though I were simple. "But *that's* what I wanted to tell the Cap'n," she said. "About the night he were murdered, and the coach."

"The coach?" I repeated.

"The one that come for Eustace in the middle of the night. I watched him get in, and that was the last I ever saw of him, living or dead."

I felt a cold thrill travel up my spine. "He went into a coach of his own accord? Though he was afraid for his life?"

"He looked like he thought it was the saving of him. 'There,' I thought. 'Eustace will be safe as houses. He's got a friend or two more powerful than mine.' "

"What time was this?"

"Middle o' the night. I don't properly remember. Maybe four or five bells."[1]

She had, after all, been raised by a boatswain.

"Was it a hack, or a private carriage?"

Nell looked uncomprehending.

"Do you recall noting any arms upon the doors?"

"I couldn't say. But the lady inside were very fine."

Jenny took a sharp breath beside me. I reached for Nell Rivers's hand.

"It was a *lady* Chessyre went to meet?"

Nell nodded miserably. "I suppose she were the death of him, miss."

---

1. Between two A.M. and half-past.—*Editor's note.*

Chapter 18

What the Orders Said

28 February 1807,
cont.

~

BEFORE PARTING, I ENQUIRED OF NELL RIVERS HER DIRECTION, AND learned that she was staying with another woman—a confederate in her trade—who lived in one of the dense streets running from Orchard Lane, not far from her father's house. It was convenient, she said, for the Bosun's Mate to look in on the children when she could not be there—and I gathered this must be often. Nell had quitted her own lodgings in terror that the lady in the mysterious coach might return to finish her off. She would not be charged with having exposed her blameless little 'uns, she added, to harm.

I forbore from suggesting that she had already done so, for most of their young lives; and commended her to caution. I urged her to plead an indisposition with the proprietress of the Mermaid's Tail, that she might better avoid her constant brush with strangers; danger could appear in any form. But she shook her head in stubborn refusal.

"I'd lose my place, miss, and they're not easy to come by. You've no notion how many women'd fight for a chance at the Mermaid's Tail. Murder or no, I must put bread in the children's mouths."

"You said that the lady in the coach was very fine," I attempted. "Can you describe her?"

"I didn't see her face," Nell answered. "She wore a black veil over all—heavy lace—and her pelisse was something dark. She was inside the carriage, and the lamps was blown out; I only caught a snatch of her cloak and a gloved hand as she opened the door."

Either the woman had doused the spermaceti candles in her globes, or she possessed oil lamps that guttered and smoked and suffocated from want of air. It was a problem common enough; but in this case, looked too much like design. The lady had intended to go unnoticed in the environs of Orchard Lane.

"Eustace went right up to the steps and said, 'My lady,' like she were a princess or summat; and she answered in a voice that told me she were his master, all right. It was low and firm, like she were used to giving orders. 'Get in,' she says; 'I have not much time.' And he got in."

"What about the nags?" my faithful Jenny demanded. "Did you not notice them? How many, and what colour?"

"Four, I think," said Nell in doubt, "and dark. But I've never paid too much mind to a horse."

It was hardly a hack chaise in local use; they were drawn by at most two horses, sometimes one alone. It must have been a private carriage, or one hired post at a coaching inn along the road. The entire matter was a puzzle; I could not believe that a woman had garroted Lieutenant Chessyre in her own equipage, much less cast him from the same into the Ditches behind the Walls.

"And you noticed nothing upon the carriage itself?" I pressed, without very much hope. It had obviously been pitch black in the lane in the middle of the night, and the lady had depended upon this to increase her anonymity.

"Naught but the diamond painted on the side," said Nell as an afterthought, "with the fist in the glove."

The fist in the glove. The bloody gauntlet accorded a baronet. I had seen one only days before, emblazoned on a coach that stood before Tom Seagrave's door. Lady Templeton's equipage.

"MISS AUSTEN!"

The voice came from the paving-stones opposite, as I made to cross to French Street. Mr. Hill, bereft of his companion of the morning. I had searched the Quay steps for Charles and Edward Seagrave, to no avail; I was desperate to be at home, in order to consult with my brother regarding Nell Rivers's rambling account; but I could not deny the impulse to enquire after Monsieur LaForge. I bade Jenny return to East Street, and her long-neglected duties in Mrs. Davies's household, and made for Mr. Hill's spare figure.

"Good day to you, sir. How did our patient pass the night?"

"Far better than we had reason to hope. I sent you word this morning, Miss Austen, but must conclude that the messenger found you from home." He peered at me kindly. "You hoped for a last sight of him? I am afraid I must disappoint you there. He is gone."

"*Gone?*" My throat constricted. "But I thought . . . you said that he passed the night . . ."

"LaForge was taken away with the rest of them this morning, at Sir Francis's orders." The surgeon pursed his lips in a grimace of frustration. "I cannot like the decision, but in this, I am utterly powerless. Sir Francis *is* the Transport Board, and before him I must bow."

"Then LaForge is not dead! Thank Heaven! Your purgatives and emetics did some good!"

"Yes," agreed Mr. Hill thoughtfully, "and I should never have attempted them were it not for you. I suspected—I feared the matter was one of poison; but I could not believe the evidence of my eyes. As every physical scientist must, however, I credit the result of my own experiment."

"You believe, then, that he was deliberately poisoned?"

"It was not a case of food gone bad," he said, "nor yet of an arsenic intended for Wool House's rats, ingested in error. His food—and his food alone—was tainted by something I have yet to name. I am as certain of that, as I am that the poor man lives. And I confess it disturbs me greatly in my mind. This threat to his life can have been no accident. It came too swiftly upon the heels of his testimony in Captain Seagrave's court-martial."

"You have questioned the Marines?"

Mr. Hill shrugged. "I have. They observed nothing untoward, and all stoutly maintain that no one but ourselves was permitted to enter Wool House. By ourselves, I would include, of course, your brother and Mrs. Braggen."

"Then the Marines are in error," I declared with heat. "Last evening, Sir Francis Farnham told me that he had visited the place the previous day. It was then he determined upon the removal of the prisoners to Greenwich."

"Greenwich?" Mr. Hill stared at me strangely. "Our patients are not gone to Greenwich, Miss Austen. They have been removed to that hulk lying at anchor in Southampton Water you may see from the quay—a rotting, foetid, and unwholesome berth if ever I saw one. It has been commissioned as a prison hulk, under the command of Captain Smallwood. An excellent fellow, but an unenviable post."

"A prison hulk?" I gasped. "But that is madness! Sir Francis told me expressly last evening that all the prisoners were to be removed to the naval hospital at Greenwich!"

"Not while the gaol-fever hangs over them," Mr. Hill grimly replied. "Greenwich would never tolerate the threat of infection to its good British sailors. Sir Francis claims that he had no choice but to isolate the sufferers; all of Southampton was alarmed at the possibility of epidemic. The French could not remain the longer in Wool House."

"He lied to me," I muttered furiously. "He made me look a fool, and himself a paragon, before the better part of my present acquaintance."

I turned and stared out at the ghostly ship, dismasted and forlorn at its anchorage in the Solent. "Etienne LaForge has been consigned to *that* misery? A man as ill as he?"

"I promised him I would row out to the hulk tomorrow, and see how he did," the surgeon said. "He was quite broken at his removal; he commended his books and walking-stick to my care, and went into the longboat as though it were a tumbril of execution."

"I should not give a farthing for his chances," I said bitterly.

"And I should not take your wager, if you did," replied Mr. Hill.

I FOUND FLY SITTING IN THE PARLOUR WITH HIS BOOTS OFF AND HIS damp socks steaming gently before the fire. He was alone—Mrs. Foote, I was made to understand, had very kindly called for Mary and carried her off for a visit to Highfield House—and he held a scrap of paper in his hands. His forehead was furled in puzzlement or dismay. I judged him to be perusing his missive for a second time.

"What is it?" I enquired as I came to a halt in the doorway. Whatever headlong rush of accusation and argument I had intended was quelled. "A letter from Tom Seagrave? Has he repented of his harsh words?"

Fly shook his head. "The note is from Tom's wife—and I am afraid I cannot make it out at all. She writes remarkably ill, Jane—a most impenetrable fist. If I judge correctly, she seems to think her boys have run away to sea! But that is absurd!"

He tossed me the single piece of paper. I took it with a sense of foreboding, and scanned it swiftly. Louisa Seagrave's handwriting was almost illegible: whether from the weight of her anxiety, or the effects of Dr. Wharton's Comfort, the words were cramped into a scrawl. The meaning, however, was clear enough.

"Naturally they have run away to sea," I retorted, and thrust the letter back at Frank. "What boy of pluck would fail to do the same? With a father consigned to gaol and a mother enslaved to opium, I should be moved to risk even so dreadful an institution as the Navy myself. You shall probably find them aboard that Indiaman riding at anchor in Southampton Water."

"The *Star of Bengal*?"

"I caught a glimpse of them on the Quay not an hour since. They wore cockades and dark blue cloaks, Frank, and each carried a seaman's chest upon his shoulders."

"Devil take them both!" he burst out. "Young cubs! That ship is due to sail with the evening tide!"

"Naturally. Charles and Edward are not Lucky Tom's sons for nothing. They meant to be long gone by the time their mother discovered their absence. Poor little souls—they *shall* be disappointed!"

But my brother did not vouchsafe a reply. He was already pulling on his boots.

FRANK WAS GONE FROM MRS. DAVIES'S ESTABLISHMENT A FULL TWO hours and thirteen minutes by the mantel clock, during which time I turned about the room in restless impatience, my brain divided between a natural concern for the welfare of the little Seagraves, and the most active anxiety on Etienne LaForge's part. Every minute spared for Charles and Edward, must be another moment of liberty denied the Frenchman. I attempted to bend my activity to the completion of a small garment for Mary's child—I took up and set down no fewer than three books—and still my gaze would travel inevitably to the ticking clock.

At last, when the hands had reached twenty-five minutes past two o'clock, I caught the bustle of entry in the front hall and heard Fly's voice raised stridently in a demand for brandy. It must have been perishingly cold upon Southampton Water today.

"I had to search into the very hold of the ship," he declared with barely suppressed rage as he entered the parlour, "and with the quantity of stuff still sitting in that Indiaman's bowels—salt pork, hardtack, biscuit, water casks, calicoes, a full complement of rats and I know not what else—it was tedious, unpleasant work, I assure you. Captain Dedlock insisted that no boys had come aboard, as well he ought—the Seagraves had paid off their ferryman to get their trunks on board, and come up themselves through the chains. They hid themselves in the hull, determined not to be found."[1]

"But you *did* discover them?"

"Only by resorting to the oldest trick in the book," Frank retorted. "I waved a burning piece of sacking through the open hatch and shouted *Fire!* until I was hoarse. They fairly tripped over themselves in their anxiety to achieve the air."

I could not suppress a smile. "I hope you were not too hard on them, Fly."

"I whipped them soundly with the bosun's switch, and then carried them back to the Dolphin. Neither Charles nor Edward shall have the use of his backside for several days, and they shall live in terror of naval justice for the rest of their lives. Or so it is to be hoped."

Jenny appearing at that moment with a large serving of brandy ("for medicinal purposes, the Cap'n having got wet through in all this cold"), my brother sighed his gratitude and could manage nothing more for several moments. At length, setting aside his empty glass, he cocked a quizzical eyebrow at me.

"What stealthy business carried you to the Quay this morning in any case, Jane? For I am not so much of a flat as to believe you were merely taking exercise when you espied the young Seagraves."

I told him then every particle of intelligence I possessed regarding Nell Rivers, and her strange tale of Eustace Chessyre's end. My brother could no more account for the insertion of a woman— much less a woman in a baronet's coach—into the business than I. Rather than dwell upon the unaccountable, however, I moved

1. "The chains" refers to the chain-wale or dead-eyes, the hardware used to secure the lower shrouds of a mast to the hull of the ship. We may suppose that Charles and Edward Seagrave climbed up the bow of the ship and entered at the spot in the chain-wale where a sailor usually stood to take soundings of water depth.—*Editor's note.*

quickly to the comprehensible: Sir Francis Farnham's perfidy regarding the prisoners of Wool House, and the manner in which I had been made to look a fool.

"It is active malevolence on Sir Francis's part," I told Frank indignantly. "Sir Francis has determined to destroy those poor men by consigning them to that hulk. They should all of them be tucked up in warm bedchambers, while instead they lie piteously below decks."

"Recollect, Jane, that most of those poor men, as you call them, have spent a lifetime in the hold of a ship," observed my brother mildly. "They may feel more at home in a slung hammock than they should in the best featherbed you could provide!"

"I doubt they have often benefitted from the choice," I retorted.

"And I must agree with Sir Francis," Frank went on, "that our convalescent British sailors should not be exposed to gaol-fever. We are too often in want of good men, to lose them in saving the French. Though I am sorry for our friend the surgeon—who seemed a good enough sort of chap—I must say that Sir Francis shows excellent sense."

"A prison hulk, Fly! Should you like to lie in one yourself, off Boulogne or Calais?"

"I might do a good deal worse," he rejoined. "I know Captain Smallwood, who has command of that hulk, and I should vouch for his goodwill and integrity without hesitation. He shall not like his duty, but by God, he shall do it!"

"Hurrah for Captain Smallwood." I sighed.

With a grunt, Frank pulled off his damp boots and tossed them against the fender. A faint frown was lodged above his eyes. "You do not suspect *Sir Francis Farnham* of having tainted the French surgeon's food, while inspecting Wool House? Surely that is carrying your grudge too far."

"I do not harbour any grudge," I said coldly. "I merely observed that the Marines were over-hasty in stating that no one but ourselves had entered the gaol. Plainly, others *have*. Sir Francis was certainly walking among the prisoners Thursday evening; and I saw him there again this morning. Any man with ill intent, and the good luck to know exactly which meat pasty LaForge would consume, might have done it."

"Or any woman?—One who drives a coach emblazoned with the arms of a baronet?"

I thrust back my chair, ignoring his satiric look, and crossed to the fire.

"We ought to go to Percival Pethering with your intelligence," Frank persisted. "Think what it may do for poor Tom! We know, in this, that Chessyre met with others before the end!"

"Nell Rivers's account, though provocative in the extreme, fails to prove Seagrave's innocence. The woman in the baronet's carriage might have dropped Eustace Chessyre anywhere, and left him prey to Seagrave's or another's violence," I replied thoughtfully. "It should not be unusual for a man to employ a woman as his lure."

Many ladies were but too willing to serve as the tool of a powerful man, and concerned themselves little with the purpose of their activity. Consider Phoebe Carruthers, for example, with her golden head bent to the words of her companion. . . .

"Fly . . . Sir Francis Farnham is a baronet, is he not?"

My brother threw up his hands. "And I suppose he veiled himself as a woman, and spoke in a voice firm and low! Next you shall be suspecting Lady Templeton of having been in both Kent and Southampton at once."

"That is hardly necessary," I retorted. "Chessyre was killed on Wednesday night, and I observed Lady Templeton in Portsmouth on Thursday. She spoke a great deal of her decision to quit the place the following morning—but no one thought to inform me when she had *arrived*."

"I should like a glimpse of Lady Templeton," Frank said drily. "She must be a formidable person, and much used to arduous travel. After strangling Chessyre with a garrote Wednesday night, we must suppose she poisoned Monsieur LaForge on Thursday. That is quite a piece of road between Portsmouth and Southampton, to traverse three times in twenty-four hours! And what motive could she have for despatching either man?"

"We should have to assume that she wished Tom Seagrave to hang; that she formed a plot with his disgrace as her object; and that she was unwilling either for Chessyre to recant, or LaForge to destroy, the delicate subterfuge she had constructed."

"But why?" Frank argued. "Because Tom married her niece against all opposition, *fifteen years ago*? It does not make sense, Jane."

"Not yet," I murmured, "but perhaps with time . . ."

"With time, you expect to learn that LaForge is a French noble-man in disguise, and Lady Templeton an agent of Buonaparte sworn to effect his ruin. Really, Jane! At times I must believe with my mother that you indulge too much in novels!"

I glared at him. "Have you a more apt solution, Frank? What did you learn from Seagrave this morning, in Gaoler's Alley?"

"Nothing to the purpose. Tom refused, without quarter, to discuss his activity Wednesday night; and he very nearly took off my head when I mentioned Phoebe Carruthers. All of Southampton was disposed to invade the lady's privacy, he said, because of her extreme beauty; she was an angel, she had suffered greatly, she deserved to be free of the wretched noose of gossip—et cetera, et cetera."

"So he *is* in love with her."

"Naturally. He managed, in every form of his refusal to discuss Mrs. Carruthers, to expose himself abominably. I only hope he does not behave thus before the magistrate."

"Did you enquire about Tom's orders?"

"I did. In this, I am happy to report, he was more forthcoming."

"Ah." I turned away from the hearth with alacrity and regained my seat. "Excellent fellow! You have disdained all *niceties* and *forms*, you have abandoned constraint, and thrown yourself into the chase! Pray tell: Whither was Captain Seagrave bound on the fateful day he fell in with the *Manon*?"

Frank's grey eyes glinted. "It is most intriguing, I will confess—the stuff of novels, as I declared before! Seagrave did not wish to disclose the whole; but when I impressed upon him the gravity of his condition, he relented. It is plain he considers the orders as having nothing to do with his fate; but I cannot be so sanguine."

"I am all agog."

"The *Stella Maris* was ordered to stand off the coast of Lisbon, between Corunna and Ferrol—a treacherous bit of coastline, which the men all call the Groyne—and signal with a lantern every half-hour of the watch between two and eight bells for three nights in succession.[2] If he received a lantern beam in return—the signal was prearranged, of course—he was to land a boat and collect a stranger, for passage to Portsmouth in the *Stella*. Seagrave was given no hint of the man's identity, but suspected he must be a foreign agent of the Crown; your fast frigates are often employed in such jiggery-pokery schemes."

"And did he collect his supercargo?"

"He did not. After the affair of the *Manon*—the battle done, the French ship repaired and despatched to port under Chessyre's management—Seagrave proceeded to the position specified in his sailing orders. He opened the sealed packet, and commenced to wait for the proper day and hour. Three successive nights he stood off the Groyne, signalling to no avail. Not an answering beam did he discover, and no stranger was hauled from the rocks. The duty done, Tom returned to port—and found himself accused of murder."

"Corunna might have been a subterfuge, I suppose."

"Designed to lure Tom within striking distance of the *Manon?*" Frank enquired. "I thought the same. The idea is fantastic, however—particularly when one considers the possibility of the two ships

2. Bells were the time-keeping system aboard ship. Struck every half-hour, they indicated by the number of strokes the tally of half-hours elapsed in the watch. Eight bells indicated midnight, one bell 12:30 A.M., two bells 1:00 A.M., and so on to eight bells at 4:00 A.M., when the sequence was repeated.—*Editor's note.*

missing each other in all that sea, the vagaries of wind and weather. No, Jane, it will not do."

"By whom were the orders issued?"

"Admiral Hastings. And he can have no reason to wish Tom Seagrave ill—he and the *Stella Maris* have won Hastings a fortune! The Admiral should be a fool to hang the goose that laid all his golden eggs!"[3]

"And were the orders written by the Admiral?"

Frank hesitated. "They were certainly transcribed by Hastings's hand. Seagrave wondered whether Hastings had noted the position in error—whether the *Stella* had missed the agent's signal, from standing off the wrong part of the Lisbon coast. Such a mistake is possible, I suppose."

"I do not understand you. You said that Hastings issued the orders!"

"He put them in Seagrave's hand, assuredly, and issued them with all his authority as flag officer in command of the Channel squadron. But the orders themselves were sent by the Admiralty telegraph. There is nothing unusual in this." Frank was attempting to marshal patience; but at his words my mind and spirit were animated as if by a shaft of lightning.

"The telegraph! Of course! A convention of the Navy bent to peculiar purpose! Why did we not see it before?"

Frank looked bewildered, but I lacked sufficient time to explain. For at that very moment Phoebe Carruthers was announced.

---

3. When a British ship seized an enemy vessel, the profits accruing from the sale of the prize were divided into eight equal parts. The captain of the victorious ship received three-eighths; one of these eighths was then turned over to his admiral. The remaining five-eighths were divided among the crew according to seniority.—*Editor's note.*

Chapter 19

A Picture of Grief

28 February 1807,
cont.

~

THE GOLDEN-HAIRED BEAUTY SWEPT INTO THE ROOM ON JENNY'S
heels, a veil of black lace all but concealing her features. At the
sight of it I nearly gasped aloud; but stifled the sound in time. It
would not do to betray a dangerous knowledge. Nell Rivers's very
life might depend upon my silence.

She lifted the veil from her face. Her eyes, I saw now, were the
green of pond-weeds in April, the green of lichens and stone.
Another woman might have encouraged the hue with silks of gold
and amber; but Phoebe Carruthers was resolute in her adoption of
dark grey. In this, at least, she was sensible of the conventions of
mourning.

"Captain Austen," she said with a curtsey, "it has been many years
since we first formed an acquaintance. I daresay you do not remember me, but perhaps you will recall my late husband—Captain
Hugh Carruthers."

Frank put his heels together and bowed. "He was an excellent man, Mrs. Carruthers; all England must feel his loss. You do not know my sister, I think. Miss Austen, Mrs. Carruthers."

I inclined my head. "Pray sit down. Jenny, be so good as to fetch some tea."

Phoebe Carruthers glanced over her shoulder at the hard wooden chairs ranged against the wall; Frank drew one of them forward and placed it near the hearth. She perched on its edge with all the poise of a figure carved by Canova.

"I am happy to make your acquaintance, Miss Austen. I was very sorry not to speak with you last night, at the Footes'; and seized the first opportunity of paying a morning call."

My surprise must have shown in my countenance; her green eyes flickered, and fell to her lap. She commenced to draw off her gloves.

I said, "You were obliged to leave the party rather early. But it was a delightful evening, was it not?"

"Or should have been, but for the manners of *one* in the room." Her cool eyes came up to meet my own. "I had not intended to appear at the Footes'. Much as I respect them, I am ill-suited to mix in company. I recently lost my son, as you may be aware. For my own part, I would fix quietly at home. But not all our obligations are matters of choice."

I glanced at Frank. The lady was dispassionate; she was contained; but this frankness she affected among virtual strangers could not fail to pique our interest. It might be a cold-hearted campaign to win our allegiance, who should find cause to suspect her of complicity in murder—but that was absurd. Phoebe Carruthers could have no idea of Nell Rivers, or what the latter had seen. She had no reason to assume our mistrust. She must be a woman of considerable caution.

"Your son's death cannot but be deeply felt," I said. "You have my sincere sympathy, Mrs. Carruthers."

She bowed her beautiful head, and could not speak for several seconds. I thought I glimpsed the gleam of tears beneath her lashes; it was all admirably done.

"I heard of your warm support for the prisoners of Wool House, Miss Austen—of your habit of tending to the sick."

Again, her tack in conversation surprised me; I inclined my head, but said nothing in my own cause.

"Tell me, are any of the *Manon*'s crew imprisoned there?" she enquired.

"There were lately four," I replied. My thoughts sprang to Etienne LaForge. If Sir Francis Farnham was somehow embroiled in Chessyre's scheme—if Phoebe Carruthers had lured the Lieutenant to his death—they would both be aware of the Frenchman's evidence at court-martial. Why, then, consult with me?

"One man died of gaol-fever, another is gravely ill, and all have been removed at Sir Francis Farnham's instruction to a prison hulk moored in Southampton Water," Frank supplied.

"Removed? By Sir *Francis*?"

The careful composure of her features was entirely torn. Her countenance evidenced shock. She stood, and moved restlessly towards the fire; grasped the mantel an instant in a desire for support—or suppressed anger—then turned, and regained her seat. When her gaze fell upon us once more, her looks were under management. The serenity of her features was as a lake no stone could ripple.

"You were not aware of the amendment," I said. "I had supposed that being acquainted with Sir Francis, you might have known all he intended."

"Sir Francis shares nothing, Miss Austen," she said carefully. "He prefers to dispose of people's lives rather than consult them. I had expressed a wish to speak with the men of the *Manon,* and he has deliberately thwarted my ambition."

"I see." She had betrayed none of this bitterness while in the gentleman's company.

Phoebe Carruthers leaned forward. "You have moved among them—the prisoners at Wool House. You have heard them talk among themselves. You speak French, I think?"

"A little."

Her lips worked painfully, and then the words came. "Do any of the French say how my poor son died? Was the shot that killed him deliberately fired? Were they so heartless as to strike down a child—so that his body was dashed upon the decks? . . . Oh, God, when I think of his father!"

She put her head in her hands and wept with a brutal abandon. Frank went to her instantly, and placed his arm about her heaving shoulders; I snatched up a vinaigrette that stood on Mary's work table, and offered it in vain.

"Tea, ma'am," said Jenny stoically from the doorway; and I motioned her towards the dining table. She set down the tray, poured out a cup, and proffered it wordlessly to Phoebe Carruthers.

The lady lifted her streaming face and accepted the tea gratefully. "I am sorry," she whispered. "I should not have so far forgot myself. It is just that this fresh blow is like a wound reopened, and carved more deeply than before. It was tragedy enough to lose Hugh—but Simon! He was such a bright and beautiful boy. Seagrave always said—"

Her words broke off; she sipped at her tea. The struggle for serenity was more obvious this time . . . and far less successful.

"I know nothing of how your son died," I told her gently. "It was not a subject I felt authorised to raise in Wool House."

"I quite understand. It was foolish of me to enquire."

Frank cleared his throat. "Mrs. Carruthers—you did no wrong in sending your son to sea. That was what his father would have wished, I am sure."

"My late husband would not have sent the boy aloft at such a time, in battle—he should have secured the child in his cabin. I must reproach myself for having entrusted the boy to Thomas Seagrave. I had not understood, at the time, what was vicious in Captain Seagrave's character. It was enough for me that he was Hugh's friend."

"They were long acquainted, I think?" Frank said.

"From midshipmen. I cannot remember a time when I did not know Tom Seagrave—he was almost a brother to Hugh. I have loved him as one, I know; but all that must be past."

She uttered the words without a blush. Whatever the naval set might suspect of Seagrave's attentions to Mrs. Carruthers, she betrayed not the slightest sensibility.

"You must not blame Seagrave," Frank said earnestly. "His present troubles aside, I believe Tom to be as good a man, and as honourable in his profession, as ever lived. The misfortunes attendant upon his engagement with the *Manon* are too many to name; but do not forget that your son spent nearly two years in Seagrave's keeping, and thrived."

"I know it." She summoned that ghostly smile I had glimpsed on her lips the previous evening. "How Simon loved that ship! He was always his father's child—haunting the seawalls and the quays, intent upon every anchorage. I could no more deny him a berth than I could cease to breathe. And I *did* regard Tom Seagrave—before I learned of his capacity for murder."

She shuddered.

Was this another calculated ploy? A deliberate subterfuge, from a lady who had enticed a man to his death?

"We had a glimpse of you on Wednesday night," I said carelessly, as though to change the tenor of the conversation. "In French Street, at the theatre. How did you like Mrs. Jordan?"

"Exceedingly," she replied. "Her antics spared me the necessity of conversation. Sir Francis had only just descended upon the town, and was most pressing in his invitation—I could not bear to entertain him in Bugle Street, where I lodge, and thus resorted to the theatre."

She endeavoured to make it plain she did not like the Baronet's attentions. I wondered at her energy in expressing so personal a sentiment, to a relative stranger; and thought the hint of design was in her words.

"How unfortunate, then, that you were obliged to quit the place after the first act," observed Frank engagingly. "We had intended to force acquaintance on Sir Francis at the interval, and were denied the privilege."

Mrs. Carruthers's nostrils flared. "I found that I was unequal to the effort of appearing in public. It is a strain, you understand, to parade as though one is insensible to grief—as though every word and look must not inspire the most painful recollections! I begged to be quit of the crowd at the first opportunity, and Sir Francis obliged me in this."

"How unfortunate! And so you fled one frying pan, only to end in the fire!"

Her delicate brows curled in perplexity. "I do not understand you, Miss Austen."

I cast a look of amusement at my brother. "To bid Sir Francis *adieu,* only to find Tom Seagrave at the door!"

"I did not know the Captain was in Bugle Street," she replied steadily. "He left no card. It is as well we failed to meet; I have not seen him since Simon's death, and might have uttered reproaches I should regret. Though Captain Seagrave may carry Simon on his conscience until he dies, I should not wish to carry *him* on *mine.*"

"And one might expect the two men to come to blows," I added sympathetically. "Thank Heaven you were spared such a scene."

For the first time, her complexion lost some of its colour. "To blows? Sir Francis and Captain Seagrave? What could you possibly suggest, Miss Austen?"

"From something Sir Francis said last night, I gathered that he holds the Captain in low regard."

"That is hardly singular. All of Southampton might say the same."

"But Sir Francis is not *of* Southampton, Mrs. Carruthers. Has he any cause for so pronounced a dislike? Some professional discourtesy, perhaps, on Seagrave's part?"

"None that I know of."

"Then perhaps he merely thinks to support *your* grief, and your sentiments."

For the length of several heartbeats, Phoebe Carruthers said nothing. Her green gaze held my own. Then she set down her cup. "Sir Francis is not always the perfect master of his temper, Miss Austen, as you have reason to know. He is often betrayed into speech he may regret. He is a man of great passions and considerable jealousies, and may imperfectly understand the circumstances of those around him."

"You have been acquainted with the Baronet for some time, I see."

"Nearly twenty years. I was governess to his little sisters when I was but eighteen, and spent nearly a year in the bosom of the Farnham family. When one has observed the formation of a man's character, one may forgive a great deal."

"Certainly one may respect the enduring nature of his regard," I observed. "Twenty years is a period! And yet Sir Francis's admiration for you is unflagging." What had Frank said? That Phoebe Carruthers had been involved in scandal while a governess . . . something to do with the family's eldest son . . . and her marriage to her cousin had followed hard upon the business. Sir Francis—jealous Sir Francis—had married and acceded to his title; but he had not forgot the golden beauty. He had waited, and bided his time—and plotted to remove his rivals. . . .

"Always his father's child," I murmured. "It is remarkable how blood will out, Mrs. Carruthers."

Her green eyes widened suddenly with alarm. She reached for her gloves.

"I must beg your pardon for trying your patience so long," Phoebe Carruthers said, rising. "It has been delightful to make your acquaintance, Miss Austen."

MY BROTHER SHOWED THE LADY TO THE DOOR, WITH MANY A FINE flourish regarding his hopes of seeing her in future, and all the assurances of his wife's regret in having lost such an opportunity to form Mrs. Carruthers's acquaintance; and when she had dwindled down the street, he rounded upon me in indignation.

"Jane, you were exceedingly rude just now. Poor Mrs. Carruthers is the picture of grief—and you must interrogate her regarding Sir Francis Farnham! It is obvious she don't like the fellow's company, and only suffers his attentions because she is too well-bred to send him packing! You might have shown some consideration!"

"She is altogether too picture-perfect for my liking, Fly," I said abruptly. "She displays her grief at the slightest urging; desires us to believe that she has no designs upon a baronet; adopts the general tone of disapprobation towards Captain Seagrave, and denies all knowledge of him in Southampton on Wednesday evening. It was a performance intended to distance her from murder, and that alone must make it suspect."

My brother's countenance hardened. "You think her afraid, Jane? You believe her bent upon deceit?"

"I think that Sir Francis determined to destroy his rival for Mrs. Carruthers's attentions. That he plotted Seagrave's disgrace by offering advancement to his lieutenant, in return for betrayal. That he used the signal line to despatch a set of orders the Admiralty never contemplated—and that when Chessyre despaired of his guilt and dishonour, Sir Francis determined to be rid of him. I believe that Phoebe Carruthers went in search of Chessyre in the Baronet's coach on Wednesday night, and carried the man away to meet with Farnham. I do not need to inform you of the result."

Frank took a turn about the room in considerable agitation. It is hard for such a man—trained up in the ways of gallantry—to credit a beautiful woman with evil.

"I could accept all this, provided Phoebe Carruthers had no notion of what she did. The wife of Hugh Carruthers should never collude to murder a man."

"Very well. Call her merely a handmaiden—too stupid to know her purpose—and she will thank you for it from the bottom of her heart."

"She don't even like that fellow Farnham!"

"Perhaps not," I agreed, "but she may feel herself in some wise bound to his purpose. How did she phrase things just now? 'Not all our obligations are matters of choice.' How soon after her marriage to her cousin was Simon Carruthers born?"

Frank stared. "I have not the slightest notion!"

"You should do well to enquire. Phoebe Carruthers might do much for the father of her dead child, however little she has cause to love him—particularly when Sir Francis's quarrel is with the man she blames for her son's death."

Chapter 20

An Episode with Rockets

28 February 1807,

cont.

~

"GOOD LORD, JANE—IF YOU WOULD HAVE SEAGRAVE THE VICTIM OF a plot constructed well before the *Stella* sailed, then you must admit Mrs. Carruthers is out of it!" Frank cried. "Her boy was yet alive when Seagrave left the Channel. She could have no cause to hate poor Tom. Indeed, she vows she loved him as a brother."

"But after she received the intelligence of young Simon's death, and learned that Seagrave was accused, moreover, of murder, her sentiments may have undergone a change. Sir Francis had only to appeal to Mrs. Carruthers's grief and sense of outrage, to secure her as accomplice."

My brother pursed his lips. "We cannot prove that either of them had anything to do with Seagrave's debacle, you know. I should look an absolute fool, did I suggest to the Admiralty that Sir Francis Farnham was Chessyre's murderer."

"We cannot risk an injury to your career, Frank—even in such a cause," I said with decision. "The Admiralty shall be left in ignorance until such time as guilt is irrefutable. We must provide our friend Mr. Pethering with evidence of so compelling a nature, that he cannot do otherwise than arrest Sir Francis and Mrs. Carruthers both."

"But how?"

"By catching them in their last desperate act."

Frank's eyes narrowed. "Have not they done enough?"

"Etienne LaForge," I said urgently to my brother. "He is in the gravest danger. Mrs. Carruthers meant to learn from us what the French canvassed, in their talk at Wool House. The appeal to her son's death was but a subterfuge: she was sent to test what we know. Sir Francis fears and suspects every sort of betrayal—this is why LaForge was poisoned after giving evidence in Seagrave's trial. And that is why the sick men have been removed to the prison hulk."

"Farnham need only exchange the French to France to be secure in their silence," Frank objected.

"But LaForge requested the right to remain in England as payment for his honesty. Does Farnham know as much?"

Frank looked all his discomfort. "The subject was generally discussed. Mr. Hill certainly knew of LaForge's plea, and I conveyed it myself to Admiral Bertie, who assured me he would try his influence at the Admiralty. As a prisoner, LaForge and his situation must fall under the authority of the Transport Board. . . ."

"Which is governed by Sir Francis Farnham. Good God, we have contrived between us to deliver the man to the very Devil!"

Frank ran his hand through his hair. "Then we must endeavour to save him, Jane. I believe I know a way."

WE FOUND THAT IT WAS NEARLY FOUR O'CLOCK, AND ORDERED DINner to be sent to my mother's room—left a note of apology and very little of explanation for Mary and Martha—and set out for Wool House thereafter.

"You said, I think, that you are a little acquainted with Captain Smallwood—the officer in command of the prison hulk?" I enquired as we hurried down the High towards Southampton Water. I spoke in part to defray anxiety; I could not help but feel we should have been hours beforehand in our apprehension of danger.

"An excellent fellow! Though quite enslaved to cards," Frank returned distractedly. "There is no one like Smallwood for playing at faro. I met with him some once or twice in Malta, and later in the West Indies; I have seen *Hamlet* in his company, too, while ashore in Gibraltar. He once put me in the way of a bang-up prize-agent."[1]

"But is Smallwood likely to oblige you in so serious a matter, without the requirement of greater authority—or at the very least, a full explanation?"

"I cannot say," Frank admitted. "The Navy is rather ticklish about—"

"—*niceties* and *forms*," I supplied. "Not to mention the conduct of prisoners of war. Smallwood should not like to risk the disapprobation of the Admiralty, in the person of Sir Francis Farnham."

"Nor should anyone, I expect—but Farnham need not come into it. We shall have Hill at our side, and a man of science may convince a fellow of anything. We must try Smallwood's character, and hope for the best. Mind the loose cobble, Jane!"

What my brother intended was fairly simple: he thought to secure Mr. Hill's support in urging the release of Etienne LaForge into Frank's care, so that the Frenchman might be removed from the hulk and placed in a room at Mrs. Davies's lodging house. The fact that LaForge was a surgeon—rather higher in his berth than a common seaman—should be strenuously represented, as well as the gravity of the man's condition. Nothing of our murderous suspicions need be disclosed to Captain Smallwood; nothing but charity and goodwill on the part of ourselves should be displayed; and with a minimum of fuss or anxiety, we might all sleep soundly in our beds this evening.

Such was the plan, and it might have gone off to perfection—but

---

1. A prize-agent was responsible for selling enemy ships seized in maritime war and condemned by the prize-court, one of the courts of the Admiralty.— *Editor's note.*

for the small difficulty of our discovering, at the moment of arriving at Wool House, that the place was locked and deserted. Even the Marines who usually stood guard before the great oak doors were fled.

"I suppose Mr. Hill can have no reason for remaining in attendance," said Frank thoughtfully, "the prisoners being taken off to the hulk. I shall have to seek him at his lodgings. He resides in St. Michael's Square, I believe—no very great distance. You might remain on the Quay, Jane, and await our return."

"I shall stare at the hulk until my eyes fail me," I promised him.

I MADE MY WAY TO THE OPPOSITE SIDE OF THE PAVING AND HAStened past the wharves towards Water Gate Quay. The heavy stone expanse thrust out into the sea had no power to cheer me, this darkening day; the distance between Quay's end and anchored prison hulk was too great to admit of comfort. I stood near a piling and felt the wind tug at my pelisse; sea birds wheeled and cried overhead like unquiet souls. As always, the activity on Southampton Water was very great, despite the late hour and lengthening shadows. Boats of every description plied their oars between mainland and moorings.

The hulk was easy to discern, dismasted and stripped of its sails, against the backdrop of the New Forest. Only this ship, out of all the others at anchor, must exhibit no purposeful movement on its upper deck; here the activity was entirely below, behind the closed portals that had once housed guns, and now sheltered the abandoned wretches tethered in chains. What sin had Etienne LaForge committed, that he must suffer so fearful a purgatory?

The Water was all chop and white-curling wave, the stiffening breeze driving the current hard against the shore. I could feel its shuddering force slap at the stones of the Quay on which I stood. The hulk would be heaving in its depths, the misery heightened for those in delirium. I narrowed my eyes, attempting to pick out even one figure against the dusk—and saw a rocket soar up near the prison ship's hull. It exploded overhead in a red arc of light.

"Young fools," muttered a voice at my feet.

I glanced around, but could discover no one.

The harsh clearing of an old man's throat assailed my ears; I peered down the steps that led from quay to water, and eventually discerned a figure familiar in its outline—a seafaring man, with a neat white queue hanging down his back and a silver whistle around his neck. He was crouched in the stern of a small skiff, smoking his pipe. A quantity of fish was neatly stowed in a basket at his feet, and his line and tackle laid by.

"Mr. Hawkins," I said.

The Bosun's Mate pulled his pipe from his lips and nodded. "Miss Austen, ma'am. Nell said as you were very kind to her. I thank you, I do, for your attention to my poor girl."

A second rocket fired out of the Water and exploded with a great report over our heads. Despite myself, I started.

Jeb Hawkins pointed towards the prison hulk with his pipe stem. "That's a sorry sight, if I may be so bold. It burns my heart to see the *Marguerite* in such a state—cut down to a stump and disgraced. The times we had in her—aye, and the battles, too!"

"You were posted once in that ship?" I enquired curiously.

"That I were, ma'am—four year and more, and many a sharp brush the *Marguerite* saw. She took fifteen French prizes in her day, and seven Spanish, make no mistake. She were a barky ship, the *Marguerite;* but it's donkey's years since she were fit for sailing."

"What cause could the crew find for signal rockets?" I asked him.

"Why, that's never the crew, ma'am! That's a few of Southampton's best, in Martin Whitsun's cockle of a boat, chivvying the Frenchies with the sound of the guns! The young lads're forever plaguing the prisoners with a fight; they think it drives the French half-mad, to have the sound of shells whizzing overhead and be prevented from offering a reply."

I strained my gaze towards the hulk's waterline, and discerned the very small craft Hawkins had described, hard in the lee of the ship and almost indistinguishable in the darkness. A sudden misapprehension seized me. What if the rockets were a diversion—a cover for greater malice about to operate on board?

I turned to stare at the Quay's end, and Winkle Lane; no sign of Frank or Mr. Hill. And at every moment the dusk grew heavier! Surely if murder were done, it would strike under cover of night! I rounded on Mr. Hawkins in his skiff.

"You say that you are familiar with the *Marguerite*. Would you be so kind as to convey me to her?"

Hawkins eyed me dubiously; between drabs and prison hulks, he no doubt thought, I possessed curious tastes for a lady.

I opened my reticule and retrieved my purse: four shillings, five pence. The sum would have to do. I held out the coins.

"You're never thinking of clambering aboard yourself," he protested. "It's right difficult for a lady, without a chair; but happen the Captain could find one—"[2]

"We shall deal with that difficulty when we come to it." I clinked the money enticingly.

He shrugged, rose into a half-crouch, and extended his palm. I dropped the shilling pieces into it.

"Have a care, ma'am, to step into the middle of the boat. I'm not so young as I was, but strong enough for all that to make the *Marguerite* in under ten minutes."

Ten minutes! It seemed ten hours, rather, as the Bosun's Mate heaved and grunted at his oars. I sat in the bow, facing the hulk, and he amidships, with his back turned to his object; I was privileged, therefore, to experience every agony of apprehension while the distant outline of the *Marguerite* loomed and grew no nearer. Eventually, however, as the darkness of late winter descended and the shouts of men flew across the Water, the hulk ceased to recede.

2. Jeb Hawkins refers to the bosun's chair, which resembled a wooden swing and could be hauled aloft when seamen were at work on the shrouds. It was routinely used to hoist women who boarded from the sea.—*Editor's note.*

I thought it came a little nearer—a little nearer—and a little nearer; the Bosun's Mate showed sweat on his brow, and at last we approached so swiftly that the dark and glistening hull of the ship filled all our sight, a mountainous wall, with the waves slapping against its anchor-chains in petulant bursts of foam. A few lanterns had been lit against the turning of the day; their warm yellow light pooled in places on the upper deck, but shed no glow in the dark under-regions, the successive rings of hell, that comprised the lower decks. From the closed gun ports came the piteous sounds of suffering men—groans, cries of delirium, the harsh cut of laughter.

Another skiff, larger than the Mate's and filled with at least eight young bucks of seafaring aspect, rowed around the *Marguerite*'s bow and roared with delight at the sight of us. One—who must be their leader—held aloft a bottle in salute.

"Old Hawkins, ahoy there! Have you come to join the merriment? And brought a fishwife, too! Are you after selling your girl, Mate?"

"She's too dear for your purse, Martin Whitsun," Hawkins retorted, "and well you know it."

"Aye, none but a fool would pay more than tuppence." Whitsun busied himself with a bulky object clutched against his chest; another rocket, perhaps. He must have a store of them at his feet. The two skiffs were drifting closer together; in a minute I should be discovered as anyone but Nell Rivers. I shrank behind the Mate's sturdy back.

"Oi, Nell," shouted a buck through the gloom, "have ye tired of good English cock, then? Do you think to dance a jig for the Frenchies' pleasure? There's many a lad would die for the sight of your arse, love!" He grasped his trousers in a lewd gesture and commenced to lurch drunkenly in the skiff, so that it rocked and bobbled perilously in the waves.

"Mangy curs!" Jeb Hawkins swung upwards so suddenly that the pranksters were taken off guard. "I'll teach you to show respect to a lady!" The blade of his oar slapped hard against the drunken man's chest, and sent him careening overboard with a terrible cry. In falling, the man clutched at one of his mates—and the scuffle and tumble that then ensued caused Martin Whitsun to drop his rocket.

It had just been lit.

There was a horrified cry, a welter of splashes and dark shapes leaping over the skiff's side, and I felt myself propelled backwards in Jeb Hawkins's boat by the violent pull of the man's remaining oar. And then, with a roar as calamitous as Judgement Day, the entire complement of Whitsun's rockets flared and shot skywards.

Boom! Boom! The light was searing, unlike anything I had ever witnessed, so that I covered my eyes with my hands and cried aloud in terror. Sparks and flaming pieces of Whitsun's ruined skiff rained down all about us. I was struck a glancing blow by one splinter, and crouched as low as possible in Hawkins's bow. Everywhere were heard the cries of *Fire! Fire!*—and when I considered with surprise how singular it should be for the drunken bucks struggling about us to sound so vigorous an alarm, I glanced up at the *Marguerite.*

A burning spark, or several perhaps, had landed on the hulk's deck, where a coil of cable or a bundled hammock had caught ablaze. Perhaps one of the lanthorns had been knocked over by a flying splinter or struck by an errant rocket. Whatever the cause, flames were now licking merrily along the deck, lurid and frightening in the darkness. Where there had been no activity before, was suddenly a handful of flitting shapes—the *Marguerite*'s skeleton crew, desperately working with sand and sacking to douse the greedy fire.

"Mr. Hawkins!" I cried. "What have we done?"

"That's not our doing, ma'am," he shouted back. "That's God's judgement on the poor *Marguerite!*"

"But the prisoners—the men in chains below! What will become of them?"

The Bosun's Mate ignored me. He was bent over the side of his small craft, fishing intently for a floating oar. Heads bobbed everywhere in the expanse of water between ourselves and the *Marguerite;* Martin Whitsun's gang, I supposed, abruptly sobered by the shock of February water. One man appeared intent upon making for our boat. He thrust an arm awkwardly above the waves and cried out, then was submerged in swell. I hoped fervently that the rogues were more adept at the art of swimming than I should be myself, and clutched firmly at the gunwale of the skiff.

Hawkins rose up from the side with a triumphant cry, and stowed his prize in the oarlock.

"Mr. Hawkins!" I shouted fiercely as the man began to pull away from the burning prison ship, "you must go back!"

"I can do nothing from the water, ma'am. It's for the crew to save her now. The fire's not so great—I've seen worse in my time—but in the event they carry powder, we would not wish to be near. If the ship blows—"

I clutched at the stem of one oar and pulled heavily against my determined saviour. "There is a man held in that hulk who must not be left to die! I beg of you, Mr. Hawkins—consider your daughter! This man might be the saving of *her*!"

Hawkins shipped his oars and stared at me. In the light thrown by the burning ship, his aged features were grotesque, like a gargoyle carved in a cathedral wall. The cries from the hulk grew more strident; I heard the splash of a body as it plummeted into the sea.

"Is that why you had me row you out to the boat? To save a Frenchie?"

"Nell's paramour, one Chessyre, was murdered a few days ago."

"I know it."

"Chessyre's murderer would exult in this Frenchman's death. He would think himself secure. He might then consider the life of a poor woman like Nell, who had the misfortune to be in Chessyre's confidence. But if the Frenchman lives—and may tell his tale . . ."

"Then Nell shall be free from fear?"

It was a gross exaggeration of the facts, but I was desperate. I nodded my head.

Jeb Hawkins turned the small craft with a few dips of the oars, and heaved his way back towards the burning ship. All around us were the remnants of Martin Whitsun's skiff, blasted sky-high and floating now in the water; and to my horror, I glimpsed an oblong shape with streaming hair that rose and fell with every swell of the current: the corpse of a drowned man. Hawkins ignored it, dipping his oars with care and maneuvering amidst the flotsam, until he came hard by the *Marguerite*'s bow.

"They have left out the ladders," he muttered. "That's just as well; I'm not the sea rat I once was. I shall go up through the sally port, and work my way down.[3] God knows how many men are held below. What is this Frenchie's name?"

"LaForge," I said tersely. "He looks the gentleman."

Jeb Hawkins threw me a grimace. "Have you any notion of oars?"

"None."

"And I have no painter—only an anchor line I'm loath to lose. I'll find a cable yon and toss it down. You must secure the skiff to the ladder."

The small boat bobbled with his weight as he grasped the rope ladder at the bow, and hauled himself up the side. I crawled forward, my anxiety extreme, and clutched at the ladder to keep the boat from drifting; but with a wave of panic I saw that I should be pulled over the gunwale.

"Oh, Fly, what I would not give for your strength!" I muttered between my teeth, and gripped the ladder with all my might.

At that moment, the gap of water widening between burning hulk and small cockle, a coil of rope thudded into the skiff's bottom. I snatched it up.

"Tie it to the ladder!" Jeb Hawkins cried. His face floated above me in the lurid darkness, and then was gone.

I know nothing of seaman's ropes, but I have embroidered many a square of lawn in my day, and may be trusted to tie off a knot that will

---

3. The sally port was an entry hatch on a warship's larboard side, not to be confused with Sally Port, a spot on Portsmouth's fortifications where naval boats and men embarked for ships anchored at Spithead.—*Editor's note.*

serve in a pinch. The rope was slippery, and my hands fumbled in the darkness; but in a little the job was done, and I had but to wait.

I then became sensible of the chaos above: the hoarse shouts, tramp of feet, fearsome swearing and shudder of blows. One seaman at least must be hacking away with an axe at the burning timbers; they would be tossed overboard to gutter in the sea. It seemed impossible that such a large vessel could founder within sight of land—but I recalled the wrecks off Spithead, and the *Mary Rose*, sunk centuries before in Southampton Water. I peered upwards in an effort to discern something of the activity on deck: I saw nothing but the great bowed curve of the hull. Great roiling clouds of smoke billowed over the side.

The skiff jerked abruptly so that I was almost unseated, and a dark, seal-wet head appeared over the gunwale. Gleaming eyes, a mouth open in a snarl, and two hands reaching for a hold. The boat bobbed wretchedly again.

I screamed aloud. The sound was lost in the general din.

"Help me," said a voice hoarsely.

Those two words spurred me to action. I reached forward and grasped the wet hands—rough, male fingers slippery with seawater—and braced myself against the skiff's bottom. I leaned backwards. He surged forward, and fell asprawl in the bottom of the boat.

Martin Whitsun.

"Who the devil are you?" the Rocketeer growled, and promptly vomited a quantity of the Solent over my boots.

AT LENGTH THERE WERE FIVE MEN HUDDLED IN JEB HAWKINS'S boat, shivering and cursing and half-dead from cold; Martin Whitsun was the most voluble of these, his vehemence sharpened by his frustration with my knots.

"Trust a woman to foul a line so bad it cannot be undone," he muttered. "If I had my knife—"

"I should be forced to scream for Mr. Hawkins," I retorted patiently. "I have no intention of abandoning him, and I shall not allow you to steal his boat."

"You'd rather see us die of exposure, I suppose."

"That is why I hauled you from the sea," I replied implacably.

"Curse you, woman! What have you done to the cable? It's lodged so tight we shall never get free."

"We might s-w-wim for it, Marty," suggested one of the rogues. His teeth were chattering, and his lips were blue. "There's the *Queen Anne* sending out a longboat, and I'll wager they've grog and blankets."

It was true. The fire could not help but be seen by the score of vessels moored roundabout, and it would not be long before a host of small craft converged upon the hulk and endeavoured to aid her survivors. Martin Whitsun shaded his eyes with his hands, and peered across the dark water; I glanced anxiously upwards, intent for any sign of Jeb Hawkins.

"I don't fancy meeting a longboat full of Navy men," Whitsun said shortly. "They might ask cruel questions, about the rockets and such. The hulk's a Navy vessel, mind."

The men stole shuddering and miserable glances at me. "Here," Whitsun demanded suddenly. "*You* fashioned the sodding knot; *you* get it undone, or I'll throw you over the side."

He looked as fierce as his words, and being vastly outnumbered in strength and desperation, I did not like to test his mettle. I propelled myself forward, and clutched at the vile cable with gloved hands and a sinking heart. The wet coils had swollen and tightened inevitably upon themselves; the knot was fixed, for all my scrabbling fingers might do. I stopped short in the attempt, and drew off my gloves, hoping to buy time.

"Longboat's c-c-coming!" cried one stuttering buck.

"What I won't do to Jeb Hawkins when I meet him," said Martin Whitsun through his teeth. He shoved at my back, nearly toppling me from the boat. I cried out and clutched at the rope ladder.

"Say that again, Martin Whitsun," demanded a voice from above.

"Happen you'd rather beat a man senseless than a poor defenceless woman—or maybe you'd rather go over the side?"

I looked up—and saw the Bosun's Mate peering through the livid gloom above. He carried a burden over one shoulder: a man, insensible and unmoving.

"Stand aside, you fools!" Hawkins shouted, and heaved one leg over the *Marguerite*'s rail. He grasped the rope ladder with his right hand, and steadied his load with the left. Such strength and grace in a man of his age must stand as testament to the hardy nature of the finest seamen. I watched with bated breath all the same, my bare fingers twisting together, conscious of Martin Whitsun malevolent at my back. If he moved—if he menaced Jeb Hawkins in any way—I was determined to shove my elbow hard into the rogue's ribs in an effort to unseat him. The Bosun's Mate torturously descended, breathing hard, his burden dangling. I could not tell for the smoke whether it was LaForge or no.

"Ahoy, there!" cried a voice across the water. "Have you need of assistance?"

The longboat put off from the *Queen Anne*. Martin Whitsun turned, his attention diverted, and began to swear viciously under his breath. I reached out and seized Jeb Hawkins's coat sleeve; his left boot groped for the skiff's gunwale.

"Don't clutch at me, ma'am—hold the rope steady," he shouted irritably. I did as I was told, and his foot found a hold. He stepped backwards into the crowded vessel, the man he carried sliding heavily into the bilge—and at that moment the skiff rose up and slapped against the *Marguerite*'s side, all but overbalanced by a sudden shift in weight.

Martin Whitsun and his fellows had abandoned us, diving into the chill waters rather than face the *Queen Anne*'s rescue party.

Chapter 21

The Frenchman's Story

28 February 1807,

cont.

~

IT WAS AS WELL FOR US THAT THE DRUNKEN BUCKS DESERTED US when they did, for the wild activity in the water alerted the men of the longboat party, who set about rescuing the unfortunate rogues much against their will. Other boats presently appearing—from the *Star of Bengal,* the *Matchless,* the *Parole,* and other vessels moored in Southampton Water—Martin Whitsun's men were soon surrounded by benevolence, and hauled out of the sea to be plied with grog and warm clothing. Their terror and shame should soon tell the tale despite their better interests, and the sailors' welcome become an interrogation; but this was not our affair.

Jeb Hawkins righted himself, squinted at me through the clouds of smoke, and pulled his knife from his pocket.

"You'll never rate Able, ma'am," he said, and sliced the skiff's painter in two.

Etienne LaForge—for it was assuredly he, in a dead swoon—lay sprawled in the bilge of Hawkins's skiff. I struggled to pull his shoulders upright, and rest his head upon my lap, while the Bo-sun's Mate settled his oars and turned our craft. He intended to slip round the far side of the *Marguerite,* and double back upon Southampton unnoticed in the general clamour; in a few moments we should be lost to view and quite safe from scrutiny.

"How did you discover him?"

"I asked where he lay," Hawkins said curtly. "Many a man in His Majesty's service has cause to know the Bosun's Mate. I've a favour or two I don't mind using, when the occasion requires."

"But weren't you questioned?"

"Every man jack on the *Marguerite* was setting about dousing the blaze; it's a small crew on a prison hulk, what with the want of sails and cordage. I told one tar that I must have the keys to the prison-ers' chains, in case the hulk should be abandoned. He never blinked twice, just said they was kept on a hook in the old ward-room. I shinned along and fetched the picks, then asked politely where LaForge was housed."

"You are a wonder, Mr. Hawkins," I observed unsteadily. The *Marguerite* was receding from us now, the flames on her decks flar-ing like an unholy sunset. Everywhere about us, Southampton Water rippled red. "I owe you a very great deal."

"He owes me a sight more, I reckon," said Hawkins with a nod to the insensible Frenchman. "There's a few in that hold won't see an-other day, what with the smoke and the fright. Screaming half fit to blow their own ears off, stark mad with fear some of 'em were." He shuddered. "That's as close to hell as I'm comfortable sitting, ma'am. A quick death and clean in the cannon's mouth's one thing—but slow roasting within sight of your neighbours is not to my relish. I opened the manacles on the lot of 'em."

I laid my hand over his where it pulled at the oar. "Thank you, Mr. Hawkins," I said.

WE ACHIEVED THE QUAY AS THE LAST FLAMES ABOARD THE *MAR-guerite* flickered and went out. Torches had been mounted along the seawall, the better to illuminate the spectacle of the burning ship; and a crowd of children and gaping onlookers had gathered. Among the horde of figures lining the stone platform I discerned my brother, and the slight figure of Mr. Hill at his side. How much time had my adventure demanded? It was now full dark—perhaps six o'clock in the evening, well past our dinner hour. Surely my mother would be grown querulous, Mary should be consumed with worry, and Martha attempting to comfort them both.

"Fly!" I called out as Jeb Hawkins pulled alongside the Quay. "Captain Frank Austen—ahoy!"

My brother started, peered down at the water, and then dashed down the Quay steps. "Jane! In the name of all that's sacred—! You were *not* out at that ship!"

"We have LaForge," I said tensely. "He requires assistance and care. Mr. Hill—"

My brother cupped his hands about his mouth and in the best sailor fashion, roared for the surgeon. The pack of onlookers, though far from weary of their public burning, divided their attention between prison hulk and skiff.

"It's a dead man! He's drownded!" cried one urchin with enthusiasm.

"There'll be more'n worse by dawn," prophesied a woman darkly.

"That's the Bosun's Mate!" shouted a third. "Eh, Jeb, are you become a Fisher of Men like the Good Book says?"

Jeb Hawkins did not reply. Instead, he grabbed a mooring and made the skiff fast to the Quay. My brother jumped into the vessel and seized LaForge by the shoulders. Mr. Hill proffered his hand and helped me from the boat.

I had never been so thankful to find good, hard Hampshire stone beneath my feet.

"I made certain you had gone back home," Frank muttered to me. "I merely stayed to see what became of the hulk—I never dreamed you were upon the Water."

"Take him to Wool House," I said tersely. "Mr. Hill will have the key."

"Of course." Hill hurried off before us, clearing a path through the curious crowd. Jeb Hawkins—who must, in truth, be exhausted—grasped LaForge's ankles and helped bear the insensible man the length of the Quay.

"How did you manage . . . to pry this fellow . . . from the depths of that barge?" Frank gasped, as we approached Winkle Street.

"The Bosun's Mate," I replied. "Mr. Hawkins is deserving of our deepest thanks and praise. He freed Monsieur LaForge and carried him to safety."

"Safety? I begin to think this man shall never be safe until he has England at his back."

Mr. Hill stood ready by the great oak portal of Wool House; he had found and lit a candle. We slipped through the door like wraiths or shadows, too swift to be clearly discerned in the pitch-black streets; the crowd's attention, in any case, had returned to the quayside where the longboats were approaching with their soggy burden of Southampton's own.

LaForge was laid on one of the old straw pallets and covered with a blanket. He moaned, and turned his head in restless dreaming; I thought perhaps his eyelids flickered, but it may have been only a chimera of the candle flame. Mr. Hill bent swiftly to feel for his pulse.

"*Geneviève,*" said a faint voice at our feet; and with a sharp intake of breath, I saw that LaForge was once more in his conscious mind.

I crouched near him and placed my hand on his brow.

"Ah, *Geneviève.*" He sighed. "*Tu vives encore.*"

"It is all right, *monsieur*—you are safe now, and we shall not let you come to harm. You may be assured of that. You are among friends."

He frowned. "*Cette voix—je la sais. Mais ce n'est pas la voix de Geneviève.*"

"It is I, Miss Austen. I am here with Mr. Hill and my brother and another man who saved you from the burning ship."

Mr. Hill had been busy at the hearth to the rear of Wool House;

he had tindered flame, and set a pot of water to boiling, and now appeared at my side with a hunk of day-old bread. "Soak it in water," he commanded, "then try if you can to persuade him to swallow a morsel."

I did as I was bid. After a little, LaForge was persuaded to eat; he appeared to recover somewhat of his strength with every sodden bite; but still he lay with his eyes closed, the symmetry of his features marred by a sharp crease between his eyebrows, as though he suffered considerable pain. He looked thinner and more drawn from his ordeal with poison and neglect than I could have imagined. Inwardly cursing Sir Francis Farnham, I bent myself to my task.

My brother had found a stool, and propped himself upon it. I slipped the last of the soggy bread into LaForge's mouth; he lay back on his pallet. Presently the surgeon and the Bosun's Mate joined us with steaming tea, which we accepted gratefully.

"I should like to know, Captain Austen," said Mr. Hill over the rim of his cup, "exactly what has occurred. Whom do you suspect of murder, and how does our friend LaForge come into it?"

We told him, then, the worst of our fears of Sir Francis Farnham, and the collusion of Phoebe Carruthers, not excepting the gentleman's motive for defaming Tom Seagrave, the possible use of the Admiralty's telegraph to transmit spurious orders, and the accidental insertion of Nell Rivers in the affair.

Jeb Hawkins, in comprehending how tangled was the plot in which his girl found herself, muttered beneath his breath and flexed his broad hands, as though he should like to seize the Baronet himself.

"You have no proof of anything, of course," said Mr. Hill pensively. "I should not like to attempt to arraign Sir Francis on so wild a charge. The equipage with the bloody gauntlet might be traced on Wednesday night—the coachman paid to disclose what he knows—"

"I have considered that," I interrupted. "What if the coachman was Sir Francis himself, suitably disguised? He had only to lure poor

Chessyre into the carriage, let Mrs. Carruthers down at a suitable spot, drive to a darkened alley, and employ his garrote."

"No one should be the wiser," Mr. Hill admitted. "The same is true of our suspected poison. It is impossible to show that Sir Francis introduced something noxious to a particular Wool House pasty; your men of the Navy should declare that the food was rotten, and be done."

"Something might be learned of those sealed orders," suggested Frank. "We might enquire at the Admiralty—as friends among friends, you understand—what purpose they thought to serve by sending Seagrave on a wild-goose chase. And if no one admits to taking our meaning—"

"Wild-goose chase?" interrupted Mr. Hill.

"Seagrave was ordered to stand off the coast of Corunna," I explained, "to take off an agent of the Crown and bear him back to England. But no one answered his signal, and after three days he turned for home."

"No one answered the good Seagrave's signal," supplied Etienne LaForge weakly from his position on the floor, "because the agent of your Crown had already been seized by Captain Porthiault, and locked in a cabin of the *Manon*."

We turned as one to stare at him. His shrewd brown eyes—replete once more with the humour I had always discerned in them—roved across our faces. "Did you not wonder why I demanded to remain on British shores? It is death to me to return to France!"

"*You* are that agent?" I gasped, finally comprehending. "But why did you not inform us earlier?"

"Because such an admission, from a prisoner of war, should sound fantastic; and because I did not know whom I could trust." With effort, he propped himself weakly on one elbow. "May I beg you, *mademoiselle*, for a little of that tea? I have had nothing hot to drink in days."

"Of course." I hastened to procure another cup. LaForge drank it down entire while his rescuers kept silence in the sharpest suspense. At last he set aside the tea and sat fully upright. His voice, when next he spoke, gained in timbre and strength.

"You must understand, above all, that nothing in my plan went as I had hoped when I fled Paris. I did not reveal myself to you when first I came to Wool House, because I have already escaped death too many times to invite it willingly. The wisest course was to wait, and watch, and turn to advantage what I could. When I heard of the good Seagrave's court-martial, I thought to bargain my way to safety by telling what I had seen during the battle for the *Manon*. I did not comprehend, *hein,* that by accusing the man Chessyre, I should *tomber de Charybde en Scylla.*"[1]

"Are you, in fact, a surgeon?" I enquired curiously. "Is any part of your testimony the truth?"

LaForge shrugged. "I told you, *de vrai,* what I had seen. As for my profession—a man may be anything his circumstance demands, *mademoiselle.* Certainly I have studied physiognomy in my day; I have worked among some of the finest men of science that Paris may offer; I am no stranger to the scalpel and saw. I have also killed a chicken and eaten him for my dinner from time to time—but if you would ask whether it is as a *butcher* that I earn my bread . . ." He smiled, and said nothing further.

"I think," Frank said sharply, "that you owe us a complete explanation, Monsieur LaForge."

"If you will give me another cup of that excellent tea," the Frenchman returned, "I shall be happy to oblige."

The tea was fetched, and placed in his hands; his back propped against a pile of empty sacks that served as a Wool House pillow; and the four of us ranged around him expectantly, Frank with his face to the door and an expression of wariness on his features.

"I was not always as you see me now," LaForge began. "I shall not wear at your patience with tales of my youth in the Haute Savoie—

1. ". . . fall between Charybdis and Scylla." This is similar to the English phrase "between a rock and a hard place," or "out of the frying pan, into the fire."—*Editor's note.*

of my father, Gaspar, Comte de la Forge; or of my mother Eugénie; I shall say nothing of how they spent their winters paying court at Versailles, and were counted among the blessed of France. You know enough of the fate of such people in our Revolution—you have heard, even in England, of the guillotine. I will begin only with myself as I was in 1792, an orphan of thirteen years, sent to live with my maternal uncle—Eugénie's younger brother, a captain of Grenadiers. He had a fine revolutionary fervour, Hippolyte; he had a fine revolutionary bride, and a fine revolutionary daughter—a girl named Geneviève, my cousin."

"Aha!" I murmured.

His brown eyes found my face. "Geneviève was a sort of perfection, to a boy of my turbulent history. She was younger than myself by seven years, a child of sweetness and laughter who grew, with time, into a beautiful young woman. My uncle, in turn, grew into one of the Emperor's most respected officers. He died last year at Jena—but by that time, Geneviève's hand had been sought in marriage by every *notable* in France. My cousin had refused them for years—I like to think because it was me she loved. But then the Emperor himself came to call."

"Buonaparte already possesses an empress," I observed. "And thus we must assume his attentions were dishonourable."

"The Empress Josephine cannot bear children," LaForge replied. "Napoléon is mad for an heir, you understand; he talks of nothing but divorce. There are some who claim he has debauched his own step-daughter, the Princess Hortense, in order to get a child of Josephine's blood—but I will spare you the sordidness of court intrigue.[2] It is enough to know that he paid his court at my Geneviève's feet, and that Napoléon was the death of her."

2. LaForge refers here to Hortense de Beauharnais (1783–1837), the daughter of Empress Josephine's first husband, a nobleman guillotined in the Revolution; Hortense was forcibly married in 1802 to Louis Napoleon, brother of the Emperor, and her third son, Charles-Louis Napoleon—whom court rumor identified as Bonaparte's—eventually became Napoleon III. He ruled France from 1852 to '71.—*Editor's note.*

"Your cousin was not flattered by the Emperor's esteem?"

"She took him in such dislike, that her father considered a complete break with his sovereign in order to protect his child. But he was embroiled in Austria, you understand. He wrote to urge my protection for Geneviève—and when I learned of his fears, I threw up my studies at the Sorbonne and fixed myself at my cousin's side."

LaForge paused, and sipped his tea.

"I had loved her for years, of course; but I could not hope for her heart in return. I was nothing—my estates had been seized, my patrimony hidden. I was not the Comte de la Forge, as I should have been, but a man of science labouring in obscurity. All seemed well, once I returned to my aunt's household; but then my uncle was killed at Jena not three months later.

"Geneviève was determined to see in his death a vengeful murder. She could not believe that her father must fall like any soldier in battle; the cannonball that sundered his frame must have been sent with diabolic purpose. It was her fault, she believed, that her papa lay dead; he had been crushed by a ghoul who was determined to have her virtue."

"Another reader of horrid novels," Frank murmured in my ear.

"I did not comprehend the depths of my Geneviève's despair. The Emperor paid a call of condolence upon his return to Paris; he kissed my cousin's hand, and uttered phrases of comfort for her ears alone. Later I learned the import of his words: since my uncle had died without a son, his fortune was entirely forfeit to the state, and my aunt and cousin would be thrown into the street. Unless, of course, Geneviève could find some way of earning her bread . . .

"She came to me that night and begged me to take her from Paris. She would go anywhere I liked, as long as we were far from the Emperor's clutches. She had not reckoned, however, with my sense of honour: I could not abandon my uncle's fortune to the rogue, without attempting to fight. I told her I would contest the forfeit of the estate, on behalf of my widowed aunt and Geneviève;

we would try what the law might do. Later, while the household slept, Geneviève threw herself from her bedroom window."

"How horrible!" I exclaimed.

LaForge stared at me, his eyes implacable now. "I had no love for the Empire. It had cost me all that was dear. But I could take my revenge. My uncle had long been intimate with the Emperor's closest counsels. He knew all of Napoléon's plans, his perfidious intentions with regard to Europe. It was within my grasp to hand these to the only power capable of crushing the Monster: the Crown of England.

"I returned to the Sorbonne and requested the aid of a person I shall not name—a fellow man of science, who knew a good deal of British politics. He sent a message to your Admiralty, which has always been in command of certain funds disbursed for the purpose of buying information. I did not require recompense. I required the satisfaction of seeing the Monster's ambitions thwarted wherever he turned. I waited a few weeks in apprehension and impatience, and at last I was instructed how to act. I must take my uncle's maps and papers, and embark upon an expedition of science—a survey of the flora native to the Pyrénées. While thus employed, I must cross over the mountains into Portugal and make my way by degrees to the coast. An English ship would await me there."

"Except that your message was intercepted," suggested Frank, "and instead of a British ship, you were collected by the *Manon*."

"Indeed. You know it all. I was seized by Porthiault himself and locked into a cabin, without so much as a word to the *Manon*'s crew. I feared the worst—my plot exposed, my uncle's name besmirched, his fortune confiscated, and my aunt degraded. My trial and execution would prove a sensation; but of that I thought nothing. I believe my most bitter sensation was one of regret. I had intended to avenge the death of Geneviève—and I had failed."

"And then Seagrave attacked," my brother said.

"—Barely six hours after I was pulled off Corunna! One of the first British balls destroyed the wall of the cabin in which I was held; I freed myself from my bonds, dashed out onto the deck, and was handed a weapon as a matter of course by the frenzied crew. I used it to despatch Captain Porthiault; he was the only man on board ship who knew the truth of my crimes. Then I descended to the cockpit hold, and made myself useful in attending to the wounded who collected there, for the *Manon* had sailed without a surgeon."

LaForge set down his teacup with an air of finality.

"I believe we understand the rest," said Mr. Hill.

Jeb Hawkins stood and extended his hand. "I should like the honour of shaking yours, mon-sewer, as a cool-headed cove and no mistake."

The Frenchman smiled faintly, and grasped the Bosun's Mate's paw.

"But, Monsieur LaForge," I attempted, "would you suggest that the Admiralty *intended* for Captain Seagrave to take you off Corunna? And that the interception of your communications by Captain Porthiault was merely a dreadful mistake—the engagement of the *Manon* an extraordinary piece of luck on your part—and the whole episode of Chessyre's treachery a matter of happenstance, rather than design?"

The Frenchman studied my face. "That is how it appears, *mademoiselle*, does it not?"

"Did the Admiralty possess any intelligence of your seizure?" I persisted. "Could they have known, at the event, that you were taken by the French?"

"I must think it unlikely."

"You made no attempt, while a prisoner at Wool House, to reveal your identity to the authorities—beyond this vague plea for sanctuary on British shores."

"I feared a spy in the Admiralty," LaForge said quietly. "Few persons were aware of my existence or plans. It was possible, I thought, that my friend at the Sorbonne had been betrayed—that he had broken under the methods of Napoléon's police—but it was equally possible that an English traitor had exposed me. Silence, and caution, appeared the only guarantors of safety. But when I heard of Miss Austen's anxiety for Seagrave—of the court-martial and its *terreurs*—I saw an opportunity to bargain. That much I might do."

A silence fell—a silence heavy with indecision and doubt.

"We must regard the sealed orders as entirely above-board," Frank said abruptly. "Sir Francis Farnham should be unlikely to risk the life of an agent—particularly one bearing such vital information—merely to despatch a jealous rival. I cannot believe that even so arrogant a man would place his affairs before those of King and Country."

"Nor can I," agreed Mr. Hill.

"Unless," countered LaForge delicately, "Sir Francis betrayed the Crown long ago. He is perfectly positioned, is he not, to play havoc with the Emperor's enemies?"

Frank's eyes widened; the idea of such perfidy—such conscious working at deceit—was utterly new and repugnant to him; he must recoil, he must refuse the knowledge. I thought fleetingly of my cynical friend, Lord Harold Trowbridge; not for him the innocence of a post captain. He should have weighed and considered the Baronet's guilt long before.

"We cannot determine whether Sir Francis is capable of both murder and high treason on the evidence of this man alone," said Mr. Hill, as though privy to my inmost thoughts. "What remains for us is to guard his life and the secrets he holds. Where, if I may ask, are your uncle's documents now, Monsieur LaForge?"

"Where they have been for the past six weeks," he calmly replied. "In the hollow interior of my walking-stick. Do you have it still?"

Without a word, Mr. Hill rose and went to a cupboard near the hearth at the rear of the room. He withdrew a slender parcel wrapped in white cloth, and unwrapped it reverently.

"The catch is designed to open at my hand," observed LaForge, turning the stick dexterously in his elegant fingers. "I do not believe the Marines of Wool House have even considered of it. There!"

The silver knob fell off into his palm, and a tight roll of yellowed papers slid from the tube. "If you will guarantee me safe passage to London, I shall carry the papers there myself."

"London!" said Frank, with an eye for Mr. Hill. "That is bearing the viper straight to Sir Francis's breast."

"Sir Francis is as yet in Southampton," returned Mr. Hill pointedly. "But I cannot be easy in Monsieur LaForge's safety. Sir Francis will know, even now, of the fire on the prison hulk; he shall enquire, and he is not a fool, as to the fate of LaForge."

"Perhaps it would be better for us all if LaForge had died," I said slowly. "Then the eyes of enquiry should turn elsewhere, and leave us all in peace."

Mr. Hill stared at me in surprise and consternation. Then he seized my meaning, and his looks altered.

"A fortunate death?"

"With a certificate affirming the hour and cause, penned by a reputable surgeon."

"—One who had seen the patient often in his care," Frank said quickly, "and must be trusted to know the man and his condition. It is imperative the news of the Frenchman's death be published at once."

Etienne LaForge thrust himself to his feet, his headless stick held before him like a sword. His face had drained of colour.

With a sudden movement, Jeb Hawkins placed himself between the Frenchman and my brother; in his hand was the seaman's knife he had used to cut my dreadful knot.

"There'll be no murder done tonight, gentlemen," he said warningly, "unless it's your blood I shed in defence of a brave man."

Frank gaped—Mr. Hill nearly choked—but I burst out in shaky laughter.

"Not *murder*, Mr. Hawkins—only its parody," I told him. "We mean to hide our friend in the surest way we know: by declaring him dead, and smuggling him out of the city."

The Bosun's Mate went still. He considered my words an instant then let out a low, admiring whistle. "The lads at the dockyard allus said as the Cap'n was a rare fighting gentleman, miss—but you're no dithering ninny, neither."

"Thank you for the compliment, Mr. Hawkins. Will you put up your knife, and fetch a hackney chaise? My brother, I am certain, will bear the charge."

Chapter 22

In Gaoler's Alley

Sunday,
1 March 1807

~

THE BOSUN'S MATE HAD ONLY TO COMPREHEND WHAT WAS WANTED, to devise a suitable plan.

"Yon Frenchman is not fit to take the mail to London," he decided. "He's as weak as a newborn lamb, and that's a fact. And though he speaks the King's English to admiration, he's not without the sound of foreign parts; there'd be those as were curious how a Frenchie came to travel our roads as free as a lord."

"A private hack might answer," said Frank impatiently.

"—but for the powers of Sir Francis," persisted Jeb Hawkins. "That roguish gentleman has only to learn of the Captain's hiring a conveyance at the Dolphin, to have the chaise followed and waylaid on the road."

"But he shall believe Monsieur LaForge is dead," I pointed out.

"He'll hear as much," said Hawkins grimly, "but don't you be certain, ma'am, as he'll believe the same, without the sight of the corpus in his own eyes. If you wish to safeguard the mon-sewer's life, you could do worse than to trust Giles Sawyer."

"Giles Sawyer?" said my brother blankly.

"He's a coffin-builder in the town, Cap'n, and a rare mate o' mine. He'd be sailing with the Hearts of Oak still, if it weren't for Boney having taken off his leg. Giles'd be agreeable, I reckon, to shifting the Frenchie in his cart to London—and if the mon-sewer don't mind a bit of confinement, and travel by the slow road, he might rest secure until Kingdom Come."

"Not quite so far, I beg of you," said Etienne LaForge; but there was laughter behind his words. "First you would have me dead, then pack me off to London in a casket, *hein?* The English—they are plotters *à la merveille. Bon.* I shall go to my death with a will, as you say. *Monsieur,* I applaud you."

It required only the addition of Nell Rivers to the cart, as principal mourner for her dead husband; Frank's note of explanation for the delivery of LaForge to the home of our brother, Henry, in Brompton; and a second note of introduction vouching for the Frenchman's probity, to Henry's acquaintance Lord Moira, who might be depended upon to convey LaForge to the First Lord.[1]

"I shall be off to nab old Giles directly," said the Bosun's Mate, and fixed his cap upon his head.

My brother paid him the courtesy of a bow. "I could wish there were more men of fibre like yourself, Mr. Hawkins, as yet in the Royal Navy. We are greatly in need of your wit and courage—and greatly in your debt."

"Now, then," said Mr. Hawkins sternly, as though Frank were an errant Young Gentleman, "none of that misty palaver. I'll have Giles bring the cart round the back of Wool House, and carry the coffin inside; he has nobbut to do but poke a few holes in the sides, so that the mon-sewer don't stifle, and we'll all be right as rain."

---

1. The First Lord of the Admiralty to whom Jane refers was Thomas Grenville. Lord Moira was a client of Henry Austen's bank—and his failure to repay substantial loans later contributed to Henry Austen's bankruptcy.—*Editor's note.*

~

I COULD NOT BEAR TO PART FROM MY CONSPIRATORS BEFORE THE conclusion of such a business, and thus found myself at home as late as nine o'clock. My mother had retired with a hot posset, but poor Mary was as yet abroad and beside herself with apprehension on her husband's part. When the door to Mrs. Davies's establishment opened to reveal only myself, the poor girl nearly fainted from fretted nerves.

"Where is Frank?" she implored, and clutched at Martha Lloyd's arm for support.

"He is making the rounds of the taverns," I told her, "in the company of Mr. Hill, the naval surgeon, and is no doubt better fed than I. Has Jenny retired for the evening?"

"Taverns!"

"There has been a fire, Mary, on a hulk moored in Southampton Water, and Mr. Hill fears the loss of one of his patients." We had determined among ourselves that if the ruse of LaForge's death was to bear weight, it must be supported in the bosom of our family as well as in the town. "The Frenchman who gave testimony at Captain Seagrave's trial is believed lost in the sea. Frank is conversing with all and sundry in an effort to learn of the unfortunate man's fate."

"Good God!" ejaculated Frank's wife. "Shall we never be free of that wretched affair? Tom Seagrave is gone to gaol, and still my husband will not accept his guilt. Hang Tom Seagrave, I say, and be done!"

"Come and lie down, Mary," interposed Martha gently. "You should have been abed long since. I believe, Jane, that Mrs. Davies left a little bread and soup on the kitchen hearth; you might enquire for your supper." And with a speaking look for me, my friend led Mary firmly towards the stairs.

FRANK DID NOT RETURN UNTIL WELL NIGH ELEVEN O'CLOCK, WHEN I was tucked up in bed with the candle already snuffed; I heard the low murmur of conversation as he entered the adjoining room, and knew that Mary had enjoyed little rest in the interval. I was very warm, exceedingly comfortable, and shockingly sleepy—but spared a thought for Etienne LaForge, shut up in an oak box with handsome brass handles, and freezing, no doubt, on his way to London. His coffin was worth all of six pounds, seven shillings, eight pence, Giles Sawyer had assured us; and as holes had been bored in the sides, thus rendering the coffin useless, my brother and Mr. Hill had felt compelled to recompense the man. They paid him as well for the loan of his waggon, the use of his horse, and several hours' cold journey north to London; no small sum for either Frank or the surgeon. Such are the sacrifices of gentlemen for King and Country. I hoped that Monsieur LaForge should survive the trip: it would be a wretched joke indeed, if the coffin-lid were removed to reveal a corpse.

Sunday morning, and all the bustle of service at St. Michael's, our parish of preference—it is close enough to Castle Square to prove an easy walk, once we are established in that house. My mother, upon observing that the day should be fine, determined to mark the Sabbath by quitting her bed. She rose in good time to accompany us into St. Michael's Square, where I had the pleasure of hearing a sermon neither too long nor too bombastic, and of meeting afterwards with Mr. Hill in the vestibule.

The surgeon appeared much refreshed, and remarkably jovial for a man so recently bereaved of a patient.

"Has your brother told you, Miss Austen, of our excellent luck last evening?" he enquired, in a voice lowered for the benefit of the milling crowd. "After touring the public rooms of the Dolphin, the George, the Star, and the Coach and Horses, we chanced to meet with Sir Francis Farnham himself, sitting over sherry in the Vine. We informed him, in the most lowering tone imaginable, of the loss of our former patient—which intelligence we had confirmed from the stories everywhere circulating, at the inns aforementioned—"

"—and which you had published in the first part yourselves. Well done!" I cried, and then subsided at a glance of curiosity from Frank's Mary. "And how did the gentleman take the news?"

"He said all that was proper—declared himself shocked at the poor conditions of the prison hulk—lamented the fate of two other Frenchmen, who had died of the fire before it was put out—and announced that the remainder should be exchanged to France to-morrow or Tuesday at the latest. In a word, Sir Francis conducted himself as a cunning rogue might be expected to do."

"That is very well," I mused, "for he must consider himself safe. Once LaForge's intelligence is known at the Admiralty, however, he shall begin to be afraid—and in his actions *then,* may show his hand."

"Such an event is what we must hope for," said Mr. Hill gravely, "because I do not think we can expect to expose Sir Francis in any other way. He professed himself determined to quit Southampton on the morrow; we must rely upon his betraying himself in London."

"Mr. Hill," said Frank, with a clap on the surgeon's shoulder, "I intend to visit my friend, Tom Seagrave, in Gaoler's Alley this morning; should you like to bear me company?"

"Gaoler's Alley?" cried Mary, with a look of pique. "But it is Sunday, Frank! Cannot you sit quietly at home, and work a little on the drawing-room fringe?"

"Sunday is a day for charity, Mary—and one must behave like a Christian to all of God's reprobates," Frank said genially. "The loss of Seagrave's principal witness in the hulk last evening has put his defence in question. I should dearly love Mr. Hill's advice and counsel—and I know that Tom should be comforted by any appearance of interest in his case."

"Then by all means take Jane," urged my mother, with a friendly nod for Mr. Hill. She was devising a match, I little doubted, between myself and the aging surgeon; like a boy who would shoot fish in a barrel, my mother cannot be in the presence of a single

gentleman of any age without hitting upon a marriage. "You cannot keep Jane at home, when there is a gaol or an inquest to be
had. I daresay Mr. Hill is exactly the same. It is wonderful, is it not,
how alike two strangers' hearts may be? Jane was always such a
charitable girl—quite a slave to the sick and downtrodden! She
should have made an excellent wife in Bengal, I always said, for
they have a vast amount of beggars there. I urged her once to
consider a bride-ship—Mr. Austen's sister took passage in one, you
know, and was so fortunate as to marry a surgeon!—but Jane could
not be persuaded."[2]

"Quite right," said Mr. Hill with a twinkle. "Such a jewel should
settle for nothing less than a true physician." And then he bowed.

GAOLER'S ALLEY DEBOUCHES FROM THE HIGH, FOUR STREETS BE-
low St. Michael's Square. For our achievement of the small prison
was required but a few moments' exertion; the sharp air of a bright
March morning hastened our steps and brought animation to our
looks. Frank swung along as though the breeze tugging at his cockade was fresh from a thousand frigates' sails, while Mr. Hill offended the Sabbath by whistling between his teeth. We were all, I
believe, feeling chuffed by our success at spiriting LaForge from beneath the gaze of a murderer; and even the sight of the low-roofed
Norman building, with its narrow slits of windows, could not
dampen our spirits.

I am no stranger to your modest house of incarceration, having
visited no less a prison than Newgate in my time; I have entered
the gaols of Lyme and Bath, and glimpsed the exterior of Canter-
bury's. Though I should never traipse through the dungeons of the

2. Mrs. George Austen refers to her sister-in-law, Philadelphia Austen Han-
cock, who went out to India in 1752 for the express purpose of finding a
husband among the employees of the Honourable East India Company.
Philadelphia was the mother of Jane's sister-in-law, Eliza de Feuillide.—*Editor's
note.*

Kingdom for a fee, as many a fashionable lady presently does, and call it a lark and a dissipation—I can find no shame in cheering an intimate of the gaol when the occasion arises.

Frank approached the heavy wooden door and peered through a small window barred in iron. "Halloo there, Constable," he cried. "You have visitors for Captain Seagrave."

"Captain Seagrave be presently entertaining a visitor, sir," called a voice laconically from within. "Ye shall have to cool your heels a bit until the lady is done."

"It must be Louisa," muttered Frank. "I thought her unlikely to condescend to such a duty. Perhaps her humours are under amendment."

He stepped back from the doorway and clasped his gloved hands together.

"Were it not Sunday, I should suggest a cup of chocolate at a pastry shop in the High," said Mr. Hill. "The sun, though bright, quite fails to quell the bite of the cold. Are you well, Miss Austen?"

I had parted my lips to reply, when a rustle at the iron-barred door brought all our heads around. The oak was thrust back and a figure appeared—a woman clothed in black, with a veil about her face. She stepped out into the alley and nodded in acknowledgement of ourselves, but made no attempt to converse.

Phoebe Carruthers.

In another instant she had turned into the High, her carriage superb and her hands encased in a black fur muff. We watched her go in silence.

Chapter 23

The Lady in the Case

"AUSTEN!"

Tom Seagrave stood with his back to the wall of his prison. His right leg was tethered to an iron ring set into the stone floor. He might travel five feet in every direction; such was the extent of his liberty—a man who had spent his life in roaming the seas. The floor was covered with straw, and smelt strongly of mould. The temperature within the cell was barely higher than in the streets, but the small space offered one advantage, in being sheltered from the wind.

"How d'ye do, Tom?" Frank bowed. "You will recollect my sister, Miss Austen—and perhaps Mr. Hill, Admiral Bertie's surgeon. He was present—"

"—at my court-martial. I remember him well." Seagrave bowed. "You are come in some state to see me, Austen—and I cannot think that I deserve such attention. I have abused you to your face and behind your back, and still you dance a faithful attendance. I owe you a very great apology, I believe."

"Not at all," my brother returned, with all the appearance of awkwardness. "I should be a scrub of the first order, did I expect one."

Seagrave shifted in his chains, the clink of metal resounding in the small space, and his eyes drifted towards me. "I understand from my wife that I owe you all a considerable debt as well—that it was you, Miss Austen, who discovered the whereabouts of my sons, and your brother who retrieved them from the *Star of Bengal*. We have put our few friends to decided trouble! I should have urged Louisa to send the children into Kent with her uncle when this dreadful business first broke upon us. They should have been safe and well cared-for."

"They are charming rogues, Tom," Frank broke in with warmth, "and you must get them to sea as soon as may be, for they will not consent to stay moored on dry land forever. They are pining for a berth in the orlop, and should do handsomely for all their pluck!"

Seagrave nodded, but without much enthusiasm or attention; his mind, I judged, was decidedly elsewhere. His straight naval figure had lost a good deal of its confidence in the ordeal of the past few days; he was as a sapped trunk, that must soon fall to the axe.

"Then your wife has come to cheer your solitude?" I enquired. "She has borne you the news of Charles and Edward herself?"

"I heard of the boys' misadventure in a note despatched from the Dolphin," he replied curtly. "No one but Captain Austen has deigned to enter this cell."

"Captain Austen," said Mr. Hill delicately, "and . . . Mrs. Carruthers, I believe?"

Tom Seagrave did not immediately reply. His dark eyes blazed an instant in his haggard face, and then he turned towards the wall of his cell with an abrupt expression of impatience.

"She means to marry Sir Francis Farnham, Frank," he burst out. "And yet, she cannot *love* him!"

"Why not?" my brother enquired in a hardened tone. "Farnham is rich—he is powerful—and his affections have endured these twenty years at least."

"Sir Francis is not unhandsome, however incongenial his manners," I added. "Why should Mrs. Carruthers remain a widow, when she might be a baronet's wife?"

"Any woman might do murder I reckon, to secure herself a similar position," Mr. Hill observed.

If Seagrave found the surgeon's words disturbing, he did not betray the slightest sensibility. Perhaps he'd become inured to shock. "I cannot believe her capable of a loveless union," he said. "She is too perfect a creature to act upon interest."

I glanced at Frank. How likely was Seagrave to credit the truth of our suspicions regarding Mrs. Carruthers? Farnham he might hate as a rival—Farnham he could believe capable of the basest infamy—but it might be as well to say nothing of the role Mrs. Carruthers had played, in luring Chessyre to his death.

"Did you meet with Farnham in Bugle Street on Wednesday night?" asked my brother wearily.

Seagrave's eyebrow rose. "I was denied the pleasure," he answered. "I will admit, now, that I went to Bugle Street—but I found no one at home. Mrs. Carruthers, I was told, had gone out to the theatre. I could not believe it—I thought it a subterfuge to put me off. But apparently she had indeed gone into Society, despite her mourning." His eyes moved absently over my face. "I had thought her more wretched at Simon's loss."

"She professes a good deal of unhappiness," I said carefully. "Indeed, she exhibits anger. She told us that she could not meet with you, Captain Seagrave, for fear of the reproaches she might rain upon your head. And yet we find her here this morning . . ."

"It is the first glimpse of her I have had since that dreadful day in January, when I engaged the *Manon*," he said heavily. "I bade Chessyre break the news of young Simon's loss when he achieved Southampton, as I could not be first myself; and how Phoebe took it I know not—for I was prevented exchanging so much as a word with my lieutenant, on account of his charges. God!" He struck a blow to his forehead, as though to blot out all that had been, and all that might be. "If only man were capable of knowing all, and ordering his days, so that a world of trouble might be prevented!"

"Then he should be as his Maker, and our world be Heaven upon Earth," I observed quietly. "Have you loved Mrs. Carruthers long?"

Tom Seagrave stared. "*Loved* her? Would you fall into the same error as my wife, Miss Austen? Do not be such a fool!"

"But, Tom—" spluttered Frank.

"I esteemed Phoebe Carruthers as the wife of a good friend— a man I regarded almost as a brother; I attempted to improve her situation in what manner I could, when Hugh was killed at Trafalgar. In Simon I cherished the father reborn in the son—and felt as cruel an anguish at the boy's death as I should feel for the loss of my own. But love, for Phoebe?" He shook his head.

I looked at Frank. My brother was gaping.

"Remorse has driven me like a madman," Seagrave told us. "A thousand times I have consulted my conscience—I have wondered, and blamed myself for failing to place poor Simon in a position of safety. I had not realised the boy was aloft—he should have been with the other Young Gentlemen, carrying powder to the guns. When I saw his body dashed upon the deck, I felt myself a murderer."

It was as though he had read his wife's thoughts for weeks past, and found no argument to refute them.

"I dreaded the admission of my guilt to Phoebe—she who has borne so much. When I returned to Portsmouth, I learned that she was thrown into deepest mourning. I rode immediately over to Southampton, but she would not receive me. I tried once more, a few days later, and still she would not consent. And so I began to write—letter after useless letter, all of them returned. I begged her forgiveness. I called myself a murderer. I told her that if I could hurl myself into death in Simon's place, I should have done so in a thrice. But she never read my words." He looked down at his clenched hands. "No one was more surprised than I when she entered my prison this morning."

Mr. Hill stirred beside me. "And why do you think she came, sir?"

Seagrave glanced up. "She said that the gossip of the naval set would have it that we were lovers. She told me that the suggestion had pained her deeply, as it must affect my wife. Her marriage to Sir Francis, she believes, may put a stop to such outrage."

I coloured. If Phoebe Carruthers had reason to fear the gossip of Southampton, then I was certainly the cause. I had thrown the implication in her face in East Street, only yesterday.

But surely, I argued, whatever the woman said was lies! We knew that she had acted as Sir Francis's lure. She merely attempted to throw Tom Seagrave off the scent, as she had attempted to persuade ourselves of her disinterested good.

"No reproach did she utter, for Simon's death," said Seagrave wonderingly. "No mention of the lad was suffered to pass her lips. The lady is remarkable in her self-command."

"Why did you seek her in Bugle Street on Wednesday night, if you knew that all entreaty—all explanation—must be in vain?" enquired Frank.

Seagrave started as though slapped by a cold sea wave. "I went in search of my wife, Austen. Surely that has always been obvious?"

"Your wife?" I repeated. "What has Mrs. Seagrave to do with Bugle Street?"

"It is she whom I have endeavoured to protect," Seagrave returned. "On Wednesday she was so unfortunate as to discover in my desk drawer the packet of letters I had written to Phoebe Carruthers—all returned. She suspected the worst of our acquaintance."

"And so you thought that Louisa was determined to confront Mrs. Carruthers?"

Seagrave hesitated, as though uncertain how much to reveal. "My wife has been exceedingly unwell for some time. Her aunt—a Lady Templeton—has lately attempted to revive her connexion with Louisa, and unsettled her nerves decidedly. Lady Templeton descended upon Portsmouth on the Wednesday morning, and having denied her visit that day, Louisa declared that she would pay her aunt a call after dinner. She walked over to Lady Templeton's inn about six o'clock, and when she had not returned by nine, I was naturally anxious. I sent a servant to enquire after my wife, and learned she had quitted the place—in Lady Templeton's carriage—some two hours earlier."

"You thought your wife fled to Southampton?"

"I did. I saddled one of the inn's horses and rode over directly to Bugle Street, convinced that Louisa intended a scene before Mrs. Carruthers. I may say that I lathered my mount unforgivably, and arrived at half-past ten."

"And found no one at home," I said thoughtfully. "And Mrs. Seagrave?"

"—Was nowhere in the vicinity. I concluded that Louisa had driven out in a wholly different direction, and at that hour was probably returned to our lodgings in Lombard Street, only to find me gone. I rode home again, at a somewhat more measured pace, and achieved my bed at half-past one."

Frank's expression was wooden. "Was your wife within?"

"Her bedroom door was closed," said Seagrave abruptly. "I did not like to disturb her. She suffers from nightmare. And as you know, I had reason to guard my sleep as well that night. I was to face court-martial in the morning."

The Captain's face was hard—as unyielding as any of the Enemy might find it. It occurred to me, as we took our leave, that whatever his failings in duty or attention, Tom Seagrave still meant to shield his wife.

WE HAD TOLD SEAGRAVE NOTHING OF ETIENNE LAFORGE'S ESCAPE, nor of our suspicions of Sir Francis Farnham. Whether the shock of Seagrave's disclosures—the surprise of his history with Phoebe Carruthers—or some inner caution proscribed the topic, I shall leave the reader to determine. It was nonetheless true, however, that we quitted the gaol without the necessity of mutual consultation, and that we breasted the High in heavy silence, each of us lost in thought.

"Captain Austen," said Mr. Hill, "it occurs to me that proper feeling might dictate a call upon Mrs. Seagrave. Would you regard such an act as likely to break the Sabbath—or entirely within the compass of these extraordinary circumstances?"

"I shall bear you company, Hill," said my brother grimly, "and regard it as a charity. Jane? Are you greatly fatigued? I confess I should welcome the presence of a lady at this interview."

"I was always a slave to the poor and downtrodden," I observed piously, and placed my hand within his arm.

Chapter 24

Incitement to Vice

MRS. SEAGRAVE LOOKED VERY ILL INDEED AS SHE WAS USHERED INTO
the Dolphin's upper parlour. Her hair in its cruelly tight knot was
lifeless, her eyes overly bright, and her countenance determinedly
sallow. If she had taken anything by way of food in the days since I
had last seen her, it had added nothing to her frame.

"Forgive me," she said without preamble. "I am not attired to receive visitors. I hardly looked for any today."

"Pray do not make yourself anxious," said Frank. He thrust himself hastily from his chair and bowed. "I trust you are well, Mrs.
Seagrave?"

"I am thoroughly wretched; but what of that? It is become my
usual condition. Miss Austen—it is a relief to see you again. I had
begun to think that the world was solely populated by hypocrites
and scoundrels."

I went to her and curtseyed. "You may remember our friend Mr.
Hill from our last meeting in Lombard Street."

"The naval surgeon." She offered him the barest nod. "I do recall. And how is your French colleague, Mr. Hill? The one who succeeded in preventing my husband from hanging?"

"Sadly—he is dead, ma'am," lied Mr. Hill with the gravest of looks. "He died most tragically in a shipboard fire last evening. You may have heard rumour of the event."

A spot of colour flared up in Louisa's cheek. "I never attend to rumour, sir, I assure you. Will you take some bread and cheese? Or a glass of wine—may I fetch you one?"

"Thank you—but no," I returned after a glance at the impassive gentlemen. For my own part, I was faint with hunger. I do not break my fast before Sunday service, and the hour was fast approaching noon.

"I can stomach nothing at present," Louisa murmured, "but I may at least ring for tea. Pray avail yourselves of chairs—" this last, with a vague gesture about the parlour, as though she were viewing its contents for the first time. At her ring, a maidservant appeared in the doorway, then disappeared in pursuit of a tray.

Frank waited for the ladies to adopt their seats before settling into his own. Mr. Hill seemed determined to stand. Louisa sank into her chair with so complete a weariness that I understood nerves alone must be animating her frame. She put her head in her hands, insensible for an instant to everything about her.

I broke the silence. "And how do the children? Charles and Edward are well?"

"Well enough in body," she said, "but low in their spirits and cowed as mice. It is something to see one's father—whom one has always considered a sort of god, from his habit of command—taken from the house under armed guard, and conveyed like a pauper through the streets. I do not know what to tell them. Every sentiment must sound false in my ears. All my words are lies."

"Not all," I urged her. "Surely you have hope for the future—and not all hope is false. Some prayers must be heard, and answered."

"But I do not know what to pray for," she said bleakly.

"Good God, woman!" my brother ejaculated. "Would you have

your husband called a murderer—when those who love him must believe the accusation false—and hang for it? I can think of several dozen prayers that might adequately serve."

"We have only just quitted your husband's cell," I told her.

A light flared in her eyes—but of joy or anger, I could not tell.

"You have seen my husband?"

"And found poor Tom quite sunk," said Frank. "It was all we could do to elicit a word from those stern lips. He bears his troubles nobly. I intend to search out a reputable barrister on his behalf tomorrow—and shall travel to London if I must, to secure such a man!"

"Did he tell you where he went on Wednesday night?"

Louisa's expression, as she asked the question, was painfully acute. Every ounce of passion in her famished countenance was directed at my brother's answer—upon his next words her very existence seemed to hang.

Frank hesitated, and his eyes found mine. "He did not."

Well done, I thought.

The tension in Louisa's body seemed to drain away. But her countenance twisted in a bitter smile. "It was hardly an honourable adventure, you may be sure. A man with nothing to hide would not now be sitting in Gaoler's Alley. I am sure he sought only *one* in this wretched town, and that she was eager to bid him welcome."

Frank snorted derisively and rose from his chair. "Forgive me, ma'am, if I must plead urgent business. I shall expect to meet you in future under happier circumstances, when we may all forget this dreadful episode, and rejoice in your husband's return to vigour and respect. I hope to find your humour and manners much improved."

A curt bow, that was almost an insult, and not the slightest softening of his angry manner. I understood Frank's regard for Tom Seagrave; but I thought my brother lamentably ill-equipped to comprehend the subtlety of Louisa Seagrave's soul. Mr. Hill, perhaps, should have done better—but Mr. Hill was fixed in his position by the far wall, his regard never wavering from Louisa's wan face.

"You think me a hard and bitter woman, Captain Austen," she said softly, "because I do not profess to love my husband. But perhaps I have loved him too well, and more than he deserves. I have sacrificed everything to his comfort; I have borne him five children, and seen two swallowed by the grave; I have endeavoured to preserve his respectability. Yet he has turned from me. He has left me bereft, who possessed nothing but his love in the world. Should you wonder that I find it hard to pity him now?"

"I wonder that any woman can fail to pity a man," returned my brother with heat. "You are all of you so much wiser and better than we. Can you not see that your husband is now in greater need of your respect and esteem than at any moment in his life? And yet it is now that you would withdraw them!"

"They were murdered, Captain—not withdrawn." Her voice was raw with stifled weeping. "He killed our love with his careless ways, as surely as he killed that poor boy."

"Call it Death by Misadventure, then," Frank persisted, "if you will call it death. Murder implies something other than mere carelessness. It suggests a cruelty and an intent to harm that I have never witnessed in Thomas Seagrave. I wonder, madam, whether you know your husband—or merely some demon your mind has formed!"

To my surprise, Louisa stared at my brother with an expression akin to horror, as though he had peered directly into her soul. "I do see demons," she whispered. "They torment my sleep. No rest do I have, by night or by day; they are ogres in form, that bear my husband's face."

Frank's brows came down in perplexity at this; but whatever he might have said was forestalled by Louisa's sharp cry. "My flask! What has become of my flask?"

Her eyes swept frantically about the room.

"Is it in your reticule?" I enquired. The article lay forgot on the parlour table. I reached for it, but Louisa was before me—she rose from her chair and clutched at the thing as though it contained her life's blood. Her efforts to free the flask from her reticule were in vain, however; her fingers shook so violently that she was powerless to withdraw the bottle of laudanum. She swayed—Mr. Hill stepped forward—and without uttering a sound, Louisa slid to the carpet in a swoon.

The surgeon felt immediately for a pulse, while Frank and I waited in suspense.

"Carry her into the bedchamber," he said abruptly. "She cannot lie here, displayed to the public eye. Quickly—help me to support her."

The door to the upper parlour opened at that moment, to admit the maidservant with the tea. Her eyes widened as she comprehended the scene—but she was collected in her wits, and merely set down the tray on a chair, rather than dashing it to the floor in the best tradition of drama.

"This gentleman is a surgeon," I told her. "Fetch cold water, and be so good as to bring a vinaigrette to Mrs. Seagrave's room."

WE LAID LOUISA ON HER BED AND PLACED A SHAWL OVER HER. MR. Hill loosened her stays, and peered under her eyelids; and then he requested the bottle of laudanum Louisa carried everywhere with her.

To my surprise, he administered a draught.

"But is not that the very thing that ails her?" I enquired.

"To be sure. But one cannot deprive the body of the evil prop it craves. Mrs. Seagrave has grown so dependent upon her Comfort that she cannot do without it."

"Then how is she to be saved? For her condition worsens. Every day that passes finds her more attached to the elixir, more despondent in her thoughts, more deranged in her dreams."

He raised a thin eyebrow. "The demons that bear her husband's face? They are common enough among your opium-eaters. The initial effects of the drug are wondrous—the portal to a world of beauty and delight; but as the mind becomes ensnared to opium's effect, the fantasies grow harsh, the dream world darkens. And still the sufferer cannot thwart the body's craving."

I met the surgeon's eyes. "You know a good deal more of the evil than is wise, Mr. Hill."

He smiled wryly. "I am not entirely a stranger to the poppy, Miss Austen, though I am happy to say that I am no longer its slave."

"How is the addiction broken?" Frank asked intently.

"The taking of opium in any form is a difficult practise to inhibit. A strong mind—a will to desist—is required; and of course, adequate diversion to free the soul of boredom. Too many physicians will prescribe complete rest, without the understanding that *ennui* is a powerful spur to relapse. Mrs. Seagrave is unlikely to procure much of either rest or diversion, however, in Southampton at present. Is she greatly attached to her husband?—I do not speak, here, of bitter words and reproaches. I speak of real feeling."

I glanced at Frank, who stood mutely by the opposite side of the bed. "That is difficult to judge," I replied. "Certainly she regards it as her duty to be near him, under his present difficulty; but she derives no happiness from braving scandal, and has never professed confidence in his innocence."

"I see," said the surgeon; and possibly he did. "How many children?"

"Three, one of them a babe in arms. She possesses a nursemaid; we must presume the woman presently in charge."

"Has she any family capable of lending support? A home to which she might go, under careful supervision, while attempting to wean herself from the vile stuff?"

I hesitated. "There is her aunt—the lady to whom Captain Seagrave referred. Lady Templeton has quitted Portsmouth, I believe, and is presently gone into Kent. She was bound for a place called Luxford House—somewhere, I think, near Deal."

"Luxford House!" Mr. Hill straightened. "Then your Lady Templeton is gone to a funeral! Viscount Luxford is very lately deceased—I read the account only yesterday in the *Morning Gazette*."

"So we understand. Mrs. Seagrave is the late Viscount's daughter."

Mr. Hill's eyes gleamed sharply. He glanced down at Louisa, who remained insensible. The draught of laudanum, however, appeared to have made her more comfortable; she looked now to be only sleeping.

"Have the maid bathe her temples with vinegar every quarter-hour," the surgeon instructed. "I can do nothing more here at present; and it is imperative I speak with you both."

"ARE YOU AWARE OF THE DISPOSITION OF THE LUXFORD ESTATE?" Mr. Hill enquired.

I glanced at Frank, who appeared as bemused as myself. We had descended to the Dolphin's downstairs parlour, the better to converse in privacy; the airy room was empty but for ourselves.

"We know nothing of the family at all," I answered. "We have only just learned the name in recent days."

"In company with the better part of England," Mr. Hill replied comfortably. "Mrs. Seagrave and her history are now the intimate concern of every reader of the *Morning Gazette*—to say nothing of the *Post,* the *Times,* and every other reputable scandal-monger in the Kingdom. The report of the Viscount's death has led to considerable speculation. For the provisions of his will—and the passage of his estate—must leave your friend in peculiar suspense."

There is no one in England, I daresay, who may resist the temptation of canvassing an estate oddly left; the various clauses and provisions of wills, while dry stuff in themselves, must lead to the most extraordinary incident. Fortunes are made and lost; heirs plucked from obscurity, or thrown into eclipse; ancient scandals revived, in all their lurid particulars; and the Dead afforded the satisfaction of disturbing the Living's peace for a decade or more.

"Pray sit down, Mr. Hill," said my brother. "Let us send for refreshment. Madeira, perhaps, and ratafia cakes?"

"I should be infinitely obliged," said the surgeon, and pulling the tails of his black coat over his hips, he sat.

The wine was brought; I accepted a glass; Louisa's maid appeared to report that Mrs. Seagrave was unchanged, however much vinegar might be pressed into her temples; and Mr. Hill was urged to a second round of Madeira. His thin face took on a bit of colour, and his small eyes did not lose their gleam.

"I often think that had I spurned the world of physick, and the adventure of the seas, I should have loved nothing so well as a tidy solicitor's office, and the management of sundry affairs," he observed. "Three or four families, in a country village—provided they be sufficiently rich or eccentric to involve the affairs of a multitude—is the very thing to work on. And so we come to the Viscount."

"I gather that he made some mention of Mrs. Seagrave in the will?" said Frank impatiently.

"So it is rumoured. The actual reading of the testament will not occur, to be sure, until after the Viscount is interred—and that is not to happen until Tuesday. But speculation is rife, I fear, and the Viscount's solicitors have not been as chary with intelligence as his lordship might have wished. Are you at all familiar with the gentleman?"

I shook my head.

"He was a very warm man, I believe," said Frank.

"So warm as to be positively scalding," agreed Mr. Hill. "Viscount Luxford inherited a very handsome fortune at his ascendancy, but rather than going immediately to ruin in the pursuit of horses, gambling hells, or the improvement of his estate—he engaged in speculation."

"Which is merely gambling by a different name," my brother observed.

"But a happier one, in Luxford's case. He first commissioned the building of a crescent, to the designs of Nash,[1] on property long held by the family in Mayfair; the buildings, when sold, garnered a

---

1. John Nash, the foremost architect of the late Georgian and Regency period (1752–1835).—*Editor's note.*

fortune. This in turn he ploughed back into commerce, by investing in ships. Luxford money has long been a considerable force in the management of the Honourable East India Company. More tea has come to England in Luxford's holds, and more opium gone from India to China, than might fill all of Southampton."

"Opium!" I cried.

"Naturally. It is a vital part of our triangular trade—though one we may hesitate to mention in polite circles. By consigning the vice to China, however unwillingly she might accept it, we may congratulate ourselves on remaining untainted."

"How dreadful, that the Viscount's daughter should now be enthralled to the very abuse he has encouraged."

"There are many hypocrisies inherent in trade, Miss Austen— and chief among them is the notion that noblemen never engage in it. They may not build their own ships or purchase their own cargoes; they call themselves investors rather than merchants; but they thrive in the mercantile world as happily as the Fashionable one."

"And so we may take it that Viscount Luxford was exceedingly wealthy at the time of his death," Frank persisted.

Mr. Hill nodded. "One of perhaps three or four of the richest men in England. There was talk of an earldom just last month, before Luxford took ill."

Frank let out a faint whistle. "And yet he cut his daughter off without a farthing when she married Seagrave."

"To say that she was 'cut off' is not entirely exact." Mr. Hill pressed a napkin delicately to his lips, as though to contain his own huge excitement. "I believe the Viscount lived in fear of his daughter's marrying a worthless adventurer; and we may judge him to have regarded Seagrave in such a light. Her portion was no less than an hundred thousand pounds, along with some considerable property in Berkshire, that came to her through her mother's line."

"Her *portion*?" I said. "But Louisa is his only child. Is the bulk of the estate entailed upon heirs male? Shall it go to a cousin, perhaps?"

"I am coming to that," Mr. Hill informed me. "Luxford settled this marriage portion upon his daughter with the express provision that she must marry with his blessing."

"Louisa eloped," I told him.

"And was thrown off by her family. I am afraid that the Viscount took then-Lieutenant Seagrave in such violent dislike, that he sought to be punitive in the management of his daughter's affairs. Louisa's marriage portion was made over to her issue, inheritable only upon her husband's death."

"The sole purpose being to keep the property from Tom," Frank said.

"Exactly. And so we proceed to the Viscount's entire estate—which, according to the knowledgeable fellows at the *Morning Gazette,* is estimated in the millions of pounds. If Louisa Seagrave is a married woman at the moment the will is read, the estate and title are to pass to her eldest son—provided she divorces her husband within the year, and her son adopts the Luxford family name of Carteret."

"Good God!" I cried, and stared at my brother. "What an inducement to unhappiness and vice! Might any woman be equal to refusing such temptation?"

"And is Louisa then empowered to act as her son's guardian and trustee?" Frank enquired.

Mr. Hill smiled thinly. "The late Viscount was hardly so forgiving. He offers his estranged daughter ample funds—some ten thousand pounds per annum—and the use of the Dower House at Luxford; but the guardianship of her son and the management of his affairs, including his vast fortune, will be undertaken by Sir Walter and Lady Templeton—trustees to the estate."

"And thus we comprehend the benevolent activity of Lady Templeton in Lombard Street," I said softly.

"Even did we charge Lady Templeton with acting in her own interest," Frank countered, "the benefit to Louisa must be considerable. She might be returned to the circle in which she was born; her sons receive every advantage presently denied them; and her infant daughter be reared in the most select society. What mother could turn aside?"

But I was hardly attending. I was in the grip of an idea so dreadful I could barely pronounce it.

"You said, Mr. Hill, that the property was disposed in the above manner, if Mrs. Seagrave were *a married woman*. There is another provision, surely?"

Mr. Hill drained his Madeira to the dregs before replying. "It is a preoccupation of your Great Man, I find, to grasp in death what he could not obtain in life. The Viscount was a very Great Man; and his spirit of fun, shall we say, was commensurately large. Louisa Seagrave will inherit the entirety of her father's fortune, and her son become the next Viscount, without recourse to guardians, trustees, or settlements—provided that when the will is read, Mrs. Seagrave is already a widow."

Chapter 25

What the Lady Knew

1 March 1807,

cont.

~

"DEAR GOD," I WHISPERED, WITH MY EYES UPON THE CEILING OF the inn's drawing-room, as though Louisa Seagrave might over-listen our words in her poisoned dreams. "We must discover what she knew."

Frank stared. "You think it possible . . ."

"That she arranged for her husband's dishonour? Paid off Eustace Chessyre to commit an act so obscene, the entire Navy must take notice, and charge Tom Seagrave with a violation of the Articles of War? Entirely within the range of her powers, I assure you!"

"But that is madness—to send her husband to the gallows! No woman could contemplate such an act! No wife could be capable of it!"

I did not reply. Restlessly, I commenced to turn about the room, my fingers smoothing the pleats of my gown. "What did Louisa know of her father's will, and when did she know it? From Lady Templeton, as lately as Thursday, when I found the two together in

Lombard Street? Or far earlier—before, let us say, the *Stella* sailed in January under sealed orders? How much time would Louisa require, to effect her husband's ruin?"

"If she were well-acquainted with Chessyre—and he had been her husband's lieutenant for many years—very little time at all," answered my brother grimly.

I wheeled upon Mr. Hill. "You said, I think, that the Viscount began his decline a month ago?"

"That is as the papers would have it. But the death itself was quite sudden."

"And the *Stella Maris* engaged the *Manon* some seven weeks since. If we would have Louisa responsible for Chessyre's plot, then we must accept the idea that she knew of the Viscount's provisions well before her father's illness. In a communication from Lady Templeton, sent during the Christmas season, perhaps? Or—if the Viscount's *sense of fun,* as you call it, extended to the torment of his daughter—in a communication from the gentleman himself?"

My thoughts raced as a fevered pulse; but the gentlemen followed as swiftly behind. We all of us spoke in lowered tones, in deference to the public nature of an inn.

"The moment of the Viscount's passing is immaterial," Mr. Hill pointed out. "What is vital is the moment of his interment—and the subsequent reading of the provisions of his will. Mrs. Seagrave today is no different than she was before; but by the dinner hour on Tuesday she might be anything."

"We may exonerate Lady Templeton of murder at least," observed my brother ironically. "You have provided her with the strongest inducement to ensure Tom Seagrave's survival. Without him, Lady Templeton gets not a farthing to administer or spend."

"We must interrogate the aunt regardless," I said, "though we must venture into Kent to do it. Without intending to incite murder, Lady Templeton may have done so with simple gossip. If she was aware of the Viscount's provisions before his death, and communicated them to her niece—"

"It cannot prove that Louisa Seagrave decided to murder her

husband," Frank insisted impatiently. "And by so contrived a means! She should better have put arsenic in Tom's plum pudding at Christmas, than attempted a hanging by court-martial!"

"Poison will out," I reminded him. "How much more to be preferred, is an official disgrace—an impartial judgement—a public hanging . . . and the widow rather to be pitied than suspected of evil. The entire affair bears the mark of Louisa's subtle mind."

"And yet, not subtle enough," opined Mr. Hill. "For Mrs. Seagrave to achieve the object you would set her, Miss Austen, she must have effected her husband's death by Tuesday at the latest; and you must admit that *that* is not very likely."

"Not if she is watched," I said, "and knows herself to have fallen under suspicion. But if she feels secure . . . we might catch her in the very act . . ."

The two men were silent.

"Death might have been achieved already if Tom Seagrave's court-martial had not been suspended," I persisted. "Thus far, Louisa's scheme marched to plan. She was listening for the gun that should mark her husband's execution when I found her in Lombard Street on Thursday."

"We may blame Eustace Chessyre and his uneasy conscience for spoiling such morbid hopes," said my brother.

"Perhaps we may congratulate ourselves, for having thrown Etienne LaForge into the fray, and complicating matters irremediably," I added. "We must certainly accept the burden of his poisoning."

"But how? Louisa Seagrave has never been to Wool House—and on Thursday, when LaForge fell ill, we know her to have been at home!"

"Remember that LaForge was present in Lombard Street on Thursday, in company with ourselves. We were served dry sherry and iced cakes, much against our will. Is it at all possible that Monsieur LaForge was poisoned *then*, Mr. Hill, and not several hours later?"

"It is possible," the surgeon said slowly, "for you will recall that

LaForge was ill en route up the Solent. Something might have been introduced, I suppose, to his victuals in Lombard Street. We ascribed his sickness to the effects of fever and the sea, but with the benefit of hindsight—"

"The lady would have to be remarkably cool!" Frank protested. "She had only just learned of Seagrave's survival—of LaForge's existence—and you would have the poison so conveniently to hand?"

"She had learned of LaForge's existence a full *two* days before his appearance in her drawing-room," I countered. "You told her yourself, Frank—in your express to Seagrave of Tuesday; and we learned from the Captain only this morning that Louisa had plundered his desk."

That fact must cause my brother to fall silent an instant. "But consider, Jane," he attempted at last, "that we believe Eustace Chessyre to have been murdered by his conspirator. Nothing you may say shall convince me that Louisa Seagrave wields a garrote. It is one thing to plot disgrace, and another entirely to strangle a man!"

"True." I halted before the hearth and stared into the flames. "But where did Louisa go, when she fled Portsmouth on Wednesday night in her aunt's carriage—a carriage that bore the arms of a baronet? To meet with Chessyre, who she feared repented of his betrayal?"

"If Louisa Seagrave was the veiled woman in the carriage, and not Phoebe Carruthers, then Chessyre was a fool to get in," said Frank bluntly.

"He may not have feared the hands of a woman. Particularly one who appeared so sickly."

Mr. Hill nodded once, as though in agreement; but my brother could not be easy.

"Why despatch Chessyre, if his death should suspend the very trial and conviction she desired?"

"Because you outlined the Lieutenant's plot in your express of Tuesday. Louisa is unsteady in her mind, as we have all observed; she may have read that letter, feared Chessyre's exposure of herself and her object—and made her plans accordingly."

Frank revolved the idea in his mind. It is something to learn that one's meddling for good might have achieved the deaths of two men.

"But *why*, Jane?" he demanded suddenly. "Do you believe Louisa to crave rank and fortune so very much? She scorned them fifteen years ago."

"Fifteen years is a period," I mused. "Louisa has become a bitter woman in the interval, and not a little deranged by opium. And she has much to resent, Frank—the rumours of Seagrave's infidelity, the threat she perceives to her sons' safety. She felt the decline in her social fortunes acutely, I assure you. All these must have led her to Dr. Wharton's Comfort in the end."

Mr. Hill cleared his throat. "I should say rather that the steady usage of Dr. Wharton's Comfort may have deluded the lady, over time, into *believing* her husband the very ogre whose face she saw in her nightmares. To kill such a beast—we might take it as Mrs. Seagrave's hidden desire to free herself from opium-eating."

"You are kinder by half than I should be," muttered my brother.

There was a knock at the parlour door, and the maidservant's visage once more appeared around the frame. "Begging your pardon, but the lady upstairs is awake, and asking for Miss Austen."

I glanced at the gentlemen with resolution. "What shall I say to her?"

"For now," cautioned Mr. Hill, "it is vital to offer comfort."

Frank held his finger to his lips. "Remember that you know nothing for certain, Jane. Do not betray your worst fears. Remember that we have told her LaForge is dead. She may exult in the idea that her secret is safe. If Louisa intends to have her fortune, she must despatch Seagrave tonight."

"Then we must watch her every movement," I cried.

SHE HAD ARISEN BY THE TIME I ENTERED, AND WAS STARING AT HER countenance in the looking glass.

"I was quite beautiful once. You would not think so, Miss Austen, to look at me now—but that summer I made Thomas's acquaintance in Brighton, I was the flower of the regiment."

"The passage of time may affect many changes, in appearance and sentiment; we are none of us immune."

"I cannot remember the name of the regiment in Brighton that year," she murmured, "but it scarcely matters. I tired of scarlet uniforms, and turned instead to blue. Thomas thought me quite the most extraordinary creature he had ever seen."

"And you?" I asked her quietly. "What did you think of him?"

Her fingers, which had been fluttering over the wisps of her dull, black hair, stilled an instant; her eyes met mine in the glass. "I thought John Donne had come again to walk the earth. *When thou and I first one another saw:/All other things, to their destruction draw.'*"

" *'Only our love hath no decay;/This, no tomorrow hath, nor yesterday,'* " I quoted. "The perfect union of two hearts, two souls, for all eternity. It is a fearful burden to answer, Mrs. Seagrave. A greater man than your husband should have bowed beneath it; for time, as we know, will exact its cost. Death only may preserve such love."

She shuddered as if with cold, and reached for her bottle of laudanum.

"Mr. Hill is of the opinion that Dr. Wharton's Comfort works viciously upon the system," I told her gently. "Do you not wish to rid yourself of its effects?"

"At the suggestion of a naval hack?" she enquired with a laugh. "When I choose to consult a doctor regarding my health, Miss Austen, he shall be a reputable London physician—not the sort of man who administers to gaol-fever. I wonder you allow Mr. Hill's acquaintance; he is hardly prepossessing."

"Take care, Mrs. Seagrave," I replied evenly. "You would not wish me to prefer one friend to another."

Her expression hardened instantly. "I am glad you are come today, Miss Austen. I should have regretted quitting Southampton without a word of farewell. I go into Kent tomorrow with my children, for the funeral of my father—Viscount Luxford—and I cannot say when it shall be in my power to meet with you again."

Had she summoned me upstairs merely to issue this dismissal?

"It is a considerable distance. Do you travel around the coast by boat—or intend to journey overland, by post?"

"My aunt is to send her carriage for me. It would not do, she insists, for the daughter of a viscount to appear at Luxford in one of the Dolphin's equipages." She turned her face before the glass once more, in contemplation of her complexion. "I shall achieve my ancestral home in good time for the funeral rites. How surprised they shall be to see me at Luxford!"

"Then you shall be in need of your rest, Mrs. Seagrave," I said curtly, and bade her *adieu.*

Chapter 26

The Uses of Letter Knives

IT WAS EVIDENT THAT LOUISA SEAGRAVE MEANT TO MURDER HER
husband under cover of darkness, before quitting Southampton altogether on the morrow. Mr. Hill and my brother were agreed that,
having employed poison once, the lady might be likely to attempt it
again—with the introduction of some noxious substance in a parting gift of food she would press upon Tom Seagrave at this last
interview. We deemed it probable that Louisa should await her children's retiring, before quitting the Dolphin; she should not be
likely to attempt any evil before eight o'clock at the earliest. The
two gentlemen agreed to take it in turns to watch throughout the
night for Louisa's appearance in Gaoler's Alley; as the duty would
be a chilly and tiresome one, I was forbidden to appear, and consented most unwillingly to remain at home in East Street.

We invited Mr. Hill to dine, and the invitation was accepted with
alacrity; like ourselves, the surgeon had consumed nothing but tea
and Madeira for the better part of the day. Mary was persuaded to

put aside her petulance, and do the honours of Mrs. Davies's table with all the flushed enthusiasm of a bride; my mother found the surgeon's attentions highly promising, and asked so many questions about the Indies, that I wondered the poor man was not driven mad. Martha was pleased to report some little information regarding the garret beds to be installed in Castle Square, and to present a letter received of Cassandra this morning, that named the very day of my sister's return to Southampton.[1]

My mother was so charmed by Mr. Hill's manners and good sense—however little she noted his fifty-odd years and wizened appearance—that she stayed below conversing in the parlour until very nearly seven o'clock. Her maternal fervour was so great that she condescended to confide in me, while ascending the stairs, that she "hoped that Disreputable Rogue, Lord Harold Trowbridge, would soon have news that should discomfit him." I judged it best not to enlarge too much upon the nature of the news, as Mr. Hill was fixed in the front hall, preparatory to quitting East Street for his frigid station. It was left to Frank to make his excuses to the long-suffering Mary, to lift his hand in farewell—and so I was abandoned to all the dreariness of solitary suspense.

I sat over my needlework to little purpose, while Mrs. Davies's parlour clock chimed round the quarters of the hour; listened with half an ear to Mary's idle chatter, and Martha's measured responses; and then at last threw down the baby's shift I was embroidering with cornflowers.

Poor Uncle Walter—how he must suffer it! . . .

He is shot of her for now . . . and must be having a jolly time of it . . .

I should have urged Louisa to send the children into Kent with her uncle . . .

"Is something amiss, Jane?" Martha enquired with an anxious look.

"Yes," I replied. "Lady Templeton's carriage is not at all as it should be."

---

1. Jane is not in error when she mentions Cassandra's letter. The post was delivered on Sundays regardless of the Sabbath.—*Editor's note.*

"I do not understand," said Martha. "Who, pray, is Lady Templeton?"

"I am sure there was a good deal amiss with the mutton," observed Mary. "Mrs. Davies is prone to boil the joint less than she ought; and for one in my condition, mutton is such a trial! I am sure we have tasted of the same old animal three times this week. How I long for Castle Square!"

"Are you retiring, Jane?" Martha enquired.

"I feel the need of a walk," I told her, with my hand on the parlour door. "Do not disturb yourself—I shall be perfectly safe. I shall employ our faithful Jenny as link-boy, and be returned within the hour."[2]

WE MADE OUR WAY PURPOSEFULLY DOWN THE HIGH TOWARDS THE Dolphin, Jenny clutching a lanthorn in one hand and the fastenings of her cloak with the other. The strong sunshine of the morning now fled, the wind off the water was cutting and sharp. I spared only a thought for my brother, crouched silently in the cold but a few streets distant; he was accustomed to exposure from more than two decades at sea. At the door of the inn, I paused.

"Jenny, be so good as to carry your light into Gaoler's Alley, and bid my brother and his friend to join me here. I have urgent need of them. Do not stay for argument, but say that Miss Austen deemed it vital."

Jenny went. I did not watch her steady progress down the street, but hastened into the Dolphin.

The broad front hall was awash in candlelight; the sound of male laughter and conversation emanated from the public room. I felt myself dreadfully exposed—a lady alone in a hotel, without even a maid in attendance—but my discomfort could not be considered of consequence. A footman passed, bearing a bottle of claret and a

2. The link-boy was an urchin paid to run before a sedan chair in its passage through the streets of a town, holding a torch or lantern aloft.—*Editor's note.*

glass; he mounted the servants' stairs off the passage. I saw a gentleman in converse with the innkeeper, and two ladies seated on a sopha in an attitude of fatigue. The length of my walk from East Street, I had struggled to determine the wisest method of approach. I could not present my card, and have it taken up to Mrs. Seagrave—but I must gain entrance to her rooms. Should I await the appearance of my brother? When every moment must be precious?

"Miss Austen?" said a voice at my shoulder.

I turned to see the stooped shoulders and balding head of the innkeeper. "Good evening, Mr. . . ." What had Frank said was the man's name? "Mr. Fortescue. I am sorry to appear at such an advanced hour, but I have only just learned that Mrs. Seagrave intends to quit Southampton on the morrow. I could not bear to let her go without a word."

"Very good of you, and I'm sure," said the fellow with a bob and a smile, "but Lady Templeton charged me expressly to refuse all visitors tonight."

"Lady Templeton?" I repeated. It was as I had feared. There was hardly time enough between Friday and Sunday to complete a journey into Kent—and certainly no time at all to achieve the distance *twice*. The Baronet's coach had been sent not from Luxford, but from Portsmouth. Sir Walter had gone alone into Kent in a hired carriage, but Lady Templeton had remained behind. Awaiting news, perhaps, of Tom Seagrave's fate?

"Mrs. Seagrave's aunt," Fortescue informed me kindly. "She intends to start for Kent quite early tomorrow, I understand, and does not wish to be disturbed. If you like, you might pen a note to Mrs. Seagrave and leave it for her—there is ink and paper in the morning-room, just off the passage."

He gestured in the direction of the back staircase.

"You are very good, Mr. Fortescue," I told him with a dazzling smile. "That is exactly what I shall do."

I turned purposefully towards the morning-room, and was careful to linger in it until I was certain that the weary ladies on

Mr. Fortescue's sopha had claimed the innkeeper's attention. The morning-room was quite empty. I examined the contents of a writing desk, then quickly made for the servants' stairs.

THE DOOR TO LOUISA'S UPSTAIRS PARLOUR WAS FIRMLY CLOSED, but a light shone through the jamb. I approached it stealthily, desperate to make no noise, and pressed my ear almost to the oak.

All was silent within. Not even the fall of embers in the grate disturbed the silence. The children's rooms must adjoin this one, as Louisa's bedchamber did—and yet I heard nothing: no shift of a bed frame, no faint whimper of unquiet sleep. It was as though the family were already fled into Kent, and for an instant—my worst suspicions assuaged—I was weak with relief.

I must have sighed, and the sound penetrated to the room beyond the door. There was an abrupt movement—as of a small metal article overturned upon a table—and then an imperious voice called out: "Who is there?"

I had heard that voice on only one occasion, but I could not fail to recognise its tone of command. There was something of the same harsh timbre—the reflexive coldness—in Louisa's voice, when she gave way to snobbery. Lady Templeton.

I drew a sharp breath, and said in my best imitation of Jenny, "It's only the upper housemaid, ma'am, with the hot water."

"We have no need of you tonight. Mrs. Seagrave has already retired."

"Will the lady be wishful of a fire in the morning?"

"If so, I am sure that she will ring. Now be off, you stupid girl, and leave us in peace."

I made a great deal of noise in retreating down the hallway, and collected my wits and my nerves in the shadows of the staircase. Were I not careful, I should be discovered in loitering by an honest servant, and made to explain myself. *Steady, Jane,* I urged inwardly; and took care to draw off my pattens and half-boots as dexterously as possible.

Louisa's bedchamber lay between my position and the parlour in which Lady Templeton worked. Undoubtedly the door should be on the latch; but I had procured a letter knife from the morning-room below, and was prepared to use it. I crept noiselessly forward, the blade concealed within a fold of my skirt. It was essential to muffle the sound of metal working against metal.

There was the bedchamber door. I wrapped the letter knife in the hem of my gown, and attempted to slide it slowly between door and frame. Once the tip of the blade was inserted beneath the edge of the latch, I might ease the fastening upwards, and gain entry to the room. Pray God Mr. Fortescue attended to his hinges. . . .

Mr. Fortescue, or someone he employed, did.

There was no squeal of reluctant iron, no betraying creak of timbers. The door opened as though a wraith desired passage; and I took this bit of luck as a favourable omen. I stepped into Louisa's bedchamber and did not trouble to secure the latch behind me. I could not hope for such good fortune again.

She should have stirred at the band of candlelight that fell across her drugget, and screamed aloud as she detected my presence: but she did not raise so much as a finger. This was no luck, I knew—this was the drugged sleep of laudanum. I cast one glance at the inert form in the middle of the four-poster, determined that she yet breathed, and moved on tiptoe to the bedchamber's far door. The parlour lay beyond. I would not require my letter knife here; the portal was already ajar.

With breath suspended, I hung in the shadows and stared at Lady Templeton's back. She was seated at the table before the fire, her hand steady and unhurried as it moved across a sheet of rag. She had, at last, all the time in the world for writing.

I understood how it should be: Louisa Seagrave, repentant of the plot she had urged against her innocent husband, would die of laudanum tonight in the bed behind me, a determined suicide. The letter Lady Templeton busily penned—was she so certain of her hand, that she could attempt to mimic Louisa's?—would admit to a wife's infamy—to the plot Chessyre had perpetrated against Tom

Seagrave, aboard the *Manon*. Only that plot was not of Louisa's invention—but Lady Templeton's. She must have known of her brother's will some months before his death; perhaps it was *she* who had reported its curious provisions to the London press. The *Morning Gazette* should seize upon this suicide, and make the obvious construction: the heiress had determined to blot out her husband, and had repented too late.

One person alone should benefit if Louisa were to die. Little Charles, of course, should inherit everything his grandfather had to leave—but with Lady Templeton as trustee. I doubted that even so sturdy a child as Charles could long survive the guardianship of such a woman.

Where, oh where, were Frank and Mr. Hill? How long before a fatal dose of laudanum must take its cruel effect?

I grasped the letter knife more firmly in my hand and eased through the door. Behind me, Louisa moaned.

Lady Templeton's back stiffened; her hand was arrested in its flight over the paper—and indeed, the sound of the woman dying in her bed was such as must make the flesh crawl. My lady, however, was a scion of the bluest blood, which is to say that she was the product of perhaps four or five centuries of harsh and ruthless breeding. She did not blench. Her forefathers had poisoned kings and princes; she had suckled at the breast of Lady Macbeth. She would have Luxford House and the late Viscount's millions, or hang in the attempt.

She laid down her pen, dusted the paper, and folded it in three. Then she rose—and at that moment there came a firm rap on the door.

"Mrs. Seagrave!" my brother cried. "Mrs. Seagrave! I must speak to my sister at once!"

Lady Templeton started, turned—and at the same moment, I leapt towards the table where the letter lay, and seized it in my hand.

"Good God!" she cried, her hand at her throat; and then she lunged at me.

I held out the letter knife in warning; she stopped short, her eyes fixed on my face.

"I know you," she muttered. "Louisa's friend—the naval woman. You were in Lombard Street."

"It is my brother at the door. Shall we open it?"

She snatched at the paper I held, but I stepped backwards, towards the outer passage. "Frank!" I cried. "The bedchamber!"

There was the sound of racing feet in the passage. Lady Templeton gave one wild look towards Louisa—glanced back at the letter—and hurled herself at my breast. I was thrust so hard against the closed door as to be nearly winded; the letter knife clattered to the floor.

"Give me that letter," she gasped, as though she had only to cast it in the fire, and save herself. She was clawing at my hand when Frank achieved the room.

Chapter 27

A Bride-Ship to India

Monday,
2 March 1807
~

"WELL, CAPTAIN AUSTEN," SAID MR. PERCIVAL PETHERING AS HE prepared to quit our lodgings this morning, "I am deeply obliged. It is something to have a murder resolved to satisfaction—and before the Assizes, too."

"Captain Seagrave, I trust, shall be released?" Frank's face was stern; he offered no quarter to the magistrate. Pethering, in his opinion, had made a mess of things; and Pethering should feel the Captain's displeasure as forcibly as any midshipman too clumsy with a quadrant.

"Captain Seagrave is at liberty even now," the magistrate replied, "and keeping vigil over his wife. Poor lady—there was little enough to be done, I suppose, in such a case."

"But what could be attempted, was attempted," Frank reminded him abruptly.

Mr. Hill had followed hard upon Frank's heels at the Dolphin last night, and while Frank held the struggling Lady Templeton, and called out for cordage and watchmen, the surgeon examined Louisa Seagrave. She was lost in a swoon—impossible to rouse—and he judged, from the appearance of her pupils, quite close to death. The pulse was fluttering and weak, her skin clammy to the touch.

"We have not much time," said Hill grimly. "You must support her, Miss Austen, and walk her about the room, to stimulate the bodily humours." And with that he went immediately to his rooms in St. Michael's Square, in search of ipecac and tartar emetic.

The maidservant, Nancy, was roused from sleep, and pressed into service in supporting her mistress; we attempted to force some coffee through Louisa's blue lips; we walked, and chafed her wrists, and waved burnt feathers under her nose—but to no avail. Rather than emerge from her swoon, she seemed determined to slide further into unconsciousness.

By the time Mr. Hill returned with his remedies a quarter-hour later, Louisa Seagrave was no more. And Lady Templeton stood accused of a second murder.

It was plain, once the letter her ladyship had written was read and understood, that she meant to implicate Tom Seagrave in the Chessyre plot. The confession ascribed to Louisa's pen—the confession Lady Templeton had sought to wrench from my hand, and cast into the fire once she knew herself discovered—named the Captain as the man responsible for garroting the Lieutenant. Lady Templeton had allowed for no possible reprieve, in her brutal scheme: she intended to see Tom Seagrave hang, and with him, all possibility of her discovery.

"It should be nothing, I suppose, for such a woman to learn Chessyre's name and direction," my brother had said, as we perused the false confession by candlelight last evening. "Lady Templeton already possessed a good deal of influence; she should soon be the mistress of a considerable fortune; and she had only to promise Chessyre the world, to gain the sacrifice of his honour."

"And everything else merely followed. Louisa, we may assume, would have told her of your express, and the events the Frenchman witnessed; Lady Templeton might have learned of them as early as Wednesday, when she appeared in Portsmouth. And so she determined to be rid of both men."

"It is a puzzle," my brother said pensively, "for you know Tom was told in Portsmouth that Louisa went out in Lady Templeton's carriage that Wednesday night. Do you think, Jane, that Lady Templeton carried her into Southampton, and made her speak to Chessyre?"

"—That she served as lure, you mean, for her aunt's murderous purpose?"

I had glanced down at Louisa Seagrave's body as I said this, and the sight must quell my tongue. Whatever Lady Templeton and Louisa had done between them was finished now. "I do not think, Frank, that we should ask that question."

MR. PETHERING BOWED; MY BROTHER NODDED SLIGHTLY IN RE-turn; and the magistrate was shown the door. I collapsed into a chair and stared at my brother.

"I believe, my dear, that we should fortify ourselves with a glass of wine."

"But it is barely ten o'clock in the morning, Jane!"

"And the sun is not yet over the yardarm." I smiled up at him. "Consider, Frank, that if you were in the Indies now—or rounding the Horn . . ."

"I should be already deep into a bottle. Ring for Jenny, my dear—we shall send round to the Dolphin for a bottle of Madeira, and drink to Seagrave's innocence. It is all the man has left to him, poor fellow."

WEEKS PASSED, AND THE MOVE TO CASTLE SQUARE WAS ACCOM-plished. We are established in this comfortable house exactly a fort-night, and know the pleasure of watching spring roll in off the Solent from the broad expanse of our very own garden. Martha and I—for Mary is grown too large for gambolling, particularly on a stone parapet that may permit of only three or four walking abreast—will stroll for hours together along the high old walls of the fortified city, staring out at the faint green of the New Forest. My mother no longer keeps to her bed, but digs at the raspberry canes that are setting out in the fresh earth; she is constantly on the watch for the Marchioness, our neighbour, so that she might have the pleasure of the lady's faerie horses, and find consolation in a fallen woman installed so conveniently to hand. Now that Mr. Hill is gone off to Greenwich, as resident surgeon for the naval hospital there, consolation must be necessary.

Cassandra is expected at home next week, and I have purchased figured muslin for a new gown.

I have been so busy throughout March, indeed, that I have almost forgot the events that opened it—or I had succeeded, perhaps, in diverting my mind from so much that was troubling, and must remain forever unresolved. But the matter was brought forcibly to my attention today, with the arrival of the morning post.

One shilling, eight pence, was demanded of me, for the receipt of a packet in an altogether unfamiliar hand. I duly paid the charge—slit open the seal—and commenced to read with a smile at my lips.

> 5 *March 1807*
> *On board the* Dartmouth,
> *in the Downs*

Ma chère mademoiselle Austen:

I write swiftly, as a mail boat has just called without warning, and we are to have our missives sent within the hour; but I know that you are familiar enough with naval life to forgive this small *bêtise*. I have been fortunate enough to obtain a position—with the help and collusion of your Admiralty, than which no institution of subterfuge and statecraft could be more honourable—as ship's surgeon aboard an American vessel bound for Boston. I am very well satisfied with the outcome of my late adventure, and may think with satisfaction that no small part of my happiness is due to having made your acquaintance. The Admiralty is now in possession of what personal property I carried out of France; and I trust that they shall continue to evidence a pleasing concern for my welfare.

Accept my deepest thanks and undying devotion for yourself, *mademoiselle*—without whom I should never have remained—

Etienne, Comte de la Forge

"The man's become a spy," said Frank shortly, after perusing this missive. "He's been despatched to inform upon the Americans. I shouldn't wonder that he will prove as wretched at the business as he did at avoiding the Emperor."

I must forgive my brother the slight bitterness of that speech; Frank is only just made aware, by the very same post, of his latest appointment. He is not to have a fast frigate—those are very dear in the Navy at present—but is to command the *St. Albans,* on convoy duty to the East Indies. In this, I suspect, we see the malice of Sir Francis Farnham, who cannot excuse my brother for Seagrave's acquittal.

"A bride-ship," Frank muttered as he read the official letter from the Admiralty. "There is certain to be a bride-ship in the convoy, Mary, awash with tittering females who cannot stand the heat of the sun. A long, desperate slog of it we shall make, with no hope of prizes, neither."

"My poor lamb," soothed the stalwart bride; and said nothing of the fact that he should be absent for the birth of his first child.

THOMAS SEAGRAVE IS TO REMAIN THE CAPTAIN OF THE *STELLA MARIS.* We learned of his acquittal on all charges considered by the court-martial a few days after his wife's burial; and even Admiral Bertie is disposed, now, to make much of him when the two chance to meet. Young Charles and his brother Edward are to be despatched to Uncle Walter and Luxford House in Kent once their father is again at sea. Seagrave has handsomely allowed little Charles to take the name of Carteret—without repining or rancour at his millions of pounds. The new Viscount accedes to all the honours and fortune of his grandpapa's estate, with Sir Walter for trustee; and I am sure that the Baronet will greatly enjoy his second childhood in Charles's keeping, once his wretched wife is no more.

The baby girl, Eliza, is to take up residence with her august relations; but Edward is destined for the sea, and when he has achieved a full ten years, is to join his father in whatever fast frigate the Captain then commands. I cannot help but wonder if the lad is not the happiest party in all of Southampton—who had least to do with the shocking events at Wool House.